# Baby Momma Drama

# Baby Momma Drama

## Carl Weber

KENSINGTON PUBLISHING CORP.
http://www.kensingtonbooks.com

DAFINA BOOKS are published by

Kensington Publishing Corp.
850 Third Avenue
New York, NY 10022



All Kensington titles, imprints and distributed lines are available at special quantity discounts for bulk purchases for sales promotion, premiums, fund-raising, educational or institutional use.

Special book excerpts or customized printings can also be created to fit specific needs. For details, write or phone the office of the Kensington Special Sales Manager: Kensington Publishing Corp., 850 Third Avenue, New York, NY 10022. Attn. Special Sales Department. Phone: 1-800-221-2647.



First Hardcover Printing: January 2003
First Trade Paperback Printing: January 2004
First Mass Market Printing: October 2005
10 9 8 7

Printed in the United States of America

*This book is dedicated to my momma.*
*Rest in peace, Bettie Jean Weber.*
*I will always love you.*

## Acknowledgments

First of all, I would like to thank God for giving me the opportunity to write another book during a hard year. I would like to thank my readers for supporting *Lookin' for Luv* and *Married Men.* Without you, I would have no career. I hope you enjoy *Baby Momma Drama* as much as I enjoyed writing it. I'd also like to thank all of the bookstores, book clubs and radio stations for all their support. Once again, I would like to thank my agent, Marie Brown, for all of her support. And last but not least, I would like to thank my editor, Karen Thomas, and the Kensington staff for a fantastic publishing experience.

To contact me, e-mail me at urbanbooks@optonline.net, visit my website www.carlweber.net, or write me at P.O. Box 3045, Farmingdale, New York 11735.

# 1

# Jasmine

My neck was stiff from sleeping the wrong way most of the bus ride, but I didn't let that bother me. The only thing I was really concerned about was that my hair was gonna look like shit from leaning up against the fogged-up window. Lord, please don't let my hair be messed up. My hair is my strength, kinda like Samson. When my hair is a wreck, I'm a wreck. But as much as I hated what these long trips did to my hair, the thought of seeing Derrick every weekend was the only thing keeping me together. Yes, I hated the fact that it was Thanksgiving Day and I'd be missing my mom's smoked-turkey dinner. And the Lord knows I didn't wanna hear my sister Stephanie or my grandmother, Big Momma, about me missing all my family from out of town for the second year in a row. But Derrick was my man, and he had to come first no matter what.

I met Derrick about four and a half years ago. At the time I was working in the downtown Richmond, Virginia, branch of the Post Office as a clerk. When he walked into the lobby my tongue nearly fell out of my mouth. He was so fine in that designer suit, I wanted to jump across the counter and tongue him down. Six foot one inch tall with an olive complexion highlighted by blue-green bedroom eyes, and hair black as coal, with big, soft curls. His face was narrow, with two of the cutest dimples I'd ever seen. He wasn't just fine.

He was *fiiine!* And I wasn't the only one licking my lips. Every woman in the lobby was staring him down, even the stuck-up old woman who always complained about our service. When he walked up to the front of the line, he must have known I was looking, 'cause he gave me a smile that could have melted Mr. Freeze's heart.

"Can I help you?" I blushed, practically begging him to come over to my counter.

"I'd like to mail this priority." He leaned over the counter with a seductive stare. I looked down at the package and noticed that it had a large white label with a James Center law office as a return address.

*Damn, fine and a lawyer! I think I've died and gone to heaven,* were the only thoughts I could muster at the time.

"I'm a lawyer," he said, showing me those gorgeous teeth as if he was reading my mind. "My name's Derrick Winter."

"Nice to meet you, Mr. Winter. My name's Jasmine. Jasmine Winter. Oh, my God, I mean Jasmine Johnson." I couldn't help but blush again.

"Well, Jasmine Johnson, you taking time off your supermodeling job or what? 'Cause baby, I've never seen a post office clerk look as good as you."

I know it was just a line, but the way he said it made me turn three different shades of red. Not only was he gorgeous, he had a way with words that made me weak. He eased me into small talk so smoothly that I ended up talking to him for five minutes at my counter. Somehow, small talk became an invitation to dinner, and a post office line full of angry customers. When I saw my supervisor walk into the building, I jotted down my address and phone number so he could pick me up later that night, and watched the man of my dreams walk away.

It took me almost two hours to get ready for dinner that night, and Derrick, unlike most brothers I'd dated, was on time. There I was, standing in front of the bathroom mirror with a curling iron in my hair, trying to decide if I should open the door or just let him wait until my hair was done. I decided on the latter and ran to the front door, shouting.

"Just a minute, I'm still getting dressed!" I ran back to the bathroom and my curling iron, praying he would understand.

I don't know how long I left him outside, but he was the perfect gentleman when I let him in. He just smiled at me with those pearly white teeth while I admired his dimples.

"Damn, baby, if I'd known you were going to look this good, I could have waited outside all night." He smiled seductively, looking me up and down.

I spun around so he could see all the curves that my tight-fitting mini dress would reveal. Taking my hand, he led me out the door to his Porsche and whisked me away to The Tobacco Company, one of Richmond's nicest restaurants for dinner and atmosphere.

Derrick treated me like such a lady that night. When we arrived at The Tobacco Company, he wouldn't even let me order. It was as if he knew exactly what was right for me from that point on. We ate shrimp scampi and drank Moët till I was silly drunk, then we walked over to the club After Six and danced until they were ready to close. Derrick was having such a good time, he bribed the owner and DJ into staying open an extra half hour. It was the most perfect evening I've ever had, and quite honestly the most fun I've had in my adult life. It was as if that perfect date would never end. By the time I awoke from my fairy tale, it was two weeks later and we were a couple. A month later, he'd moved in.

Derrick had shown me romance in ways I'd never dreamed of, showering me with diamonds and furs. He even bought me a new car. There is no question that those were the happiest six months of my life, and if you knew my life, you'd know happiness was rare. Yeah, those were happy times, all right. That is, until Big Momma got involved. God, I remember it like it was yesterday. Big Momma was at the house eating dinner when Derrick looked at his watch.

"I've got to go to court," he said, kissing me as he got up and put on his sport coat.

"What kind of lawyer did you say you were?" Big Momma asked him with that tone she used when she thought we were lying.

"I'm a defense attorney. I do mostly legal aid work through the night courts," he answered, no doubt expecting Big Momma to shut up. But he didn't know Big Momma at all. She never said anything unless she was going to make a point.

"Ohhhh, so that's why you leave my grandbaby every night and don't come home until the wee hours of the morning?"

She lit a cigarette, and that scared the hell outta me. 'Cause when Big Momma lit a cigarette, one thing was for certain: trouble was about to raise its ugly head.

"Big Momma, why you askin' Derrick all these questions?" I interrupted.

"Hush, child. Let the boy answer for himself. He's a grown man." She smirked at Derrick. "Well, Derrick, is that why you leave my grandbaby all alone at night?" I could see Derrick sensed trouble, but he still played it pretty cool.

"Yes, ma'am, night court doesn't close until four o'clock in the morning."

I sighed with relief. Big Momma was up to something, but Derrick seemed up to the task.

"So I guess you know Judge Jackson and Judge Jones?"

"Yes, ma'am. I've had a chance to be in both their courtrooms quite a few times," Derrick answered with confidence, although he did look a little agitated.

"Then how come neither of them seem to know you? They both belong to my bridge club, and I asked about you." Big Momma tilted her head as she released the smoke from her lungs.

"Well, there's a lot of lawyers in Richmond, especially in night court. You know the night court judges are pretty busy men." Derrick was visibly nervous as he glanced back and forth from Big Momma to me. "They probably don't pay attention to a young lawyer like me."

"That's not what Judge Jones said. He told me that night court was actually a very small world and he made it his business to know every lawyer that came into his courtroom." Big Momma took a long drag on her cigarette, then blew the smoke in Derrick's face. "How old are you, young man?"

"Twenty-four," he answered meekly.

"And how old were you when you finished college?" I could see Derrick doing the math in his head.

"Twenty-two." It sounded almost like a question rather than a statement.

"Lord have mercy. Either you're the smartest man in the world or the dumbest! 'Cause in addition to college, law school takes three years to complete, and your math don't add up." Big Momma shook her head and stared Derrick in the face. "Now, young man, what do you really do for a living?"

Derrick was so embarrassed that he walked straight out the door without saying another word. I got up from my chair to chase him, but Big Momma grabbed my arm.

"Child, if I told you and your sister once, I told you a thousand times. A good man is hard to find, and that is not a good man." I sat down reluctantly and listened to her lecture.

Derrick didn't return home for three days, and I was sick to my stomach with worry. It didn't matter what Big

Momma said; it didn't matter what anyone said. Derrick was a good man. He was probably just a night watchman or factory worker who got caught up in a lie he couldn't get himself out of. I promised myself right then and there that if God sent him home to me, I would forgive all his lies and be supportive in whatever he really did for a living. But I must admit I never expected what he would finally tell me.

"Hey, baby," he mumbled, walking past me into the bedroom. I followed behind him and sat on the bed as he opened the closet and pulled out his suitcase.

"What's that for?" I asked, taking the suitcase out of his hands.

He looked at me like I'd just asked the craziest question.

"You're not leaving me, Derrick. I love you too much to let you leave me."

"Look, Jazz, I'm not a lawyer. I'm the furthest thing from a lawyer." I could see he was embarrassed.

"I know, and I don't care if you're not a lawyer. You lied to impress me? Well, baby, I'm impressed. Not with you being a lawyer, but with you as a man. I love you, Derrick. I just want to be with you." I walked over and placed my arms around him.

"Jasmine, I love you, too." He hesitated before continuing. "But baby, I'm a hustler, a drug dealer. When you first met me I was leaving my lawyer's office trying to beat a possession charge. My lawyer asked me to do him a favor and mail a package."

I'd be lying if I said I wasn't shocked. For some stupid reason, I never even imagined that he could possibly be a drug dealer. I suppose the tons of cash he always carried should have tipped me off, but I was blinded by my love for this man. He always seemed so mature, nothing like those roughneck gangbangers whose pants hung halfway down their backsides. I looked up at him. Nothing about him said "drug dealer."

"Our whole relationship is built on a lie, Jasmine." He reached for the suitcase.

"That's not true. Our relationship is built on love." I felt compelled to reassure him of my love. So without thinking or caring I said, "If you're a drug dealer, Derrick, then so be it. Just make sure you're the boss and not some unimportant street-corner gangbanger. Be the best drug dealer you can be, 'cause I don't want my man to be anything but the best." I could see the shock on his face as I pulled him onto the bed. We made love right there, sealing a relationship that would end up with Derrick spending three years of his life behind bars and me traveling up every weekend to see him.

I was stunned out of my thoughts when the PA system for the bus blared, the driver's voice announcing that we had arrived at Roanoke Regional Prison. As usual, I got the chills when I looked at the tall, castlelike structure of the prison. This place gave me the creeps. Thank God Derrick only had six months to go.

It took almost an hour before I finally reached the visiting room. By then I was dying to see him. I smiled, eagerly telling the captain I was signing in to visit Derrick Winter. A brief look of jealousy came across his face but disappeared just as quickly. I bet he was wondering why a five-foot-eight-inch-tall, caramel-colored Tyra Banks look-alike would be visiting a convicted drug dealer. Well, it was none of his fucking business. I hated black correction officers more than any law enforcement officers, mostly because of the stories of abuse Derrick had told me. They always seemed to be harder on the black inmates because they needed to prove to the white officers that they weren't cut from the same cloth. I wanted them all to know that someone like me was out of their class.

The captain flipped through his book, managing to keep one eye on my chest at all times before he found Derrick's sign-in page. He smirked as he handed me a pen. I almost cursed out loud right then and there when I looked down at the sheet. There on the sign-in sheet for the previous day was Wendy Wood's name. She was Derrick's baby's momma, and I couldn't stand that bitch. She'd been trying to take Derrick away from me ever since we started goin' together. I sighed heavily, tempted to turn around and not visit him at all, though I quickly changed my mind. I had traveled three hours to see him, so I was going to stick around to have the satisfaction of cursing his ass out. I stalked into the visiting room and found Derrick sitting at a table, waiting for me.

Even in those orange prison overalls he was so damn fine. I almost wanted to forgive him for Wendy's little visit. But I couldn't let him get away with that. I had made too many trips to see him and brought too many pairs of sneakers, not to mention the two and a half years of celibacy I was going through. He wasn't gonna play me, especially not for that big-ass, weave-wearing bitch he had a baby with. Hell, no!

"Damn, baby, you think you could look any better? Every week you seem to get finer and finer. Mmm, mmm, mmm, come 'ere and give your man a kiss." He smiled flirtatiously, and I almost melted at the sight of his gorgeous dimples.

He was doing it to me. He was making me blush even though I was mad at him. God, I hated the power he had over me. I was mad. He had done me wrong. Nonetheless, a smile was creeping over my face and I was about to give in as I felt his hands wrap around my waist.

"What the fuck was Wendy doing here?" I pushed him away as I regained my resolve. I could have plenty of attitude when I wanted, and I needed it then. I had to, because he was going to kiss me, and if he did it would have been all over. "I asked you a question, Derrick! What the fuck was Wendy doing here?" He raised his eyebrows in surprise, then looked around to see who was watching.

"Sit down and I'll tell you," he ordered me through gritted teeth. "What you tryin'a do, make me look like a punk?" He guided me into a chair.

"This had better be good, Derrick, or this is the last time I bring my black ass to visit you." I sat down but wouldn't let him touch me. My hands were trembling with anger.

Derrick was silent for a minute. I was tempted to slap him across that pretty-ass face of his, but I waited for his explanation. Finally, he spoke in a whisper.

"A couple o' the fellas and I started a little business selling weed to the other inmates. Part of our agreement was that each of us would recruit someone to bring weed up to us each month. Now, baby, you're my woman, so there was no way I was gonna ask you. I don't want you gettin' into no trouble." He smiled.

"But Derrick, why did you have to ask her? You know I can't stand that bitch." I was indignant.

"Because she's stupid enough to do it. Wendy's not smart like you, baby. She's nothing but a ho from the street. You're a college-educated woman."

He covered his face up with his hands. I wasn't sure, but I think he was trying to hide some tears. I hated times like this. The last thing I wanted was for my man to feel like he was less than a man.

"Jazz, I love you, baby. It brings tears to my eyes just thinking about you coming up here to see me." He reached over and touched my hand. "I'm just using Wendy so I can do business. She brought me two ounces of weed yesterday. Do you know how much that's worth in here?"

I didn't care how much it was worth. I didn't like it.

Derrick only had six months left to see the parole board. If he got caught, they'd give him another two years as sure as I was looking at him.

"Derrick, this is stupid. You have more than enough money in your commissary. Why do you have to do this?"

"Baby, I can make twenty grand easy in the next six months. I'll be able to start up a legit business with that kind of cash." His eyes lit up.

"I thought you were going to college. We don't need any money. I'm making good money now that they made me supervisor at the post office."

"Hey, lemme decide what's right for us. I *am* supposed to be the man in this relationship, right?" He waited for an answer. "Right, Jasmine?"

I nodded my head weakly.

"Now, that's my girl." His voice brightened as he changed the subject. "Come gimme a kiss." He opened his arms, and I went to him. I sat on his lap and just melted against his chest. Suddenly, Wendy and her little visit were the last things on my mind.

"I miss you, Derrick. I can't wait till you're at home."

"Baby, not as much as I miss you." He kissed me, and I held on tight. I didn't want to ever let him go, but the captain had a different idea. He interrupted us with a loud bang on the table with his nightstick.

"Winter, you know the rules. No physical contact after the first five minutes. Don't make me cut this visit short," he threatened.

I slid off of Derrick's lap reluctantly and made sure the captain saw me pouting as I walked back to my side of the table. He made sure I knew he didn't give a shit when he repeated his warning before walking away.

"I hate him," I whispered.

"Man, fuck that Uncle Tom motherfucker. I got something for his ass when I get outta here." Derrick waved his hand like he was swatting flies behind the captain. Then he changed the subject. "Did you bring my comic books?"

"Yeah, I brought them." I smiled.

Derrick and I shared Thanksgiving dinner in the special mess hall that had been set up for inmates and their visitors. It wasn't my momma's smoked turkey but it was all right. Then we went to what they call the rec room and made small talk for the rest of our visit. There was lots I wanted to say that I couldn't. I wanted to tell Derrick how much I loved him, how hard it was being without him every day. But I knew I had to keep things casual while I was there. Derrick was hurting as much as I was while we were apart. There was no need for both of us to break down and get all emotional. Especially with all those other inmates around. Derrick let me know early on he couldn't afford to look soft in front of these people. So there were no tears, just lots of hand-holding and promises about how things would be when he was back on the outside. We would be together again, inseparable. I couldn't wait for that day. Until then, I'd have to be satisfied with these visits and the small comfort they offered.

# 2

# Travis

It was Thanksgiving Day and I looked across the dinner table and smiled at my very pregnant girlfriend Stephanie, who was helping her grandmother, Big Momma, with dinner. Stephanie and I met a little over three years ago at a club in Richmond called The Satellite. The Satellite was without question Richmond's hottest black singles bar and club. It was situated right between cigarette manufacturer Philip Morris, the only place a brother could get a job making over twelve dollars an hour, and the Southside Projects, home of some of the finest single black women in Richmond. The Satellite had the reputation of being the perfect place to find a one-night stand, and that's exactly what I was looking for the night of my twenty-eighth birthday.

Stephanie was hanging with a couple of so-so-looking sisters, smoking weed, when I pulled into The Satellite's parking lot. I'd just bought myself a brand-new burgundy Expedition for my birthday, and my army buddy Matt had offered to buy me a few drinks to celebrate. Matt and I were both stationed about twenty minutes south of Richmond at Fort Lee army base in Hopewell. He was married and not really interested in hooking up with anyone but was happy to take the ride and get away from his wife for a few hours. I was hoping to get lucky. I'd just gotten out of a long-distance relationship with this sister in Germany about six months ago and it had been a long, long time since I'd gotten any. So you can imagine how eager I was to hook up for the night.

When Matt and I hopped out of the truck, the so-so sisters were all smiles.

"This your car?" one of them asked.

"Yeah, why?" I smiled.

" 'Cause I wanna ride." She said it like it was an order.

"So, what am I gonna get if I give you a ride? Today's my birthday." I was testing the waters. I could tell she wasn't the brightest woman in the world by the way she smiled at that stupid-ass line I'd thrown at her. But at the time I didn't give a shit about her IQ. Only thing I cared about was how fast I could get her to a hotel and between the sheets.

"What you want, birthday boy?" She opened up her coat, showing me her skintight spandex outfit. I surveyed the sister real quick. She was about five-eight, with an almond color. A little thin for my taste, but doable. I figured she was about twenty-two. Her friend, who turned out to be her blood sister, was the same complexion, a little thicker, with a much nicer body. I figured she was probably the older of the two.

"You wanna ride, too?" I turned my attention to her sister.

She nodded, trying to avoid eye contact with her sister, who had placed her hand on her hip and was sucking her teeth. That's when Stephanie got out of their car. She was five foot five with heels on. Her chocolate skin was so pretty she didn't need a drop of makeup, and wasn't wearing any other than lip gloss. Her chest was small, but her hips made up for it tenfold. I hadn't even seen her from the rear, but I knew she had one of the nicest asses I'd ever seen. There was no doubt in my mind she had it going on, and if I was going to take somebody for a ride it was definitely going to be her. She was fine in every sense of the word, with just enough attitude to keep a brother on his toes.

"Come on, y'all. He ain't takin' your sorry asses for no

ride." Stephanie stepped out of the car and took two steps toward the club.

"Only 'cause you'd be the one in my car, sweetheart." I smiled until I realized how corny the line was.

She stepped between her friends and looked up and down my six-foot-three-inch frame. "I doubt it, baby. I don't even know you. And don't think you could handle me if I did." She swung her head toward her friends, gesturing for them to follow her to the club.

"Hey, why don't you let me buy you a drink so we can get to know each other and find out?" She turned back to me with this confused look. She was probably trying to figure out where the hell I was coming up with these corny-ass lines. I was so embarrassed I wanted to smack myself.

"You buying them a drink, too?" She looked at her friends, who were now battling for Matt's attention.

"Only if you want me to," I said sincerely.

"Fuck 'em. Let 'em buy their own drinks." She smiled at me. I have to admit I was in shock. I couldn't believe that stupid-ass line worked. Those were some of the corniest lines I'd ever used and she actually went for it. I put my arm around her and guided her toward the club. *This might actually be a happy birthday after all.*

Two hours and damn near a sixty-dollar bar tab later, Stephanie was sitting next to me with her arms around my neck. She was drunk. I was even drunker. Her two friends had found some other playmates for the night and Matt had left. He took his marriage vows pretty seriously, so when the so-so sisters offered to do a two-on-one he decided to grab a cab back to base before he did something stupid. I didn't go with him, but I wasn't expecting to get laid anymore, either. I was just hoping to get Stephanie's phone number and possibly take her out to dinner later in the week. She wasn't as ghetto as I first thought, though she was rough around the edges. From what I could tell from our conversation, she was the kind of woman I wanted to get to know long-term. She was a woman with real dreams, and unlike some of the sisters I'd met, she actually had a plan to achieve them. I liked that.

"What's up with that ride?" she asked.

"Baby, I like you, but I'm not in any shape to drive. That's a brand-new truck out there, and I don't plan on crashing it." Matt was the designated driver, and before he would leave I had to promise to catch a cab back to base if I didn't get lucky. And that definitely didn't seem to be in the cards. I'd tried to kiss Stephanie on the dance floor a few times but she just pushed me away. I was sure she liked me, but she wasn't gonna make it easy. I was probably in for quite a few cold showers before she would give me some.

Stephanie looked at me with a grin. "You sure you can't drive? I only live about four blocks from here. Don't you want your birthday present?"

"Huh?" I raised an eyebrow in confusion. "What birthday present?"

"Damn, they don't let you out much in the army, do they?" She laughed.

"What's that supposed to mean?" I slurred.

"If you don't take me home, you can't get no ass. That's what it means." She kissed me gently on the lips.

Suddenly, I felt like I was sober. I hadn't had any in over six months, and on the first night this fine woman was offering to give me some. I had to control myself from leaping out of my seat.

"Let's go. I can drive." I grabbed her hand and she almost fell on the floor as I tried a little too eagerly to help her from her seat.

"Okay, but maybe we should walk. We're both a lot drunker than I thought." She tried to regain her footing. I didn't argue with her, but the truth is, new truck or not, I would have driven to hell and back to get some from her. I don't know why, but it just felt right.

When we got outside the club, the night air felt good for February. It was more like an early spring night. Stephanie wrapped her arm around my waist and I did the same to her, massaging her beautiful hips as we walked in silence. It only took about five minutes to walk to her apartment. When we arrived at her door she kissed me. I kissed her back, slow and passionate.

"Travis," she whispered, still holding onto my waist.

"Yeah," I whispered back.

"You don't do this very often, do you?"

"Do what?" I leaned back so I could see her face.

"Go to clubs and pick up girls."

"No, I don't. How'd you know?" My voice was low, and I was afraid she would hear my embarrassment.

"The way you kissed me. Like I was your girl or somethin'." I looked at her and smiled. She was right. That's exactly how I was trying to make her feel. That's just the kind of guy I was. I wanted her to feel safe and comfortable, even if this was just a one-night stand.

"Did you like it?" I smiled. She smiled back.

"Yeah, but it scared me. Only one man's ever kissed me like that before. My daughter's father."

"You've got a daughter?" I raise my eyebrows. She hadn't mentioned a kid all night.

"Yeah, she's nine months old. She's at my mom's for the weekend." Nine months old? Damn, she just had the baby. Where the hell was the father?

I watched her walk into the apartment and throw her jacket on the sofa. I hesitated at the front door, looking inside. Lord, please don't let this girl's baby have some crazy, deranged father. 'Cause the last thing I wanted was to get caught doing the nasty with some other brother's woman.

"What are you doing out there? Come on inside," she ordered when she realized I hadn't come in. I obeyed but entered tentatively. I was seriously thinking about backing out. I wanted some from her real bad, especially after she bent over to pick up something off the floor and gave me a full view of that beautiful backside. But I wasn't sure if it was worth the stress. She lived in the projects, had a kid, and probably had a baby's father somewhere close.

"You ain't got no man, do you? I mean, where's your daughter's father?" I asked warily.

"No, I ain't got no man. I don't want no man. I just wanna have a good time. And my daughter's sorry-ass father ain't been around since she's been born. He's up in D.C. tryin' to be a rap star. You ever heard of a group called KRN? It's short for Kill'a Richmond Niggas."

"Nope, never heard of them."

"Neither has anyone else. But they've been opening for a go-go group in D.C. called Top Side. Would you believe that nigga left me right when my baby was born?"

I shook my head. I'm not sure if it was because I was horny or what, but I believed her and calmed down. I wrapped my arms around her.

"Kiss me like you did before." She smiled.

I did what she asked, this time kissing her even more passionately.

"Wow, a girl could get used to that." She led me up the stairs and before we entered the bedroom I kissed her again.

"I'm not looking for a man," she repeated. "Just a good time."

I hesitated. I'd never had a real one-night stand before. Any time I'd ever slept with someone it ended up becoming a long-term relationship. Since I was fifteen years old this was the longest gap I'd had between serious girlfriends. The truth was, I wanted a woman in my life. But at that moment, I'd take what I could get. After all, it was my birthday and we could talk about tomorrow when the sun came up.

She said it again, this time a little more serious. "I'm not looking for a man."

I exhaled. "That's good. I'm not looking for a woman. It's my birthday. I'm just looking to have a good time, too."

I massaged her ass, trying to reassure her it was all about the sex. She looked up at me with a smile. I think she knew I was fronting. She knew I wanted more.

"Why don't we pretend I'm your woman just for tonight, okay?"

I nodded and she led me into her room. It was small and needed to be painted. The only furniture she had in it was a dresser, a full-size bed, and a small crib. I sat on the edge of the bed and kicked off my shoes. There were condoms on the dresser, so I guess she had planned on bringing home company. I watched her pull down the shades to the two tiny windows. Then she spun around and unbuttoned her blouse in one swift motion.

"I don't have much, but they need lots of attention," she said as she displayed her bare breasts.

I nodded as I sat back to enjoy the rest of her show. She slid her black stretch pants and her panties down to the floor. I couldn't take my eyes off of her perfectly rounded hips. I glanced at her stomach and thighs. Incredibly, not one stretch mark on this woman who just had a baby.

It was my turn. I pulled my sweater over my head and flexed my biceps nonchalantly.

"Damn, look at you! You are one big boy. Where did you get this body?" She approached me and slowly slid her hands along my chest. "You're built like a brick shithouse." She grinned.

I didn't reply; I just flexed again. My smooth chocolate-brown complexion and tall, muscular body had always been admired by the opposite sex. I stood up and she unhooked my pants, letting them slide to the floor. Then, with a smile she looked down. My heart almost stopped beating when she started to laugh.

"Damn, I guess we both planned on getting some tonight, huh?"

I finally looked down and blushed. I'd completely forgotten I was wearing my red G-string underwear. I felt like a fool, but at least she wasn't laughing at the size of my dick.

"To be honest, I need to do laundry. These are my only clean drawers," I told her, and it *was* the truth.

"At least you have somethin' sexy to wear. When that happens to me, I gotta wear my old granny briefs."

We both laughed as I slipped out of my G-string.

"Where you from? I know you're not from Richmond. You sound too country."

"Georgia."

"So you one of those big-ass corn-fed niggas, huh?" I didn't even answer her. I hated the word *nigger.*

"I got a cousin lives in Georgia. She's from Atlanta. You from Atlanta, big man?" She was still rubbing her hands across my chest.

"Nah, I'm from Waycross."

"I don't know where that is."

"Well let's put it this way: Waycross is way across Georgia."

She laughed then changed the subject. "What's your favorite position, Travis?"

"Sixty-nine."

She laughed hard. "You the first country nigga I ever met that admitted to eating pussy. I like your honesty."

"Thanks. But if you ask me that question in public, I'm gonna lie." We both laughed and I kissed her again.

"What about you? What's your favorite position?"

"I like a sixty-nine," she said, smiling. "But nothing beats a nice, long pony ride."

"Pony ride? What's a pony ride?"

She pushed me on the bed and straddled my legs. Ripping a condom open, she slid it onto me effortlessly. She took my penis into her soft hands and rubbed it against the warmth between her thighs.

"Dammmn! That feels so good," I moaned. She slid all the way down on my manhood, letting out a soft moan when it was all the way in.

"A perfect fit," she purred.

"Yeah, a perfect fit," I moaned.

"Now that I'm saddled up, it's time for a nice, long ride."

Stephanie and I made love that night in every imaginable position. She was down for anything and everything, and I'm not embarrassed to say she taught me a thing or two. What she thought was going to be a one-night stand turned out to be an all-weekend thing. I hate to sound self-serving, but once I slept in her bed and she wrapped her arms around me, I got comfortable and I didn't wanna leave.

She was serious about not wanting a man. Her daughter's father had turned her off to the thought of relationships and love. At least, that's what she told me. Somehow, despite what she said, I found my way over to her place every night and she never turned me away. She called it a sex thing, but Stephanie and I had a bona fide relationship going on. It was fine with me if she never wanted to admit it. A few of the local brothers I'd met living in her project tried to warn me about her reputation, but I didn't really care. I knew she was a freak the first night I met her. But now she was my freak.

We played that little game for almost nine months. I guess after a while Stephanie started to realize what I already knew, that she wasn't getting rid of me so easy. So that Thanksgiving, out of nowhere she invited me to her grandmother's house for turkey dinner with all the trimmings. To my surprise, she introduced me to her grandmother as her boyfriend, and from that point on that's who I was. Her boyfriend. Not that I'm complaining. It's been a wonderful three years we've shared together, and with the baby coming in the next few weeks, I'd decided to make that couple of years a lifetime.

I smiled at Stephanie as she set the large pan of macaroni and cheese down on the table. She'd just finished helping Big Momma bring out the last few trays for this year's Thanksgiving dinner, and sat down next to me. In the three years we'd been together she'd traded in her shoulder-length perm for long box braids, and her skintight clothes in for more conservative skirts, slacks, and blouses. Except, of course, when she went out to the club. But even with her new, conservative look she couldn't hide the fact that she had a big ass. Matter of fact, ever since she got pregnant that ass seemed a little bigger. Not that I minded. Like most black men, I liked a big ass. As far as I was concerned, my girl had it goin' on. Not just in the looks department, either. Her shit was together in all aspects of life. She was going to school to be a nurse, working at Wal-Mart to help pay the bills, was a great mother to her daughter. And she showed me all kinds of love. She was a great woman and I loved her for that. That's why I wanted to make her my wife.

"Travis, would you mind blessin' the food?" Big Momma set the steaming tray of greens down on the table and took her seat. A big, heavyset old woman, Big Momma was the head of Stephanie's family and had an opinion about everyone and everything. She was the kind of woman you did not want on your bad side. And since Stephanie had gotten pregnant and we weren't married, guess where I was. But that was about to change.

"Sure, Big Momma, I'll bless the food." I looked over at Stephanie's Uncle Mark, who was staring at Big Momma. For as long as I'd known Stephanie, Mark had been blessing the Thanksgiving table. And from what she told me, he'd been doing it ever since his father died twenty years ago. So I know he wasn't too pleased with Big Momma asking me to bless the food.

"Momma, why he gonna bless—"

Big Momma cut Mark off with a quickness.

" 'Cause I said so. That's why. Now, bow your heads, so we can give the Lord thanks." Like everyone in this family, Mark obeyed Big Momma. He lowered his head so she couldn't see his scowl. "Now, Travis, you bless the food. It's Thanksgiving, and we hungry."

I bowed my head and took a deep breath before beginning my prayer. I made it short, sweet, and to the point, and ended it with a chorus of amens. When I lifted my head I tried to smile at the fifteen adults and five children sitting at three tables reaching for food, but it was hard. I was about to make the most important speech of my life. I tapped my spoon against my glass to get everyone's attention. They all turned toward me like I'd lost my mind. All except for Big Momma, who'd been expecting my announcement.

"I know y'all hungry, but before we eat I'd like to say something important." I stood and ignored the grumbling among some of the hungrier people at the tables. "Unofficially, I've been a part of this family for three years. Y'all been more of a family to me than my own down in Georgia. So I wanted you all to be here when I did this." I turned to Stephanie and took her hand. With my other hand I reached into my pocket and slowly knelt down on one knee.

"Stephanie, I love you more than anything in the world and I want you to be my wife. Will you marry me?" You should have seen the look on her face when I took out the half-carat diamond ring from my pocket.

"Oh, my God." She looked over at Big Momma, who was smiling and nodding. "Yes, yes, Travis, I'll marry you." I slid the ring on her finger and we both stood to embrace. Stephanie wrapped her arms around my neck and kissed me to the sounds of a few family members applauding, the others grabbing for their Thanksgiving feast.

# 3

# Dylan

I was so full, I thought I was going to burst. I unhooked my belt buckle to give my stomach some room to breathe as I drove down River Road, back to my house in Petersburg. My girlfriend, Monica, and I had just left her parents' place in Chesterfield County, Virginia, where her mother had put together one hell of a Thanksgiving feast. Turkey, ham, candied yams, collard greens. You name it, we ate it. Mmm-mmm, it was some kinda good.

I looked at Monica in the passenger seat. She was staring into space, no doubt still upset about the argument we'd had at her folks' house. Even angry she was a beautiful woman. At five foot nine, Monica was a good two inches taller than me. Her body was slender with long, sexy legs, and beautiful curves in all the right places. Big, dark-brown eyes highlighted her smooth mahogany complexion. As far as I was concerned, she was the sexiest woman on earth, and I'd traveled quite a bit.

"You still mad at me, boo?" I asked.

"What do you think, Dylan?" She cut her eyes at me, then turned away.

"Look, baby, I think you're blowing this whole thing out of proportion." She whipped her head around and pointed her finger in my face.

"How can I be blowing it out of proportion? You humiliated me in front of my family."

"All I did was answer your mother's question. You're acting as if I farted at the dinner table or somethin'." She wanted to laugh. I could see it in her face. But she stifled it and shouted instead.

"I spent six, almost seven years of my life with your ass! And you can't tell my ma when we're gonna get married? You ain't shit, Dylan Taylor!" She turned her head back toward the window.

"Come on, Monica. You know I love you, baby. You know I want to marry you. All I want you to do is finish school. Why is that such a big deal?"

Monica sucked her teeth and crossed her arms tight against her chest. She didn't intend on answering my question. Hell, we'd been arguing about marriage for almost two years. She knew I wanted to marry her. I wanted to start a family more than anything in the world. I just wouldn't give her an engagement ring until she graduated college. Yet she still insisted on starting this same argument at least once a week.

Monica and I met almost seven years ago, when I was a junior and she was a freshman at Virginia State University. We quickly fell in love, and when I graduated, instead of moving back to New York I decided to stay in Petersburg while she finished her two remaining years of school. Well, she changed her major three times with less than a semester to go each time. I think she was afraid to graduate. Graduating would have meant getting on with her life. She would have to find a job and cut the financial ties with her parents. I don't think she wanted to do that until she had a committed replacement, and that meant a wedding ring from me. But my parents had taught me the power of an education, so I kindly explained to her, over and over, that upon graduation

I would present her with a rock that would make her eyes pop out. For whatever reason, that didn't motivate her. She wanted things done her way.

"Look Dylan, me finishing school has nothing to do with us getting married. If you really loved me, you'd marry me no matter what. One day you're gonna wake up and my black ass is gonna be gone. Then what are you gonna do?"

"I'm not going to justify that with an answer. You know how I feel about you, and if you don't, maybe you should leave." I was getting tired of this argument. I pulled into the parking lot of Colonial Plaza, in front of my business, Colonial Comics.

"What the hell are we doing here?" She threw her hands in the air.

"I just wanted to make sure Brett packed all the boxes for the comic convention in D.C. tomorrow." I stepped out of the car as I spoke.

"Goddamn it, Dylan! Can I have one day with you that you're not worried about one of your fucking stores?" She got out of the car and slammed the door. "Why couldn't you just have stayed an accountant—"

Monica shut up when I shot her a look. There were very few things that could piss me off without a thought, and my old career in accounting was one of them. We'd had more than our fair share of fights about that. You see, Monica was a very materialistic woman and she liked having—no, she *loved* having—a man to show off. Someone she could brag about, who fit society's idea of a successful man. For my first two years after college I fit that role perfectly. It didn't matter that after I left accounting I made sixty grand a year as a comic book dealer. She always looked down on me because I didn't wear a suit and tie to work every day. This was the same woman who couldn't seem to finish her own degree.

I'll never forget the expression on Monica's face the day I

told her I'd quit my job at PricewaterhouseCoopers and rented a small store to sell comic books. It was a mixture of shock, anger, and disappointment all wrapped up into one.

"Wh-why'd you do that?" was all she could stutter. She took my career change as a personal insult.

"Well, there are three reasons, actually," I smiled, ready to state my case. I was happy about my decision and wanted her to understand and support me. "First of all, you know that I hate being an accountant. Do you have any idea how horrible it is to wake up every morning and go to a job you can't stand? Second, I'm not the kind of guy who can work for someone else. I need to be my own boss. And third, I like comic books."

She gently held on to the lapels of my suit jacket and kissed me. I suppose she thought she could sweet-talk me into changing my decision. "Look baby, I understand you wanting to own your own business. To be perfectly honest, that's what I want for you. But you're an accountant, a CPA, a man of prestige. You're not some insignificant shopkeeper. Why don't you open up a tax office? Hey, I'm even willing to take my classes at night so you won't have to pay a secretary."

"Monica, I'm going to open up a comic book shop with or without your blessing." I folded my arms defiantly.

"*Comic books?* You keep talking about how much you want a family. How the hell do you expect to support a baby selling comic books? Jesus Christ! Southside projects here we come," she mocked.

There is no word to describe how much that hurt me. Ever since the day we met, Monica knew how much I wanted to have a child. Now she thought I'd put that child in the projects if I wasn't a suit-and-tie man. It was like a knife in my back, and it just proved that she had very little faith in my ability to be successful.

"Thanks for the glowing endorsement, Monica." I shot up my middle finger and turned to walk away.

"Dylan, comic books are a hobby, a fad. Do you really want to place our future in the hands of ten-year-old boys and drugged-out teenagers?"

I was still too pissed off to answer. What she didn't know was that before I handed in my resignation, I had sold my personal copy of *Fantastic Four #1* to a man in D.C. for seventy-five hundred dollars. Would you believe I only paid ten dollars for it in 1973? I had started collecting comics when I was six years old. My stamp-collecting father forced me to keep my comics in protective plastic bags after I read them. Sixteen years later I was still collecting comic books, and my personal collection was worth a small fortune, thanks entirely to dear old Dad. During college I began selling and trading comics at flea markets and small shows around the Richmond-Petersburg area. Unbeknownst to Monica, who thought I was just going through a childish phase, I was making more money selling comic books than I was as an accountant, and having a lot more fun at it, too. I had developed quite a local following in Petersburg. Not only were the kids my customers, but I also sold to many die-hard adult collectors. It only made sense to me that if I gave my comic book business my undivided attention, I would quickly be on my way to prosperity.

Despite Monica's objections, I did open my first store, and then two more followed. I also traveled to conventions almost every weekend, where I made some of my biggest profits. Monica hated that I traveled so often, which is probably why she started yet another fight with me as I started checking the work my store manager had done for the D.C. convention.

It had taken me about ten minutes to check the work that

Brett had done. Before I could finish, Monica was already getting fidgety.

"What the hell is Teddy Harris for, decoration?" She sighed loudly, checking her beeper.

"Look, Monica, you know as well as I do that Ted isn't worth shit. Why don't you just let me finish what I have to do here so we can go home?" I guess she didn't like my tone of voice, because she turned around and walked right out the door. I really hadn't meant to upset her, but any time someone mentioned Teddy Harris's name lately, I got pissed.

Teddy Harris was my business partner and full-time pain in the ass. I met him at the annual three-day Chicago comic convention a few months after I opened up my first store. We were both young and living in Virginia, so we hung out after the show closed each night. Teddy, a tall, wiry white man, was a master salesman. He could sell you your own toothbrush three times and you'd end up leaving his booth thinking you got a great deal. He was without a doubt the smoothest talker I have ever met. Matter of fact, he was so smooth that over a pitcher of beer he talked me into forming a partnership to open my second and third stores.

The partnership was great at first. Ted, who lived in Spotsylvania County, ran our Fredericksburg location, and I ran our Richmond location. Both of us worked shows each weekend, and we split the profits fifty-fifty. For a while it was like printing money. But after a year the Fredericksburg store was making less and less money. Well, at least that's what Teddy was saying. The truth is, if anyone other than Teddy had been running that store I might have believed it. But like I said, Teddy Harris was a master salesman. There was no way that store was not making money. What had started out as a great partnership had quickly become a mess, with me doing most of the work and Ted sticking his greedy hands out for more money. We were making money, but nowhere near what we should have been. This is why the mere mention of my partner's name made my blood pressure rise.

When I finished in the store, I expected Monica to be waiting for me in the car, but she was nowhere to be found. I searched the entire area for about fifteen minutes, finally driving over to the cabstand two blocks away. It wasn't unlike Monica to take a cab home when she was upset with me. I went in and asked the dispatcher if he'd seen a young lady fitting Monica's description. Bingo! She had just left in a cab headed to Riverside, Petersburg's most expensive condominiums. Just what I didn't wanna hear.

I was fuming as I drove over to Riverside. I didn't know what Monica's problem was lately, but I was getting sick of it. She was going to give me some answers or we were through. As much as I loved her, the last few months had been one big, constant argument. Not just about getting married or us having a baby, but about stupid things like me watching too much football, or the toilet seat being left up. The only arguments started by me were the ones about her so-called friend, Jordan.

Jordan Brown was every faithful boyfriend's worst nightmare. A six-foot-tall pretty boy, Jordan was the heir to the Brown Funeral Home business in Petersburg. Proud of his reputation as a ladies' man, Jordan was known to carry on six and seven different relationships at the same time. Most of them were with other people's wives and girlfriends, and lately I suspected he'd been after mine.

I had tried to stop their friendship on several occasions by explaining to Monica that he was planning on seducing her, after which she'd be thrown to the side like a used condom. But for months she kept telling me that he was just a friend and that I should grow up. Maybe I was acting like a jealous teenager, but I had been warned about Jordan Brown.

My best friend, Joe, who had grown up in Petersburg,

knew Jordan well. He told me in no uncertain terms, "Keep your woman as far away from Jordan as possible. He's a master street psychologist and he preys on weak-minded, materialistic women."

Of course I responded as most overconfident brothers would. "My girl is too smart to fall for that pretty boy's shit. She gets everything she needs right here from me."

Joe, being the true friend he is, quickly burst that bubble.

"Dylan, man, I don't know how to tell you this, but Monica's the most materialistic woman I've ever met. I can just envision Jordan pulling up in that brand-new Mercedes sport. Monica would be daydreaming about how to spend his parents' loot as soon as she got in his ride. She's a prime candidate for a brother like him, 'cause she can't see past the green."

I didn't admit it to Joe, but it took me exactly five seconds to realize he was right. I looked over at my Ford Taurus. Monica always hated that car, even though it was less than a year old. I guess after being with her for six years I had put aside what I really knew to be true. Monica didn't come to college to get an education; she came to get her M.R.S. You know, as in Mrs. Filthy-Rich Doctor's Wife. She came to meet a husband, a rich husband, and although I was on the right track, I wasn't there yet, and she sure didn't believe I was gonna get there.

Because I knew how much Monica craved wealth, I didn't trust her around Jordan. I tried to put my foot down and forbid her to see him. Finally, she quit the bowling team they were on and swore that she would never hang out with Jordan Brown again. Matter of fact, she said that they weren't even friends anymore. At the time I had been relieved, but as I drove to Riverside on Thanksgiving night, I decided it must have been a well-calculated lie just to get me off her back.

"That sneaky fucking bitch!" I yelled as I passed the cab that had probably dropped her off.

Monica hadn't walked out of the store because I yelled at her. When we were in the store her beeper went off just as plain as day. But instead of running to the phone in the store as she normally would, she must have gone outside to use a pay phone. Now there was no doubt in my mind that it was Jordan who had beeped her.

I pulled into a space in front of Jordan's town house apartment and thought about how much Monica really meant to me. I was nervous about losing her, and afraid of what I was about to discover. Maybe it was all my fault. Maybe I should have just given her an engagement ring so that we could get on with our lives and have a baby.

But that weak shit didn't last long. I couldn't believe that I was actually contemplating buying an engagement ring for a woman who had just left me a half hour ago without a word to go see some other brother. I stormed toward the apartment intending to pull her ass out of there. But I stopped dead in my tracks when I looked at the window and spotted a silhouette of two people embracing. Taking a deep breath, I slowly crept up to the window, peeking through the space where the curtains met. What I saw next was much worse than a simple embrace. It was tragic. Monica was naked, bent over Jordan's coffee table with a straw up her nose, snorting cocaine like it was going outta style. Jordan was sitting next to her with a straw in his hand, eagerly waiting for her to finish.

"Monica, you stupid bitch! What the fuck are you doing?" I yelled at the top of my lungs.

I must have scared the shit out of them, because Monica let out a piercing scream.

I was about to put my fist through the glass when Jordan poked his head through the curtain to see what was going on.

There I was, staring angrily at the man who was about to screw my girlfriend, and the only thing between us was a pane of glass. I wanted to put my fist right through that glass and punch him in the fucking nose, but the last bit of common sense I had told me that I'd cut my hand to shreds. I'm sure Jordan suspected I was about to do something crazy, because he took a step back. He was scared; I could see it in his eyes.

"Tell Monica to come outside, motherfucker!" I screamed as he quickly closed the curtain.

I wasn't sure if I'd be able to control the rage that was building inside me if I saw Monica. For the first time in my life, I truly understood why some guys hit women. I was so full of anger that I just wanted to hurt somebody, and Monica was my first choice. I pounded on Jordan's front door.

"Open this fuckin' door, Jordan, or I swear I'll kick it in!" I kicked and screamed as I pummeled the door. "I want my woman back, you cokehead motherfucker."

I raced to my car and leaned on the horn. Jordan pulled back the curtain, and his eyes widened as he saw the autographed baseball I snatched off my dashboard. I threw it right at him. It felt so good to watch it shatter the window right in front of his face.

"That's right, motherfucker!" I returned to his door. "Send my woman out here right now or I'll throw somethin' else!"

To my surprise, a few seconds later I heard the click of the lock and the door open. She was coming out easier than I thought. But it wasn't Monica who opened the door. It was Jordan. He must of taken another snort for courage, 'cause I could see the white powder all over his upper lip.

"Tell my girlfriend to come out here. I want to talk to her," I demanded.

"Well, she don't wanna talk to you." His voice was cold

as ice. "Now get your black ass outta here 'fore I put a cap in yo' ass."

"Is that so, motherfucker?"

I clenched my fist, planning to smash it against his head. Now granted, he's six feet tall and I'm only five foot seven. Most people would think he had a pretty big advantage against me. But I was a semifinalist in the Virginia Golden Gloves 140-pound weight class my senior year at college, so as far as I was concerned, Jordan was in for one hell of an ass-kicking.

"You must be one stupid-ass motherfucker," Jordan said flatly. He lifted his right hand and pointed a black nine-millimeter handgun at my face.

I couldn't believe I had been so stupid. Never once in my arrogance did I look at his hands. Now I was face-to-face with the wrong end of a gun and scared shitless. I was sure that if I moved he would have blown me away and claimed self-defense. I could feel the sweat beginning to form on my brow, and the anxiety attack I had when I first saw them embrace was nothing compared to what I was going through now. I couldn't move, so I did the only thing I could think of to be sure I'd live to see the next day. I begged. That's right, I begged. I looked Jordan in the face and I pleaded for my life.

"Don't shoot me, Jordan. . . . Please don't shoot me." I was shaking, and tears slid down my cheeks. "Look, man, you can have Monica. . . . She ain't worth dying over. Just don't pull that trigger, man." I must have looked pretty damn pathetic, because Jordan started laughing.

"Look at you, you little punk. I thought you were supposed to be some tough guy from New York. You ain't shit. I should shoot your ass just for cryin'." He cocked the gun and I could hear a bullet slide into the chamber. "Motherfucker, you broke my window, didn't you? Who's gonna pay for my window?"

"I will. I'll pay for it. Just don't shoot me," I begged.

"Oh, my God! Put that gun away, Jordan!" Monica yelled from behind him. At least she had managed to cover herself up, even if she was wearing a man's bathrobe.

"Please don't let him shoot me, Monica. I don't wanna die," I whispered, choking on the salt from my tears.

"He's not gonna shoot you, Dylan." She tried to reassure me with her calm tone. "Please, Jordan. Put the gun down. He ain't worth it. I already made my choice. I'm stayin' with you." Monica put her hand on Jordan's arm and slowly brought it down to his side.

At that point I hauled ass the twenty feet to my car, jumped in, and put the car in reverse. I nearly drove right into the crowd of tenants that had come out of their apartments to watch the free show. Before I could put the car in drive, Monica was at my window, knocking frantically. Looking past her, I could see that Jordan was still busy inspecting his broken window. I rolled down my car window.

"Dylan, are you all right? I'm sorry about the way this happened. I never wanted to hurt you." She had tears rolling down her cheeks, and I almost wanted to feel sorry for her.

"I told you this was gonna happen, Monica."

"Dylan, I'm sorry, but it just wouldn't have worked out," she said sadly. She only looked back once as she returned to Jordan's side. He put his arm around her and led her into the apartment.

"I'm sorry, too, Monica," I muttered as I slammed my foot on the accelerator. "I'm sorry, too."

# 4

# Jasmine

I'd been driving around Woodhaven projects with an attitude for nearly twenty minutes. I was trying to find building 10, but the numbers weren't running consecutively and it was confusing the hell outta me. I was so frustrated I was about to give up and head to work, which I was already late for. But of course, that's when I spotted the building I was looking for right in front of me. I pulled over to the curb and got outta my car with my attitude still intact. This was the last place I wanted to be on a Friday morning. Derrick was gonna owe me big-time for this.

You see, at the end of our visit on Thanksgiving Day, like most of my other visits, I was on the verge of tears. The inmates were allowed five minutes of physical contact to say good-bye to their loved ones. For Derrick and me, it was usually one five-minute kiss, and we had to be torn away from each other when our time was up. But this time Derrick broke our kiss prematurely because he had something to say. Something he knew I wouldn't like.

"Baby, I need you to do me a favor." He lowered his head.

"Sure, boo. What is it?" I tried to kiss him again, but he'd only let me give him a peck.

"Well, I . . ." He paused.

"What is it, Derrick? You know I'll do anything for you."

"Would you?" He looked directly into my eyes. "Would you really do anything for me?"

"Yes, Derrick." I nodded without hesitation. "You know that. You know I'd do anything for you."

"Yeah, I guess you would. But this is different."

"Different how? Haven't I proven myself over the years? Haven't I shown you that my love is unconditional? Whatever you want, I'll do it."

"You sure?"

I took a deep breath before I answered him. I was praying he wasn't going to ask me to bring him drugs like he'd done Wendy. 'Cause I was not about to do that.

"Yes, Derrick, I'm sure."

"God." He exhaled loudly. "I can't believe I'm about to ask you this."

"Don't worry about it, boo. Just ask me."

"Ah'ight." He paused and I waited silently. Finally, he asked me, and I knew why it was so hard for him to get around to his question. "Would you . . . Would you bring Wendy a hundred dollars? I didn't get nothin' for Tyler's birthday, and she spent all her welfare check on his birthday party, so she ain't got no money."

"Are you serious?" I leaned as far away from him as I could get. "You want me to give my hard-earned money to your baby's momma? Have you lost your mind? I ain't bringing that bitch shit!"

I glared at him. He had set me up with his little humble act. He knew he could get me to say I would do anything. To say I was insulted by this blatant lack of respect was an understatement. I was flabbergasted. What the hell made him think I'd bring that bitch anything other that my size 8½ Timberlands? And the only reason I'd bring her those was to put my foot in her ass.

"Don't act like this, baby. She needs the money for my son. You know I wouldn't ask you something like this if it wasn't important." I stayed out of reach as he tried to hug me. That wasn't gonna work, so he tried another angle. Guilt. "I thought you said you'd do anything for me. What happened to that unconditional love you were so adamant about a few minutes ago?"

"I came to my senses when I realized you was tryin' to play me for your baby's momma." No guilt here. "How you sound, asking me to bring another bitch some money? A bitch I can't stand, at that!"

"Will you keep it down? There's other people around here. And I'm not tryin' to play you. The money's not for Wendy. It's for my *son.*" He was getting an attitude now, but I didn't give a shit.

"That's bullshit, Derrick." I put my hand in his face. "That bitch ain't getting her hair and nails done with my money." I pushed him away and he stared at me. His eyes were getting smaller with anger by the second.

"You know what? Just forget it. Just take your selfish ass on the bus and don't come back. I knew I shouldn't have asked you to do shit for me. I'll get somebody else to help me. Somebody that cares about me." He got up and turned away from the table. *Damn.* He always could find a way to get to me. I hated the thought of leaving before we made up, and he'd just made it very clear the only way we were gonna settle this was for me to say yes.

"Okay," I sighed finally, giving in. "I'll do it. I'll bring her the money. But don't ask me to do this again."

He turned around. "You mean it?"

I nodded, but I wasn't about to take the pout off my face. He tried to kiss me but I resisted. I was willing to do this 'cause I didn't wanna fight with Derrick, but his request left such a bad taste in my mouth I didn't want him to touch me.

He knew he was sending me to deliver money to Medusa herself. That bitch was gonna throw me nothin' but attitude, and he knew it. There was nothing left for us to talk about, so I said good-bye, gave him a quick peck, and got the hell out of there. The ride back to Richmond was the longest one of my life.

"Who?"

I was jilted out of my thoughts as a female voice boomed through the apartment door. That was no easy feat, considering the stereo was playing loud enough for the entire complex to hear.

"It's Jasmine. Derrick's girlfriend. Is Wendy here?"

The sound of the stereo faded as someone called Wendy to tell her I was there. I heard footsteps approaching.

"What you want?" Wendy snarled as she swung the door open. Her nappy-headed friend, a size 20 if she was anything, was standing behind her with hands on her hips. I wanted to laugh. The two of them looked like supermodels for *Projects Weekly*. Both of them were wearing beat-up housecoats, and Wendy had a weave I'm sure she'd done herself. "I axed you a question. What you want?"

"Derrick asked me to stop by and drop off a birthday present for Tyler and—"

Before I could finish my sentence and tell her about the money, she snatched the gift bag I was carrying.

"Hey, what's wrong with you?" I demanded, but she ignored me. She took the wrapped present out of the bag and shook it.

"I bet she bought something cheap," she mumbled to her friend.

"Only if you consider a Game Boy cheap," I replied. "That thing cost me almost seventy dollars."

"Seventy dollars! You spent seventy dollars on a Game Boy?" Wendy laughed and her friend joined in. "I coulda got Little Gerald to steal one from Kmart for twenty. Damn, you stupid."

"I don't deal with stolen merchandise."

"I don't deal with stolen merchandise," she repeated sarcastically. "Well, you better stop dealing with Derrick, 'cause everything he buys is off the back of a truck. Where you think he got those chains you wearing around your neck?"

"From Zales," I lied. "I was with him when he bought them."

"Whatever." She waved her hand at me. "Come on, Stacey. Jerry Springer is about to come on."

Yes, she was about to walk away without even so much as a thank-you for the gift. I wondered if her son would even get it. Probably she'd already thought of some way to sell it and keep the cash for herself. Speaking of cash, I still had some in my purse that I was supposed to be giving to her. It took every ounce of strength not to just turn and leave right then. But I had promised Derrick I'd give her the money, and I did not want another fight with him if I didn't follow through.

"Wait a minute. Derrick wanted you to have this, also." I reached in my bag and handed her an envelope with her name written on it. She grabbed it, ripped it open, and smiled.

"Well, Stacey. It looks like I'm going to Summer Jam with y'all after all." Again she didn't bother to thank me, or even speak to me, for that matter.

"For real?" her friend asked with excitement.

"Yup, 'cause Derrick came through like I knew he would." She high-fived her friend, then the two of them started dancing in the doorway like I was Ed McMahon and they'd just won Publishers Clearing House.

"Um, I hate to break this to you." I interrupted their stupid dance. "That money's not for you. It's for your son."

"Don't worry about it. I'll make sure he gets it," Wendy snickered as they both looked at each other and burst out laughing.

"Look. Tell Derrick I said thank . . ." She stopped herself. "Forget it. I'll probably see him before you do. I gotta bring him a package Thursday."

"He didn't tell me you were going up there this week."

"Honey, let's get something straight so we both understand each other. You may be Derrick's girlfriend, but I have his son. He ain't got to tell you shit we do. Girlfriends come and go, but baby mommas? We here for life. Now, run along to work. I might need you to bring me a hundred fifty next week."

With that, she smirked at me and swung the door closed in my face. I stood frozen on the doorstep for a few seconds, trying to decide if I wanted to kill her or Derrick first. Wendy acted exactly the way I expected she would. The girl had absolutely no class. She couldn't handle the fact that she was no longer Derrick's woman, so she tried to make it seem like being his baby's momma made her more important. That was the last time I'd bring that bitch anything, no matter how much Derrick begged.

# 5

# Stephanie

I just ran through two stop signs and planned on running through a third. I had to get home and get home with a quickness, 'cause I had to pee. I had to pee so bad my knees were shaking, and I didn't think I was gonna make it in the house without peeing on myself. God, I hated being pregnant.

I don't know how I made it, but somehow I pulled in front of my apartment without creating a puddle in my seat. I was trying my best to get out from under the steering wheel and into the house when I spotted my sister Jasmine's car parked out front.

*What the fuck is she doing here?* I wondered as I ran up the walkway.

Call it sibling rivalry, immaturity on my part, or just plain jealousy, but I couldn't stand my sister. Ever since we were kids, she always seemed to get all the breaks and all the attention. And my mother and grandmother always treated her like she was better than somebody, especially after she graduated college and got that job at the post office. The happiest day of my life was when she came over to Big Momma's house one Sunday with her tail between her legs after that fine-ass drug dealer she was fuckin' with was sent to prison. That's when Miss Perfect stopped being so perfect and everyone started to see her for the phony she really was. And let me tell you, I really drove a knife in her back by inviting Travis over to Thanksgiving dinner that year and introducing him as my boyfriend. It was only a week after her boyfriend's conviction and it made her look like such a fool. Big Momma was so disappointed in Jasmine that I became her new favorite granddaughter.

The second I hit the door I headed for the bathroom, and my daughter, Maleka, was right on my heels. "Mommy! Mommy! Guess what Auntie Jazz brought me?"

"What?" I whined, closing the bathroom door then quickly pulling down my panties so I could relieve myself. Maleka slid into the bathroom as the door shut.

"Skiing Barbie and her snow lodge!" She shoved a Barbie in my face.

"Damn," I mumbled as I relieved my bladder. I'd just put the same Barbie and ski house on layaway at Wal-Mart this morning. It was the only thing that Maleka had asked Santa to bring her for Christmas, other than a swing set, and where the hell was I gonna put a swing set living in the projects? Now, what was I gonna get her for Christmas? I pulled my maternity pants back over my huge belly and waddled into the living room, where Travis was sitting in front of the TV.

"What's up, baby? I got a surprise for you." He patted the cushion next to him.

I ignored his smile. I didn't give a shit about his surprise. "You know what Jasmine did? She went and bought Maleka the Barbie stuff I was gonna get her for Christmas."

"So get her something else," Travis said nonchalantly. He knew how I felt about my sister but he just couldn't understand why. If I didn't know better I'd think they were fuckin', 'cause the two of them acted way too chummy whenever they were together.

"What do you mean get her something else? The only other thing she asked for was a swing set. Where do you suggest we put a swing?" Travis just shrugged his shoulders, never taking his eyes off the TV. I waved my hand at him in disgust. "Where the hell is my sister, anyway? I saw her car parked out front." Travis pointed to the ceiling.

"She's upstairs in your room."

"What the fuck is she doing in my room?" My eyes got wide.

"Well, when she came over to drop off Maleka's toy she asked if I knew where her diamond earrings were. Something about she was going to a club in Petersburg. So I told her they were in your jewelry box upstairs."

"You told her what?" I became one big attitude. "What'd you do that for?" I headed for the stairs without waiting for his excuse.

"They were her earrings and she wanted them back. What's the big deal? She loaned them to you for the NCO ball at the base last month." I could hear him talking but I didn't pay him any mind as I walked up the stairs. I loved Travis, but for a sergeant in the army he could be so stupid sometimes. When I reached the second floor I took a deep breath before I peeked into my bedroom. My worst nightmare had come true. There was my sister, with about fifteen outfits laid across my bed. Damn, why'd he let her upstairs?

"Umm, what are you doing?" I placed my hand on my hip.

"I was just about to come downstairs and ask you the same thing." She grabbed a pile of clothes that I had borrowed and never returned. "I thought you said you couldn't find these."

"I couldn't. Where'd you find them?" I tried to look surprised, but she wasn't buying it.

"In your closet." I didn't say anything. I just stared blankly at her as she picked up three more outfits. "And how the hell did you get these out my house? I never even wore them."

"I did. They looked cute on me." I smiled and Jasmine grabbed the rest of the outfits off the bed.

"You know what, Steph? If you wasn't pregnant I'd whup your ass." She pointed a finger in my face and I laughed.

"You mean you'd try. You might be a few inches taller than me, Jasmine, but you can't beat me. You never could." I took a step closer and she took a step back. Jasmine was a real wimp. She was scared of my big, pregnant self. "What the hell are you doing going through my closet, anyway?"

"I came over here to get my earrings 'cause me and Becky are going to a club in Petersburg tonight. Not only did I find my earrings but I also found my two gold chains, an ankle bracelet, and another pair of earrings that belong to me. So I decided to see what else you had of mine."

"Well, you got your shit. Now get out my apartment." I turned the attitude up high now, especially since I had a lot more of her stuff in my dresser and wanted her outta my room as quickly as possible.

"You don't have to have an attitude, Steph. I know you were just borrowing this stuff. I just wish you'd return them, or at least tell me you got 'em. I mean, it's just stuff. If you really need it, you can have it. You are my sister, you know." Would you believe she said that shit with sincerity? She just didn't get it. She never got it. I couldn't stand her ass.

"Just get your shit and get out." She tried to reason with me but I kept on my bitch face and led her out my room. I followed her down the stairs then straight to the front door, where my daughter ran up to her, hugging her leg.

"Thanks, Aunt Jasmine. You're the best auntie ever."

"You're welcome, baby." Jasmine tried to bend down and kiss her but I grabbed Maleka by her dress and pulled her toward me.

"Maleka, get in your room," I told her.

Jasmine looked at me and tried to smile but I could see she was finally starting to get pissed off, and I was glad. She thought she was all that 'cause that drug dealer of hers left her a little money. Fuck that bitch. At least my man was home to keep me warm at night.

"And why the hell did you buy Maleka that damn Barbie less than a month before Christmas?"

"Look, I was in Toys 'Я' Us buying a gift for Derrick's son. Big Momma said Maleka was asking for it. Don't you remember that's what Aunt Lynn used to do when we were kids? She'd just surprise us with new toys whenever she came by. Remember how much we loved her for that? That's the type of auntie I'm trying to be."

"Ohhh, so you trying to buy my daughter's love?"

"No, but I know things are tight with you going to school and all. I mean, come on. You been living in the projects for four years. Maleka's only got two Barbies. I'm just trying to help out."

"Well, we don't need your help. And you don't have to worry about me living in the projects no more, 'cause as soon as we're married Travis is gonna move us on base. Then he's going to buy us a house."

"Well, then you're a lucky woman, Steph. And Travis is a good man. Just don't blow it, okay?"

"You don't have to worry about that. I love my man. Now don't be coming by here when I'm not home. You ain't got no reason to be around him when I'm not here."

"Oh, please. You have got to be kidding me. You been with Travis three years and you don't trust him?" She shook her head and gave me a pitiful look.

"I didn't say I don't trust him. It's you I don't trust. Him, I trust completely." I smirked at her. A look of shock crossed her face.

"You know what, Steph? I hope Maleka doesn't grow up to be like you, 'cause you can really be some kinda bitch." Finally the girl had a reaction other than that nicey-nice shit.

"Is that so? Well, let's pray she doesn't grow up to be like you and fall in love with a drug dealer who pretends to be a lawyer." I started to laugh as she fumed. I'd really struck a nerve. I was gonna have to remember to use that one again. I watched her get into her Lexus, then looked over at my beat-up '92 Honda Civic. God, I hated her.

When I walked back in the living room Travis got up and kissed me. I liked the way he kissed. His kisses had a way of making everything better, and I loved him for that. The funny thing is, when we first met, I was just using him because I didn't have a car and he seemed like he had a little cash. Don't get me wrong. I thought he was cute, and the sex was good, but I was into bad boys. Hell, probably the only thing my sister and I have in common is our love for thugs. If it wasn't for Big Momma, Travis woulda been history a long time ago. Thank God she talked me into staying with him, 'cause I really love the guy now. Although I have to admit I still wish Tupac was my baby's daddy.

"What's up? I saw your sister walk out of here with those dresses. If you need clothes, boo, you know all you gotta do is ask." He gave me that big smile of his.

"I know. It's just that she gave those dresses to me," I lied. "And now she comes over here taking them back just because I'm pregnant. I hate her, Travis." He looked at me with a frown.

"I guess your sister's not the good soldier I thought she was."

"She's not. She's a real bitch, and I don't want her in my house when I'm not here."

"Okay, but I want you to forget about that for a while. I

told you before, I've got a surprise for you." He smiled. I grinned. Last time Travis said he had a surprise for me, he asked me to marry him.

"What kind of surprise?" I started jumping up and down like a kid, I was so excited.

"A big surprise. A real big surprise. Now go get Maleka so I can show it to you."

When I got back to the living room with Maleka, the front door was open and I could see Travis was standing by his truck, holding my pocketbook.

"Come on," he yelled.

"Where we going?"

"Don't worry about that. You'll see when we get there. Now, get in." I got into the truck and Travis helped Maleka into her car seat. It took me a while to get my seat belt around my belly, but I managed. When I was all settled in, Travis handed me a black scarf.

"What's this for?" I looked at him strangely.

"It's a blindfold. I told you this was a surprise."

"This had better be good, Travis." I smiled at him as I tied the scarf over my eyes.

"Don't worry, it is. It's big. Real big." He checked the scarf to be sure I couldn't see, then pulled off.

I knew he wasn't lying when he said the surprise was big. Whatever he was up to, he was really going all out to keep it a surprise. I felt like a little kid who was waiting for daylight so she could run downstairs and see what Santa Claus had brought her on Christmas Day. We couldn't have driven more than ten minutes when I felt the truck stop. Travis eased it into park. By now I was going crazy trying to figure out what he was up to.

"Can I take this thing off now?" I pleaded. Travis had jumped out of the truck and let Maleka out.

"Not yet." He opened my door, grabbed my hand, and

guided me out of the truck. "Steph, I love you, and what you're about to see is the first step to showing you how much I really love you and Maleka."

"Okay, okay. I love you, too. Can I take this thing off now?" I was going crazy. I couldn't take it anymore. He was telling me my present was right in front of me.

"Yeah, you can take it off." I reached up and ripped the blindfold off, and what I saw left me speechless. I turned to him with my mouth wide open.

"Is that for me?"

"It's for us. Me, you, Maleka, and the baby. Merry Christmas, baby." I couldn't help it. I started to cry. Travis had done a lot of things for me the past few years. He'd paid for me to go to nursing school, paid for Maleka's day care, and brought groceries every Friday when he left the base. But this was more than I could have ever asked for.

"Do you like it?"

"Do I like it? It's everything I ever wanted." I was standing in front of a brand-new white colonial house with burgundy shutters. It wasn't huge, but it was just what I'd always wanted.

"I'm serious, Steph. If you don't like it I can always tell them we don't want it. I haven't signed all the papers yet," Travis chuckled.

"Don't you dare! It's perfect." I turned around and took my man by the waist, planting a giant kiss on his lips. "I can't believe you bought us a house! I can't wait to tell Big Momma. When can we move in?"

"We close in about a week. I figured you'd want to have Christmas dinner with all your family at our house this year." My face burst into a smile, then a frown.

"We can't have Christmas dinner here. We don't have a dining room set—"

He cut me off. "We don't have a lot of things, but I guess

that's why Visa was nice enough to send me this new gold card." He reached in his pocket and pulled out the card. He looked at Maleka, who was running around to the back of the house. "We've got a little more than a quarter acre. Think we have enough room for a swing set?" Travis laughed and I joined in. He made me so happy. I felt like a queen.

"Travis?" I said softly.

"Yeah, babe?"

"I don't think I can ever repay you for the things you've done for Maleka and me."

"You already have repaid me. You're having my child, remember?" He smiled. So did I.

"I know we're having a baby together, but I wanna give you more. I wanna—"

He cut me off. "You really wanna give me something that I'll always cherish?"

I nodded.

"Give me her." Travis pointed in the backyard at Maleka. "Let me adopt her, Steph. Let me give her my name so she has the same last name as her siblings."

"You mean that? You really wanna adopt Maleka?"

"More than anything in the world. Hey, she already tells her friends I'm her dad." He smiled.

"You know what? Now I know why I love you. You're the sweetest man I ever met. I love you, Travis Thomas."

"I love you too, Stephanie Johnson." I reached my arms up and kissed my man. No matter what, I was never gonna let him go.

# 6

# Dylan

I drove into the jam-packed parking lot of the Ramada Inn and decided to park across the street at the Waffle House. It was ladies' night at The Copper Mine, the small club in the basement of the Ramada, and it looked like everyone in Petersburg was out to have a good time. Everyone but me, that is. I wasn't in the mood to party. I didn't even know why I had let Joe talk me into meeting him at the club. But he told me it was time for me to get out of the house, so I finally agreed. I had been bored and lonely since Monica and I split. For five years I had spent my Sunday nights in Chesterfield, having dinner with Monica and her family. Now I had nothing to do but sit and imagine Jordan in my place at their dinner table.

God, I missed Monica. It had only been ten days since the gun incident, and I was lost without her. All I could think about was getting back with her. I tried leaving messages on her beeper. I even tried calling her folks, but she never responded. The only sign I had that she was even alive was that all her clothes had been taken out of my house one day while I was at work. She didn't even leave a note. She just left her key on the table by the front door.

It defied all reason, but I was still deeply in love with that girl. Even after all that went down, if she had walked up to me and asked me to take her back, I would have. I realized she had her faults. Hell, so did I. But she had been a part of my life for too long to just let it go. Once I parked my car, I sat for a few minutes to get myself together before meeting Joe at his usual booth inside the club.

Joe was a big, six-foot-five, three-hundred-pound, light-skinned man with handsome features and a bald head. He moonlighted as head of security for the club to supplement his income as a dispatcher for Petersburg's Public Bus Corp. Joe loved his job at the club. He hired members of the Nation of Islam's FOI, and their mere presence kept the crowd under control. All Joe had to do every night was sit in his booth and watch the dance floor. It left him plenty of time to play mack daddy. It always amazed me how much play he would get, too.

"My main man, Dylan! What up, brotha?" He smiled, patting my back with his huge arm.

"I'm doing ah'ight, Joe. How you doin'?" I forced a smile as I took a seat across from him.

"I was doin' okay till you showed up with that sour-ass look on your face. Monica is wrong for doin' you like this."

"Yeah, well, I'm over her." Joe knew I was lying. I could see it in the look he gave me. But I wasn't in the mood to talk about my broken heart, so I changed the subject. "All I wanna do is get that son of a bitch Jordan for pulling that gun on me."

"That, my brotha, you don't have to worry about. I've got something in the works that'll make Mr. Jordan Brown wish he'd never met you or your woman." I knew whatever Joe had planned, Jordan was in for a world of hurt. Joe was the type of brother that liked to play games. When it came to revenge, he was the master. Somehow, I felt better knowing he was on the job.

"Look, man, I need a little favor," he asked, changing the subject again.

"Name it."

"Remember that woman Rebecca from the post office I met at your store?"

"Yeah, the one who came in with that brown-skinned wench, looking for the Brotherman comics."

"Yeah, that's her."

"What about her?"

"Well she's coming down from Richmond tonight"—Joe hesitated for a minute—"and she's bringing her friend Jasmine with her. I was hoping that you might—"

"Ah, hell no, Joe! You know I can't stand that bitch!"

"Come on, Dylan. It's just one night."

"No way, Joe. No way am I baby-sitting the customer from hell."

"How many times do I ask you for a favor, Dylan?"

He was right. Joe never asked me for much. He'd just offered to take care of Jordan for me. Still, asking me to spend an evening with Jasmine was like asking me to cut off my right arm. Rebecca and Jasmine had been customers in my Richmond store a few days before. Rebecca, a dark-skinned cutie with dimples to kill for and a short finger-wave hairstyle, was fine as hell. She was wearing a Post Office uniform, but it didn't matter, 'cause baby had all kinds of back. Straight up, she was the only woman I'd met since Monica and I separated that came close to piquing my interest, and she was flirting with me from the minute she walked in. I was just about to make a move when good old Joe walked into the store. Well, that was the end of that. I don't know if it was his light skin or his height, but he definitely stole Rebecca's attention from me. Before I knew it, they'd walked away and left me with Jasmine.

While Rebecca was all temptation, Jasmine was all business, and to be honest, I don't really remember much about her physical appearance. But I do remember her mouth. She was a real bitch. I didn't make a habit of using that word to describe a woman, but in Jasmine's case it fit. She had asked me for some hard-to-find comics called *Brotherman*. I brought her to the front counter and explained to her that they were expensive. She didn't seem concerned about the price until I rang them up and asked her for $130.00. That's when she turned into the kid in *The Exorcist.* As God is my witness, that woman cursed me out in ways I never thought possible. She called me a nigger, an Uncle Tom, a sellout, a black motherfucker. All because she thought I was trying to rip her off with the price of a comic book. She made such a scene, the other customers dropped their comics and left. I gave her the price guide to prove I wasn't cheating her, but she threw it back at me. I probably could have dealt with all that. We had customers every day that didn't understand the collectibles market. But she took things to another level. Would you believe that ignorant bitch had the nerve to tell me, "That's why I don't shop in black businesses. 'Cause niggas never do shit right!" She stomped out of the store, grabbing her friend Rebecca. On her way out the door, she said she knew where a white-owned comic book store was and that she'd get what she needed there.

I could feel my temples throb just thinking about that shit, so I turned to Joe and refused his request. "Read my lips, Joe. No fucking way!"

I wasn't about to give him time to talk me out of leaving. I was about to slide out of the booth without another word, but as I turned to leave, there they were, Rebecca and her friend Jasmine, the customer from hell.

"Hey, Joey," Rebecca squealed, sliding into the booth next to him.

"Hi, Dylan." Jasmine actually sounded timid as she sat next to me.

"What's up?" I mumbled rudely. I didn't make eye contact with her as I kicked Joe's ankle beneath the table.

"What'd you do that for?" he yelped.

"Damn, Joe. I'm sorry. It was an accident." I gave him an evil look. "Anyway, I'm outta here." But instead of moving so I could get out of the booth, Jasmine put her hand on my arm.

"Dylan, before you leave, can I speak to you?"

"You already called me a nigger and a sellout. I don't think there's anything else to be said unless you've learned to curse in another language or something. Now could you get out of my way?" I demanded, barely able to look at her face.

"Please, Dylan. It'll only take a minute. What are you afraid of, anyway?"

"Afraid of? Do you know where I'm from?" I took a deep breath, rolling my eyes at Joe. "Look, Jasmine, I'm already mad at one woman, okay? So unless you want me to take my aggravation out on you, let me pass." The two of us were now locked in an angry stare.

"Dylan, man, do me a favor. Just talk to her." Joe tried to intervene before we had a repeat of the other day.

"For what, Joe?"

"Because I asked you to, that's why. I didn't hesitate when you asked me to help you with Jordan, did I?"

I pointed my finger at him weakly. "This shit ain't fair and you know it."

"Life ain't fair, Dylan." He smiled as he put his arm around Rebecca.

"Come on, Jasmine." I glared at her. "You got five minutes to speak your piece. And don't be cursing at me."

"Hey, you can have all the privacy you need right here." Joe stood and grabbed Rebecca's hand. "Come on, baby, I been waiting all night to see you dance."

"Is that so?" she giggled.

"You damn right! My daddy told me once, you can always tell how good a woman is in bed by the way she dances."

"Well, then, baby, you're in for one hell of a treat," she pulled him closer and winked, "'cause I damn sure can dance."

The two of them moved out to the dance floor, and Jasmine nervously moved into Joe's seat across from me. I was amazed at how attractive she was. With all the attitude she had given me when we first met, I never really bothered to take a good look. She had big, light-brown eyes and a dark-caramel complexion. Her hair was the same color as her eyes and she wore it feathered back over her shoulders. It was hard to judge her figure, because she was sitting, but I did get a good view of her ample cleavage. I was so busy admiring her looks that for a second I forgot what I was so mad about.

"Dylan," she interrupted my fantasy. "I'm not used to doing this. . . . I guess my personality can be a little overbearing. But I want to apologize about the way I acted in your store last week. It was very immature. And I figured out you weren't cheating me when I went to three other stores that tried to charge me almost twice what you did. I'm really sorry I was so ignorant."

"Okay, let's say I accept your apology. Why the big change? Where'd all this come from? You were ready to take my head off the other day. Now you come all the way to Petersburg to apologize?" I'm sorry, but call me a skeptic. I wanted to know why I was so blessed. I just didn't believe she didn't have another motive.

"Look, Dylan, I'm woman enough to admit when I'm wrong. You're a black business owner who I embarrassed in front of a store full of white customers. You don't know how bad I felt about that when I got home."

"Not half as bad as I felt."

"I can imagine. That's why I wanted to apologize. I truly believe black women need to raise up our men, not tear them down. I was out of line and I'm sorry."

I was blown away as she finished her minispeech. In less than five minutes this woman had gone from the outhouse to the penthouse in my book. She was genuine. So I figured I'd accept her olive branch and perhaps extend one of my own.

"Apology accepted. Matter of fact, why don't you come by and pick up those *Brothermans*? I'll give you ten percent off."

"Thanks. I just might do that." She smiled.

"Well, now that that's settled, can I buy you a drink?" I lifted my hand to get the barmaid's attention.

"Okay, but you'd better make it a double." She pointed to Joe and Rebecca, kissing on the dance floor. "I have a feeling we're going to be spending a lot of time together tonight." Our laughter was a signal that the tension between us had lifted.

"So, you're obviously not a comic book collector," I said as we chitchatted over our drinks. "Who are the *Brothermans* for?"

"My boyfriend, Derrick. He's got about ten boxes full of comic books in our apartment. He's a real collector. He's even got a *Superman* comic book from nineteen sixty-nine."

Whoever this brother was, she must have really liked him, 'cause she was grinning from ear to ear at the mention of his name. I didn't wanna tell her that a 1969 *Superman* comic was worth less than the *Brotherman* comics she had refused to buy in the first place. So I just listened to her talk about her man's comic collection while I sipped on my drink.

"Sounds like this Derrick is a pretty cool guy. There aren't too many brothers who collect comics seriously. Why don't you bring him by the shop?" She was unusually silent, which made me suspicious. "He is a brother, isn't he?"

"Yeah, he's a brother," she sighed. "But he's away for the next six months."

"Oh, yeah, what's he in? The Army or Navy?"

"He's in the Na—" she started to say. "No, I'm not going to lie to you. Derrick's not in the Army or the Navy. He's in prison."

I wasn't sure if she was serious. She just didn't seem like the type to date a brotha in jail. Then again, if it were up to her, he probably wouldn't be in jail in the first place.

"I'm sorry to hear that. It must be tough not having him around."

"It's like I'm doing time myself," she lamented.

"I don't mean to be nosy, but what'd he do to get locked up?"

She took a long sip of her drink before she answered.

"Derrick was arrested for possession of cocaine with the intent to distribute. They gave him six years. But he should be coming home in six months." She looked so sad, I was sorry I had even brought it up.

"Hey, I'm sorry. I didn't mean to pry. We can drop the whole thing right now." I placed my hand on hers.

"No, it's all right. I'm surprised you're not trying to judge me like everyone else."

"That's not me. To tell you the truth, I have a lot of respect for you. At least you're sticking by your man. My old lady left me for the biggest player in Petersburg."

"I'm sorry."

"That's nothin'. After he took my woman, that son of a bitch had the nerve to pull a gun on me."

"Don't worry. Her loss is gonna be someone else's gain. I know quite a few women at the post office that would go crazy for you. You should just forget her. A woman like that isn't worth it."

For the better part of an hour we shared basic get-to-know-you facts about ourselves. We discovered that we had graduated college in the same year and actually had a lot of common interests. When I asked her what kind of music she liked, Jasmine mentioned that we hadn't danced yet. Once we hit the floor, we didn't stop for an hour. And man, could she dance. As I watched her I couldn't help but think about what Joe had said earlier about dancing and sex. Joe must have seen some good things on the floor himself, because when we got back to the booth, he and Rebecca were kissing like lusty teenagers.

Jasmine and I hadn't even warmed up the chairs when I felt a soft tapping at my ankle. I knew it was Joe. We had been using this type of signal for years. I looked at him discreetly as he cut his eyes toward the door, so the girls wouldn't notice. I turned my head in that direction and almost passed out. It was Monica, and right behind her, being frisked by security, was Jordan. The only thing that went through my mind at that moment was that if security let him pass, it meant he wasn't carrying his gun. I smiled at Joe, hoping he'd be up for a good fight. He shook his head to let me know he wasn't.

"Why not?" I asked loudly, no longer caring what the girls noticed.

"Excuse me, ladies, but Dylan and I have something to discuss in private." Joe stood and waited for me to follow.

"Is everything all right?" Jasmine asked.

"Oh, everything is just fine," Joe answered for me, placing his huge arm around the back of my neck and dragging me away from the table. As soon as we were out of sight, Joe put me in a painful headlock and whispered in my ear as he led me into the men's room.

"Listen to me, Dylan, and listen to me good. I know I promised to help you get Jordan. But tonight's not the night, man." He loosened his grip so I could breathe.

"Come on, Joe. He's right there. He ain't got no gun, no nothing."

"No! I'm the head of security in here, Dylan. I'm not gonna jeopardize my job!" he shouted, putting his thumb and forefinger an inch apart. "Besides I'm this close to getting some tonight from Rebecca. You're not going to blow this for me, Dylan, you hear?"

"Joe, the guy pulled a gun on me! I'm not letting him get away with that."

"I'm not asking you to let him get away with it. All I'm asking is that you trust me. We've known each other a long time. Have I ever let you down?"

"No."

"Then let me handle Jordan. I promise you he's gonna get his."

I looked at Joe and shrugged my shoulders. As much as I wanted to kill Jordan right then, I had to respect Joe. My revenge would have to wait.

"Look, let's get out of here. Why don't we take the girls back to my place and see if we can get lucky?" Joe gave me a big smile as we walked out of the bathroom. "That Jasmine sure is fine, isn't she?"

"Yeah, but she's got a boyfriend," I said with a shade of disappointment.

"Damn, that's too bad. But you're not gonna let that stop you from getting some, are you?"

"I'm not gonna do that shit, Joe. You seem to forget somethin'. Jordan's doing the same shit to me right now."

"Suit yourself. Just make sure you keep her entertained when we get to my place. The last thing I need is her cock-blocking me."

As soon as we were out of the bathroom, I spotted Monica slow-dancing with Jordan. She was wearing my favorite dress, a tight-fitting navy blue cocktail dress that I bought her when we were on vacation in Jamaica. She looked stunning in that dress. When Monica looked up and we made eye contact, she smiled nervously, then placed her head back on Jordan's shoulder, closing her eyes. I couldn't believe what I was seeing. Was she really happy with him? Naw! She was just trying to make me jealous. She had to be.

As we returned to the table, Jasmine gave me a huge smile. I decided that two could play Monica's little game. So I stuck out my hand, and without a word, Jasmine followed me onto the dance floor. I wrapped my hands around her slender waist and pulled her in close enough to feel her breath on my neck. She placed her head on my shoulder. I took a deep breath, taking in the freshness of her hair.

"Gee your hair smells terrific," I said half-jokingly.

"Thank you," she laughed.

She took her fingernail and ran it down the back of my neck, sending shivers of pleasure down my spine.

"Dylan?" she whispered.

"Yes."

"Who was that woman at the door you and Joe were staring at?"

"You noticed that, huh?"

"Yeah, Becky did, too." She didn't sound jealous, just curious.

"That's my ex."

"I kinda figured that. She's really pretty. Do you wanna get back with her?"

"I'd like to. Why?"

" 'Cause I think she's staring at us."

I turned Jasmine slowly as we danced so that we could

both see Monica. She was right. Monica was trying to be subtle, but she was definitely staring.

"Wanna have some fun with her?" Jasmine asked, squeezing my butt with both her hands before I could answer. She started grinding her hips into mine. I glanced over at Monica, who was no longer trying to hide her stare. It was blatant. Her eyes were practically bugging out. I couldn't help but turn the other way and smile.

"Did you see the look on her face?" Jasmine giggled. "Now that was funny."

She was laughing, but I had serious things on my mind. All I could think of was that Monica still cared. She had to care. There was no way she'd ever grit her teeth like that if she didn't.

"What d'you think, wanna really piss her off?" Jasmine asked.

"Sure. What do you have in mind?" I was enjoying Monica's obvious jealousy after all she had put me through.

In one fluid motion, Jasmine placed her hand behind my neck and pulled me toward her. I was so surprised that I didn't even realize we were kissing until I felt her tongue in my mouth. Not that I'm complaining. She kissed me with such passion and desire, I swear it felt like that kiss would never end. When our lips parted, I stared into her eyes, still savoring the effects of her kiss. I'd never had anyone kiss me like that before, not even Monica. I wanted to know if it was a fluke, so I kissed her again, and I must admit I was pleasantly surprised when she reciprocated. A few seconds later, she broke the kiss, and all I could do was stare into space. It was definitely not a fluke. She was the best kisser I'd ever met.

"What's she doing now?"

"Huh? What's who doing?" I was still in a daze.

"You know who. Your girlfriend, silly." She laughed,

pulling herself away from me a bit. It was a good thing she did. I was about to kiss her again.

"Oh, her. I don't know." I glanced over at Monica, who had now stopped dancing and was staring at us with both hands on her hips. Jordan was standing next to her muttering curses under his breath, looking like he was about to lose his cool with her. It sure felt good to witness that scene. I held Jasmine's hand and smiled at Monica as we walked back to the booth. Joe and Rebecca were waiting with their coats already on.

"I see Jazz helped you with your little problem," Joe chuckled quietly.

I helped Jasmine with her coat, then took one last look at Monica. She was dancing with Jordan again, and he seemed to have calmed down. But she was also staring at me from over his shoulder. I couldn't help but feel good about what had just happened. I loved her, probably always would, but now I felt free. I'd been obsessing over her since the breakup, like I was powerless to do anything but think of her. To see her get jealous gave me back some of the power, made me feel like I could go on with my life. Who knows? Maybe even with Jasmine. The way she kissed me, maybe that boyfriend in jail didn't mean all that much to her. I took her hand and we followed Joe and Rebecca out of the club. It was time to move on with my life. Time to start a new chapter.

# 7

# Jasmine

After we left the club, we all went over to Joe's apartment to play cards and listen to music. It wasn't the type of thing I did on a regular basis, but it was still early and I loved to play spades. Plus, Becky had made it clear that she was going to Joe's with or without me. I didn't wanna desert my friend, so I went along hoping to keep her out of trouble. Besides, I was having a good time with Dylan. He was smart, funny, and even more important, respectful. And he wasn't bad to look at, either. If I didn't already have a man . . .

When our card game was finished, Joe must've been bored, because he tugged on Becky's sleeve and whispered something into her ear. Next thing I knew, they were headed for his room so they could have a *private* conversation. I tried to get her to stay in the living room with me, but she just waved her hand, telling me to mind my business. At that point I just shut up and let her do what she wanted. She was a grown woman and I was sick of being her conscience. If she wanted to be a hoochie and sleep with Joe on their first date, well, that was on her. I just hoped he was around in three months so I didn't have to listen to her cry on my shoulder.

While Becky and Joe were having their so-called conversation, Dylan and I were left sitting on the living room couch. He was drinking a beer and I was sipping on some wine, telling him about Big Momma and the rest of my family. He was really a great listener. It felt as if we'd been old friends for years. He just sat there stroking my hair, which I loved, as I told him my life story. I knew I probably should have gone home as soon as Becky decided to go in the back with Joe, but I felt comfortable with Dylan, and it had been a long, long time since I'd had any kind of male company. I knew I was playing with fire, letting him play with my hair, and especially with me enjoying it so, but I just kept trying to convince myself it was a totally innocent conversation between two friends. Besides, I was having a good time and wanted to stay.

It wasn't until about three in the morning that things became a little uncomfortable. That's when we heard the bed squeaking and Becky moaning like she didn't care if the whole neighborhood heard.

Now, I'm not gonna lie. I'm not into vibrators or threesomes or anything kinky like that, but I was getting aroused listening to Joe and Becky make love. I'm sure Dylan was, too. Not only was he stroking my hair, but he also began to gently rub his fingers along my body. It felt like an eternity since someone had touched me that way, and his fingers were reminding me of things I'd almost forgotten. I closed my eyes, and an image of our kiss on the dance floor flashed into my mind. At the time, I'd convinced myself that the kiss was nothing more than a practical joke to upset his ex-girlfriend. But now just the mere thought of his tongue in my mouth was making me breathe heavy.

When I opened my eyes, Dylan's lips were inches from mine and I wanted him to repeat what we'd done on the dance floor. I wanted him to kiss me so bad I could taste it. But thoughts of Derrick quickly took that taste away. I'd never cheated on Derrick before. Hell, I'd never even thought about it. I loved him too much for that. At least I thought I loved him that much, but Dylan's touch was hard to resist. And I knew I had better do something fast, but when I decided to stop him it was already too late. He'd pressed his soft lips against mine and I felt the warmth of his tongue enter my mouth. At that moment, my love for Derrick was like a distant memory, and my lust and passion for Dylan was overwhelming.

We lay on that couch kissing like teenagers for what seemed like eternity. I'd probably be there right now if Dylan's hand hadn't found its way under my dress. Trust me, after the way he'd been kissing me I contemplated letting him continue, but images of Derrick alone in his prison cell flashed into my mind. I grabbed Dylan's wrist, but like when he kissed me, my timing was off. He'd already pushed his fingers inside me and they were doing things to me I'd only dreamed of. I moaned, easing my legs open so that he could continue what he'd started. Hell, I might as well. I'd already crossed the line between the faithful and the unfaithful. And I must admit, it felt good.

I imagined what it would feel like to make love to Dylan; then I scolded myself for being so weak. I damn sure didn't want him to stop, but at the same time I knew I shouldn't let him continue. And it didn't help matters at all that Dylan knew exactly where to touch to make me shout.

Finally I just said, "Fuck it." It had been so damn long since I felt like this, and I was entitled to feel some pleasure, wasn't I? Even if it was only for one night. I mean, there was Becky in the other room, getting her swerve on like she did every weekend. And yet here I was, in my third year of voluntary celibacy, worried about Dylan's fingers. And for what? Derrick? Sure, I loved him, but I was still a woman with needs and wants, wasn't I?

God, I wanted to be footloose and fancy-free just one time. I just wanted to see how the other half lived once. I wanted to be reminded that I was a desirable woman and that the loneliness I had inside was only temporary. So without thinking, I arched my back, letting Dylan know that I was fully ready to give in to whatever his fingers had in store and maybe a little bit more. He pulled my panties down to my ankles and slid to his knees. A few seconds later I was pleasantly surprised when his warm, wet tongue began to lick the inside of my thigh, making me gush with moisture. I swear to God, he sent shivers down my spine when he touched the spot that I thought only I knew. I gently took hold of his head so he wouldn't get away and deprive me of the pleasure he was giving. A few minutes later I felt an eruption between my legs that was more powerful than the fireworks on the Fourth of July. Maybe it was because I had just gone through such a long dry spell, or maybe it was his skills, but I swear I was experiencing one of the greatest orgasms of my life, and I was powerless to do anything other than enjoy it. When I finally regained my composure, Dylan was above my face, resting his weight on those gorgeous, muscular arms. He kissed me and I pulled him against my body, still enjoying the lingering warmth from my orgasm.

"You like that?" he smiled.

I nodded but was too spent to speak. I loved that feeling that comes after a powerful orgasm, when every inch of your body feels like you just had a massage, and you're so relaxed you don't want to move a muscle. You just want to sleep. And it would've been easy to lie there and do just that with Dylan on top of me. Unfortunately, I was forced to come to my senses when I heard the jingling of his belt buckle. That's when I realized the mess I'd gotten myself into. How could I have been so stupid? Sure, Dylan was a nice guy, but did I really believe he was gonna give me that kind of pleasure without expecting some in return? Hell, no. Just like any man, he was ready to get his now. And I guess I couldn't blame him for it, but I sure as hell wasn't down with it. Especially after Derrick marched back to the forefront of my thoughts.

"Stop. I can't do this," I practically screamed as I struggled to get out from underneath him.

"Don't worry. I've got a condom right here." He was trying to show me the condom and soothe me with his tone, but I wasn't having it.

"I don't care. Stop!" I tried to push him off me but he was too heavy or didn't wanna be moved. I wasn't sure which one. All I knew was, his frown was making me nervous. Real nervous.

"What's wrong?"

"Get the fuck off me! Don't you understand? No means no!"

He still didn't budge. At that point the only thing going through my mind was that I was about to become a rape victim, and I had no one to blame but myself. Jesus, how stupid could I be? I'd been preaching to Becky for years about leading men on, and there I was doing the same damn thing. The only thing left for me to do was beg.

"Dylan, please. Please get up. I don't want to do this," I cried.

"What's the problem?" He sighed loudly and lifted himself off of me. I ran to the other side of the room as quickly as I could. "Did I do something wrong?"

Can you believe he put an innocent look on his face as he asked that question? It took a few seconds for me to finally gain my composure, but when I did I lit into him.

"You damn right you did something wrong, you fucking phony! A few hours ago in the club you were lovesick over your ex-girlfriend. But you were really just scheming to get some ass, weren't you? And when I wasn't givin' it up fast enough you figured you'd just take it, huh?"

"Take it?" His face was full of astonishment and anger. "You trying to say I took advantage of you? You gotta be kidding! If anyone got taken advantage of, it was me. 'Cause I sure as hell didn't hear you complaining when my face was between your legs and you was begging me not to stop. Guess it's all good as long as you're gettin' yours, huh?"

He picked up my panties and threw them at me. I felt like a fool when they hit me in the face. Especially when I thought about how easily I'd let him take them off.

"You know what, Jasmine? You're a real dick-tease."

Don't get me wrong. Some small part of me knew I was being unfair to Dylan. I wasn't some young, naive church girl. I knew you couldn't get naked with a man and expect him to put his dick away as soon as you ordered him to. Hell, guys just can't turn it on and off like that. And the more I thought about it, he never really tried to put it in; he just kept staring at me. It probably just took some time for his big head to start thinking for his little head. Something told me this guy was genuinely confused by my actions.

Problem was, I was so full of guilt about what I'd done, and that guilt was stronger than any sense of fairness I might have toward him. Even if it was wrong, I wanted to make it all his fault. If I took part of the responsibility, then I had to admit to myself that I wasn't the faithful girlfriend I'd been claiming to be for so long. I was no better than Becky now, and who the hell would want to admit to that?

"Everything all right out here? Rebecca thought she heard . . . Oops!" Joe walked into the living room and let his eyes wander up and down my half-naked body. He didn't even try to hide his smile. Why should he? There I was standing there like an idiot, balancing on one foot with the other halfway into my panties.

"Sorry, didn't mean to interrupt," he chuckled.

"You're not interrupting anything," I snapped, trying to

sound in control. And that was no small task as I tried to pull up my panties and close my shirt all at the same time. "Tell Becky I'm ready to leave."

"You ain't gotta leave. Y'all can spend the night if you wanna. I got an extra bedroom." Joe winked at Dylan, which pissed me off even more.

"Don't wink at him like I'm some fucking ho. I ain't no ho, and he ain't get none. Did you?" I turned toward Dylan, but before he could answer, Joe cut in.

"Hold up. Ain't nobody call you a ho. I was just asking if you wanted to spend the night. Damn, what's with the stink attitude?"

"Ask your friend." I pointed at Dylan, who glared at me evilly. "Look, just forget it. Tell Becky it's time to go."

"I don't believe this shit," Joe mumbled under his breath. He was obviously pissed off, but I didn't care. He was just another horny asshole lookin' to get laid, and Becky sure fit that bill. The worst part was, as far as they were concerned, so did I.

"So you gonna blame this whole thing on me, huh?" Dylan finally spoke.

"I'm not blaming this on anyone. All I know is that it was a mistake to come here. I just wanna go home."

"Yeah, well, so do I."

Becky walked into the room with her dress all crooked and buttoned wrong.

"Why we gotta leave?" Becky shouted. Her hair was sticking out every which way. "Why don't we just go to work from here?"

" 'Cause my work clothes are at your house and I'm ready to leave *now*. That's why." I sucked my teeth.

"Damn, Jasmine, you could fuck up a wet dream, you know that? Why don't you lighten the fuck up for once?" She headed for the door, followed by an angry Joe. I was about to follow them to the car when Dylan put his hand on my shoulder. I wasn't sure what he was up to, so I turned to face him with my fist clenched.

"What do you want?" I snapped.

He shook his head with a frown, then spoke very frankly. "You were wrong for the way you treated me. And I want you to know I wasn't trying to take advantage of you. I was feeling you, Jasmine. I was really feeling you and I thought you were feeling me. Now I mighta got caught up in the moment, but I would never rape any woman."

I stared in his face for a few seconds and I could feel his sincerity.

"I know that, Dylan," I finally admitted. "And I'm sorry. I guess I got caught up in the moment, too. Let's just call it a misunderstanding on both our parts."

"Ah'ight. But aside from our little misunderstanding, did you have a good time tonight?"

I gave him a weak smile. "Yeah, believe it or not, I really did have a good time. I guess that's the problem."

"What's the problem?" I wasn't about to tell him that he was right, that I was feeling him, too, so I made up an excuse.

"Look, I gotta go; Becky's waiting. I'll stop by your store some time and pick up those *Brotherman* comics."

"You do that," he replied.

I waved at him, wondering if this would be the last time I ever saw him. Most likely I wouldn't get up the nerve to stop by his store. It was too dangerous. As much as I wanted to pretend it wasn't so, lying on that couch with Dylan had awakened feelings I was not ready to deal with. I had to wonder what it was about this guy that had made it so easy for me to forget Derrick, even if it was only temporary. I had been so sure my relationship with Derrick was like a rock, and now my commitment to him seemed about as solid as

Jell-O. His request for money for his baby's momma sure hadn't made things any stronger between us, and now Dylan comes along. I was afraid my relationship with Derrick was about to hit some serious bumps in the road.

I took one last look at Dylan and silently promised myself I would just stay away from that temptation. Once I walked out that door, it would be back to my life as I'd known it.

It was hard being at work the next day. Not only was I tired as hell from being out all night, but I couldn't get my mind off Dylan. It had been so long since I'd had a man to hold me and make me feel desired. I had to force myself not to daydream about him, and the more I did that the more he crept into my mind. I kept thinking about the way he talked to me, the way he kissed me, and the way he went down on me. Not that I wanted to admit it, but my panties were getting wet just thinking about how it felt when he was doing his thing. I tried to convince myself that it was just oral sex, not like it was my first time or anything. But I don't think I've ever met a man with as much skill as Dylan.

I was so grateful to get home at the end of the day. I couldn't wait to put my feet up and get some much-needed sleep. But that plan was ruined when the phone started ringing before I could even put down my purse. I knew right away it was Derrick calling. My life was pretty predictable since he'd been locked up, so he knew he could always catch me at home around this time. Truth is, usually I was happy to hear from him and would run to the phone. But today was different. I definitely didn't want to talk to him.

Derrick seemed to have this sixth sense when it came to me. He knew right away if I wasn't telling him the truth. And I knew he'd be trippin' about why I hadn't answered my phone last night. Once he started interrogating me, I'd have to lie. Then I'd have to deal with the consequences once he figured out I was lying. On the other hand, if I didn't answer now, he'd be calling me all night until I did pick up the phone. I had to choose between letting the phone ring all night or dealing with it now so I could get some sleep later. Might as well get it over with, I decided.

"Hello?" I was trying to think of a lie fast.

"Jasmine?" I let out a thankful sigh when I heard Big Momma's voice. "Where you been, girl? I was callin' your house all night. I must've left fifteen messages. Why ain't you call me back?"

I looked down at my answering machine and the number 20 was flashing. That was not a good sign. Big Momma was not the type to leave one message, let alone fifteen, so something must be really wrong.

"I spent the night at Becky's house last night, Big Momma. Why? What's wrong?" I braced myself for bad news.

Big Momma released a sigh that made it clear she knew I wasn't telling the whole truth. She had probably called Becky's house as many times as she'd called me. I was sure she'd ask me for the real story another time, but now Big Momma had more urgent things to tell me.

"Your sister had her baby last night, child! A big ol' nine-pound baby boy!"

"Oh, that's great, Big Momma. What'd she name him?" I tried to sound enthusiastic, but it wasn't working. I was happy for Stephanie and Travis, but more than that I was jealous. I'd been wanting a baby for a long time. Derrick and I had even started trying to have a baby, but of course that all came to an end once he got locked up. So it wasn't that easy for me to share my grandmother's joy.

"Travis Jr. They're gonna call him T. J." Big Momma ignored my lack of enthusiasm and kept talking a mile a minute. She was like that. Wasn't no one or nothing gonna spoil her good mood. "Yeah, my first great-grandson. I can't wait to see him. I want you to come over here and pick me up so I can see my great-grandbaby. You hear?" she ordered.

Going out again was the last thing I wanted to do, especially since I'd have to put on a happy face for everyone else's benefit. But Big Momma was not the kind of person you refused. So I promised I'd pick her up as soon as I took a shower and changed. At least with the birth of Stephanie's baby I had an excuse for where I was last night when I did finally talk to Derrick.

Before I could kick off my shoes and head to the shower, there was a knock on my door.

"Who is it?" I sighed wearily.

"It's me, girl. Open the door!" It was Sabrina, my best friend and next-door neighbor. She and I had been friends for years, but we really got close when her husband, Richie, got locked up and sent to prison for armed robbery around the same time as Derrick. I liked Sabrina. It was nice having a friend who understood what it was like to have her man in jail. The only difference between us was Sabrina was sick of traveling up to Roanoke every weekend and was looking for a new man. You see, along with being my best friend, Sabrina was also the biggest slut I'd ever met. She'd slept with about half of Richmond, and the other half was on standby.

"I hope you got that twenty dollars I loaned you the other day." I opened the door. " 'Cause girl, I'm broke."

"Please, Jazz," she sucked her teeth as she entered my apartment. "You know Uncle Sam don't pay 'cept on the first or the fifteenth. And it ain't neither one of those days. So you just gonna have to wait till next week like the rest of the bill collectors. I'm as broke as you, if not broker." She held out a vase filled with the prettiest red and white roses I'd ever seen.

"So where'd you manage to get them roses, then? Seems

to me if you got a man who can afford roses, he should be able to help you pay me back," I teased. I knew when I gave Sabrina that twenty dollars I wasn't gonna see it anytime soon.

"Shiiit! Ain't nobody give me these flowers, girl. I was coming up the steps from work when the florist came knockin' on your door an hour ago. He asked me if I'd give these to you when you got home." Sabrina smirked. "He was kinda cute, so I told him, 'Sure, but you gotta give me your phone number.' "

"Well, I guess you got the number?" I took the vase from her and walked over to the sofa. Sabrina was right on my heels.

"Yeah, he gave it to me, all right. Then he said if his wife answers the phone to tell her he was on his way home with the milk." Sabrina sucked her teeth while I laughed. "Can you believe that shit?"

"Not really, but that's the kinda man I wanna marry."

"That's 'cause you a player-hater," Sabrina replied, and we both laughed. "Okay, girl, give it up. Who you talkin' to that would send you roses?" She placed her hand on her hip.

"I don't know. I'm surprised you didn't read the card."

"Trust me. I wanted to, but it was sealed. And last thing I wanted was for you to get an attitude."

"I know that's right, 'cause that's exactly what I would do." I sat down and opened the card.

*Dear Jasmine,*

*Sorry about our little misunderstanding last night. I meant no disrespect, and I hope you'll accept these flowers as an apology.*

*Your friend,*
*Dylan*
*555-9988 (call me)*

I took another look at the beautiful roses, then read the card again, with Sabrina begging for details over my shoulder. Dylan must have been truly sorry for what happened to spend this kind of money at the florist. It made me smile to know my original opinion of him was right. He really was a nice guy. Maybe a little too nice to be safe for a woman whose man is locked up. This kind of treatment could tempt a girl to do things she'd promised she wouldn't.

"So?" Sabrina was staring at me impatiently.

"What do you mean, 'So'?"

"So who the flowers from?" She rolled her eyes at my obvious question.

"Just a friend." I smiled unconvincingly.

"Ohhh, hell, no! Don't you dare hold out on me, Jasmine. As much shit as I told you the last couple o' years?" She was right. She had shared enough dirt about herself for me to blackmail her ass for the next twenty years. Guess the least I could do is throw the girl a bone. It wasn't like he was my new man or anything.

"Oh, all right. His name is Dylan Taylor." I tried not to sound too excited as I said his name. "Becky and I hung out with him and his friend Joe last night. We had a really nice time."

"And?" she stared at me.

"And what? He's a nice guy, but he's just a friend." I gave her an innocent look.

"Just a friend, huh? I ain't never heard of a man laying out the money for long-stem roses unless he wanted to be more than just friends. You musta given him some reason to buy these flowers." Sabrina gave me a skeptical smirk. "Is he fine?"

"He's cute," I smiled as I thought of him on the dance floor. "And girrrrrll, he had this pretty dark-chocolate skin."

Sabrina loved her some dark-skinned men. The darker the better.

"He got a job?" She got to the heart of the matter.

"Yeah, he owns his own business."

"What? Oh, shit! Girrrrlll, you done hit the jackpot!" Sabrina's eyes got wide. Lately, her first criterion was that the brother had to have a job. Probably because her husband, Richie, could never keep one. Richie's philosophy was, if you want it, I'll steal it. That's why he's doing a five-to-ten-year bid for armed robbery.

"He got a brother?" Sabrina asked.

"Don't know. We never talked about his family. Just mine."

"What about a friend? He's gotta have a friend," she pleaded.

"Sorry, Becky's already got him." I felt sorry for her. She actually looked like she'd just missed the lottery by one number.

"Damn, story of my life. Every decent man in Richmond belongs to somebody else." Sabrina shook her head and inspected her fingernails as she got back to her game of twenty million questions. "So this Dylan, is he nice?"

I smiled because the answer made me feel so good. "Yeah, he really is. He's probably the nicest guy I've met since Derrick's been locked up."

Sabrina raised her eyebrows. She knew me well enough to know what that meant. In all the time Derrick had been away, I'd never had anything good to say about another man. But there was something about this one, and she knew it as well as I did.

"Well, he sure has good taste." Sabrina reached down and took a white rose out of the vase. She smiled as she inhaled.

"He sure does." I leaned over the flowers to enjoy the

sweet fragrance. "I hate to admit it, but I could really get used to this."

"Tell me about it. Wish it was me." She frowned jealously. "So what you gonna do about Derrick?"

"What do you mean, 'do about Derrick'?"

"You know. You gonna tell him about this dude or you just gonna have you a little fun on the side? It ain't like you and Derrick is married or nothin'."

I shook my head. "Sabrina, you're trippin'. All I said is that he's nice. That don't mean I'm givin' up on Derrick."

"No, actually, you said he was the nicest guy you'd met since your man went away. Now if that don't mean you're interested, I don't know what does."

I sucked my teeth. She was pissing me off, mostly because she was speaking the truth I wasn't even trying to admit to myself.

"Look, what the fuck you interrogating me for? I told you he's just a friend. Damn, give me a break. I got a man, remember?"

"From the look on your face every time you say this guy's name, maybe I should be asking you to remember you got a man. So you gonna tell Derrick, or what?" she repeated the question. I rolled my eyes at her. To be my so-called friend, she could really get on my nerves.

"Hell, no, I'm not gonna tell him. What should I tell him for? So he can blow things out of proportion like you do? Dylan is just a friend."

She looked me straight in the eye, and then she got this gleam, like a lightbulb just went off in her mind. "Ooooooh, girl. You got laid, didn't you?"

"No, I didn't," I answered in a hurry as I remembered just how close that was to the truth.

"Yes, you did! You fucked him. That's why you didn't

come home last night." There was a momentary silence before either of us spoke. Then I got indignant.

"Hold up. How you know I didn't come home last night?" This girl was starting to sound like the damn CIA or something. "Stay out my business, Sabrina. I'm a grown woman. My momma don't keep tabs on me—"

She lifted her hand to stop me. "Well, your grandmother sure does. I know she keep tabs on you, 'cause she the one who called my house askin' me to knock on your door at three o'clock in the morning."

"Big Momma called you?" I felt like screaming. Big Momma was always blowing somebody up.

"Yeah, she called. Now, stop trying to change the subject." All of a sudden her tone softened. "Don't get me wrong, Jazz. I ain't mad at ya if you did get you some. Three years with your man upstate is a long time. I don't know how you did it. Hell, I didn't last three months." She hit a nerve with this little speech. As much as I had been playing it cool for three years, I had to admit it had been hard. There were plenty of nights I cried myself to sleep. Now I was beating myself up over one moment of weakness.

"Sabrina, I swear I didn't fuck him. But I wanted to." I finally admitted it to her and myself. "I couldn't help it. We were just talking and the next thing I know he's giving me these soft, toe-curling kisses. Girl, he was touching me in all the right places. Have you ever . . ." I hesitated, almost afraid to admit out loud how good Dylan had made me feel. "Have you ever been with a man who could make love with his tongue better than any other man could do with his whole body?"

Sabrina's eyes widened, and so did her smile. I could tell she was reminiscing about some past love. "Yeah, once. And I wish I could find him now. Right now."

"Well, girl, that's what happened last night."

"Damn, he was all that?" There was envy in her eyes.

"Was he?" I exhaled. "Girrrrrll, I thought I was gonna pass out."

"Damn!" Sabrina sat up and leaned toward me. "You sure he ain't got no brothers?"

I laughed. "Not that I know of."

"So what about Derrick? You gonna kick him to the curb for the man with the golden tongue, or what?"

I looked at Derrick's picture on the mantel.

"Nah, I can't. I love my boo. He's the only reason I *didn't* sleep with Dylan. Sex is important, but it's not the most important thing. Love means more. And I'm not about to risk five years of my life for a one-night stand or some meaningless affair. Not when I've already found love with Derrick."

"Hmmph, you better than me, girl. 'Cause if I were you, I'd be picking up the phone right now to invite Mr. Wonderful over for dinner. And the main course would be me."

"Please, girl, I ain't no better," I admitted. "I picked up the phone five times to do the same thing when I was at work, but I kept thinking about Derrick and hanging up. I never been so damn confused in my entire life. Do you know that last night, after he did his magic on me, I actually cursed his ass out?"

"You what? Why?"

" 'Cause I couldn't curse myself out for being so damn weak. And because he made me feel so damn good. Too good."

Sabrina laughed at me. "You cussed him out because he made you feel good? I know he musta went off on you."

"Yeah, we had some words," I explained. "But he sent the roses to apologize." Sabrina's expression made it clear she didn't think I was for real, so I handed her the card from the flowers delivery. "Here. Read the card."

"Shit," Sabrina was shaking her head. "A black man who's

cute, romantic, owns his own business, and admits he's wrong even when he's not? Where do I sign up? If you don't want him, I'll take him." The thing about Sabrina was, I know she was more than half serious. She'd do anything to find a replacement for Richie. I rolled my eyes at her.

The phone rang, and I realized just how long I had been sitting there with Sabrina. I was supposed to be at Big Momma's already.

"Shit." I stood up. "Can you get that? If it's Big Momma, tell her I'm in the shower."

"Hello?" Sabrina waited as the caller spoke. "No, this isn't her. Can I ask who's calling?" A smile came across her face. "Okay, hold on a second."

Her grin remained as she placed her hand over the receiver.

"Do you wanna speak to a Dylan Taylor?"

My heart was in my mouth, but that didn't stop me from snatching the phone from her with a mile-wide grin on my face. I took a deep breath and tried to compose myself. I didn't want him or Sabrina to know just how excited I was.

"Hello?"

"What's up, Jazz?" His voice sent a shiver through me.

"Hey, Dylan." I tried to stay cool. "Thanks for the roses. You didn't have to do that."

"I know. But I wanted to."

"How'd you get my number? Becky give it to you?"

"Nah. Actually, in the world of unlisted numbers, yours is listed."

"You know, you're right. I completely forgot that," I laughed, feeling like a schoolgirl with a crush. It had been a long time since anyone had made me feel that way.

"Hey, what're you doing tonight?" he asked.

"I gotta take my grandmother to see my sister's new baby." That was already something I didn't want to do, even more now since it sounded like Dylan had other plans in mind. Then I realized I better check myself. I was letting my little romantic fantasy get out of hand.

"Too bad you've got plans," Dylan sighed. "I was hoping you'd come to Captain George's with me for dinner."

"Dinner at Captain George's, huh?" I repeated for the benefit of Sabrina, who was hanging on my every word, jealousy written all over her face.

"Yeah, and then maybe a movie. But if you're busy . . ."

"Well, I do like seafood." Immediately, I was plotting the quickest way to get out of the maternity ward with Big Momma so I could go out with Dylan later. Of course, I knew this was just what I had promised myself last night I wouldn't do. I was supposed to be staying away from this man and his temptation. While I was busy wrestling with my conscience, the call waiting beeped on my phone, buying me a little time.

"Hold on a second, Dylan. I got another call."

I clicked over.

"Hello?"

*"This is an AT&T operator with a collect call from Derrick. Will you accept?"*

"Oh, shit." I threw my hand over the receiver and gave Sabrina a look of terror.

"What the hell is wrong with you?" she asked.

"It's Derrick. He's on the other line," I whispered.

"You better get yourself together and talk to him," she told me without a hint of sympathy. Guess her jealousy had gotten the best of her, 'cause she sure wasn't handing out any supportive advice right now. She folded her arms and waited to witness how I got out of this one.

"Yes, operator. I'll accept." I tried not to sound too disappointed.

"Jazz?"

"Hey, baby," I replied nervously.

"What's the matter?" Guess I didn't disguise my mood so well. All I could do was try harder.

"Nothin'. Why would you think something was the matter?"

"Don't play dumb, Jasmine. I heard you say 'Oh, shit' and it took you long enough to accept the call."

"Oh . . . I dropped my cigarette on the sofa. That's all."

"Where were you last night? I called like five times."

"I was at the hospital. Stephanie had her baby." At least that lie came quickly. But I wasn't prepared for the next question.

"What about this morning? I called you at six o'clock."

"We were at the hospital all night. She didn't have the baby till this morning." I closed my eyes and prayed he'd believe me. A call-waiting beep reminded me I'd left Dylan on the other line. "Oh, Dylan. Hold on a minute."

"Dylan! Who the fuck is Dylan?"

I shot a look at Sabrina, who had her head in her hands, laughing up a storm. Shit, with friends like her, who needs enemies?

"Did I say Dylan? I'm sorry, boo." The lies were getting easier, coming faster. "I was just talking to Sabrina about her new man. His name is Dylan. I just got a little confused."

"What the hell is going on, Jasmine?" His sixth sense was kicking into high gear, and I knew it was only a matter of time before he went off on me. The phone beeped again and I took advantage of the escape.

"Nothin', Derrick. Hold on a second." I clicked over. "Hello?"

"I guess you forgot about me." Dylan's voice didn't make me tingle this time. It gave me a headache.

"No, I didn't forget you. I'm just on an important call."

"Okay, well, I'll let you go then." Damn, he was still

being the gentleman. If he were an asshole, I wouldn't be in this shit right now. "So what's up with dinner?" he asked.

"I don't think that's a very good idea. Not after last night." I did another 180-degree turn with my attitude. Just a minute ago I would have agreed to go anywhere with him. Now I just wanted him off the phone. And yet, once again, he dealt with my changing personality and persisted.

"Jasmine, we can go just as friends. I swear, no funny business."

"I appreciate the offer, Dylan." *More than you know.* "But maybe some other time, okay?"

"Hey, we're still gonna be friends, aren't we?"

"Yeah, I'd love to be your friend. Look, I gotta go. Thanks again for the flowers." I clicked over before he could try to change my mind.

"Derrick?"

"Who is Dylan?" He was still on that. Shit.

"I told you. He's Sabrina new boyfriend." I took on some serious attitude. Maybe I could distract him from the issue if I got him mad about my bitch factor.

"Stop lying to me, Jasmine." Damn. He still wouldn't give up. It was time to turn up the volume.

"Fuck you, Derrick!"

"What'd you say?" I could hear the shock in his voice.

"I said fuck you!" Sabrina was still nearby, giving me mock applause for my performance. I'm sure this shit was better than Ricki Lake as far as she was concerned. "I'm not a liar, Derrick, and I don't appreciate you calling me one. Now, I'm tired from being up all night. I had a hard day at work, and I still gotta take Big Momma to the hospital to see Stephanie's baby. So if you wanna call me a liar, I'ma hang up the fucking phone, 'cause I don't need this shit!" There was silence on the line for a second as I waited to see if my performance had done its job.

"Hold up, baby. Relax for a minute." I did relax, 'cause I knew I was finally safe. "I'm sorry. It's just hard bein' in here, knowing you're out there with all them brothers who might be trying to take advantage of you. I mean, look at Sabrina. Her poor Richie is doing his time, trying to hold on to his sanity, and Sabrina's out ho'in' with some guy named Dylan. That shit ain't right. You can see how I could get a little suspicious, can't you?"

"I guess. But if you don't know I love you by now, you never will." I tried to sound like he'd hurt my feelings. All I was really feeling was guilty, 'cause doubts about my love had definitely crossed my mind in the last twenty-four hours.

"I know, I know. I'm sorry." Derrick sounded like he'd had enough of this roller-coaster ride for the moment. "Look, I gotta go to chow, but I'll call you later, okay?" I didn't answer. I was relieved I'd been able to distract Derrick's suspicious self, and I didn't want to risk another word. "Come on, Jazz. Don't do this."

"Make it around seven. I gotta take Big Momma to the hospital."

"Ah'ight, boo. I love you." He actually sounded relieved that I'd told him to call me back. It wasn't often I felt like I came out on top of one of our little squabbles.

"I love you, too, Derrick." I hung up and looked at Sabrina, knowing she'd be dying to give me her two cents now.

"Damn, girl, they should be giving you an Academy Award, 'cause that was one hell of a performance." She wrinkled her brow when I didn't thank her for the compliment. Maybe she thought I wasn't done when I picked up the phone again. "Who you calling now? Dylan?"

"Hell, no! I'm callin' the telephone company. This time tomorrow I'm gonna have a new unlisted number. I can't handle this kinda stress."

# 8

# Travis

It was our first Christmas in our new house, and we were halfway through dinner when the doorbell rang. Both Stephanie and I glanced at each other, hoping the other was gonna get up and answer the door. I had a good reason for wanting her to get it. I knew who was at the door, and he was delivering Stephanie's Christmas present. The plan was for her to answer the door and get her big surprise while all her family was here to witness the look on her face.

Unfortunately, it didn't look like things were gonna go according to plan. Stephanie was on a mission at the moment. She was sitting at the kids' table trying to get Maleka to eat her vegetables, and she was finally making some headway. She had actually gotten her to eat a few bites of greens, which was no small feat. If it were up to Maleka, her diet would consist of hamburgers, hotdogs, and french fries. Getting up to answer the door would signal escape for Maleka, and Stephanie was not about to go for that.

*Ding-dong, ding-dong.*

"Baby, can you get that, please?" She gave me a pleading look.

"Sure, hon." I handed my son, Travis Jr., to my soon-to-be mother-in-law, Miss Betty. Now I'd have to think of another plan.

"I bet you that's Jasmine's sorry ass," Big Momma grumbled from across the table. "That girl should be ashamed of herself. She ain't never on time unless she's trying to catch a bus up to that jail in Roanoke. Who in the world ever heard of showing up three hours late for Christmas dinner?"

"Oh, she probably just had car trouble, Momma." Miss Betty tried her best to defend her oldest daughter.

"Please, Betty Jean." Big Momma sucked her teeth. "She could've at least called. She was probably up at that prison with that drug dealer. The Lord only knows what she sees in that boy."

"I don't think the Lord even knows, Big Momma," Stephanie interjected with a laugh.

"Wait a minute, Stephanie. Didn't she . . ." I was about to remind her that Jasmine had called this morning to tell us she wasn't coming to dinner, but Stephanie shot me a look that shut my mouth in a hurry.

"Travis, go get the door, and mind your business." Stephanie rolled her eyes at me and I rolled mine right back. I knew what she was trying to do, and I didn't like it one bit. She wanted me to shut up about the call 'cause she always enjoyed when her family talked shit about her sister. I could have put a stop to it, but I'd told myself a long time ago that I wasn't gonna get involved with their little feud. Besides, I had other things on my mind.

*Ding-dong, ding-dong.*

I opened the door and smiled when I saw the sparkling Ford minivan parked next to my Expedition in the driveway. A giant Christmas bow hung from the rearview mirror and another from the hood ornament.

"Matt, where you at, man?" I stuck my head out the door and whispered loudly.

"Over here behind the van," he whispered back. "I thought you said Stephanie was gonna answer the door."

"Don't worry, she's coming. I just gotta figure out how." I

stepped out onto the porch. "Now, fix the bow on the hood. It's crooked." I watched him adjust it. "How's she drive?"

"Like a dream. She's really gonna love it, T. Wanda wants me to buy her one now." He handed me the keys.

"Speaking of Wanda, how is she?" I waved to his wife, who was sitting in their car, parked in front of a neighbor's house.

"She's good, man. But I know she's wondering why it's you at the door and not Steph. She was dying to see the look on Stephanie's face when she saw that van."

"Well, I'm gonna go get Steph now," I told him as another plan came to mind. "Why don't you go get Lisa and the two of you can come in and have dessert?"

"Thanks, man, but I can't. I've gotta get up the road. I was supposed to be at my in-laws' in Fredericksburg an hour ago."

"All right, then." I reached out and we grasped hands. "Thanks again, man. I really appreciate you keeping the van at your place until today."

"After all the shit you've done for me? Please, this is nothing. I'll see you at work." I watched Matt walk down the driveway. He was a good friend. I don't know too many people who would take time out of their holiday to do what he did.

I glanced at the minivan one last time and swelled with pride. Nothing in the world could make a man feel good about himself like being able to provide for his family. Now Stephanie would have a shiny car to park in the driveway in front of our new house. But first I had to surprise her, and I wanted to make it good. I stepped into the house and slammed the door as hard as I could behind me.

"Goddamn it! Stephanie, get out here," I screamed. Stephanie came running into the foyer, followed by Big Momma and the rest of her family.

"What is it, baby? What's the matter?" She had a look of fear on her face. No doubt she was expecting some terrible news, so I guess my performance was pretty effective. It took everything I had not to burst out laughing.

"Don't play stupid with me." I masked my laughter. "You know exactly what's the matter! What the hell is that in our driveway?"

"I don't know." Stephanie shrugged her shoulders and looked to Big Momma for some help. Miraculously, this was the one time Big Momma's mouth didn't seem to work. Maybe she was in shock. This sure wasn't the Goody Two-Shoes Travis they were used to seeing, and I was kinda enjoying the act.

"You must think I'm a fool." I faced her and tried to look grim.

"Look, Travis, I don't know what you're talking about, so stop playing games and tell me what's going on."

"Oh, so now you don't know what's goin' on, huh? You think I'm playing games? Well, what's that parked in our driveway? A horse and buggy?" I opened the door dramatically and made a grand, sweeping gesture with my arm. Stephanie stepped past me, and her family wasn't far behind, everyone peering outside to see what horror I'd been screaming about.

"Merry Christmas, baby," I murmured into Stephanie's ear as I moved beside her.

"Oh, my God!" she squeaked, placing her hands over her mouth. She looked at me then back at the van, a smile covering her face. "Is that—is that for me?"

"Yeah, it's for you." I kissed her and handed her the keys. "Only the best for my baby."

There were plenty of *oohs* and *aahs* coming from her family members. They'd all been impressed by the house, so this present was just icing on the cake. How could I be anything less than Superman in their eyes right now? I was taking care of Stephanie, taking care of Maleka and the baby, and showering my family with gifts they'd never dreamed they could own. But somehow, I guess Stephanie wasn't as impressed as her family members, 'cause she handed the keys back to me.

"What's up? Why you givin' the keys back?" I tried to put them back in her hands, but she kept her fingers curled tightly.

"I can't accept this, Travis," she said quietly. Now there was plenty of murmuring coming from her family behind us. Talk about blowin' up my spot.

"Stop playin', Steph." I tried to give her the keys again, but she still wouldn't take them.

"I'm not playin', Travis. Take the car back." She looked at the van one more time, sighed, and tried to head to the door. I wasn't letting her go anywhere without an explanation. To say I was hurt is an understatement. I'd gone to a lot of trouble to get that car by Christmas, and this certainly wasn't the reaction I'd been expecting.

"You been saying you wanted a new car for over a year." Talk about some shit. All of a sudden I felt like a used-car salesman when I should have felt like Santa Claus. "Come on. You didn't even look at it. It's the van you were talking about last week. It even has a VCR for the kids just like you wanted. Is there something wrong with the color or somethin'?"

"No, the color's fine and so is the van," she sighed again.

"So what's the problem?" *Enough with the sighing shit; just get to the point.*

"We can't afford a new car. You just bought me a house and you're still paying off your truck. How we gonna afford another car?"

*Huh?* This couldn't have been the same girl I met in that club. As long as she got what she wanted, that girl couldn't have cared less how the bills were getting paid. Now here she was, the voice of financial reason. This was funny. She was either seriously maturing, which I liked, or she was frontin' for her family members. Either way, I could play her game, too.

"Okay," I told her with finality. "If you really want me to take it back, I will. But I made my last truck payment on Friday." She studied my face.

"You're serious? The truck's paid off?"

"Uh-huh." I nodded while she studied my face.

"Well, shit! In that case, gimme them keys!" She gave me a quick peck on the lips, snatched the keys out of my hand, and ran for the van. "Come on y'all, let's go for a ride." Now, that was the Stephanie I knew and loved. Guess I wasn't the only one with a flair for the dramatic.

"Look at her. She sure loves that car." Big Momma eased her rather large backside into a wicker chair on the porch while the rest of the adults followed Stephanie and piled into the van.

"I sure hope so, Big Momma." I strolled over to the chair next to her and sat down. "How come you're not over there with the rest of them? It looks like they're about to go for a ride."

"I know, but my feet been botherin' me a bit lately. So I'ma sit right up here on the porch with you for a while, Travis. Besides, I'm gonna have my fair share of rides in that van. Trust me." Big Momma gave me a smile of certainty.

"I know that's right."

"Travis, keep an eye on Maleka and the rest of the kids. We're goin' for a ride," Stephanie yelled out the window of the van, where she'd quickly settled in the driver's seat.

"Ah'ight, baby." I leaned back and smiled proudly. Big Momma and I waved as she pulled out of the driveway.

"Travis?" Big Momma leaned toward me as she cleared

her throat. "I heard what you said to Stephanie, but you sure you can afford this house? And them cars? You know, if money's tight you can always come to me."

"I appreciate that, Big Momma, but we can handle it. I only had to put three percent down with my VA loan. And with the interest rates being so low, my mortgage is only twelve hundred a month. With my housing allowance from the army and all the money I've been saving over the years living on base, we've got more than enough to get by. Just don't tell Stephanie. She might not wanna go back to work."

"I ain't tellin' her nothin'." Big Momma grinned. "But now that y'all got a new house and two fancy cars, when y'all plannin' on settin' a date for this weddin'? I'm not gettin' any younger, you know." This woman sure didn't waste no time when she had something on her mind. Luckily, I had an answer for her.

"Stephanie didn't tell you?"

"Tell me what?"

"We set the date last week. Fourth of July. We wanted to have it Memorial Day weekend, but Stephanie's lawyer said it was gonna take at least six months for my adoption of Maleka to go through."

"You adopting Maleka?" Big Momma was grinning from ear to ear. Apparently, Stephanie hadn't told her a thing, but I was glad to see she approved.

"Yes, ma'am. I love that little girl and I want her to have my name." Hell, I was the only father Maleka knew, and I know she loved me as much as I loved her.

"You know, Travis, I'll be eighty-five on June tenth, so I'm not sure how much longer the Lord has for me in this world." She hesitated, patting my knee. "But I'm glad I met you. You're a good man. I pray my granddaughter's smart enough to realize what she's got." We shared a smile, though I was a little surprised to hear the lack of confidence she had in

Stephanie. I guess judging from Steph's track record with roughnecks and hoods, Big Momma had reason to wonder. Not me. I knew that with all the love I was showering on her, there was no way she'd even think about steppin' out on me.

"Thanks, Big Momma. Coming from you that means a lot. And I want you to know I love Stephanie more than anything in this world."

"Believe me. I can see that . . ." The rest of her sentence was swallowed by the blaring rap music coming from a souped-up Honda Civic that passed by. The bass made the floorboards of the porch rumble. "Lord, these young people act like they ain't got no sense!" Big Momma shouted.

"And no eardrums neither," I shouted back as I watched the car pull into my neighbor's driveway. My eyebrows rose as it backed out and pulled in front of my house.

"Somebody you know, Travis?" Big Momma asked.

"No, ma'am." I shook my head. "Nobody I know." I stood, wondering who the hell would be dropping by unannounced on Christmas Day playing their music so damn loud. About a minute later I got my answer when a tall, thuggish-looking brother with an almond complexion stepped out of the car. Big Momma almost fell outta her chair when she saw him.

"Lord have mercy! What's he doin' here?"

I'd never seen the brother before, but it didn't take a genius to figure out who he was. He was Maleka's biological father, there was no doubt about that. He looked like he could've spit her out.

"Travis?" Big Momma was struggling to get out of her seat. "Don't you step off this porch. You hear me? Travis!" I didn't answer her because I was already halfway down the walkway, headed for Maleka's father. In less than a month we were supposed to go to court to have his parental rights rescinded so I could start adoption proceedings for Maleka. This guy had been missing in action for the better part of

Maleka's life, and now he decides to show up at my door? Wasn't no way I was gonna let him mess up my little family. Not without a fight.

"Can I help you?" I stopped about two feet in front of him, flexing my arms. I wanted to be sure he got the message from the start. He was not welcome.

"I'm lookin' for my baby's mom. Stephanie. She live here?" He spoke with that street thug cockiness. I guess he was trying to intimidate me.

I stepped in a little closer, put a little more bass in my voice, and gave him the same attitude right back, army-style.

"Yeah, she lives here. What you want her for?"

"That ain't none of yo' business unless your name's Stephanie. And I can't remember fuckin' anyone as ugly as you." He leaned to the side, checking out the house.

"I'm gonna ask you one more time, man. What you want with Stephanie?" I moved closer to block his view of the front porch.

He stepped back, eyeing me from head to toe with a devilish grin. "Oh, I get it. You must be her new man."

"No, I've been around for quite a while. Playin' daddy to your daughter," I smirked, hoping to piss him off, but he had a few comebacks of his own.

"Well you can stop playin' now, dawg, 'cause her real daddy's here. And I'm not planning on leaving anytime soon."

"Her real daddy, huh? Why don't you ask her who her real daddy is?" I scoffed. Malek clenched his fists like he was about to take a swing at me, and believe me I was ready for whatever he was about to bring. But Big Momma's interruption put us both in our place.

"Malek Robinson! What are you doin' here?" Big Momma huffed angrily, glaring from Malek to me and back to him. She was out of breath after running from the porch. "Both of you! Put them damn hands down, now!"

I don't know if Big Momma was worried about what I would do or not, but she must have known Malek well enough to know she might have to break somethin' up. 'Cause it wasn't every day you saw Big Momma moving her large frame so fast. A few more seconds and we would have come to blows, but Malek's hands dropped instantly when he heard her voice. It always amazed me how easily she could command respect, even from a punk like Malek. His hard-ass tone became choirboy-gentle when he spoke to her.

"It's Christmas, Mrs. Washington. I just came by to see my daughter. I'm not here for no trouble. I swear. I just wanna see my daughter." He lifted the shopping bag he'd been carrying. I could tell Big Momma was not impressed.

"What daughter? You ain't got no daughter around here." She nudged me to the side and pointed her finger right in Malek's face. "It takes a man to raise a child, not some fool who ain't been around in four years. So don't be comin' 'round here talkin' 'bout your daughter, 'cause you gave up that privilege when you walked out on her years ago. Now get your sorry ass outta here 'fore I call the police." Malek's expression changed. I guess not even Big Momma was allowed to disrespect him like that, 'cause he lost his passive stance and started demanding.

"I ain't leavin' here till I see my daughter, Mrs. Washington. So you might as well point me to her or call the police." Malek turned toward the children playing on the swing set.

"What you mean point you to her? You don't even know which one she is, do you?" *Damn!* From the embarrassment on Malek's face, it was obvious Big Momma was right. She just threw her hands in the air. "Lawwwd, the boy done come over here talkin' 'bout his daughter and don't even know which child she is!"

Big Momma started in on him with a litany of insults about what kind of sorry excuse for a father he was. What surprised me was that he actually stood there and took it for a few seconds, which I thoroughly enjoyed witnessing. Just when he looked like he was ready to interrupt her, Stephanie pulled the van into the driveway. I turned in her direction, anxious to see how she was going to handle this. From everything Stephanie had ever told me about her ex, I was sure they wouldn't be exchanging pleasant holiday greetings. And if he wanted to act stupid I'd be right there by my girl's side to act stupid with him.

# 9

# Stephanie

"Oh, God! Momma? Is that who I think it is? Is that Malek?" I almost drove into the mailbox when I saw him standing in the walkway. Big Momma was huffin' and puffin' next to him, her arms waving all up in his face. I had no idea what Malek was doing there or how he even found my new house, but one thing was for sure: his presence meant trouble. Big trouble.

"Girl, it sure looks like that fool. What's he doin' here? You tryin' to mess things up with Travis?" My mother's tone was accusatory, like I had something to do with all this shit. God, I could feel a migraine coming on with a vengeance. Not only was my mother already jumping in my shit about him, but Travis would no doubt have plenty to say about it, too. He was already glaring at me with his arms crossed. Made me wanna put the van in reverse and back out of the driveway.

"Stephanie, I think you better get out there and do something," my mother urged as if she'd read my mind and knew I was close to fleeing.

"I ain't goin' out there, Momma. Big Momma looks like she's got everything under control." I tried to sound like it was a joke, but I would have driven away in a hot second if she had even smiled at me in response.

"She looks like she's about to slap that boy silly." Momma

shook her head. "Now get out there and get rid of that fool before he ruins what's left of the holiday. We ain't even opened the presents yet."

"How am I supposed to do that? You know Malek ain't got good sense." I just wanted to crawl under the dashboard.

"You the one who had a baby with him, so don't be complainin' now." She gave me a light shove. "Now get out there and handle your business."

I sighed in protest but knew she was right. Malek wasn't going anywhere until I talked to him. If there was one thing that boy had always been, it was persistent. He could stand there and face Big Momma's berating all day if he set his mind to it. And from the look on his face, he was ready to do just that. I reluctantly opened my door and stepped out, gathering my strength as I marched toward the group.

"Malek! What the hell are you doing here?" I pushed my way past Travis and Big Momma and got right in his face.

"What's up, Shorty? You lookin' mighty fine." I swear it took everything I had not to smack the shit outta him when he eyed me from head to toe with that arrogant grin.

"Don't 'what's up?' me, Malek. And my name is Stephanie. Not Shorty." I glared at him. "What the hell are you doing here? And how did you find out where I live?" I added that last part for Travis's benefit, who had yet to speak, though he was standing by, watching every move I made. I wanted to make it completely clear I had nothing to do with Malek's arrival. Unfortunately, Malek also decided it was time to invite Travis into our little discussion.

"Yep, that's my Shorty. She sure got a lot of spunk, don't she?" he smirked at Travis. "You know, that's why I started messing with her in the first place, because she had a lot of spunk. That and a *phat ass*." He grabbed my arm and spun me, his eyes traveling down my backside. "Mmm-mmm, she always did have a nice ass."

"You better back the fuck up 'fore I put my foot in your ass!" Travis roared, taking a step toward Malek. He looked like he was about to hit him.

"Oh, my God. Travis, no!" I grabbed tight onto his arm to keep him by my side.

"Come on and bring it, big boy. You don't know who you fucking with. I will fuck your big ass up!"

"That supposed to be a threat, punk?" Travis lifted his fists, grinning. "C'mon, let's see what you got."

"Travis! Please don't! Malek's sorry ass ain't worth it. He's still trying to prove he's a man."

"Shut up, Shorty," Malek growled. I ignored him as I looked into Travis's eyes.

"Baby, you got me and the kids. Don't stoop down to his level." I kept my hand on Travis's shoulder, though he had relaxed enough that I knew there wouldn't be a fight. "I asked you a question, Malek. What are you doing here?"

"I came by here to see my daughter." His fists were down, but he was still pretty agitated. "And if *you* didn't want me to know where you live, you shouldn'ta put it on this." He pulled a rolled-up paper from his back pocket and waved it at me.

"And? What's that supposed to be?" I was in no mood for guessing games.

"It's the subpoena you sent to Ma's house. You tryin' to get my rights as a parent taken away?" He shook his head. "You think you're real slick, don't you? Sending this to Ma's house instead of Nana's. You knew I wouldn't get it." He was right. I didn't want to deal with his ass when it came time for Travis to adopt Maleka, so I had purposely sent the papers to his mother's house. That woman was so cracked out, I figured there was no way he'd ever see the subpoena. Then we could just claim him unreachable and everything would be smooth sailing. Malek took great pleasure now in telling me how my plan had failed.

"I guess you didn't know my ma ain't on crack no more. She lives with me at Nana's now." I knew Travis was gonna be pissed about this. He'd told me to just make up an address, but I had to be stupid and put his mother's. Who would have ever expected that lifetime crackhead to get straight? I'd have to deal with Travis later, but for now I still had to get rid of Malek.

"So you're living with Nana, huh? I thought you lived in D.C., Mr. Big-time Rapper," I smirked.

"Yeah, well things didn't work out," he mumbled.

"Somebody finally tell you that you can't rap?" That got a laugh from Big Momma, who was still standing nearby, ready to jump back in if I needed her.

"Very funny, Shorty. You should be on the Queens of Comedy." He could front all he wanted, but I knew I'd just hurt him. Once upon a time I had been his biggest supporter. That time was long gone.

"Well, if you don't like the jokes, get the hell out my yard." I jerked my head in the direction of his souped-up hoopty.

"I'm not going anywhere till I see my daughter." Back to that. Damn, he wasn't playin', no matter how many people he was up against.

"I told you. You ain't got no daughter around here. Now get the hell outta here 'fore I call the police." Big Momma was heated. Malek ignored her and spoke to me.

"Look, Shorty, you know how I get down, so don't make this hard on yourself. You might as well go get my daughter and bring her over here. I just wanna give her my Christmas present, then I'll leave." Malek gave me a wicked smile that sent chills down my spine. He was right. I did know how he got down. Things were bad enough already, but he was prepared to turn it up a notch if he had to; and the trouble he could bring was much worse than a little fight with Travis. I did not need this bullshit, especially on Christmas. Time to give him what he asked.

"You wanna see your daughter, Malek?" My eyes got small and they never left his.

"Yeah." He nodded.

"You *really* wanna see your daughter?"

"I said yeah."

"Okay." I nodded. I could see the disapproval on Travis's face, but he didn't know Malek like I did. "You got two minutes; then you're gonna leave, or I'll be the one calling the cops. You got that?"

"Ah'ight." His body language relaxed a little.

"I wouldn't let him see shit." Big Momma sucked her teeth.

"Please, Big Momma, let me handle this." I gave her a pleading look. She didn't answer, so I said it again. "I know what I'm doing. Let me handle it."

"Ah'ight, child. It's your life." She looked at Travis as she said this. I knew what she was thinking, but I could smooth things over with Travis as soon as I proved my point to Malek. Maleka knew who her family was, and I was about to prove that to her father. I just had to let him put his foot in his mouth one more time.

"Maleka! Maleka! Come here, baby!" I called to my daughter. She came skipping over to us.

"Yes, Mommy?" She looked a little nervous. No doubt she'd picked up on the tension in our group. I stroked her hair to calm her and introduced her to her father.

"Maleka, this is Malek."

"What's up, Maleka?" Malek bent down on one knee to be at her level.

"Hi." She waved. "Your name sounds kinda like mine."

"That's right." He looked at Travis and smiled smugly, then turned back to Maleka. "You're a very pretty girl."

"Thank you," she replied bashfully, twisting as she spoke.

"You're welcome. This is for you." He tried to hand the shopping bag to her, but Maleka pulled back. She looked up at me uncertainly.

"What's wrong? It's a doll baby. Don't you like doll babies?" Malek was confused. I guess he'd expected to buy his daughter's affection with a lousy doll.

"I like dolls, but I'm not allowed to take things from strangers," Maleka told him.

My grin was a mile wide. I knew my child, and I knew what would happen when Malek demanded to see her. He brings his triflin' ass around after all this time, expecting his daughter to jump in his arms. Please, maybe that woulda happened if she knew who the hell he was, but she already had a family, complete with a daddy and a new baby brother.

"I'm not a stranger, Maleka. Ask your mommy." Malek's expression softened. He was looking for some help from me all of a sudden, and I was more than willing to oblige.

"Oh no, honey, he's not a stranger at all. Are you, Malek?" Our eyes met, and I know he got the point. He was out to sea and I would not be throwing him a life jacket. At least not one that would work. "Matter of fact, why don't *you* tell her who you are, Malek?" I smirked.

"I'm your daddy, Maleka." He said it without much conviction. Could it be he already knew he'd lost this battle?

Maleka screwed up her face and shook her head at him adamantly.

"No, you ain't! You ain't my daddy." She grabbed Travis's arm with both her hands. "Travis my daddy, right, Travis?"

"That's right, baby. I'm your daddy." He scooped her up into his arms and kissed her cheek.

Everything seemed to stand still after that for a few seconds. No one said a word, but Malek's mind was spinning, I'm sure. He was breathing heavy, probably getting angrier by the second. I could tell by his eyes that his male pride had been wounded. I was afraid he might try and attack Travis while he was holding Maleka. I think Big Momma had the same fear.

"Don't you do nothin' stupid, Malek. Not unless you wanna spend the night in jail." Big Momma positioned herself between Travis and Malek.

"Big Momma, will you take Maleka in the house and give her some ice cream?" Travis asked.

"Uh-huh, I think that's a good idea. Come on, child. Big Momma wants some ice cream, too." She reached for Maleka's hand and led her toward the house.

"You know this is some foul shit, Shorty? You ain't had to do this. You coulda made sure she knew who I was." If I didn't know better I would have sworn he was about to cry.

"No, you didn't." My eyes were wide with amazement. "No you didn't just try to blame this on me. I raised that girl by myself for four years without your sorry ass. You ain't brought her a pack of Pampers or sent a birthday card since she was born. Matter of fact, do you even remember when she was born? When's her birthday Malek?"

He glared at me, tryin' to be a hard-ass, but he sure didn't have an answer.

"I didn't think you knew. So don't you dare come around here telling me what I should've done. If you wanted Maleka to know who you were, then you should've brought your black ass around." There was a momentary silence while I let my words sink in. "You've seen your daughter. Now it's time to leave."

"Don't play yourself, Shorty, 'cause this ain't over. I'm still her father."

"Yeah, but as you can see, that don't make you her

daddy!" I took hold of Travis's hand, and the two of us began to walk toward the house without even bothering to look back at Malek.

"You're not gonna win in court. I'll still have my rights!"

I stopped in my tracks and turned toward him as I let go of Travis's hand.

"Maybe so. But not until you pay some of that child support you owe the state from when I was on welfare." That felt good. Finally, I knew I'd had the last word. He didn't have nowhere near the money it would take to get straight with the state. "Oh, and by the way, Malek, now you know how *I* get down. Remember that for future reference." I turned to Travis. "Come on, boo. All of a sudden I've got a taste for some of Big Momma's sweet potato pie."

Travis smirked at Malek. "I'm right behind you, baby. I'm right behind you."

# 10

# Jasmine

I'd been on my living room floor, curled up around a pillow, crying hysterically for most of the morning. After five years of going together, Derrick and I had finally broken up. My girls, Becky and Sabrina, had come over to give me moral support and comfort me in my hour of need. But to be honest, I was wishing they would go home. I needed to be alone to think, to be miserable and hateful.

The phone rang.

"Want me to get that?" Becky reached for the phone.

"No, let it ring." I grabbed her wrist.

There was no reason to answer the phone. I knew exactly who it was. It was Derrick. He'd been calling all day, and I hadn't accepted one of his calls. Why should I? There was no reason to speak to him after the way he'd treated me yesterday. I reached up and touched my eye, which was swollen where he'd smacked me. The pain was still intense, and I had to jerk my hand away. Before now you couldn't have paid me to believe Derrick would ever put his hands on me, but now I had the proof on my face.

I'd gone up to Roanoke thinking I was gonna surprise Derrick by spending the day with him. I was supposed to go to my sister's house after my nephew's christening, but Derrick had been whining about how I'd been neglecting him lately. He was right, too. I had missed a few visits because of family obligations and overtime at work. But Derrick knew just the right words to make me feel guilty. Not that I didn't feel guilty enough on my own after what happened with Dylan.

Of course, I caught hell from Big Momma when I told her I wouldn't be at the party. But I did what I thought was right. Stephanie would have plenty of friends and family around for her, but my man was all alone up there in that prison. He needed me more than they did. So right after the baptism I caught the bus up to Roanoke, ready to make Derrick's day.

Well, I shoulda kept my black ass in Richmond and spent the day with my family like I was supposed to, 'cause when I got up to the prison I got a surprise of my own. Once again, Wendy Wood's name was on the sign-in sheet for Derrick. Only thing was, this time the bitch had signed in not less than five minutes before me! She was probably on the same damn bus, watching me sleep the whole ride to the prison.

Of course, you know I was heated. Wendy had been there just a week before, supposedly bringing him drugs. Derrick had promised me she would only be coming up once a month. Now it seemed like the bitch was there every damn week. And here I was thinking he was so damn lonely up in this place.

I was even more pissed when I tried to sign in and the captain informed me inmates were only allowed one set of visitors at a time. I wasn't gonna let that stop me, though. I told him if I couldn't see Derrick I wanted to see Richie Santiago, Sabrina's husband. I'm sure the captain knew what I was up to, but he let me sign in anyway. He probably didn't give a shit about the rules, but I didn't wait around for him to decide he should stick to them. As soon as I signed the last letter in my name, I stormed into the visiting room in search of Derrick.

My plan was to curse both Wendy's and Derrick's asses out. I know I had agreed to let her bring that crap up to him, but this was getting ridiculous. They were taking my kindness for weakness, and I sure as hell never expected what I saw when I walked into the visiting room. There they were, tonguing each other down. Derrick had his hands around Wendy's waist, palming her ass like it was a basketball. I was so hurt to see them locked in an embrace like that, I didn't stop to consider my actions. I just ran up behind Wendy and pulled half that cheap-ass weave right outta her head. I was about to rip out what was left of the other half when Derrick stepped in between us like Superman to the rescue. I tried to scratch his fucking eyes out, but now I realize that wasn't such a good idea. He slapped the shit outta me. When I finally came to my senses, Derrick was being dragged away by three corrections officers and I was being led to the infirmary.

The deputy warden tried his best to get me to press charges against Derrick, but I refused. There was no doubt I hated him. Hell, I wanted to kill his ass right about then. But I knew he'd end up doing more time if I pressed charges. I'm sorry, I just didn't have the heart to do that to him, no matter how bad I felt. I guess I'm just weak. Once he finally realized he wasn't gonna get his way, the deputy warden let me go home. But he warned that if I didn't press charges the prison would no longer be responsible for my safety. Not that it mattered. I didn't plan on coming back anyway.

The tears had been streaming down my face most of the day. I felt incredibly lonely. All my dreams were shattered. I had really thought Derrick and I had something special together, something that could withstand the pain of our separation. I'd been faithful to him the whole time he was locked up, except for that little incident with Dylan. As I wallowed in the pain of my failed relationship, Sabrina walked over from the sofa and rubbed my back.

"You all right, girl?"

"I hate him, Sabrina. I hate him more than anything in the world." I sobbed uncontrollably.

"I know, baby. I hate him, too," she commiserated.

The phone rang again, and I could feel Sabrina's and Becky's eyes bore through me. They both wanted me to answer the phone and curse Derrick's ass out. I was starting to think that maybe they were right. Maybe getting some answers would make me feel better. I reached for the phone. Of course it was the operator with another collect call. I almost hung the phone up when I heard the operator's voice, but I managed to get out a weak "uh-huh" and accepted the call.

"Jasmine, I'm sorry about what happened yesterday, baby—"

I cut him off. "Fuck you, Derrick!" My girls smiled at me and nodded in a show of support.

"How can you talk to me that way, baby? I love you." He was using that sweet and innocent voice that usually made me melt, but now it was pissing me off. I wanted to reach my hand through that phone and wring his fucking neck.

"You don't love me! You never loved me. If you loved me, you wouldn'ta put your hands on me. God, I hate you. I hate you so much!" I touched my eye and flinched at the pain. "Good-bye, Derrick. I don't have anything else to say to you, ever."

"Baby! Baby! Please. Don't hang up, please!" He was begging so loud, Becky and Sabrina could hear it, and they started mocking him with pitiful looks on their faces.

"What do you want, Derrick?" I sighed, trying to ignore my friends.

"I want you to listen to me, Jasmine." He sounded so desperate. At least that made me feel a little better. "You know I would never hurt you, but you were the one who tried to pluck my eyeballs out. I was just defending myself, baby."

"Yeah, right. So now it's all my fault?"

"I didn't say that."

"So what the hell are you saying, Derrick? What did you expect me to do, stand by and watch you jam your tongue down Wendy's throat?"

"I can explain that if you let me."

I laughed out loud. "You can? Well then go right ahead, 'cause I haven't heard any good lies today. And you won't be able to tell them to me tomorrow, 'cause I'm having my number blocked."

Derrick was quiet. Probably trying to decide if my threat was serious so he could know how to make his next move. To a man in prison there was nothing worse than losing his connection to the outside world. I was the only one Derrick had left. Everyone else had already wised up and blocked their numbers a long time ago, including his precious Wendy. So I knew my threat was the perfect way to get even with him.

"Don't do that, baby. Please." Guess he'd decided to take me seriously. He was pleading. "This is all just one big misunderstanding. Wendy was passing me the drugs. She brought the shit in little balloons wrapped up in her hair and after she got searched she went in the bathroom and put them in her mouth. We were just exchanging them when you walked in. We weren't kissing."

"Yeah, right, whatever, Derrick." I wasn't about to believe him, especially with my girls in the room, but he was determined to state his case. He spoke quietly into the phone. I don't know who else was standing near the phone booth, but Derrick was definitely taking a risk telling me this story. Hell, the lines could have been tapped.

"It's true, baby. Everything was going cool till you showed up. When you grabbed Wendy, one of the balloons fell on the table. You could have cost me my parole."

He got real quiet and started sniffling. I hated times like

this. The last thing I wanted was for him to feel like he was less than a man. On top of that, you can call me stupid, but his story actually sounded believable. I heard girls on the bus talking all the time about how they carried in drugs in all kinds of places to get them past prison security. So it wasn't impossible to think Wendy was carrying hers in her hair.

Deep down, I really wanted to believe Derrick. He'd hurt me, yeah. But you can't just throw away five years with a man because of one stupid mistake. I mean, it wasn't like he'd ever hit me before or anything. I needed this story to be true so I could forgive him and we could move on. Deep down, I didn't wanna lose my boo. There was just one thing that was still bothering me. Actually, two if you count the looks my girls were giving me. They knew I was getting weaker by the minute.

"Jasmine, I love you, baby."

"I don't like this, Derrick. I don't like this one bit. And I'm still not convinced you're telling me the truth."

"Hell no! He's not telling the truth," Sabrina yelled, and Becky laughed.

"Baby, I swear to God I'm not lying to you. And who's that in the background?"

"It's just the TV." I covered the receiver and glared at my friends.

"Jazz, I need for you to believe me."

"I don't know, Derrick. This is all so confusing. You really hurt me, you know. I mean, damn! You didn't have to hit me."

"I know, baby, I know. And I am so sorry for that. I just got scared, that's all. You know how bad I wanna get outta here to be with you." He was laying it on thick, using that smooth, sexy voice he knew always made me weak. And the truth was, I wanted him out of there as much as he did. But I didn't answer him right away. I wanted to hear him beg some more after yesterday.

"Come on, Jasmine. You know I would never lie to you, baby. Why would I want Wendy when I'm gonna marry you? You know I love you. Don't you? You know I want you to marry me."

"Marry you, huh?" We had talked about it before, so it wasn't a surprise. I just wanted to hear him repeat it, 'cause the thought made me so happy. Once he married me, I wouldn't have to worry about none of this mess with his baby's momma. He would be my husband and she could just step with her nasty ass.

"Do you love me, Jazz? Do you wanna be my wife?"

"Yes, Derrick," I tried not to sound too enthused. He wasn't completely out of trouble yet, plus, I didn't want Becky and Sabrina to know I'd given in so easily.

"Come on, now. You can say it with a little more enthusiasm than that, can't you?"

"I can't do that until we get something straight, Derrick."

"What?" He sounded worried.

"If you want me back, I don't want Wendy coming to see you again," I demanded. "If you need to see your son, I'll bring him up there. You know Wendy won't mind as long as I give her twenty dollars to get her nails done."

"No problem, baby. Wendy's history." I closed my eyes and thanked God. That was easier than I expected.

"Do you really mean it?"

"Of course I do. As long as you're willing to bring me an ounce of weed next weekend I don't have any use for Wendy."

"Huh?" He couldn't have said what I thought he said. Could he? "You didn't just ask me to bring drugs up to you next weekend, did you?"

"Yeah, I did." Gone was that sweet, sexy tone.

"I can't believe you, Derrick! I'm not gonna do that!"

"Damn right, she ain't," Sabrina shouted loud enough for Derrick to hear. He ignored it.

"I'll tell you what, Jazz, either you're going to bring up the weed or Wendy's gonna bring it up. I'd much prefer she did it because I don't want you getting in no trouble. But business is business, and you told me a long time ago that you'd never get in the way of my business."

Damn, he was right. Those words were sure coming back to haunt me now. He was being the best damn drug dealer he could be, just like I'd told him.

"So it's up to you. If Wendy's out, you gotta step up and take her place."

He waited a few seconds, but I couldn't answer him. I didn't know what to say. I had given him my approval a long time ago, so I couldn't exactly protest his drug dealing now, could I? But just the thought of bringing the shit to him myself made my heart pound. I didn't want to say yes, but I didn't know how else to make him get rid of Wendy.

"Look, I can see you need to think about this." He sounded impatient. "I'll call you later so you can tell me what you want to do. I love you, baby. But like I said, business is business."

He hung up the phone and I was left with the receiver in my hand and my jaw on the floor. I didn't know what to do. Derrick was my life. He was everything to me. I didn't want to lose him to Wendy or any other woman, but I didn't want to be a drug trafficker either. I couldn't believe he was putting me in this position.

"What happened? What he say?" Both Sabrina and Becky walked over to where I was standing.

"He asked me to marry him."

"And? What else?" Sabrina raised her eyebrows and twisted up her mouth.

"I really don't wanna talk about that right now," I answered weakly, hoping she would let me drop it, at least for the time being. I was still trying to figure it out myself. He should've just left it alone once I said no, but he was gonna press the issue. I damn sure had some thinking to do.

"So what'd you say?"

I felt like I was gonna throw up. I didn't know if she was talking about the drugs or the marriage proposal. I really didn't want to answer either.

"Nothin'. He wants me to think about it." I walked toward the bathroom. "I'll be right back. I gotta pee." I got up and went into the bathroom.

Becky and Sabrina stuck around about an hour, asking me fifty million questions before I was able to get rid of them. They were good friends, but I just wanted to be alone. At least I thought I wanted to be alone until they were gone. What I really wanted was to be around someone who wouldn't ask a whole bunch of questions. I needed someone to just listen to me. Kind of like Dylan did that night at the club and when we were at Joe's. That was it! Dylan. I could talk to Dylan. Of course, he was probably a little upset because I changed my number and never called him back, but there was something about him. I thought it was worth a little attitude from him if it meant I could talk to him. I picked up my purse and searched for the card with his number. I came across my keys first and just headed for the car. A phone call just wouldn't do. I had to see him.

I parked my car outside Colonial Comics and flipped down the visor to fix my hair and makeup in the mirror. When I finished I reached for a pair of Jackie Kennedy sunglasses I had hanging from my rearview mirror. The makeup helped, but I needed to hide the black eye Derrick had given me. There was no way I was gonna go inside Dylan's store looking like something the cat dragged home, even if that was how I felt.

Besides, I was excited about seeing Dylan again. I'd be lying if I said I didn't want to look my best. It had been almost a month since I'd seen him, and I'd actually thought about him pretty often. Most of the time it was when I was lying in my bed horny as hell from reading a Mary Morrison or Zane novel. Between those books and my memories of Dylan's magic tongue, I'd had quite a few frustrating nights in the past month. I even broke down and picked up the phone a few times to invite him over for a booty call. But that was as far as I ever got. I'd think of Derrick and chicken out before I even dialed. Still, I couldn't help wondering what he was doing and who he was doing it with. Lots of times those thoughts led to wishes that he was doing it with me.

I was snapped out of my thoughts when a car door slammed. I watched a minivan pulling out of the parking lot. *Well, it's now or never,* I thought as I stepped out of my car.

I was nervous as hell. I hadn't had this many butterflies since my crush on Maurice Hood in high school. My butterflies started doing flips when I walked in and saw Dylan sitting behind the counter, engrossed in a comic book. He was so handsome with his strong African features and smooth dark-chocolate skin. Until that night with Dylan, I'd never found myself attracted to dark-skinned men. Now I caught myself taking second and third looks whenever an ebony brother walked by. I hated to admit to myself that Dylan had done that to me with just one night.

"Excuse me, sir. Do you carry *Brotherman* comics?" I smiled when I saw his eyes light up.

"Jasmine!" He smiled with excitement, but his smile disappeared within seconds and his voice became testy, almost cold. "It's been a long time. I take it you've come for those *Brotherman* comics?" He reached under the counter and pulled out a plastic bag. "I got 'em right here."

"I didn't come for any comic books, Dylan. I came to see you." I used my most sincere tone.

"Oh, so I guess you finally changed your mind about us being friends, huh?"

"I never said I didn't wanna be your friend," I protested.

"Come on, Jasmine. You didn't have to. Rebecca told me everything I needed to know. I know you don't like me."

"I never told Becky anything like that, Dylan."

He sucked his teeth. "Whatever."

"I swear to God I didn't tell Becky I didn't like you. . . . I just mentioned that I didn't think we should see each other again."

"That's an understatement. The day after I called you, your number became unlisted. It didn't take a brain surgeon to figure that you didn't wanna talk to me."

I tried to look innocent, but he wasn't goin' for it. It hurt to see him shake his head with another frown. I know I should've expected it, but it didn't make it any easier to deal with his accusation or his sarcasm.

"Look, Dylan, you're actin' like I purposely dissed you."

"Didn't you?" he said rather frankly.

I inhaled deeply. "Okay, okay. Maybe I did, but can't we let bygones be bygones? I didn't come here to fight. I came to see a friend."

"A friend? I tried to be your friend before."

"I know. And I really did want us to be friends. I was just scared. That's all." I stepped closer to him, though the counter still separated our bodies. I was grateful for that, 'cause I really felt like throwing my arms around him.

"Scared of what?"

"You. I'm scared of you."

"Me?"

"Yeah. I'm scared to death what happened at Joe's is gonna happen again." It actually felt good to be honest to him and myself about that.

"Haven't we already been through this?" He looked frustrated. "I told you, I got caught up in the moment."

"So did I. That's the problem."

"Look, Jasmine, I'm dating someone, okay? I'm just looking for a friend. Someone I can talk to. So if you can't handle that, just tell me, ah'ight. . . ." Talk about the shoe on the other foot! I barely heard a word he said after 'I'm dating someone,' because a wave of jealousy hit. As unreasonable as I was being, I wanted to scream at him. How could he be seeing someone? It had only been a few weeks since we'd seen each other. This had been a bad idea. I'd just gotten there, but now I was ready to leave. I should have stayed home and cried myself to sleep.

"Jazz?"

"What?" I snapped. He didn't deserve it, but I was still pissed.

"What's up with your boyfriend? You two still together?"

I felt like a fool. The whole purpose of me coming to Dylan's store was so that I could talk to him about Derrick. Now here I was getting jealous of some other woman. What was wrong with me? I had to get my shit together. Besides, it was probably for the best that he was seeing someone. It would help keep both of us in check. If I could get my jealousy under control, maybe I did still have a friend.

"Derrick? He's the reason I stopped by to talk to you. Do you think we could get outta here and talk? I really need a good listener."

"Sure. Why don't we get something to eat?"

I gratefully agreed, and he headed into the office to get

his jacket. He came back out with a smile, followed by a nerdy-lookin' white guy who took Dylan's place behind the counter. I was relieved as Dylan put his arm around my shoulder and guided me to the door. I sure felt like I was on a roller-coaster ride whenever I was around this guy, but at the moment I was so happy to have him by my side.

# 11

# Stephanie

I'd just punched the time clock and walked outside to smoke a cigarette when I heard a familiar voice calling me. It was my first week back at Wal-Mart after being out on maternity leave for six weeks, and it was my afternoon break. I'd been up all night with the baby, and to be honest I did not wanna be there. And I knew things were about to get worse when I heard that voice.

"Yo, Shorty. What's up? I need to talk to you."

I crushed the cigarette under my feet and turned to see Malek leaning against his car, a blunt hanging from his mouth. I really thought that after the incident at my house on Christmas Day he wouldn't be showing his sorry face. I guess I was wrong.

I tried to pretend like he wasn't there, but he wasn't having it. He got up off the car and headed toward me.

"Yo! What's up? You tryin'a play me or somethin'? I know you heard me."

He was right. I had heard him, and the second I did I should've taken my ass back in the store, but I was afraid he was gonna follow me inside and make a scene. Malek was known for showing out in public. So I just stood there with my arms folded, eyeing him from head to toe. Would you believe after all the shit he'd put me through, I still found his ass attractive? I hadn't really noticed his looks at the house that day 'cause I was too busy tryin' to get rid of his ass before Travis lost his mind. But now I had time to get a good look at him and reminisce as he approached. I had to admit he was still cute, in a thuggish kind of way. Especially with those cornrows he was wearing in his hair. They made him look like Latrell Sprewell of the New York Knicks, and Latrell was fine as hell. I had to bite my lip just to remind myself I was supposed to hate him.

"What do you want, Malek?" I sighed and rolled my eyes. No way was I gonna give him the satisfaction of knowing he still looked good to me.

"Yo! Why you always gotta have an attitude?" He tossed what was left of the blunt to the ground, shaking his head.

"I don't know, Malek. Why you always gotta show up where you're not welcome?"

"Oh, so now I'm not welcome? Used to be a time you couldn't get enough of me." He was so damn sure of himself. I refused to even begin to discuss what used to be with him.

"That was a long time ago. A very long time ago."

"Wasn't that long ago." He took a step closer and tried to touch my face.

"Will you stop it?" I slapped his hand away and stepped back. "How the hell did you find out where I work, anyway? I don't like nobody following me."

He sucked his teeth and made a face. "Please, ain't nobody following you. My man Kenny told me you was workin' up here, so I thought I'd stop by and hit you off with some loot for Maleka. I was trying to do you a favor by coming here instead of your house."

"You were trying to do me a favor? " I couldn't help it. I had to laugh. "Boy, if you show up anywhere near my house Travis is gonna shoot your ass."

"Yeah, right. That nigga ain't gonna do shit." He looked

like he was about to say something smart but changed his mind. "Look, you want this money or what?"

"Oh, so you gonna give me some money, huh? You ain't gave me shit in damn near four years. What makes you think I need your little chump change now?" I folded my arms over my chest and glared at him. His expression said he wasn't happy with my attitude, but he just shook his head as he pulled out a big wad of money and started counting it. I guess he was trying to impress me. If he really wanted to impress me, he would be handing me the whole thing instead of a couple o' tens and twenties like I was expecting. He must have read my mind, because as soon as he stopped counting he folded up the money and handed it to me. I was so shocked I almost dropped it on the ground.

"Here. This is three-fifty. I'll try to hit you off with a little more next week." He sounded confident. I didn't answer him right away because I couldn't take my eyes off of the money. I'd heard through the grapevine that he'd given up on his rap career and was hustling for a living. As far as I was concerned, this proved it. Malek had never had more than a few dollars in his pocket in all the time I had been with him. He was always buying DJ equipment or records, and what was left always went to weed.

"Who'd you rob, Malek?" I was tempted to give it back to him.

"I ain't rob nobody," he snapped.

"Yeah, right. Whatever." Even if he hadn't robbed anybody, Malek sure as hell got this money some kinda shady way. Of that I was sure. However, I wasn't gonna argue. If I gave it back to him he'd probably end up spending it on weed anyway. All I had to do was forget about where the money came from and put it to good use for my daughter. That girl deserved something nice from him after all the years he'd neglected her. I just had to make sure Travis never knew about it, 'cause he sure as hell wouldn't let me keep it.

"Thanks for the money, Malek. I'll buy Maleka something nice with it." I wanted to make a quick exit. "I gotta go back to work."

"Wait! Hold up a minute, Shorty. Why don't you buy yourself something, too? You always looked good in red. Matter of fact, take this for you." He reached into his other pocket and pulled out a hundred-dollar bill.

He just had to go there. I was gonna take the money and run, no strings attached, no guilt. But he just had to make this about more than our daughter. He had to make this about us. I was not about to let him use our child and this too-little, too-late child support to work his way back into my life. Not when I was trying to build a new life with Travis.

"Hold up! Let's get something straight, Malek. Money for Maleka is one thing, but *I* don't want shit from you. I got a man, and he takes real good care of me."

"I know you got a man, but that don't mean I can't look out for you." He held the hundred out to me. "We got a daughter together. We should be friends."

"Malek, what are you up to?" No matter how sincere his voice sounded, I couldn't help but be suspicious.

"Look, Shorty, shit is really fucked up in my life right about now and I could use a friend. You used to be my best friend and—"

I stopped him before he could continue with this sentimental bullshit. "The key words are 'used to be,' Malek. I'm sorry to hear that you're having problems, but any problems you got I'm sure you brought upon yourself." *And gone are the days when I make those problems mine,* I thought. "Now, I appreciate the money for Maleka, but that's it. I'm not your friend. I'm not your lover. I'm just your baby's mother and I really don't wanna be that. So don't play yourself, 'cause I will hurt your feelings." I headed for the door to Wal-Mart, promising myself that I wouldn't turn around till I was at my register.

"Yo, Shorty. Don't do this. Come on, now. I got something important to tell you . . . ! Shorty!"

I just kept walking, praying that he wasn't gonna follow me.

"Stephanie, don't do this! Please!"

I stopped dead in my tracks. He was actually pleading. *And* he called me by my real name, something I don't think he'd done since our first date. I turned around and sighed in frustration. He was wearing me down.

"What, Malek?"

"Nana's dying."

"What'd you say?"

"I said Nana's dying."

"Don't play with me, Malek. That ain't nothin' to play about."

"I'm not playin'. The doctors don't think she's gonna make it more than a month or two. That's the real reason I came by here. To tell you she's been askin' about you."

Malek's grandmother was a wonderful woman. Me and her were close once. Real close. I'd lived in her house for almost two years when Malek and I were together. For a time she was more of a mom to me than my own mother. But that all came to an end when I had Maleka. That's when Malek moved to D.C. and I moved into the projects.

Nana had tried to get me to stay so she could help me with the baby, but I couldn't do it. I was devastated after Malek left me. Being around his family would have just made it hurt worse, so I left Nana's house, and pretty much her life. She'd only seen Maleka a few times over the last few years, and only I was to blame. I knew Nana wasn't well enough to leave her house to visit the baby. After the first few months, I just stopped going to see her. I guess I called myself going on with my life, but deep down I knew it wasn't fair to Nana. Just 'cause Malek turned out to be a sorry excuse for a father didn't mean his family couldn't know Maleka. I'd always felt guilty, and promised myself that someday I'd get over there with my daughter and let Nana get to know her. Now it might be too late.

"What happened? What's wrong with her?" I could barely speak.

"Lung cancer, among other things. But you know how sick she was. You used to take care of her." Another stab of guilt hit me.

"What hospital's she at?"

"She was on the hospice floor at MCV Medical Center, but the doctors let her go home so she could die at home. Want me to take you over to the house?"

"No," I told him, "I'll meet you over there. I got a few things I gotta do first." *Like call Travis and make an excuse why I can't pick up the kids.*

Twenty minutes later I was standing in front of the gate at Nana's small white house, trying to gather the strength to go in. Just the sight of the front door gave me a rush of fond memories. As sad as the circumstances were, this felt like a homecoming for me. I'd cooked my first Sunday dinner in that house and had Maleka's baby shower there. Hell, I'd even lost my virginity in Malek's bedroom the night of our junior prom. This place was special to me.

Malek came out on the front steps, and I knew it was time to stop reminiscing.

"How is she?" I stepped up onto the porch.

"She's weak, but she's awake. She's waitin' for you." He held open the door and I entered the living room. "You got here fast. No problem getting off work?"

"Nah. I just told them it was a family emergency. Travis was the problem. I had to get him to leave work a little early to get the kids."

"You told him you were coming here?" Malek shot me a look of surprise, and maybe even a little smile. But he had no reason to get all hopeful. Did he really think after all I'd said to him at my job that I would take that kind of risk?

I had actually thought about telling Travis the truth, that I was going to visit Nana. But that would probably start a war in my house that I wasn't prepared to deal with. After Malek left our house Christmas Day, Travis was not exactly happy with me. Sure, he realized I didn't have anything to do with Malek stopping by, but it was my fault that he had our address. So I guess he felt I should take part of the responsibility. He reminded me that if I had never been involved with a thug like Malek, that situation would have never happened. I knew his pride was a little hurt that Big Momma stopped him before he beat the shit out of Malek the way he wanted to, so I just nodded and kept my mouth shut. I didn't need no more confrontations on Christmas Day. I did remind him later, though, that if I had never messed with Malek, then we wouldn't have Maleka right now, would we? He couldn't deny me that truth, but he did make sure to tell me he better not catch that shady brother anywhere near me or Maleka ever again.

"No, I didn't tell him. If I did, we'd both be dead right about now." I walked past Malek. "Where's Nana at?"

"In her room. First door on the right." He pointed down the hall.

"I know where it is." I rolled my eyes. "I used to live here, remember?"

"How could I forget?" He grinned. Guess he was taking his own little trip down memory lane. "I'll be out here in the living room if you need me."

"Okay," I whispered. All of a sudden I was so nervous. I knew Nana had always had health problems, but I was afraid to see what cancer had done to her. She'd always been such a vibrant woman, and I wasn't sure I was prepared to see her weakened. I peeked my head into her room and called out her name softly. "Nana?"

"You gotta get up close to her, girl." A voice came from across the room.

"Oh, hey, Miss Janet." I hadn't expected to see Malek's mom sitting there. Last time I'd seen her, she'd been about forty pounds thinner, strung out on crack. Looked like Malek was telling the truth when he said she'd cleaned herself up. Good for her. At least that meant someone was there for Nana now. Maybe later I'd spend some time with Miss Janet, but for now I had to do what I came to do.

"Nana?" I called a little louder as I stepped closer to the bed. Nana lifted her head with a faint smile. Poor Nana. She looked like only half of her former self. Her face was all sunk in around her cheekbones, and her nightgown looked big enough to fit two more people in it.

"Stephanie? Is that you?" Her voice was raspy but recognizable.

"Yes, ma'am. It's me." I took her hand, trying not to shudder at how bony it had become.

"How's my great-grandbaby?"

"She's fine," I smiled, hoping to mask the feelings of guilt that were overwhelming me. "She's at school right now."

"She must be getting big. Malek told me how pretty she is."

"Yes, ma'am. She sure is." Dear old Nana. It looked like she wasn't even going to ask why I hadn't been around with Maleka. I always knew Nana had a heart of gold.

"Malek said she has his nose."

"Yeah, that and more. She looks just like him." Nana's

faint smile was now a wide grin. "I'll bring you some pictures next time I come, Nana." Nana placed her head back on the pillow and closed her eyes for a few minutes. I just sat quietly and watched her labored breathing, wishing I could ease her suffering somehow.

"Stephanie, you seen Malek today?" Nana asked after a while.

"Yes, ma'am. He's the one who told me you were sick."

"I'm not sick, baby. I'm dying." She said it with such certainty.

"No, you're not. You're not dying." I waved my hand and tried to sound lighthearted.

"Yes, I am. But that's okay. I had a good life and it's time to go home." She gave me that faint smile again and took another short rest. "Stephanie? I want you to do me a favor." She stared up at the ceiling as she spoke to me.

"Sure, Nana. What do you want?" I sat up a little, expecting her to ask me to get her a glass of water or something. I was not prepared for her actual request.

"I want you to spend some time with Malek." She turned her head to look at me, her eyes suddenly more alert than they'd been. "He's not taking all this very well, and you're the only one I know who could ever keep a smile on his face. So can you do that for me, baby? Can you spend a little time with him?"

I just stared at her. She couldn't possibly know all that she was asking. I hated to disappoint her, especially since I was already feeling guilty enough, but I didn't think I could take the risk involved with her request. Now I just hoped she'd understand.

"I don't think I can do that, Nana. There's still a lot of bad blood between me and Malek. He walked out on me with a two-month-old baby and I still haven't been able to forgive that."

"I know, baby, but that was a long time ago. Life is too short to hold on to hurts from the past," she chided gently. Her words rang true as I realized how easily she'd forgiven me for keeping Maleka away from her. "All I'm asking is that you spend a little time with him. You may find he's grown up a little more than you think."

"I have a fiancé now, Nana. I don't think he'd appreciate me spending time alone with Malek." I was trying to come up with every possible argument not to be around Malek. It wasn't just that I was afraid of Travis finding out. I was a little afraid of myself. As bad as he'd treated me, I couldn't deny that some small part of me was still drawn to Malek. After all, we had a history together.

"I'm not asking you to get back with him, child. Just spend some time with him. Tell him about his daughter. Go out to the movies." She coughed weakly. "Just take his mind off my cancer. Can you do that for an old, dying woman?"

Shoot. Now she was laying on the guilt. In the back of my mind, I wondered if Nana and Malek hadn't planned this all along. I don't mean to say she wasn't sick. Just that she seemed to regain a little of her strength when she talked about me and Malek. And she was sure working pretty hard to convince me. But whether it was planned or not, she was right. I couldn't deny her dying wish. Nana had been good to me, and it was time to repay her.

I exhaled loudly with a nod. "Yes, ma'am I can do it. I just hope my boyfriend will understand."

"If he doesn't understand that you're granting a dying old woman her last request, then maybe you need to rethink your engagement." She was awfully feisty all of a sudden.

"I don't know about all that. But I'll find a way to make him understand." At least I hoped I would.

"Then it's settled. You'll do it?"

"Yes ma'am. I'll do it."

"Good," Nana smiled and closed her eyes. Her face looked much more peaceful now as she rested. Either she was glad her grandson would have some comfort, or she was proud of the game she had just worked on me. I sat and watched her rest, wondering just how I was gonna grant her request with the least complication. I'd just have to give it to Malek straight and let him know this was a favor for Nana, nothing more. I knew I was playing with fire spending any kind of time with him. I just wanted the flame to be as small as possible.

I left Nana's room an hour later, promising to return another day with pictures of the kids.

"Okay, child. And don't you forget your other promise, too." It was clear where her priorities were.

I found Malek sitting on the living room sofa in front of the TV. He was struggling to take his braids out, ripping at them with a comb. That shit looked painful, but he had a big smile on his face as he watched me enter the room.

"Did Nana tell you why she wanted to see me?" I was even more suspicious now that I saw how damn happy he looked. Not the suffering boy Nana had made him out to be. Whose wish was I fulfilling, anyway?

"Nah. Why? What'd she say?"

"Nothin'," I mumbled. For now I would just play dumb. I still needed to figure out just what I was gonna do about this situation. "Why you taking out your braids anyway?"

"LaKeisha Nixon's supposed to redo them for me tonight."

"LaKeisha Nixon?" That girl had been trying to get with Malek ever since we were in high school. "Please don't tell me you mess with that bitch."

He paused before he spoke. "Nah. She just gonna braid my hair."

"Ohhh, really," I rolled my eyes. "You know she burnt Little Rob and Jeffery Owens, don't you?"

"She did?" he lifted an eyebrow. He may not have fucked her, but he'd obviously been thinking about it. The question I had to ask myself was why was I so concerned about it. It wasn't like Malek was my man or nothing. I was treading in dangerous waters and I knew it. The last thing I wanted was for him to think I was interested. Or cared. Time to change the subject.

"Goddamn it! Will you give me that comb?" I snatched the comb out of his hand after I watched him rip through another patch of hair. "Damn, watching you take these things out is painful to the eyes. Sit down there." I motioned to the floor in front of the couch and he sat with his back against my knees. I went to work loosening his braids, much more careful than he was.

"You sure you don't mess with LaKeisha?" I asked him cautiously. I wasn't tryin' to make him think I was jealous or nothing, but I couldn't get the image out of my head. Old rivalries die hard.

"Nah, I ain't mess with her. But I could hit it if I wanted to."

"You and everybody else with a dick." He spun his head around and studied my face. I avoided his eyes. "Will you turn around? I'm tryin'a get these braids out."

He faced forward and neither of us said another word until I finished combing out all his braids. I was lost in my own memories. Malek had been my first love, and even though he'd left me, we'd had plenty of good times. It was bittersweet, remembering them now, especially when I was about to be married to another man. A man who I knew was much better for me and my children.

"So what's up? You want me to braid these for you, or you want LaKeisha to do it?"

"You can do it." He handed me a jar of grease.

"What style you want?"

"I don't know. Whatever you think's gonna make me look cute," he chuckled. Malek and his damn ego. He must've known I still thought he looked good. But I wasn't gonna play that game with him now.

"Hey, Shorty, can I ask you a question?"

"No."

"Why you gonna be like that?" He turned his head.

"Because my name ain't Shorty. My name is Stephanie. I'm not a sixteen-year-old kid you trying to run game on anymore, Malek. If you wanna ask me a question, use my name."

"Okay, Stephanie," he tried again. "Can I ask you a question?"

"Go 'head." I was afraid I was gonna be sorry, but I knew he wasn't about to give up.

"Is he as good as me?"

"Is who as good as you?"

"You know. What's-his-name. Your boyfriend." He was right. I did know who he was talking about, just like he knew damn well what his name was.

"His name is Travis, and he's my fiancé, not my boyfriend," I reminded him.

"Okay. This Travis, is he as good as me?"

"Good as you at what?" I wasn't gonna make this easy for him. Men are so self-centered sometimes. Always comparing themselves to one another in the bedroom like it's some badge of honor. When we first started going out, Travis must have asked me the same question a hundred times. None of them would ever think to ask if he was as good a friend to me, or some shit like that. They seemed to think all that mattered was the almighty dick.

"You know what I'm talking about. Does he fuck you as good as I did?"

It would have been easy to deflate his ego and be done with it. But just like I did with Travis four years ago, I decided to keep that little secret to myself.

"Do you really think I would tell you that, Malek? Matter of fact, do you really wanna know the answer to that question?" I couldn't resist that little jab at his ego. Although I forgot just how big his ego was.

"Hell, yeah, I wanna know the answer."

"Well, you're not gonna get one."

"Ah'ight, then answer this for me. Is he as big as me?" He turned his head and looked up at me with a grin. He was holding his hands about a foot apart.

"I am not gonna answer that either!" I shook my head again and tried to suppress a smile.

"Come on, Stephanie. Admit it, my shit is bigger than his, isn't it?" He laughed and lifted his eyebrows suggestively. I couldn't help it. I smirked a little, waving my hand. Malek was bigger than Travis. Hell, he was bigger than anyone I'd ever seen.

"You are so stupid, Malek."

"But I got a big dick, don't I?" he teased. I couldn't help but laugh a little this time.

"I knew I could make you laugh. It was just a matter of time." He looked proud. "Remember how it used to be back in the day? You'd braid my hair while I cracked jokes and rolled a blunt." He leaned back against my knees and I started greasing his scalp again.

"Yeah, I remember." I smiled. "We'd smoke it then go to Ryan's Steakhouse. I used to love me some Ryan's."

"Oh, hell, yeah. Ryan's was the bomb." He shook his head. "Damn, I ain't been to Ryan's since we broke up."

"Neither have I," I said quietly. There were still certain things I avoided doing since Malek left me, and going to

Ryan's was one of them. Our nights there had been part of a happier time between us. Malek obviously shared some of my memories.

"Hey, do you remember how much fun we'd have when we came home from Ryan's? You used to do some freaky shit when you were high." He gave me a devilish grin.

"Don't go there, Malek."

"Don't go where? I don't know what you're talking about."

"Like hell, you don't. You trying to take me on your little trip down freaky-memory lane." *And doing a good job, I might add.*

"No, I'm not," he protested weakly.

"Yes you are. And if you keep it up, you gonna be walking around here with half a braided head, 'cause I'm gonna be out."

"Okay, okay. Sorry," he said casually. "Can I say one thing, though?"

"As long as it don't have to do with sex."

"It doesn't."

"What is it?"

"We should go to Ryan's again, after you finish my braids. My treat."

"Your treat? Where you getting all this money from? You selling drugs?" Better to change the subject than think about how tempting his offer really was.

"Hell, no. I got a real job. I been working over at Home Depot for almost two months. Yesterday was payday." He looked at me and smiled. "Never thought I'd get a real job, did you?"

"No, I never did." I was impressed, even though it looked like he was still spending his money as soon as he got it. "It's too bad you couldn't have got a real job four years ago. We might still be together."

"I can't do anything right without you bringing up the past?" He sounded genuinely offended, and I remembered my promise to Nana. This was not the way to make her grandson feel better.

"I'm sorry, Malek," I offered as an apology. "Congratulations on your new job. I'm proud of you."

"Thanks. So what's up? You wanna go to Ryan's, or what?"

"Yeah, we can go." I tried to ignore the little voice that told me to run.

"Well ah'ight! Maybe we should stop and get a bag of weed on the way."

That little voice was screaming at me now, but I just turned it off and agreed. I had just put myself on the fast track to trouble, and I wasn't turning back now.

# 12

# Travis

You ever have that feeling that something was wrong, but you didn't quite know what it was? Like your life was about to be turned upside down and there wasn't a damn thing you could do about it? That's how I felt as I searched the city for Stephanie. I wasn't sure what was going on, but I was starting to believe that she was cheating on me. Why would I think that? It was mostly a gut feeling. That and a whole lot of circumstantial evidence. You see, it all started earlier this afternoon. I'd just returned to my post from a meeting with my lieutenant when my buddy Matt, the duty sergeant, called me over.

"Yo, Tee! Phone line one." I walked over to an unoccupied desk and picked up the phone.

"Sergeant Thomas. How can I help you?"

"Well, hello, Sergeant Thomas. How you doin', handsome?" It was Stephanie and she was using that sexy voice that always turned me on.

"I'm fine, and you?" I tried to look professional for the benefit of the other soldiers in the room.

"I'm doin' all right, but I need a favor. Can you pick up the kids? They want me to do overtime tonight."

"No problem. I'll have them fed, bathed, and in bed by the time you get home." I was proud of her for getting back to work so quickly after the baby's birth, without one complaint.

She really was a trooper, trying to pull her own weight to help out with the bills.

"Thanks, sweetie. I'll call you later, okay?"

"Ah'ight, but don't forget we have a little unfinished business to take care of tonight."

"We do? What unfinished business?" she asked.

I glanced around the office to see if anyone was close enough to hear, before I whispered seductively into the phone. "Come on, Steph. You know we're supposed to get our groove on tonight. Mr. Happy hasn't been to the amusement park in months and he wants to ride the roller coaster."

"Well don't you worry, handsome, 'cause the amusement park was checked out by the engineers this morning and we're open for business tonight. All you gotta do is show me your ticket and I'll let you ride all night long." Her teasing was turning me on and I could feel myself getting aroused.

"Damn." I reached in my pocket and felt the pack of condoms I'd bought earlier. "I got my tickets right here. You sure you gotta do overtime? Cause we could hook up for a quickie right before the kids get outta day care."

"I wish I could, boo, but I already told my boss I'd work. Don't worry, though. I'll make it up to you tonight."

"You know I'm gonna hold you to that."

"You do that, sweetie. I'll see you tonight, okay? I love you, Travis."

"I love you too, babe. Bye."

At the same time I hung up the phone, I remembered that today was the first day of my classes at Virginia State University. I'd been going to night school, working on my degree in business administration, and was supposed to be taking a computer class at the university. I could still have time to pick up the kids. The only problem was that I was gonna have to drop them off at Stephanie's mom's and have Stephanie pick them up on her way home. It was a small change of plans, but I still had to run it by Stephanie. I picked up the phone and dialed Wal-Mart, hoping I could catch her before she went back to her register.

"Thank you for calling Wal-Mart. This is John speaking. How can I help you?"

"What's up, John? This is Travis, Stephanie's boyfriend." John was one of the nicer managers they had at the store.

"Hey, Travis. What's up?"

"Nothing much. Listen, Steph just called me a minute ago. Can you grab her before she gets to her register?"

"I'm sorry, Travis, but Stephanie left for the day about an hour ago. She said something about a family emergency. Is everything okay?"

"What? What do you mean, she left for the day? She just called and told me she's doing overtime."

"Overtime?" he laughed. "We haven't had any overtime since Christmas."

He had to be wrong. Why would Stephanie lie about something like this?

"Are you sure she left? Maybe she's working in another department with another manager?"

"If she is, it's a mystery to me. But I'll check her time card for you."

"Thanks, John. I'd appreciate that."

"Okay, hold on . . ." The line went silent as I waited for John to return.

"Travis, you still there?"

"Yeah, I'm here."

"Stephanie clocked out at two-thirty." He said it matter-of-factly, but it made my stomach queasy.

"You sure about that?"

"Positive. I've got her time card right in front of me."

"Okay, John. Thanks."

"No problem. Anything I can do?"

"No. I just wanted to tell her where I was dropping off the kids. Talk to you later." I hung up the phone and slowly lowered myself into a chair. My mind began to absorb what had just happened. Where the hell was Stephanie, and why did she lie to me? I slammed my hand down on the desk as my suspicion grew. This was not supposed to happen. Not to us.

"You okay, Tee?" Matt walked over and patted me on the back.

"Hell, no, I'm not okay," I told him angrily. "I think my old lady's stepping out on me."

"Stephanie? No way. She wouldn't do that." He hesitated as he saw the pained look on my face. "Would she?"

"I wouldn't put it past her. She's been acting awfully strange ever since that pain in the ass Malek came back to town. And she just lied to me about doing overtime. I can't believe this shit is happening to me."

Matt lowered his voice. "Look, man, you wanna go somewhere and talk about it?"

"Nah, not right now." I shook my head. "I need to go drop the kids with her mom and then go look for her. Think you can cover for me?"

"Yeah, I'll cover for you. But you sure you don't want me to go with you? I don't want you to do anything stupid, Tee."

"I'm cool," I insisted. "Just pray I don't find her with another man."

# 13

# Dylan

Jasmine and I left my store and drove to Ryan's Steak House in Chesterfield. We both ordered steaks and fries then sat down at a quiet table in a corner where no one would disturb us. Something about her voice in the store made me sure she had some pretty heavy stuff to share with me, and I didn't think she'd want to do it surrounded by other diners.

As I settled into my seat, I smiled at how good it felt just having her next to me. I hadn't been able to get her off my mind since that night we spent together at Joe's. That's why I told her that lie about me dating someone. I figured she'd feel more comfortable being around me if she thought I was involved. After she changed her number, I thought I'd never see her again. It was a welcome second chance when I saw her walk into my store, and I wanted to do whatever it took to keep her from bolting again.

I thought I actually saw a look of jealousy cross her face when I said I was seeing someone. She tried to hide it pretty well, but it gave me a glimmer of hope. Yeah, I knew she had a boyfriend, but I was still holding out hope that we might someday be involved. As long as her man was locked up, I was going to do whatever it took to make her mine. Besides, with her being so eager to talk to me, maybe they'd already broken up.

"What's going on, Jasmine? What'd you need to talk to me about?"

She frowned and hesitated before sliding her sunglasses off. I grimaced at the sight of her blackened eye.

"Jesus Christ! What the hell happened to your eye?" I didn't mean to sound so freaked out, but her eye really did look fucked up. "Who did this to you?"

"I don't even know where to start, Dylan." She covered her eye again with the sunglasses. I scooted my chair closer and rubbed her back and shoulders.

"It's okay, Jazz. Just take your time and start from the beginning."

"All right," she sighed, stabbing one of her fries with a fork as she started to explain. It took her about thirty minutes to tell me the whole story. I tried to hide my emotions and just listen, but the more she told me, the more pissed off I got. No woman deserves to get hit by a man.

"That's one hell of a story. You've really been through a lot the last few days, haven't you?" I know she had come to me just looking for a sympathetic ear, but it was hard to sit still and keep my emotions in check. I wanted to be the knight in shining armor coming to her rescue. I wanted to kill that son of a bitch up in that prison.

"Yeah, it's been pretty rough," she agreed. I still wasn't sure if I should speak my true opinion of the situation, so I just rubbed her back to let her know I was there for whatever she needed.

"Hey, you okay?"

"No," she said softly as tears ran down her face. I wiped them away with my napkin.

"You're still in love with this guy, aren't you?"

She nodded her head slowly with half a frown. She looked into my eyes and could probably read my thoughts. "I know you don't understand why I would stay with him, but he's a good man, Dylan. And he's all I got. He's just a little confused."

As far as I was concerned, she was the one who was confused if she thought this brother was a good man.

"You willing to take that chance on going to jail for him? 'Cause that's where you gonna end up if you start bringing him drugs." It wasn't like I was telling her something she didn't already know, but she actually looked like she had to think about it. What was there to think about? She wouldn't go to jail for him, would she?

"I'm not sure. I might still bring them." She ran her fingers through her hair and stared at me nervously. "You expected me to say, 'Hell, no, I won't go to jail for him!' Didn't you?"

"Yeah, I did." I shrugged my shoulders.

"So did I." She lowered her head sadly. "But the words just wouldn't come out my mouth. The more I thought about it, the more I realized I would do anything for Derrick. Don't get me wrong. The thought of going to jail scares the hell outta me. But I guess I'm more scared by the thought of being without Derrick."

I wondered why Monica couldn't have been as loyal to me. It hurt me to see this great woman standing by such a lowlife, but I knew I wasn't going to be able to change her mind. She had come to me looking for a sounding board, not for someone to talk her out of it. As much as I hated to do it, I would help her stay with Derrick if that was what she truly wanted. All I could do was hope that sooner or later she would realize how bad he really was. Then I'd be right there to pick up the pieces.

"All right," I sighed. "Let's see what we can do about keeping you out of jail, then." She gave me a stunned look and I smiled. I would've paid a million dollars to take her home and make love to her right then, but that wasn't what she wanted. She wanted my advice. She wanted my friendship. She wanted me to tell her it was all right to be with Derrick.

"You're really gonna help me? You don't think I'm stupid?"

"Of course I think you're stupid. But when you're in love you do stupid things. Trust me, I know."

She gave me a sad smile as she placed her hand on my knee. "You really do wanna be my friend, don't you?"

"Yeah, I do."

"Okay, so what's next? What do I do?"

"You're not gonna like it, but you're gonna let that Wendy woman carry the drugs up to your boyfriend."

"No, I'm not." She sat back in her chair and folded her arms. "I thought you said you were gonna help me."

"I am helping you, and yes, you are gonna let her do it."

"No, I'm not," she insisted.

"Look, Jasmine, I'm sorry, but I've gotta agree with Derrick on this one. If Wendy's stupid enough to bring him the drugs, then let her do it."

"But—"

I cut her off. "But what? You told me you trust Derrick, that you have faith in him. Didn't you?"

"Yes, but . . ."

"But what?" I shouted this time.

"But I hate that bitch and I don't want her near him," she admitted.

"That woman is only going to do what Derrick allows her to do. Besides, you can't keep her away from him."

"Why can't I? That's *my* man."

"Yeah, but that's her baby's father. She's got a ticket into his life anytime she wants until that kid turns twenty-one. Whether you like it or not. So if you wanna be with him, you best get used to that."

"I don't want him to see her, Dylan." She wasn't giving up.

"I know, but if you think about it, you can't stop it. Not unless you wanna go to jail."

She stared at me silently for a few seconds. "I don't wanna go to jail, Dylan."

"Then let her take the drugs to him."

It took me the better part of an hour to convince Jasmine that what I was saying was in her best interest. She finally agreed to let Wendy take the drugs up to Dylan, and it was a good thing, 'cause I was starting to get a headache. As much as I liked the girl, I was about to call it quits and let her dig her own grave.

"Dylan, can I ask you a question?" We'd just walked up to her car and she'd gotten in.

"Sure." I leaned in through the driver's-side window.

"How come you never tried to talk me out of being with Derrick?"

" 'Cause you never woulda listened to me. Just like I never listened to people who tried to talk me out of being with Monica. No one knows the good things about Monica and Derrick like we do, Jasmine. All they see is the mistakes they've made."

"You just said exactly what I feel." She looked astonished. I just smiled.

"You told me earlier that you were seeing someone. Are you back with Monica?"

I shook my head and frowned sadly. "Nah, I haven't seen her since that night we were together at the club."

"You still miss her, don't you?"

"Yeah, I do. More than I wanna admit."

"What about the girl you're seeing? Is she nice?" That jealous look was back on her face. I hesitated, trying to think of a lie.

"Yeah, Tonya's cool. But it's more a sex thing than a relationship."

"And you want a relationship?"

"Well, yeah. Maybe not with her, but I wanna get married and have kids. I'm twenty-seven years old. I want to be able to play ball with my kids, not watch them from my porch."

"You don't have any kids?" She reached out and touched my hand.

"None that I'm claiming," I joked.

"So you like kids, huh?"

"I love kids. I just haven't met anyone stupid enough to have any by me."

"You're a trip, Dylan," she laughed.

"Yeah, I know. But I'd rather be a vacation. It lasts longer." She laughed again and handed me a folded-up piece of paper.

"Here, I wrote down all my numbers. You can call me any time. I don't wanna lose this friendship."

"Neither do I, Jasmine. Neither do I."

I bent over to kiss her, and she turned her head so my lips met her cheek. That was okay, but I couldn't believe what I heard next.

"What the hell are you up to, bitch?"

"Excuse me? What did you call me?" I gave her an evil glare. "All I did was kiss you on the cheek. You didn't have to get nasty about that."

"Oh, Dylan, I'm sorry." She turned to face me. "I wasn't talking about you. I was talking about my sister."

"Your sister?" I looked around. "What about your sister?" This woman definitely kept me on my toes with her mood swings.

"See that green van over there with the MS. THING license plates?"

"Yeah." It was parked under a light across the street.

"That's my sister's van."

"And?" I shrugged my shoulders.

"And I wanna know what her car's doing in the parking lot of a motel that rents rooms by the hour."

# 14

# Stephanie

I had what most sisters would call a perfect life. A brand-new house, a new car, a good man at home, and a wedding that was less than six months away. Life was good. So why the hell was I waking up in a cheap motel in the arms of a man who'd walked out on me four years ago? I didn't have a clue.

I rolled over on my side and Malek was staring at me, his face inches away. His full, soft lips gently touched mine. I closed my eyes and savored the taste of his kiss. Yeah, I had everything a woman could ever want waiting for me at home, but all I really wanted was for Malek to make love to me one more time.

"I was wondering when you was gonna wake up. We only got about thirty minutes left before our three hours is up." He smiled as he slid on top of me, pushing his way inside me for the third time.

The first two times I had an excuse. I'd been high off weed. But this time I was sober, so there were no excuses. I just wanted to do it. I took one hand and held onto Malek's firm, muscular ass while my other hand massaged the corn-rows I'd braided a few hours earlier. Malek had been a terrible boyfriend and an even worse father, but I had to give him his props. He was an awesome lover. And every time he slid inside me I was reminded just how awesome he was.

"Whose pussy is this?" I felt him slide deeper.

"It's yours, baby. It's your pussy," I shouted back instinctively.

"Whose pussy is it?" This time he asked louder.

"It's yours, baby! It's all yours! So tear it up, 'cause I'm about to come!"

He was moving inside me like a jackhammer that just met hard cement, and it didn't take long before I was screaming so loud I'm sure everyone in the motel could hear me. I swear to God I ain't come like that in years. And it only made it better that he started moaning like he was ready to come, too. When our little trip to heaven finally ended, Malek collapsed on top of me. I held him contentedly, savoring the phenomenal moment we'd just shared together. That is, until I felt his sperm run down my leg. That's when I panicked.

"Oh, shit." I reached down and felt the warm, sticky liquid oozing out of me. "Get off me, Malek." I tried to wiggle free from underneath him.

"What's wrong?" He rolled off me and glared as he sat on the edge of the bed. "Don't tell me you're having regrets all of a sudden."

"No, not regrets," I told him a little more calmly. "But we should have used a condom."

"What? You think I'm gonna give you somethin'?" He frowned.

"No, but I ain't take my pill this morning or yesterday."

He smiled, reaching across the bed to pat my stomach. "So what's the problem? We make good-looking kids."

"You know damn well what the problem is. I can't get pregnant by you." I shoved his hand away and reached for my bag. I was hoping that maybe if I took yesterday's pill and today's pill I might be all right.

"Why can't you get pregnant by me?"

" 'Cause I just had a baby with Travis, stupid." I popped

the pills in my mouth. "I'd look like a fool if I had a baby with you."

"Why you gonna look like a fool? We already got a daughter together."

"Yeah, but I don't live with you, Malek. I live with Travis. Everybody and their brother knows we're getting married in a few months. How'd I look having a baby with you ten months after I had my son?"

"What you saying?" He slammed his hand down on the night table, scaring the hell outta me. "You still gonna marry this fool even after we just made love?" He stood up, then looked down at his penis as if I'd insulted it. "I thought you said it was my pussy."

"Jesus Christ! Why do you men take everything so literal?" I shook my head at his stupidity. "We were having sex, Malek! It was good. *Real* good. What did you expect me to say? 'No it's not your pussy, but I'm coming anyway?' "

"It woulda been better than lying to me. If you didn't wanna be with me, why'd you give me some? Or did you just plan on playin' me? Damn, I feel used." He actually sounded hurt.

"Don't you dare act like you're the victim here. Ain't nobody play you, and I damn sure ain't *use* you. You know how I get when I smoke weed. That's why you wanted to smoke with me in the first place, isn't it?" My eyes never left his and he got quiet. "That's what I thought. So don't act like I played you, Malek. 'Cause if anyone played you, you played yourself."

"Yeah, maybe I did play myself. But you played me, too."

"Please, how'd I play you?" He was getting on my nerves now.

"If weed makes you so horny, why'd you smoke with me? You could've said no."

Now it was my turn to be quiet, because he was right. I

could have said no. Truth is, there was no good reason why I didn't stop myself. I hadn't smoked weed in years.

"You know why, Shorty. Because you wanted me to fuck you. You wanted it the whole time. You just needed an excuse to do it." His words stung, but only because they were accurate.

"Maybe you're right, Malek. Maybe I really did wanna go to bed with you. But I wasn't tryin'a play you. And I damn sure don't have no regrets."

"If you don't have no regrets, then why you still gonna be with him?" He looked so pathetic, I almost wanted to feel sorry for him. But I wasn't about to let his little pout get in the way of my future with Travis.

" 'Cause we have a family together. We have plans for the future. And more important, I love him, Malek. Don't you understand that?"

"No! I don't understand shit. If you loved him as much you say, you woulda never given me the pussy." His stare challenged me. I didn't know what to say. Maybe there was a little truth to what he was saying, but I wasn't about to deal with that now.

"I know he doesn't make love to you like I do, does he?"

"Why are you making this so difficult?"

"I'm not making shit difficult. You are. Now just answer the question. Does he make you feel like I do in bed?" Suddenly, Malek was regaining control of the situation.

"No, Malek!" I blurted out honestly, regretting it as soon as I said it. "Nobody makes me feel the way you do in the bedroom."

"Then why the hell would you marry him?" He threw his hands in the air.

"Because sex ain't everything, Malek. Sex don't buy groceries. Sex don't buy a big house in Chesterfield County, and sex don't buy security. As good as you make me feel in bed, you don't make me feel secure. You never did." Admitting all of this to Malek and to myself was like a big weight lifted. "But Travis makes me feel secure, and that's why I love him. So get this in your head. I'm not leaving Travis. Not for you or anyone else."

"So you're willing to sleep with me but not be with me, is that it?"

"That's a good way to sum it up." I shrugged my shoulders. "Look, Malek. We can hang out, maybe even screw once in a while. But we can't be together. I got a man. So don't be getting any mixed messages."

"We belong together, Stephanie. You know it and I know it. So if you wanna waste your time with this guy, then be my guest." He was full of confidence. "Because me and Mr. Johnson here will be waiting. It's only a matter of time. Trust me." He leaned over and kissed me passionately. I'm not gonna lie. Just the feel of his tongue in my mouth got me excited again, but I wasn't about to give in to the passion. I had to show him I could be strong.

"You know what your problem is, Malek?" I moved to the edge of the bed and sat in front of him.

"What?"

"You and Mr. Johnson here worry too much about tomorrow instead of dealing with today."

"Oh, yeah, what's so great about today?"

"You got me here today, don't you? And we never know what tomorrow might hold," I reminded him.

"You got a point there," he smiled. "Now, here's something you can hold." Malek guided my hand between his legs, where he was quickly growing erect. For a second I tried to resist, but I was weak when it came to Mr. Johnson. Besides, shouldn't I follow my own advice and deal with what was in front of me today?

I gave him a wicked smile, then bent down and took Mr.

Johnson in my mouth. Malek let out a satisfied moan and stroked my hair gently. But before I could really get started, the phone rang.

"Who the hell is that?" I lifted my head and whined.

"Probably the front desk trying to tell us our time is up." He reached for the phone, but I wasn't letting go of Mr. Johnson.

"Tell them we want another three hours," I purred.

"We do?"

I bent over and gave him another French kiss as an answer.

"Mmmmmmm," he moaned with newfound excitement. "I guess we do. I'll be right back." I let go of him and he grabbed his pants. On his way to the desk to pay for more time, he gave me a quick kiss and promised to hurry back.

That's when I started to think about Travis and what Malek had said about me not being in love with him. Yeah, I still had feelings for Malek. There was no question about that. But I was in love with Travis. Wasn't I? Jesus, after all these years I had better be. We just had a baby together. And I'd have to be one stupid woman to mess up the good thing I had with Travis. I mean, shoot, how many women can say their man bought them a house and a car? And we weren't even married yet.

My thoughts were interrupted by a knock on the door. Malek's wallet was on the dresser, so I figured he must have forgotten his money. I picked it up and went to the door.

"Let me guess. You forgot your money, didn't you?" I opened the door and struck a pose. Unfortunately, it wasn't Malek standing in front of me, getting an eyeful of my naked body. It was somebody I never would've expected.

# 15

# Jasmine

I parked my car in the motel parking lot and waited. It had taken me a while to get rid of Dylan. He wanted to hang around and help once I saw my sister's car at the motel, but I finally convinced him this matter was best left to the family. You see, I wasn't sure what I was gonna say when I saw Stephanie, but I was sure I didn't want Dylan to hear it. Especially since I was probably gonna use a lot of profanity. Don't get me wrong. I didn't want to create a scene, but sometimes my little sister could be a bit stubborn, and a few choice words were needed to straighten her out. I was really hoping that just the embarrassment of being busted would make her realize how big a mistake she'd made by cheating on Travis. Although I doubted it would be enough.

Of course, it was possible that it was Travis with her. I had seen an Expedition parked out front, too. Maybe, just maybe, they were trying to spice things up. Then again, that was pretty unlikely once I saw her ex, Malek, walk out of one of the rooms, buttoning his shirt. I was praying it was just a coincidence, but in my heart I knew what was going on. Malek had always had some type of controlling power over Stephanie. As far as she was concerned, he could do no wrong. Even after the bastard left her with a two-month-old baby and no choice but to move into the projects and go on welfare, she still rarely talked bad about him. Shit, she wouldn't even let us talk bad about him. "Don't be talkin' 'bout my baby's daddy," she used to always say. Thank God she met Travis. If it weren't for him, who knows where my baby sister and my niece would be right now?

I watched Malek go to the motel office; then I headed straight to the room he'd come out of. I stood outside the door for a minute, wondering if I should knock. But I had to know if it was my sister in there. And it was little surprise when she opened the door, 'cept for the fact that she was butt-ass naked.

"Oh, my God, Jasmine! What the fuck are you doin' here?"

She had the nerve to be actin' all indignant as she stood in the doorway, butt-ass naked, steppin' out on a good man with that lowlife she call her baby's daddy. I know I was the last person she expected to find at the door. She just stood there and stared like I was some kinda space alien. Shoot, I know she musta been in shock, 'cause she didn't even attempt to cover herself.

"Bitch, I know you ain't the one who need to be askin' that question." I sucked my teeth. "What the hell are you doin' here with Malek? You oughta be ashamed of yourself."

Stephanie lowered her eyes and stepped back to finally get something to cover herself. I shouldered past her and sat down on the bed. The funk in the room made my stomach turn, but I had to stay and straighten this girl out. I never did understand the hold that Malek had over her. That's why I had such a bad feeling after Big Momma told me Malek came by on Christmas Day. Sure, Stephanie probably put on a good show for Travis, all up in Malek's face, tellin' him to get lost. But I knew my sister well enough to know how hard that was for her. Part of her probably wanted to jump in the car and ride away with that no-good nigga. Something told me it was just a matter of time before there would be trouble. And now I was staring at trouble in the form of my naked sister in a sleazy motel. I just hoped I could stop her before she lost the best man she could ever hope to have.

"Jesus, Stephanie." I shook my head in disgust as she stood before me wrapped in a sheet. "What were you thinking? You're supposed to be getting married in a few months."

"You're not gonna tell Big Momma, are you?" was her nervous reply.

I had to give Big Momma her due. Even when she wasn't around, she was around. Here was Stephanie, busted in a motel room with her ex-boyfriend, with not a stitch of clothing on, and all she could think about was if I'm gonna tell Big Momma.

"Big Momma is the least of your worries, Stephanie. You had better pray I don't tell Travis. How could you do this to him after all he's done for you? Do you know how many sisters would trade places with you right this minute? And you over here with that no-good nigga Malek. Please!" I frowned. "Will you stop starin' at me and put some clothes on? Don't nobody wanna see your naked ass."

She turned her back to me and started to pick up the clothes that had been scattered across the room. The air in there was thick and musty like they'd been going at it all day. I couldn't wait to get the hell outta there.

"Jasmine, please don't tell no one 'bout this. Please," she was pleading as she hurried to get dressed.

"You know, Steph, you've done some stupid shit over the years, but this is the stupidest." I turned to face her, hands on my hips. "How in the hell could you cheat on Travis for Malek? That's like choosing a Ford Escort over a Mercedes Benz."

She didn't answer me. She just sat on the bed and cried. I swear that was the first time I'd ever seen my sister speechless.

A minute or so later there was a knock on the door. Her

body language made it obvious she was dying to answer the door, but she looked at me sheepishly to see what my next move would be.

"Don't you even think about it!" I pointed at her as I stood and marched to the door.

The expression on Malek's face was priceless when he saw me. His mouth 'bout dropped to the scuzzy motel floor, and his knees buckled. For a second I thought I might have to catch this fool if he passed out. Either that or I was gonna have to go get him some paper, 'cause he sure looked like he was gonna shit on himself.

"So the criminal returns to the scene of the crime." I place my hand on my hip. Malek looked past me, searching the room for Stephanie. She was fully dressed now, sitting on the bed with tears streaming down her face. He figured out real fast he wasn't gonna get no support from her, so he took an attitude with me.

"I ain't no criminal," he snapped. "Yo, Short—I mean, Stephanie. What's up? What's she doing here?" Stephanie couldn't answer him, so I did.

"I came to get my little sister and take her home to her *fiancé*. You got a problem with that?"

Malek was definitely not happy that I'd screwed up his little booty call, but it wasn't like I cared. Wasn't shit he could do to me. He knew damn well that if he tried anything stupid, I just had to make one call to one of Derrick's friends and his ass would be pushing up daisies at Bland's Cemetery.

"Let's go, Stephanie," I ordered.

She stood up and walked to the door, her head hanging low. When she passed Malek she whispered, "I'll call you later."

"No, she won't," I assured him as I closed the door behind us. When we got to the parking lot, Stephanie turned around and watched Malek walk to his car. There was longing in her eyes, and that scared me. She was so much better off with Travis, and I did not want her to mess that up.

"You are taking your ass home, aren't you?" I used my most parental tone.

"Yes." She answered absentmindedly, still staring at Malek. As she opened the door to her van, she asked one more time, "Please, don't tell no one about this, Jasmine. I ain't gonna mess with him again, I swear. You're always talkin' about how we're sisters and we should look out for each other. Please don't say nothin'."

I looked at her but didn't answer. Let her sweat it out for a while. Truth is, I had no intention of telling Travis. She was right. Even though we didn't get along all the time, we were still sisters, and she had to live with Travis, not with me. But I did want to tell Momma and Big Momma. At least they could help me keep an eye on Stephanie so she didn't mess things up with Travis. Her kids needed someone like him in their lives, and if she wasn't gonna protect their interests, then we would.

"I thought you and Travis were happy, Steph."

"We are."

"Then why mess with Malek?"

"I don't know," she said softly. "Haven't you ever done something with a man that felt so right at the time but was so wrong when you were done?"

I nodded my head slowly. That was exactly how I felt the night Dylan and I spent at Joe's.

"Yeah, I guess I have, but not with anyone as low-life as Malek. Haven't you learned yet that he's bad news?"

"He's not a lowlife, Jasmine," she tried to convince me. "He's just misunderstood. Isn't that what you tell everyone about Derrick? "

Damn, she was killing me with my own words. When she put it that way, I guess I did understand what she meant. My entire family hated Derrick even more than they hated Malek. I had spent plenty of energy trying to convince everyone of the good that I saw in him, and I guess Stephanie felt the same way about Malek.

"You still love him, don't you?" She didn't answer. She was too busy watching Malek's car leave the motel parking lot. "Stephanie?"

"Hmm?" She finally turned to me.

"I asked you a question. You still love Malek, don't you?"

She hesitated before speaking. "I still care about him, Jasmine. I can't lie about that. But I'm not in love with him. Not anymore."

I wasn't able to tell if she was truthful.

"You for real?"

"Yeah," she nodded. "That's why I need you to keep this between us. I made a mistake today, Jasmine. I realize that now, but it was a mistake I had to make if I was gonna marry Travis. I had to be sure I wasn't still in love with Malek."

"And you're not?"

"I would've never left that room if I was in love with Malek, and you know it. I would've told you to kiss my ass."

I couldn't argue with her logic. From the start, everyone was busy telling her how perfect Travis was for her. Including me. Why shouldn't we? He's a good man. But the only one who needed to be more than sure was Stephanie. If you're gonna get married, you gotta make sure the love is real.

"So are you in love with Travis?"

"More than you can ever know," she responded with sad eyes. "I can't believe I did this to him. It all started out so innocent. I was just supposed to be hanging out with Malek and next thing you know, we ended up here." I stopped her. I really didn't wanna hear any more.

"All right, little sister. I'll keep your secret. But you've gotta promise me you're gonna stay away from Malek."

"I promise, Jasmine."

"Hold on." My cell phone was ringing. "Hello?"

"Jasmine?" I recognized my mother's agitated voice right away.

"Yeah, Momma. What's up?"

"Have you seen your sister? I been looking everywhere for her."

"She's right here. What's the matter, Momma?"

"Nothin'," she snapped. "Just put your sister on the phone."

"All right, Momma. You don't have to get indignant with me." I shoved the phone at Stephanie. "Here, Momma wants to talk to you."

"Hey, Momma. Whatzup?" It seemed like a full five minutes Stephanie just stood and listened to Momma, who was yelling so loud I could hear bits and pieces of her tirade as I stood next to my sister. Stephanie finally interrupted. "I know I need a new cell phone, Momma. But I ain't paid the bill on the last one I had, so you know they ain't gonna give me a new one. Is that why you called looking for me?"

Stephanie looked agitated, but whatever Momma told her after that had her worried, 'cause she just stood there babbling things like, "What? . . . Oh, shit! . . . What did he say? . . . Damn, Momma! . . . Why didn't you? . . . Okay, I'll be there in ten minutes."

Stephanie clicked the phone off and handed it to me. She looked even worse than she did when I busted her.

"What happened?"

"Travis dropped the kids off at Momma's."

"So?"

"She said he left them there so he could go lookin' for me. He talked to someone at my job and found out I wasn't doin' overtime."

My sister was in a whole heap of trouble, and I hoped for her sake she could think fast enough to get herself out of it.

# 16

# Travis

I stopped searching for Stephanie and headed home once it got dark. I was so heated when I walked in the house and she wasn't there that I went straight to the living room bar and poured myself a shot of tequila. I threw it back and finished it in one gulp, then poured myself another. I'm not really a drinker, but I needed something to calm my nerves. I musta drove around Richmond for three hours trying to find Stephanie's ass. I stopped by every friend, relative, and acquaintance I could think of. The only place I didn't stop by was that punk Malek's house, and that was only because Stephanie's mother said she didn't know his address.

I gulped down what was left of my second drink, then poured myself a third before I sat on the living room sofa. I sat there for a good five or ten minutes, staring a portrait of Stephanie hanging over the mantel. I was trying to figure out why the hell she'd lied to me, but I just couldn't come up with a logical explanation. I mean, it wasn't like I was unreasonable, and I had definitely been good to her. In all the years we'd been together, I hadn't even looked at another woman. So why the hell was this happening to me? In my frustration I started to scream at the portrait.

"Why? Why the fuck would you do this to me?"

Stephanie smiled out at me from that picture as if to say, *I'll do what ever I want. You're in love with me, remember!*

Maybe it was the alcohol or maybe it was just my pent-up anger, but I snatched that portrait from the wall and threw it to the ground. It shattered into a hundred pieces and I was about to stomp on what was left of it when I heard a car pull into the driveway. A few seconds later I heard Stephanie's voice coming form the front door.

"Travis! You home, baby? Travis!"

"I'm in the living room," I grumbled. It took everything I had not to explode on her like I did the portrait when she walked in the room.

"Hey, baby. I didn't . . ." Her eyes took in the broken glass all over the floor. She didn't budge, but her expression told me she was concerned. I was hoping she was scared. "What happened to my picture?"

"I broke it. What does it look like?" I slurred belligerently.

She eyed me strangely. "Travis . . . are you drunk?"

"You damn right I'm drunk! And I'm gonna get drunker. Now where the hell have you been?" I shouted.

"Um . . . well . . . I . . ." She wouldn't make eye contact, and that just made things worse. As far as I was concerned, it just proved she was doing something she had no business doing. An image of her and Malek flashed in my mind and I just lost it. I knocked everything off the bar to get her attention.

"Look at me, goddamn it! I already know you weren't at work. Now, where the hell were you?" My hands were shaking and I was trying my best to control my temper, but it was getting hard. I guess I was expecting her to act shocked or pretend she didn't know what I was talking about, but she just lowered her head without a word. "Answer me, Stephanie! Where the fuck were you?"

When she didn't answer, I kicked the coffee table in my rage, and the wood splintered with a loud crack. Stephanie screamed loud enough for the entire neighborhood to hear. But I didn't care who was listening. I just wanted answers. And the fact that she wasn't giving me any was pissing me off even more.

"Goddamn it, I asked you a question!" I reached for her and she stepped back out of my grasp.

"What the fuck is wrong with you? Have you lost your mind?" She was scared, real scared, and believe it or not, so was I. Scared of what I might do if I got my hands on her.

"Yeah, maybe I have lost my mind. But if I have, it's your fault!" I reached out to grab her again. This time I wasn't letting her get away. "I'm not gonna ask you again. Where the fuck were you?"

"Let her go, Travis! She was with me." The voice came from behind me. I turned around and there was Jasmine, holding my son with one arm and Maleka's hand with the other. I let Stephanie go and she ran to her sister's side.

"She wasn't with you. She can't stand you. Why the hell would she lie to me about being with you?" I really hadn't meant to say it that way. It wasn't Jasmine I wanted to hurt, but the alcohol was talking.

Jasmine frowned in Stephanie's direction. "She was with me 'cause no matter what you say she feels about me, she's my sister and I needed her."

"Ha! What do I look like, a fool? I may be drunk, but I'm not stupid. Do you really expect me to believe that shit? I don't know what she has on you, but I don't believe a word you're saying."

"Are you calling me a liar, Travis? I don't have to lie to you." She actually looked insulted.

"Neither does Stephanie. If she was with you, why'd she lie to me about doing overtime? She could've told me the truth. I wouldn't have stopped her."

Jasmine released Maleka's hand, then handed the baby to

Stephanie. She marched over to me and stood inches away from my face.

"You wanna know why, Travis? This is why." She removed her sunglasses.

"Damn! What happened to your eye?" She looked like she'd just gone ten rounds with Muhammad Ali.

"The same thing I just stopped you from doing to my sister," she sighed as she placed the glasses back on her head. "Look at this place, Travis. I can't believe you. I never thought I'd ever see you act this way. Is this the example you wanna set for your son?"

I felt like I was shrinking in front of her. I surveyed the damage I'd done in the room: the broken picture frame, the splintered coffee table, and the frightened look on Maleka's face. I felt like a fool. I'd jumped to conclusions about Stephanie's whereabouts a little too quickly. I should've had a little more faith. I should've trusted her more. And to make matters even worse, T. J. was crying and Stephanie was on the verge.

"She was really with you?" My voice was humbled and unsure, sorry I had rushed to judgment.

"Yes," Jasmine nodded. "She's been with me ever since I left Ryan's."

I lowered my head and stepped toward Stephanie. She flinched backwards, so I froze. I'd really fucked up. I had to proceed very carefully now.

"Is that true, Steph? Were you with Jasmine?" She glanced at her sister before she nodded at me.

"Oh, shit." I covered my face as I lowered my head. "I'm sorry, baby. I'm really so sorry. You know how much I love you. I just thought . . ." I took a step forward, then stopped.

I expected her to curse me out after I was so stupid, but she burst into tears and wrapped her arms around me. The baby squirmed between us as we held each other tight.

"I'm sorry, baby. I love you, too. I'm never gonna lie to you again, not even for my sister." She looked up at me and I kissed her tears away.

I said a quick prayer to thank God for giving me back my family. I coulda sworn I heard Jasmine suck her teeth behind me, but I wasn't gonna get into that. She was probably just jealous that she was the sister stuck with a no-good jailbird and one hell of a black eye. Oh well, maybe me and Stephanie could set a good enough example that she'd wake up and dump that guy someday soon.

# 17

# Stephanie

It was late, almost midnight. I couldn't fall asleep because Travis had been rubbing his thing up against my butt for the past hour. I was trying to pretend I was asleep, but I knew it was only a matter of time before he got frustrated and started shaking me to wake up. Even worse, I was afraid he might try to get my panties down far enough so that he could slip himself inside me. Not that I could blame him if he did. I'd promised him this morning that I was gonna give him some tonight. He'd been back from maneuvers in the field for over a week, and with the kids sick with colds and both of us taking night classes, we just hadn't had the time or opportunity to be intimate. Travis had let me know this morning that he couldn't wait any longer. The bad thing about all this was that I had an itch that needed to be scratched myself, only I hadn't waited for Travis to take care of it.

Earlier in the day, I stopped by Nana's house to drop off some pictures of the kids and ran into Malek. The next thing I knew we were in bed together. You'd think after all the shit that happened with Jasmine and with Travis nearly losing his mind that I'd have enough common sense to leave Malek alone. But that wasn't the case. Every time I looked at him I'd get weak and throw common sense to the wind.

"Steph? You awake?" Travis whispered as he kissed my neck.

"I am now," I told him groggily, pulling the covers up around my neck. My neck was my weak spot and Travis knew it. If he kissed me there and I didn't respond, he'd get the message.

"Baby, don't go to sleep. I want some," he pleaded as he gently shook me.

"You want some?" I sighed loudly.

I was tempted to just turn around and go down on him, but he always took so long to come that way. It'd be just my luck he'd get frustrated and tell me he wanted to put it inside me. And I'm sorry, I know I'm wrong, but after three rounds with Malek and his big dick, I was just too damn sore.

"Travis, do you know what time it is?" I was hoping the fact it was late might change his mind. No such luck.

"Yeah, I know what time it is, but I still want some. Come on, baby, I thought I told you this morning how much I want you. It's been a long time." He was whining like a teenager looking for his first piece of ass. I rolled over to face him.

"I know it's been a while, boo. But I'll give you some tomorrow, okay? I promise. I'm tired." I closed my eyes and tried to snuggle up next to him, hoping that would satisfy him. He backed away, sucking his teeth. I could feel an argument coming on.

"That's what you said last night and the night before," he griped. "How come you're always making excuses? You ain't gave me none since I been home."

"Look, Travis, I'm tired. I already told you tomorrow's our night. So go to sleep, all right, baby?" This was getting bad. I was gonna have to give him some soon or he was gonna drive me crazy.

"Come on, Steph." He was trying his best to grind up against me. "All I want is a quickie. You don't have to do anything. I'll do all the work."

"Damn it, Travis! How many times I gotta tell you I'm

not in the mood?" He was starting to get on my nerves. "Now, you can go to sleep, take a cold shower, jerk off, or go out there and find you a piece of ass in the street. I really don't care. Just let me get some sleep, okay?" I rolled over, my back to him. If he didn't get the message now, he never would.

"You're fucking him, aren't you?" he huffed.

"What'd you say?" I hoped I hadn't heard him correctly.

"I said, you're fucking him, aren't you?" he repeated loudly. "You're fucking Malek." It's a good thing I had my back to him, because the look on my face would have been all the proof he needed. I couldn't believe he'd figured it out.

"Are you crazy? Why would I fuck with Malek when I've got you?" I held my breath as I waited for his response.

"I don't know. Why'd you lie to me about doing overtime last month?" I turned back over to face him with a huge sigh.

"Are you back to that shit? Didn't Jasmine explain that to you?"

"Yeah, but that doesn't mean I believed her. I had a lot of time to think out there in the field."

"Too much time," I groaned. "Where's all this coming from, anyway?"

"It's coming from you. You've been acting funny ever since Malek showed up Christmas Day. And it's only gotten worse the last couple o' weeks." Damn, was I that obvious? Or maybe Jasmine had gone back on her word and put a bug in his ear. I wasn't sure what was going on, but I wasn't admitting nothing. For all I knew, he was just guessing anyway.

"I'm not acting funny, and I damn sure ain't fucking Malek. If this is about sex, I told you I'm gonna give you some tomorrow. If you thought you could get me hot tonight, you sure picked the wrong approach."

"You expect me to believe that?" he said loudly. "You been saying that all week."

"You act like I've been neglecting you or somethin'." I sucked my teeth in mock indignation. In truth, I had been avoiding him for quite a while now. Hell, it was hard keeping two men satisfied.

"You have! You don't spend time with me anymore. Shit, I tried to take you out to dinner and the movies before I went out in the field and you told me you had to go to the gym. The gym, for crying out loud! You hate the gym. But you'd rather be at the gym than with me." He glared at me suspiciously. "Or were you with someone else?"

"No, I wasn't with someone else. And you're blowing this whole thing out of proportion."

"Am I, Steph? All I know is, you never used to lie to me. Now everything that comes out your mouth is a lie."

"Oh, please! What have I lied about?"

"Where were you this afternoon before you came home?"

"I told you where I was. . . ." I hesitated. "I was out getting my wedding dress fitted. Why, do you wanna call them?" I tried to laugh the situation off.

"Yeah, maybe I should. Where's the number?" Damn! I didn't think he'd take me seriously about checking my story.

"You know, Travis, maybe I should give you some right now, because this lack of sex is warping your brain." I glared at him.

"You think so?" His tone was nasty. "Well, was something wrong with Maleka's brain when she told me you took her to Malek's house while I was in the field?" My jaw must've hit the ground. I'd told Malek that it wasn't a good idea to bring Maleka over to see Nana. Now my fears had been confirmed. Maleka had told Travis about it even though I'd bribed her to keep quiet by promising her a new toy.

"What's wrong? Cat got your tongue? Or you trying to think of another lie?" That was right. I was trying to think of a good lie.

"I was gonna tell you about that, Travis. It just slipped my mind. It's a good thing Maleka told you." He rolled his eyes at my pathetic attempt to look innocent.

"Did it also slip your mind to tell me you dropped the parental rights case against him? And that I'm not going to be able to adopt Maleka?" My heart was in my mouth and my nightgown was becoming soaked with sweat. How did he know that?

"Who told you that?" I asked nervously.

"Does it really matter? *You* should have told me, Steph!" He got out of bed. I looked at him and saw tears glistening in his eyes. "You used to tell me everything, Stephanie. Now you only tell me lies."

"Travis . . ." I had to stop myself. I didn't know what to say to him.

"You know, I waited all week for you to tell me that you saw Malek and dropped the case. So don't you dare try and tell me I'm blowing things out of proportion or that you don't lie to me." We stared at each other silently. "Are you fucking him, Steph? Are you fucking Malek?"

"No, Travis," I protested weakly. "How could you think—"

He raised his hand to stop me. I knew it wasn't worth it to make up another story. He wouldn't believe me now anyway.

"How could I think that? Maybe because I don't even know you anymore, Stephanie. You're not the woman I fell in love with."

He grabbed his pants and shirt off the back of a chair and shut himself in the bathroom. I ran behind him but I heard the click of the lock as I grabbed the doorknob. Suddenly, I felt a sense of insecurity I'd never felt before with Travis. I was losing him. I'd never before imagined he could leave me, but now I was afraid he would. It was finally becoming clear to me just how important he was in my life.

I sat down on the bed and stared at that bathroom door for

a good ten minutes before I finally got up enough nerve to knock. Travis was fully dressed when he emerged. I was scared for our future together, but it was so easy for me to fall back into my old ways with him. I immediately took on an attitude to show him who was really in charge.

"Where you going?"

"I'm going out to get a piece of ass," he smirked. "Isn't that what you told me to do?"

"Look, Travis." I softened my tone. It was time to take a new approach, since he didn't seem to be playing by the old rules, when I was always allowed to win. "I'm sorry I didn't tell you I dropped the case, but Malek came to my job offering to pay child support. Then he told me he was going to fight us every step of the way. We can't afford that. And when I told the lawyer, he said we probably wouldn't win. Ask him." I grabbed his shirt.

"I don't have to. I already spoke to him." He slipped on his shoes and stood to face me. "You don't get it. This isn't about the lawyer. It's really not even about Malek. It's about you and me. It's about how you keep lying to me, Stephanie. I can't trust you anymore, so I don't even know if I wanna marry you."

"What?" My heart was in my stomach, and my eyes full of tears. "You can't be serious. You don't know what you're saying."

"Oh, I'm serious, all right. I might just pack up my shit and move back onto base tomorrow. Now, would you let me go?" He shrugged my hand off of his shirt.

I was so stunned. My arms dropped to my side and I stepped back. Maybe he'd expected me to put up more of a fight, because he drove the knife a little deeper to see if he could get a rise out of me.

"Don't wait up. I might get lucky." He winked.

"Are you serious? You're gonna go sleep with another

woman?" I was so hurt by how callously he'd said it. This was not the Travis I knew. He was supposed to worship the ground I walked on.

"I ain't getting none here." He walked out of the bedroom door. "And I'm sick of that shit."

"Travis, don't do this!" I called after him. "I'm sorry, baby. Please, don't do this. Travis . . ." I was scared. He was mad enough to make good on his promise. And even after all the shit I'd done with Malek, I couldn't bear the thought of Travis being with another woman.

# 18

# Travis

My head felt like someone was playing a game of pinball in there. I don't think I'd ever had a worse hangover. But what could I expect after how much I drank last night? I knew it wasn't possible to drown away my sorrows, but I damn well tried after I stomped out of the house last night. In all the time we'd been together, I'd never been so mad at Stephanie or so serious about ending things between us. Usually, she could just bat her beautiful eyelashes at me and we'd be making up. But this time I wasn't having it. She had told me one too many lies, and it hurt me to the core that she had changed her mind about me adopting Maleka. She seemed to be more concerned about her daughter's father than she was about me. It was enough to make even the most secure man nervous. So where I was usually the one to make peace in our house, this time I set out to hurt Stephanie the way she'd hurt me. I told her I was going out to find me some ass, but really I was just planning on going to the NCO club on base to get drunk. Now I was the one hurting as I lay in bed, my head pounding. I was afraid to open my eyes, 'cause I knew the light would only make the pain worse.

"Steph?" I mumbled desperately from under the covers. I was rubbing my temples to relieve the pain. "Can you please get me some aspirin? My head is killing me."

She didn't answer, so I shook her. I knew she was up, because I'd just heard her hit the snooze button on the alarm a few seconds before. She probably wasn't speaking to me because of the way I cursed her out last night. I'd said a lot of things I probably shouldn't have, but at the time I didn't give a shit. I meant every word. And I still meant a lot of it, especially the part about packing my shit and moving back onto the base this morning. I was just praying that she wasn't gonna have an attitude when I asked for the ring.

"Stephanie? Did you hear me? I need some aspirin." I was about to shake her again until she spoke.

"Yeah, I heard you. But my name ain't Stephanie."

"What? Oh, shit!" My response wasn't exactly Shakespeare, but they were the only words that came to mind when I realized that something was seriously wrong. I slowly pried my eyes open, praying I was just having a bad dream. But once I adjusted to the light, I saw my ex-girlfriend, Sergeant Brittany Collins, sitting on the edge of the bed, looking like a Victoria's Secret supermodel.

"Brittany, what the hell are you doing in my guest room?"

"Your guest room? You better look around, 'cause I pay the rent here." She rolled her eyes and I surveyed the room, decked out in pastels and ultrafeminine furniture. She was right. I wasn't in my guest room or even my house, and that meant I was in trouble. Big trouble, 'cause I wasn't any better than Stephanie and her cheating ass.

"Oh, God." I sat up gingerly and rubbed my eyes. "What time is it?"

She pointed to the clock on the nightstand. "Quarter to eight."

"In the morning?" My head was pounding so loud I could barely hear my own voice.

"No. The sun shines through my window all night," she answered sarcastically. "Of course it's morning. Are you still drunk?"

"No, I'm not still drunk. Just got one hell of a hangover," I groaned. "I gotta get outta here. I gotta get home. I can't believe I did this. Stephanie's gonna kill me." I didn't even wanna think about what might have happened between Brittany and me. No matter how angry I was at Stephanie, my conscience wouldn't let me get out of this situation without heaps of guilt. She was the cheater, not me. At least I didn't think I was until now, with Brittany's half-naked ass sitting on the edge of my bed. Now I wasn't quite sure if I did or not. Especially since the last thing I remembered was her sitting down next to me at the bar and offering to buy me a drink. "How the hell did I get here, anyway?"

"Damn, I must be losing my touch if you don't even remember." She slid the strap of her lingerie back onto her shoulder. I was glad, 'cause the last thing I needed was a view of her exposed breast to get me into even more trouble.

"To be honest," I admitted, "the only thing I remember is sitting in the NCO club drinking a tequila sunrise."

"That's it? You don't remember begging me for some last night?" She looked insulted.

"I'm sorry, Brittany, but I don't remember any of that." I covered my face in shame. "God, I've really gotta stop drinking tequila."

"No, you really gotta stop making promises you can't keep." There was anger in her eyes.

"I do?" I raised an eyebrow. "Oh, Lord. What'd I promise?"

"A hell of a lot more than I got. If I remember correctly, you said something about sending me to the stars and the moon if I let you come home with me." She smirked at me. "Sweetheart, I didn't come close to the moon, and the only stars I saw were outside my window."

"For real? I was that bad?" Male ego is a fragile thing. Once Brittany insulted my performance, I was more concerned about her criticism than I was about getting home to

Stephanie. And like any self-respecting man, I had an excuse ready. "Well, it was probably because I was drunk. If I was sober, I would've handled my business. You can believe that." I winked at her, tempted to offer proof right then until she laughed out loud.

"What's so funny?"

"You are." She shook her head. "Do you really think we had sex last night?"

"Why else would I be in your bed?" I was feeling stupider by the second. One second I was worried that I had slept with Brittany, now I was worried that maybe I hadn't.

"To sleep." She stopped laughing and stared at me. "We didn't do anything. I was just joking, Travis. Can't you see you're still fully dressed?" I noticed my rumpled clothes for the first time and sighed thankfully.

"How the hell did I get here, anyway?"

"I took your keys after your sixth tequila sunrise. I didn't know where you lived, so I drove you and your truck over here."

"For real?"

"Yeah. I slept on the couch last night. I just walked in here to turn off the alarm clock."

"But you were in the bed. I was shaking you, wasn't I?" This was too confusing for my hungover state.

"No. You were shaking my pillows, Travis." She laughed as I noticed just how many damn pillows were on her bed. I musta really been hurting if I thought one of those was her, but she did say I'd had six tequilas last night. And who knows how many I had before she got there.

"Thank God," I sighed pitifully now that my ego was in check, and I realized it was a good thing that nothing had happened. "I don't think I could deal with it right now if I had."

"Please, even if I wanted to get with you last night, I

couldn't. All you did was talk about your fiancée and how you wanted to go home but she was cheating on you. I don't know what she's got between her legs, but I sure as hell wish she'd share her secret, 'cause your ass is whipped."

"Yeah, I know," I agreed. "That's part of my problem. I'm totally whipped."

"Hey, that's not necessarily a bad thing," she smiled. "Stephanie's a lucky girl. She just has to wake up and figure it out."

"I don't know, Brittany. I'm starting to think she's never gonna figure it out."

"Yeah, you told me that last night."

"What didn't I tell you?"

"I got the *Reader's Digest* version of your whole four-year relationship. From your first date to her ex showing up Christmas Day to—"

I cut her off. "Damn, I really gotta stop drinking. Shit makes me talk too much."

"It sure does." She smiled. "Look, I'm about to make breakfast. You not no Muslim or anything, are you? 'Cause I don't cook breakfast unless it's got pork."

"No, I eat pork. But I'm gonna pass. I need to get home and straighten a few things out before I head to the base."

"Well, if you need somewhere to stay, you can stay here for a few days. But from now on, you get the couch."

"You know, Brittany, you're all right. Thanks." I gave her a sad smile. "Who knows? The way things are going, I might need to take you up on that offer."

"My door's always open."

"Travis," a weak voice called from the living room when I got home a little after nine. I wasn't looking forward to the confrontation I was sure was about to go down. Still, I went into the living room to deal with our problem like a man. Stephanie was sitting on the love seat, looking nothing like what I expected. I had expected her to be ready for a war of words. Instead, she looked like she'd already been defeated. Her hair was wrapped in an old scarf and she was wearing baggy sweats. But her face was the most surprising. Trails of black mascara started at her puffy eyes and streaked all the way down her cheeks. She looked like she'd been crying all night.

"Travis, I'm sorry. I'm really sorry. I know I shouldn't have lied to you. Please don't leave me."

"Don't worry." I stepped closer to her. "I ain't going nowhere. This is *my* house. But shit's about to change around here. Do you understand me, Stephanie? Shit's about to change or you can get the fuck out." She jumped up and wrapped her arms around me as soon as I was within reach.

"I know. I understand. You didn't mess with no woman last night, did you?" During the ride home I'd convinced myself that I should tell Stephanie the truth about getting drunk and winding up at Brittany's. Hell, it was completely innocent. But now that I was looking at her tear-stained face, I didn't think it was such a good idea.

"I had a few offers, but no, I didn't mess with any—"

Before I could finish my sentence, her lips came down on mine and we were kissing like it was our first date.

"I want you, baby. I want you right now," she purred like a sex kitten.

She let go of me and pulled her sweatshirt right off. Two seconds later she was standing in front of me naked as the day she was born. She grabbed my hand slowly and backed up until she was sitting in the love seat with her legs open.

"It's all yours, baby. Any way you want it."

But I wasn't as enthusiastic as she was. I took a step back.

"What is it? What's the matter?"

"I can't live this way, Steph. I can't be paranoid all the time. Worried about where you are or who you're with. As much as I love you, it's not worth it to me. So you do whatever you have to do to get your boy Malek straight. 'Cause you got one more chance and only one chance. You screw it up and we're through. And you can try me if you want to."

"I'm not gonna screw up, baby. Now, come here so I can show you how much I love you."

"Where are the kids?" I whispered as I unbuttoned my shirt.

"I already took them to day care. We've got till five o'clock this afternoon." I smiled at her answer as I unbuckled my pants.

"Well then, back that ass on up."

# 19

# Jasmine

It was a little after noon and Dylan and I were sitting in the Red Lobster on the West End having lunch. We'd been spending most of our free time together and I must say I was really enjoying it. I was getting more and more attached to him with each day. Sure, I still loved Derrick, but after the incident with Wendy at the prison, things just hadn't been the same. Especially after I refused to bring him the drugs and Wendy started visiting him every week.

In some ways Dylan had taken over in Derrick's absence. I actually relied on him so much more than I'd ever relied on Derrick. As much as I loved Derrick, and as well as he treated me when he was free, he never listened to me the way Dylan did. Whenever I'd had a bad day at work, or another fight with my sister, Derrick always acted like he didn't have time to hear it. His so-called business was much more important to him. He always made me feel like my concerns were so trivial. Not so with Dylan. He had a business of his own, too, but it seemed like he could listen to my problems and my stories for hours. And the most beautiful thing was, he never judged me. There was this unconditional acceptance from him that I barely even got from my own family. Besides, it was nice having someone around to spoil *me* for a change.

In the few months I'd spent with Dylan, he'd learned more

about me than Derrick had in all the years we'd been together. Dylan was so understanding, I couldn't help but want to tell him everything. And because of that, we had no secrets. Well, almost none. I wasn't about to tell him I was sexually attracted to him and that the two of us were just one kiss away from getting in between the sheets.

Every once in a while, I'd think about just forgetting Derrick and admitting my feelings to Dylan. But he kept telling me about this woman named Tonya he was messing with, so I kept myself in check. Of course, I wasn't sure I believed Tonya was more than a figment of his imagination. Sometimes I suspected he was making her up to keep some distance between us. When we were together, he'd hug me a little tighter or stare at me a little longer than he would if everything were truly platonic. Besides, as much time as we spent together, there was no way in the world he could have another woman in his life. She'd have to be stupid. Whatever the case, we were both making an effort to keep things friendly and avoid another night like we had at Joe's. My greatest fear was that we'd end up having some frivolous spur-of-the-moment affair that would ruin our friendship, and I didn't think I could bear that. So with Derrick's release date getting closer and closer, I was torn.

But no matter how much we tried to be just friends, most people who'd seen us together took it for granted that we were an item. To be honest, I didn't discourage it. Other than the fact that we weren't having sex, we might as well be a couple. Even the grocery store clerk got so used to seeing me there with Dylan that she commented one night when I was shopping alone. She told me she hoped we hadn't broken up, 'cause he sure was a nice young man.

Yep, Dylan had that kind of effect on people. Unlike Derrick, everyone seemed to like him, especially Big Momma.

I swear, if she were a few years younger she'd have pushed me to the side and gone after him herself. I couldn't believe the way she acted when I brought him over to her house for Sunday dinner a few weeks ago. The minute we walked in the door, she started acting the fool. I never dreamed she would embarrass me like that.

"Lord have mercy, Jasmine! Who is this *fine* young man?" Big Momma asked the second Dylan and I walked in the door. She looked Dylan over from head to toe and nodded her approval with a wide grin. "Well, Jasmine, aren't you gonna introduce us? I know I taught you better than that."

"Yes, ma'am. Big Momma, this is Dylan Taylor. Dylan, this is my grandmother, Mrs. Washington." I had to keep from rolling my eyes at all the formality. When she met Derrick for the first time, Big Momma had barely allowed herself to make eye contact with him, and she made it clear from the start she was watching his every move. But as much as she hated Derrick was as much as Big Momma seemed to love Dylan, and she didn't even know the guy.

I had no doubt, though, that she'd done as much checking on Dylan's background as she could with all her connections in the community. After Derrick had us all believing he was a lawyer, Big Momma wasn't taking anyone's word on anything. She probably learned Dylan was a legitimate business owner, and that was enough to make him worthy in her eyes. Big Momma's biggest concern was getting me to end things with Derrick. She probably thought Dylan was a pretty good prospect to help her reach that goal. And Dylan, with his polite self, was making Big Momma's eyes light up right about now. He reached out to take her hand in his.

"It's a pleasure to meet you, Mrs. Washington."

"The pleasure's all mine, Dylan. And around here all the young people just call me Big Momma, because we family."

This time I did roll my eyes, but I made sure to turn my head away first. Big Momma never let Derrick call her anything but Mrs. Washington.

"Big Momma, huh? Well Mrs. Washington, that's kinda personal." Dylan let go of her hand. I held my breath, 'cause for a second I thought he might say something insulting, and then Big Momma would have to show her true self. "But if you want me to call you Big Momma, I'd consider it an honor. But you better come over here so I can give you a big kiss like we really are family."

Well, Big Momma looked like she could just about melt. Her face got two shades deeper after Dylan planted a huge, wet kiss right on her lips. I just stood there in shock. I'd never seen my grandmother blush before.

"Lawwwd have mercy! I ain't had a man kiss me like that in thirty years!" Big Momma grabbed her chest, pretending to have a heart attack á la Fred Sanford. She knocked over a few chairs and fell over onto the sofa. Poor Dylan was so confused by her apparent heart attack that he looked as if he were about to bend down to perform CPR. It was a good thing my look stopped him, too, 'cause Big Momma probably would've had a real heart attack if he'd pressed his lips up against hers again. It was one hell of a show, and we'd just barely walked in the door.

The rest of our visit with Big Momma was more of the same love-fest. Big Momma's eyes lit up every time Dylan spoke about himself. I could see her taking mental notes about all his good qualities, and I just knew once she got the chance, she'd be doing her best to sell me on him. So it was no surprise when she woke me at six the next morning tryin' to play matchmaker. I wasn't about to tell her she was preaching to the choir, that I'd been sold on Dylan since that first night at Joe's. I just had too much invested in Derrick to drop him. So I just let her get it off her chest.

"Now, Jasmine, baby, he sure is a good man. Don't you let him get away, you hear? Men like that don't grow on trees."

"Big Momma, I know he's nice. But he's just a friend. You seem to forget I've already got a man."

"Shoot. That boy ain't no good. He ain't nothin' but a drug dealer. A convicted one at that. He ain't brought you nothin' but grief since the day you met. Now, men like Dylan, or your sister's man, Travis? Good men like that don't come around but so often. You'd better jump on Dylan like your sister did Travis. Otherwise you'll end up being a bridesmaid at his wedding tryin' to figure out what the hell happened."

Big Momma kept me on that phone nearly two hours telling me what a fool I'd be to let Dylan go. She couldn't have made it more clear how much she despised Derrick and how much she loved Dylan. It was enough to make my already confused emotions even more jumbled.

"What're you thinking about?" Dylan interrupted my thoughts.

"You and Big Momma," I laughed. "You know y'all getting married one day, don't you?"

"Well," he smiled, "the way things have been going, I guess I could do worse. Only problem is, she probably don't wanna have any more kids."

I reached across the table and touched his hand as I laughed. "You really wanna have kids, don't you?"

"Yeah, I'd love to have a family." He stared at me momentarily before changing the subject. "So, miss, you got any plans for tonight?"

"None that I'm aware of. Why?" I wondered if my face revealed how much I was hoping his next words would be an invitation to spend some more time together. Thankfully, he didn't disappoint me.

"Well, you know my birthday is Saturday, but I'm gonna

be outta town most of the day. So I was wondering if you and your girls would mind celebrating with me and Joe tonight at Joe's club in Petersburg."

"I can't speak for Becky and Sabrina, but I'll be there. So, birthday boy, what do you want for your birthday?" He smiled wickedly, raising both eyebrows as he looked off into the distance. I was about to press him for more details when my cell phone rang. "Damn it, hold that thought." I reached for the phone in my purse.

"Hello," I said sweetly, smiling across the table at Dylan.

"Jazz?" The voice was barely audible.

"Yes, this is Jasmine. Who's this?"

"It's Stephanie."

"What's wrong, Steph? You sound like you been crying. I can barely hear you."

"Jazz, I need your help. It's important." Her voice was sounding more desperate. I was worried. If she was asking for my help, then whatever was going on must've been real important, 'cause we both knew she didn't really like me. Hell, I'd damn near single-handedly saved her engagement to Travis a while back and I was still waiting for a thank-you.

"Okay, Steph. Where you at?"

"Um, I'm at home," she told me between sniffles. "I need your help, Jasmine. Please."

"Don't worry, Steph. I'm gonna help you." I looked at Dylan and apologized with my eyes. He knew I was getting ready to cut short our lunch date. "Where's Travis? Did you call him?"

"No! Oh, my God, no! Don't call him. Please, don't call him," she pleaded. "I just need you, Jazz. I need my sister."

"Alright, Steph. Calm down. I'm on my way, okay?" I hung up my phone and gave Dylan a weak smile. "I'm sorry, I gotta go. Family emergency again."

"Everything all right?" He sounded genuinely concerned.

"I'm not sure," I sighed. "It's my sister. She's in some kind of trouble. She says she needs me."

"Want me to come along?"

"Nah, I better go by myself. You never know what kind of drama Stephanie is involved in." I stood and gathered my things. "But thanks for the offer. I'll call you if there's any problem." I gave him a quick kiss on the cheek, though I can't tell you how much I wanted to kiss his lips. I was going to have to make a decision about us soon. There was only so much a woman could take.

"You be careful, okay?" He squeezed my hand. "I'm only a phone call away if you need me."

"I know." I smiled. "And I appreciate it. I'll see you tonight at the club."

When I arrived at Stephanie's, she was standing at the door waiting for me. Though she looked calm at first, she burst into tears as soon as I asked her what was wrong. Out of instinct, I wrapped my arms around her to comfort her. I couldn't remember the last time we hugged, but she really looked like she needed one. For a good five minutes she cried like a baby in my arms. I told her everything was going to be all right, though I still didn't have a clue what was wrong.

"What is it, Steph?" I finally asked when the flow of tears seemed to slow. "What's the matter?"

"Travis is gonna kill me. He's gonna kill me," she mumbled between sobs.

"What do you mean, he's gonna kill you? Travis loves you, Steph. You know that." I tried to reassure her, but after what I'd witnessed at that motel, I braced myself for the worst possible news.

"I know he loves me. That's why he's gonna kill me." She

pulled herself away from me, and I followed her to the couch. I rubbed her back and waited patiently for her to calm down enough to tell me her story.

"I broke that promise I made to you," she said. "I kept seeing Malek even after you busted us. Now Travis is gonna kill me."

"It figures," I replied, shaking my head.

Things were finally starting to make sense. I had hoped that Stephanie would be smart enough to stay away from Malek. She might be able to fool Travis once, but I knew if she kept it up it would only be a matter of time before he found out. As it turned out, she had a little more time still. "Does Travis know about Malek?"

"He suspects, but he doesn't know for sure."

"Well, that's good." I sighed. "So, then what's the problem? Just stop seeing him. Ain't you got no self-control, Steph? He can't be that damn good."

"Look, Jasmine, I asked you here to help me, not lecture me." She cut her eyes in my direction. Probably regretting that she had called me.

"You're right," I sighed again. "So tell me what's wrong, then." She glanced at me, then looked down in embarrassment.

"I've been having unprotected sex with Malek."

"Oh, shit! Girl, have you lost your mind? Are you crazy? What is wrong with you?" I threw my hands in the air. She deserved a lecture whether she wanted one or not. "Jesus! You're not pregnant by him, are you? Please don't tell me you're pregnant by him."

It took a few seconds, but she finally spoke.

"No. I'm not pregnant. I had my period last week."

"Thank God for small favors. So what's the big deal?" I couldn't imagine what could be worse than another baby with that idiot.

"Malek called me this morning after Travis went to work. We were supposed to hook up for lunch, but he had to go to the doctor instead."

"For what?" I was afraid to ask as I guessed where this conversation was about to go.

"He'd been complaining about a urinary tract infection the last couple o' days."

"And?" I cringed as I waited for her to finish.

"It turns out it wasn't what he thought." She lowered her eyes and whispered, "Malek's got gonorrhea."

"Gonorrhea! Oh my God! Did he give it to you?" Just the sound of it made my skin crawl. I freaked out when I got a yeast infection, and here was my sister telling me about the man she's been freaking and his nasty STD. I couldn't even look at her.

"Jesus, Stephanie! Why didn't you make him wear a condom?"

"I don't know," she answered pitifully, bursting into tears for the umpteenth time. "Jazz, he tried to say I gave it to him."

"Well, did you?" I hated to ask her a question like that, but I had to know. Shit, if she was stupid enough to be messin' with Malek, who knows how low she was capable of going?

"Hell no," she whined like she had a right to be insulted. "I ain't mess with nobody but him and Travis. And I been messin' up with my birth control pills so bad, Travis and I was using condoms until last night."

My hand flew to my mouth and I gasped. It hadn't dawned on me just how serious this could be. It wasn't just nasty, it was probably the end of her relationship with Travis. No wonder Stephanie was so afraid he was gonna kill her. Shit, I'd kill her ass too if she gave me an STD.

"Jasmine?" She spoke quietly. "What am I gonna do? I really fucked up this time, didn't I?"

She sure had, but I didn't have the heart to jump on her case now. There'd be plenty of time for that later. Right now she needed some help, or she really was gonna lose everything.

"Look, we need to get you checked out. Maybe Malek's lying."

"I doubt it. I think he was messing with that nasty-ass LaKeisha Nixon."

"Oh, Lord. Not that nasty heifer? Damn, Steph, you sure can pick 'em."

"I know, I know," she whined. "Now what am I supposed to do?"

"Just grab your things and come with me," I ordered. The first thing we had to do was get to the clinic. After that I didn't have any idea what to do, except maybe to pray.

# 20

# Stephanie

"What the hell's taking them so long?" I was wearing a hole in the waiting room floor, I'd been pacing back and forth for so long. I slumped down into the seat beside my sister, who was being so damn calm I wanted to smack her.

"I don't know, Steph." Jasmine patted my knee. "There's a lot of people in here. You're just gonna have to be patient. It shouldn't be too much longer."

"I don't wanna be patient. I wanna know if that motherfucker burnt me."

"Will you calm down?" Jasmine hissed. "People are staring at us." She gave a weak smile to two women sitting across from us. They'd been all up in our conversation ever since we sat down.

"I don't give a shit who's staring. Everybody in here's got the same damn problem as me, so they need to mind they fuckin' business 'fore I take my frustration out on them." I glared at the women until they turned away.

Yeah, I know I was being a bitch. But we'd been sitting in that damn clinic lobby waiting for my test results for over an hour. And Jasmine had the nerve to tell me to calm down. How the hell did she expect me to do that? She wasn't the one waiting to find out if she had gonorrhea. Just thinking about some microscopic shit crawling in between my legs gave me the heebie-jeebies. How the fuck did I let Malek do this to me? I slumped over and held my head in my hands until I finally heard the nurse call my name.

"See, I told you it wouldn't be long." Jasmine picked up her bag from the seat next to her, stood up, and offered me her hand.

"Yeah, but why the hell's she yelling my name like I won the lottery? I don't want these nosey-ass people to know who I am." It felt like every eye in the place was on me as I walked toward the nurse.

"Please, these people aren't worried about you," Jasmine sighed. "They got their own problems."

"Are you Stephanie Johnson?" The nurse was staring at Jasmine.

"Who, me? No, I'm not Stephanie. She's Stephanie," Jasmine said it loud enough for everyone in the lobby to hear. I wanted to smack her hand out of my face, pointing at me like the nurse couldn't see me standing right next to her ass.

"Oh, I'm sorry." The nurse directed me into an office. "Have a seat in here, Ms. Johnson. The doctor will be with you in a moment."

"Damn. Put me in another room to do some more waiting," I grumbled. Really I was just trying to hide how nervous I was.

The doctor finally came in, shuffling some papers as she sat behind her desk.

"Hi, Ms. Johnson. My name is Dr. Reed. I'm sorry I didn't have a chance to introduce myself when I examined you earlier. But as you can see, it's a little busy around here."

"Look, I don't wanna hear all that shit. I just wanna know if that motherfucker burnt me."

"Stephanie," Jasmine growled in embarrassment, "don't be rude."

"No, it's perfectly all right, Miss. Under the circumstances, I understand her being a little impatient. So why don't we get to the point." The doctor glanced down at a folder in front of her. The sympathetic smile she gave me told me all I needed to know, but it hurt even worse when she said the words. "I'm sorry to have to tell you this, Ms. Johnson, but you've tested positive for gonorrhea."

"Oh, God!" All of a sudden Jasmine wasn't so calm. She covered her face with her hands. The way she was acting, you'd think she was the one with the shit. I sat as still as I could in my chair, trying to hold back tears. The only thing I could think of was how much I regretted sleeping with Travis the night before.

"How do I get rid of it?" I asked in a grim tone.

"I'm going to give you two prescriptions. One is Zithromax for the gonorrhea. It's four pills that you take at once. It's probably going to make you pretty nauseous, but that should subside in about a day." She scribbled on a prescription pad. "The other prescription is to treat chlamydia."

"Chlamydia? I've got that too?" I yelled. "I swear to God I'ma kill Malek."

"Well." The doctor shifted uncomfortably in her chair. "We're not sure about the chlamydia. We don't do the test for it here. We send it out to a lab. What happens in a lot of cases is that chlamydia piggybacks on gonorrhea. The prescription is just precautionary, but better safe than sorry."

"So I don't have to take this one until you get the results?" I stared at the two slips she handed me.

"Well, we suggest you take it right away since we won't have the results back for a few days, and it's better to treat these things quickly. We also suggest that you refrain from any sexual contact for at least ten days."

"You don't have to worry about that. I don't wanna see another dick the rest of my life." I stared at her, dying to get out of there. "Is that it, Dr. Reed?" As if that wasn't enough.

"Yes. The only other thing I need to know is how many sexual partners you have. I know it's a little embarrassing, but it's a health department requirement."

I was about to lie and say one, but Jasmine cleared her throat to get my attention. Out of the corner of my eye I saw her fold her arms across her chest, daring me to lie.

"Two." I lowered my eyes.

"Have they been notified? Because if you'd like, we can notify them for you. Sometimes it's easier that way."

"No, I'll take care of it," I mumbled, not looking forward at all to the prospect of telling Travis that he had VD.

"Okay, Ms. Johnson." The doctor stood. "Good luck."

"Thanks, Dr. Reed." I glanced at the picture of Travis on my key chain. "I'm gonna need it. Let's go, Jasmine. I wanna get to the pharmacy and take these pills as quickly as possible."

Jasmine pulled into my driveway, then turned to me with an ominous look. We'd just made a quick stop at the pharmacy to fill my prescription. I was about to go in the house and wait for Travis when she asked the most obvious question.

"You all right, Steph?"

"What d'you think, Jasmine?" I snapped. "I gotta go in that house, fix dinner for Travis, then wait till he gets home with the kids so I can tell him I gave him gonorrhea. So you tell me. Do you think I'm all right?" Tears were welling up in my eyes as I waited for her reply.

"No, I guess you're not." She took my hand and smiled weakly. "If you'd like, I'll go in and wait with you. Travis might not act so crazy if I'm here when you tell him."

"Nah, it's not gonna make any difference." I shook my head. "You go on home. Besides, I made this mess by myself, so I gotta clean it up by myself. I just hope I can think of a way to do that before Travis gets home."

"Don't play games with this, Stephanie," she advised. "Tell him the truth. Lying is just gonna make it worse." She grabbed my hand as I moved to step out of the car. "I love you, little sister. I'm here if you need me."

"You know what, Jasmine?" I smiled at my sister with newfound respect. "I'm really starting to believe that. But why? I've been a bitch to you all my life."

"Yeah, but you're also my sister. Except for Momma and Derrick, you're all I got."

"I hope you feel that way after I tell Travis about this gonorrhea. 'Cause I might be knocking on your door to sleep on your couch."

"I don't think it's gonna come down to that." Jasmine tried to sound upbeat. "But if it does, you're always welcome."

"You're serious, aren't you?" This newfound sisterhood was hard to believe, although it was touching me. Me and Jasmine had never been close, but it was great to have someone to lean on, especially now that I'd made such a mess of my life.

"Yeah, I am serious," Jasmine said.

I leaned over and kissed my sister's cheek.

"Thanks, Jazz, for everything. I don't think I coulda made it through this without you." I stepped out of the car but stuck my head back in when a thought came to me. "Listen. I'm not sure if I'll still be gettin' married after all this, but if I do, I'd like you to be my maid of honor. I was gonna ask LaShawn, but with everything that's happened, I want it to be you." I smiled at my sister. "Think you can handle the job?"

"You damn right. I'll be the best maid of honor a sister could ever have. I'ma throw you a shower you'll never forget," she promised.

"Good." I felt good until I remembered the CVS package I was holding. "Lemme go inside and take this medicine. "

"I love you, Stephanie."

"I love you, too, Jasmine." I closed the car door and walked toward the house, dreading the rest of my evening.

Today had probably been the worst day of my life. I had made a big mistake messin' around with Malek, and now I was payin' for my mistakes big-time. And I knew things would only get worse once I told Travis the truth. But as bad as things were, I was glad. I'd made a new friend today. I just couldn't believe it was my sister.

# 21

# Jasmine

I walked into the house and collapsed on my couch. I was so tired, I felt like I was gonna pass out right then and there. Becky, Sabrina, and I had gone down to Petersburg to celebrate Dylan's birthday, and I don't think I've *ever* had that much fun celebrating a birthday, including my own. Unfortunately, I was paying for it now. By the time we left the club and had breakfast at the Waffle House, it was almost seven o'clock in the morning. I didn't get home until seven-thirty, which left me barely enough time to take a shower and drag my ass to work. I should've called in sick like Becky and Sabrina, 'cause I can't remember the last time I'd been this damn tired.

I felt like I was glued to my couch. Thankfully, Dylan was going outta town for the weekend. Usually, on Friday night we would go out to dinner and see a movie. Just the thought of getting up made me wanna cry. Of course, whoever started banging on my door didn't care how damn tired I was. I tried to ignore it, but the knocking just got louder and louder.

"Who is it?" I finally whined from the couch.

"It's me!" Sabrina let herself in, looking spry and energetic. I wanted to slap her. She probably slept all day.

"Damn, girl. Think you coulda waited for me to say 'come in' or something? I coulda been in here getting my groove on." She didn't have to know I didn't have the strength to undo a zipper right about now.

"Gettin' your groove on with who, yourself?" Sabrina shoved my feet aside and sat next to me.

"Very funny, Sabrina. I coulda had a man in here," I protested.

"Please, Jasmine. I already know Dylan went outta town."

"Why you always gotta bring up Dylan?" I tried to sound offended as I hid the grin on my face. "Like he's my man or somethin'."

"He is," Sabrina said matter-of-factly as she lit a cigarette. "You know you luuuuuuuuv him."

"Girl, please. He is just a friend. I got a man, remember?" I waved my hand, hoping to put an end to the conversation.

"How could I forget," she mocked. "The almighty Derrick." She exhaled her smoke. "So you don't want Dylan, huh?"

"I told you. We're just friends."

"You didn't answer my question, Jasmine." Sabrina rolled her eyes. "And you sure wasn't acting like you were just friends last night at the club. I was about to go upstairs and see about getting y'all a room."

"Sabrina, you need to stop. We were just dancin', that's all," I insisted.

"Just dancin'! Girl, you were all over that man. You two looked like Siamese twins joined at the hip. Y'all didn't even separate on the fast songs."

I blushed. She was right. We were dancing kinda close.

"Joe said you was shaking your ass so much you mighta been havin' an orgasm," Sabrina laughed.

"Oh, please. Joe needs to mind his business." I turned my head, hoping she wouldn't see my embarrassment. I wasn't that lucky.

"Oh, my God! He did it, didn't he?" Sabrina shouted,

eyes wide with a grin from ear to ear. "He made you come on the dance floor, didn't he?"

"No, he didn't."

"Yes, he did." Sabrina wasn't giving up that easy.

"No, he didn't. But . . ." I knew she wouldn't let up until I confessed. "But there was a couple o' times there that I came damn close to an orgasm. I had to stop myself."

"You call a man who can do that to you 'just a friend'?"

"Mmm-hmm." I nodded. I know it sounded ridiculous, and Sabrina definitely felt the same.

"Girl, you crazy." Sabrina took a long drag of her cigarette. "So tell me again why you don't want him."

"It's not that I don't want him. Believe me, I lose sleep at night thinking about that man."

"Then what is it? It's obvious he likes you, too. And don't tell me you don't wanna cheat on Derrick, 'cause girl, whether you like it or not, you crossed that line a long time ago." Her words were true, and my conscience ached from the guilt I'd been struggling with ever since I met Dylan. Sabrina was not the one to worry about feeling bad or staying faithful.

"You might as well just go for it. Find out if he's the one for you, before Derrick gets out," was her advice. "Hell, as fine as Dylan is, you might fuck around and learn something new."

The phone rang and I groaned. My body was sore from all the dancing, but I stretched to reach the phone. Even though it hurt to move, I was thankful for a break from Sabrina's interrogation. I didn't really mind her questions so much. Hell, that was the way me and my girls got down. I'd done the same thing to her and Becky many a night. What was bothering me was that she was right. My feelings for Dylan *had* crossed the line a long time ago, and everyone could see it. I wasn't fooling anyone but myself.

"Hello?"

*"This is the AT&T operator with a collect call from Derrick. Will you accept?"*

I thought about hanging up the phone. This was just what I didn't need right now. I was tired, frustrated, and, thanks to Sabrina, heavy with Dylan on my mind. The last thing I needed was to talk to Derrick.

*"Miss, will you accept the call?"*

"Yes, operator. I'll accept."

"Hey, baby, guess what?" Derrick didn't waste any time with formalities. He sounded too excited for even a hello.

"What?" I stifled a yawn.

"I'm coming home on Sunday."

"That's not funny, Derrick."

"I'm not joking. They're releasing me early." I found that hard to believe.

"But you got two months to go." This news was so sudden. Maybe I was just overtired, but he wasn't making much sense.

"Not anymore." I could hear him smiling through the phone. "They said something about the prison being overcrowded. They need the beds. Everyone who's on parole had their release date moved up two months," he explained, his voice like a child on Christmas morning. "Baby, I'm coming home!"

"Oh, my God. You're serious, aren't you?" I wanted to be happy for him. For us. And before I had met Dylan, I would've been. This would have been the happiest day of my life. But now I had to watch my tone so I didn't sound too disappointed. Or at least confused. I didn't know whether to be happy or sad. I was still trying to figure out my feelings for Dylan, and I damn sure thought I was gonna have more than two days to do it. Life just wasn't fair.

"Yeah, I'm serious, baby." Derrick got quiet for a second. "God, I can't believe I'm going home!"

"Neither can I," I replied, not nearly as overjoyed as he was. "Neither can I."

I talked to Derrick for about twenty more minutes. He'd done most of the talking, and thankfully, I don't think he noticed how quiet I was. I just listened. My mind was too preoccupied. I was nervous about how his release would affect my relationship with Dylan. Derrick would never stand for it if he knew Dylan and I were friends. That much I was sure about. He was too jealous for that. Problem is, I don't think I could stand not being able to talk to Dylan.

"Did I hear you right? Derrick's coming home early?" Sabrina was staring at me as I hung up the phone.

"Sunday," I mumbled. "He's coming home Sunday. I've gotta pick him up at nine o'clock."

"Damn. What are you gonna do about Dylan?" She waited for a reply, which, of course, I couldn't give. I had some serious choices to make all of a sudden, but I had some serious thinking to do first.

"To be honest, Jasmine," Sabrina offered her opinion, "I think Dylan's the one for you. I just wish you could see how you two look when you're together."

I laughed, "That's exactly what Big Momma said."

"Well, you know what they say. Old people are wise people when it comes to the ways of love." She patted my leg, then stood to leave. "Ultimately, you gotta do what's best for you. 'Cause whatever decision you make, you're the one who's gotta live with it. You can't have both of them."

"I know. I just wish I knew what I was gonna do. I love them both."

"Well, then, girlfriend, you got a problem."

* * *

I fell asleep on the couch right after Becky left, but I wasn't asleep more than an hour before I heard a knock on the door. I was still totally exhausted, so I damn sure wasn't in the mood for company. I figured it was Sabrina, back with relationship advice for me, so I just ignored it. But unfortunately, the knocking didn't stop and Sabrina didn't let herself in again, so I finally got off the couch and went to the door.

"Who?" I shouted.

"Wendy." I looked through the peephole, and there was Derrick's ex, standing at my door with her son. She must've heard through the grapevine that Derrick was coming home, 'cause this was the first time she ever showed up at my door. And if she knew what was good for her, it would be her last.

"What do you want, Wendy?" I opened the door with a clenched fist. Last time I ran into her was at the prison when I ripped half that cheap-ass weave outta her head.

"Derrick said that if I ever needed anything I should come by here." She shoved a small knapsack in my arms. "Well, I need a baby-sitter."

"So, what's that got to do with me?" I stared at the knapsack.

"Look, I gotta catch the bus up to Roanoke to bring Derrick a package. My mother's drunk and I can't find Derrick's mother anywhere. You're the only one I know who'd be home on a Friday night. So you're my baby-sitter."

"I am, huh? Well, contrary to popular belief, I do have a life. So you're gonna have to find another baby-sitter." I tried to hand her the knapsack but she refused to take it.

"I ain't bringing my son up to no prison while I'm carrying five ounces of weed. So either you're gonna watch Tyler or you're gonna explain to Derrick why he didn't get his shit." She folded her arms and waited for my answer.

That damn woman was so low. Talking about that shit right in front of her son. And the kid just stood there with a blank look on his face. I guess he was used to hearing that shit out of his mother's mouth. I almost felt bad for him. But that didn't mean I wanted to take him in. I wasn't doing Wendy no favors like that.

"Why does he need that stuff? He's getting out in a few days."

"I don't know. Maybe he wants to make one last score before he gets out. From what I hear, they're making *stupid* money up there. . . ." She stopped herself abruptly as if she had said too much already. "But that's none o' my business. I do what I'm told. Something you better learn to do if you plan on being with Derrick."

I rolled my eyes at her. That bitch had some nerve, trying to tell me how to keep *my* man.

"You gonna watch Tyler or what, 'cause I ain't got time to be teachin' 'How to Be a Drug Dealer's Girlfriend 101.' " Wendy placed her hand on her hip and smirked.

I was about to tell her to kiss my ass and give her a little more of what she got at the prison. But her son was standing there looking up at the two of us like he was waiting for all hell to break loose. At least one of us could act like an adult in front of him. Besides, with Derrick coming home in a few days, it wasn't worth the aggravation. Once he was out, he wouldn't need her to make deliveries. Then he could put Wendy in her proper place. She was getting entirely too comfortable making demands. Anyway, Tyler wasn't such a bad kid. I should get to know him a little since he'd probably be spending a lot of time here with Derrick soon.

"Come on, Tyler." I motioned for him to come in, but he didn't move.

"Go 'head, baby. Go with Auntie Jasmine. Mommy will see you at Grandma's tomorrow." Wendy bent down and kissed her son, nudging him into the apartment.

"He ain't had nothin' to eat, so make sure you feed him. And don't let him drink too much or he'll pee in the bed."

"When you coming to get him?"

"You can drop him off at Derrick's mother's in the morning. She should be home by then." Wendy didn't give me time to refuse. She waved good-bye to her son and headed for a waiting cab.

"Well, Tyler," I sighed, "I guess it's you and me. What do you want to eat?"

"McDonald's."

Well, you ain't getting no McDonald's, so you can forget that. How 'bout some peanut butter and jelly?"

"I hate peanut butter and jelly." He sounded angry. I can't say I blame him, with a mother like that.

"Okay," I sighed. "What about pizza. Do you like pizza?"

His eyes lit up. "Yeah, I like pizza. And can I have some Kool-Aid?"

"Yeah, I think I've got some Kool-Aid." I walked to the kitchen and he followed me. Thank God Dylan had brought an extra frozen pizza on one of our video nights. It wasn't like I had kids over here all the time, so my kitchen definitely wasn't stocked with kid-friendly food.

While Tyler was eating, I made a bed for him on the sofa in front of the TV. I was still exhausted and in need of some serious sleep. I figured that if I put on the Cartoon Network he'd watch TV until he fell asleep. I smoothed the blanket over the sofa and went back in the kitchen. He'd eaten half the pizza and drunk an eight-ounce glass of Kool-Aid.

"Wow, you really were hungry, weren't you? You want some more pizza?"

"No, but I want some more Kool-Aid." He pushed his glass toward me and I poured him some more. He gulped it down.

"Okay, time for bed." We both got up and walked to the living room.

"Auntie Jasmine, you're not really my auntie, are you?" he asked.

"No, but sometimes you call family friends 'uncle' and 'aunt' out of respect. You know what I mean?"

"Yeah, I guess. But what if you don't respect them?"

"Then I guess you don't call them aunt or uncle."

"Well, I'm not calling you auntie, then."

I raised my eyebrows. "Excuse me? Why not?"

" 'Cause I don't like you."

"You don't like me? Why don't you like me?" I was trying to be patient, but this kid was getting on my last nerve.

" 'Cause you're a conniving bitch. And if it wasn't for you, my daddy wouldn't be in jail."

"What did you just call me?" I had my fists clenched. I was trying to restrain myself from slapping the shit out of that little boy. "Where did you hear words like that?" Like I didn't already know the answer.

"My mommy," he said proudly. "She told my Auntie Joyce that if my daddy had stayed with her instead of running off with you, he'd never have gone to jail."

"That's not true, you know. Your daddy left your mother way before I ever met him. And I'm—"

He cut me off with a scream. "No, he didn't! He didn't leave my mommy! You made him leave. My mommy wouldn't lie."

"Yeah, she woul—" I had to stop myself in midsentence. I hated that bitch, but I refused to disrespect her in front of her son. "You know what, Tyler? I think it's time for bed." I think he was glad to drop the subject, 'cause he calmed down and climbed under the covers right away. That poor kid was full of so much anger thanks to his mother.

"Jasmine!" he shouted as I walked away.

"Yes, Tyler." I turned to the sofa.

"I hate you."

"I can see that, Tyler. I can see that." I hoped his little outburst made him feel better, 'cause I sure felt like shit now. I wished Derrick was there to see this. Maybe he would appreciate just how much I did for his ass.

I left Tyler in the living room and went up to my room. I was still exhausted, but it took me a while to fall asleep. My mind was on Tyler and what he had said. He really did hate me, and I could understand why. Wendy had been corrupting him since the day she found out about Derrick and me. The thing that bothered me the most was that now that Derrick was coming home, I was afraid Tyler's attitude would affect my relationship with Derrick somehow. I fell asleep worrying about it.

"Auntie Jasmine?" Tyler woke me up as he stood in my bedroom doorway and called my name.

"What, Tyler? What is it?" I sat up.

"I'm scared. I wanna sleep with you. My mommy always lets me sleep with her when I'm scared."

This kid was really working my last nerve. An hour ago he was telling me how much he hated me. Now he was back to calling me "Auntie" and asking to sleep in my bed. I was tempted to send his ass back to the couch, but then I realized I wasn't being fair. It wasn't Tyler's fault that his mother was such a bitch. If he had a better mother, he wouldn't be such an angry little kid. I pulled back the cover and told him to come on. He climbed in bed without another word and was snoring within minutes. He looked so peaceful, and I was relieved. I was happy that I had decided to give the kid a break. Happy, at least, until I woke up in a puddle later that night.

"Tyler, wake up! Did you pee in my bed?" I turned on the light and looked down at him. His eyes were twitching like he was struggling to keep them closed. This kid was definitely awake, but he had the nerve to be pretending to snore. "Tyler!" I shook him.

He rubbed his eyes like a damn actor. "What's the matter, Auntie Jasmine?"

"You peed in my bed, that's what's the matter." I pulled back my satin sheets to expose the huge wet spot that covered my mattress. From the way he was smiling, I think the kid had actually done it on purpose. I was speechless. At first I wanted to wring his little neck as I sent him into the bathroom to get cleaned up. But as I stripped the sheets off the bed, I started thinking. That's when I realized Tyler's little stunt had just put me one step closer to making the most important decision of my life.

# 22

# Stephanie

Two days after my visit to the clinic, I was in the kitchen doing the breakfast dishes when Travis walked in holding his stomach. He should've left for work over an hour ago, but he hadn't been feeling well since he woke up. Every time I turned around, he was either in my face whining like a child or in the bathroom moaning and groaning on the toilet. I'll tell you. When it comes to being sick, that man is just one big baby.

"Hon, I don't know what type of virus you had last night, but whatever it is, I got that shit now." He was hunched over the kitchen counter. "I feel like someone opened up a can of whup-ass and made me drink it. My stomach is *killing* me."

"I know," I told him sympathetically. "That's how I felt last night. Did you try to use the bathroom? That made me feel better."

"Girl," Travis said, frowning, "I just spent the last half hour on the toilet. That ain't no help."

He grabbed his stomach and grimaced. I actually did feel sorry for him. He really did look sick, with his face all flushed, sweat dripping from his brow.

"Oh, my poor baby," I soothed him. "Why don't you go upstairs so I can take care of you? I'll call over to the base and tell them you're not coming in." I walked over and rubbed his back, hoping he'd refuse my offer. I still wasn't feeling too well myself. I'd taken that medication the doctor had prescribed for my little problem yesterday. I felt better than I had last night, but my stomach was still queasy.

"Shit, I wish I could, but I got a meeting with Captain Jenkins this morning and you know how he is." Travis sounded so unhappy. "I'm just gonna have to pick up some Pepto-Bismol on the way over to the base and pray." He kissed my forehead as he headed out the door.

I felt so bad watching him walk down the driveway, clutching his stomach. Oh, I was sure he'd be fine by the time he came home from work this afternoon, but I still hated that it was my fault he was feeling that way. Luckily, the phone rang before my guilt could get the best of me. Only problem was, the caller ID showed Jasmine's number, and I knew she was calling just to make sure I *did* feel guilty.

"Steph, you okay? Can you talk? Is Travis there?" she whispered.

"Yeah, I can talk. He just went to work."

"So what did he say? Is everything all right? Are y'all staying together?" Jasmine sounded sincere, but I knew she was just calling to be nosy. I was starting to like my sister, but she just asked too many damn questions.

"Yeah, everything's fine."

"Thank God." She sighed, "What did he say when you told him?"

"Told him what?" I really didn't wanna get into this. I know I had felt all sisterly with her the other day, but now I was not in the mood. My stomach was starting to do flips, and if she started in on me it would only make me feel worse. She had been so insistent that I tell Travis the truth. I didn't feel like hearing her mouth when I told her I'd made other arrangements to solve my problem.

"Stop playing, Steph. You know what I mean. Did you tell Travis about the gonorrhea?"

Might as well just tell her. Maybe if I put enough attitude into it, she wouldn't bother trying to tell me how wrong I was.

"Hell, no! I ain't tellin' him shit. Are you crazy? I ain't ruining my relationship. I'm about to get married."

"What do you mean? You gotta tell him, Steph! That man needs to know so he can go to the doctor and get checked out," Jasmine scolded. "Didn't we agree about this the other day?"

"He don't need to know," I insisted. "I've got everything under control."

"Girl, have you lost your mind? You can't let that man walk around with gonorrhea. You know that's not right." She waited and I waited, both of us silent. I was hoping she'd get mad enough and hang up the phone, but she kept right on lecturing. "Besides, sooner or later he's gonna find out about this. Men have symptoms, Stephanie. And when he gets them, that's gonna be your ass." I hoped she was getting some pleasure from her little speech, 'cause she was buggin' the hell out of me. In a matter of days my relationship with my sister had gone right back to square one. I did not have time for her tryin' to be my momma.

"Look, don't you worry about my man, okay? I told you I've got everything under control. Travis ain't gonna have no symptoms, and he ain't gonna find out about me giving him gonorrhea. That is, unless you tell him."

She raised her voice. "You know I'm not gonna tell him."

"Well, then I guess everything's all right, isn't it?" There was a hesitation before Jasmine answered.

"What are you up to, Stephanie?" Her voice was full of suspicion.

"Nothin'. What makes you think I'm up to something?" It was time to shut up. She might be a pain in the ass, but Jasmine was far from stupid, and I did not need her all up in this business. The fewer people who knew my plan, the better.

"I know you, Stephanie. I know you like a book. Now, stop playin' games and tell me what you're up to. 'Cause we both know you're up to something."

"Trust me, Jasmine. You do not wanna know."

"You're probably right, but tell me anyway," she sighed impatiently.

"Okay, but I swear you better not tell anyone about this. And that includes Becky and that Dylan guy you been hangin' out with lately. What's up with y'all, anyway? You break up with Derrick, or what?"

"Don't try to change the subject. And I'm not gonna tell no one," she insisted.

"You better not." I took a deep breath and began my story. "After you dropped me off the other day, I got to thinkin' about what you said about Travis and me. Believe it or not, Jasmine, I really do love that man."

"You've sure got a funny way of showin' it when you keep messin' with Malek," she interjected.

"Yeah, well everyone makes mistakes. Even you." I was about to get in her shit about bringing Dylan to Big Momma's house every Sunday, but she jumped in before I could continue.

"Let's get something straight. This is not about me, so don't even go there. Now tell me what you're up to," she demanded. Like I didn't know how anxious she was to keep the spotlight off her own shit right now.

"Well, after you left I went inside and took my medicine," I started innocently. "Then I started to fix dinner. I figured I'd make his favorite lasagna. I was hoping to put him in a good mood before the bad news."

"And?"

"When he got home, I got nervous and decided to wait

until morning to tell him. I don't think I slept a wink. I musta tossed and turned all night. I finally got up and sat in the living room until the sun came up. I was feeling so sorry for myself, Jasmine, I was a nervous wreck. I just knew Travis was gonna leave me if I told him I'd given him VD. So I decided to take my chances with not telling him."

"Stephanie! I can't believe you!"

"Will you calm down and let me finish?" She shut up and I continued. "I knew I couldn't let him walk around with gonorrhea. I also knew I didn't have much time before his symptoms started showing up."

"That's right," she nagged. I ignored her and continued.

"So I knew I had to come up with a plan to get me outta this mess. And believe me, it wasn't easy. I must have racked my brain half the day trying to come up with the perfect plan. Thank God I finally did."

"You did?" Jasmine's voice perked up. "What kinda plan?"

"Yep, I sure did. I got in my car and drove back to the clinic to see that doctor. I had to wait over an hour, but when I finally saw her I told the doctor that in my frustration I somehow lost my prescription and needed another one. Would you believe she didn't even hesitate to write me a new one?"

"Okay, so now you've got some more medicine. Who's that for, Travis?"

"Yep."

Jasmine laughed. "You know, Stephanie, you are one slick bitch, you know that? I would've never thought about doing some sneaky shit like this."

"That's cause you're not me."

"Okay, miss slick-ass, how'd you get him to take it? Was he 'sleep?"

"Now, that's where I really got slick." I grinned as I told her. I was pretty damn proud of my plan. "Remember that old medicine grinder Big Momma used to grind up Granddaddy's medicine?"

"Yeah, poor old Granddaddy couldn't even swallow his pills toward the end. Big Momma had to grind them up to powder and put them in his food. . . . Oh, shit!" Jasmine was silent as she put the pieces together.

"Stephanie Johnson!" she finally gasped. "You spiked Travis's food with that medicine, didn't you?" She sounded like she was gonna have a heart attack.

"I did what I had to do to save my family, that's what I did," I answered calmly. "You would've done the same thing if you were in my place. If you had thought of it. Wouldn't you?"

"I guess." Jasmine answered. "I just think it's kinda devious."

"Not devious, Jasmine. Desperate. I was desperate. And desperate times call for desperate measures."

"But—"

I stopped her. I was in no mood for another lecture. "Look, I think the baby's awake. I'll talk to you later."

"Okay, but call me back."

I said good-bye, relieved to get off that phone even though I was sure this conversation wasn't over. Jasmine had a tendency to talk about shit from the past, and this was some shit she wasn't gonna let die so easy.

# 23

# Dylan

Even though it was almost midnight when I got home, the first thing I did when I got in the house was pick up the phone to call Jasmine. I'd just returned from a two-day business trip to Atlanta, and the entire time I was there I couldn't get my mind off her. She was everything I'd ever wanted in a woman: smart, funny, loyal, educated, and of course, beautiful. Basically, she was a hell of a lot of fun to be with, and I was falling for her more and more every day. It was getting to the point that I couldn't hold back my feelings much longer.

Only problem was, I was scared I would get hurt if I revealed my true feelings to her. The last thing I wanted to do was have my heart broken again. It still hadn't healed from my breakup with Monica. But no matter how nervous I was emotionally, I couldn't wait to talk to Jasmine. I dialed her number.

*"Hi, this is Jasmine. I'm not home right now, but if you leave your name, number, and a brief message, I'll get back to you as soon as possible."*

And just what did she mean by "as soon as possible"? I'd been leaving messages for her all day on both her home and cell phone, and she hadn't returned one of my calls. I was trying not to take it personally, but it was bothering me that she was probably up in Roanoke at that jail, visiting Derrick. She always went up to see him on Saturdays. Now it was way past visiting hours, so I would've expected a call back.

With my luck, she'd probably decided to spend the night up there so she could go see him on Sunday, too. She'd done that a few weeks ago when Derrick laid some BS guilt trip on her about her not spending enough time with him. Shit, if he'd really wanted to spend time with her, he wouldn't have got caught selling drugs in the first place. It was his own damn fault he was in jail, not hers. If she was my woman, she wouldn't have to worry about me doing anything stupid that might separate us.

"But she's not my woman," I thought out loud. "And it's not my place to be jealous." Not yet, anyway.

*Beeeeep!*

"Hey, Jazz, this is Dylan. I just got back in town and I wanted to see if we were still on for church tomorrow. I'm gonna be up pretty late tonight, so don't hesitate to call. Talk to you later. Peace."

I was pretty disappointed when I hung up the phone. I'd really wanted to talk to her, even if it was only for a few minutes. These last few days away from her, I had just felt a little less complete. She was really becoming a part of my world, and I liked it that way.

I picked up my bags and headed upstairs. Despite the message I left on Jasmine's machine, I was tired as hell and in need of some serious sleep. The six-hour drive from Atlanta had worn me out. The only thing that was going to stop me from getting a good eight hours' worth of rest was if Jasmine called back. And it looked like the chances of that were about as good as my chances of hitting the lottery.

Well, when I walked in my bedroom, I decided I *should* run down to the store and play Lotto, 'cause I was either the luckiest man in the world, or dreaming. I turned on the light to behold the most beautiful sight. Jasmine was there! Lying in my bed with a smile a mile wide.

"Hey, handsome, was the traffic bad? I was expecting you hours ago," she purred.

I never answered her question. Once I got past the shock of the fantasy right before my eyes, I asked a question of my own.

"Jasmine, what're you doin' here?"

She yawned and stretched her arms as she sat up. The covers slipped lower to reveal an incredibly sexy negligee. There was no way she was here for a chat with her buddy. That was quite evident by the thong she was wearing.

"Take a guess," she laughed. "What do you think I'm doing here?"

I didn't answer. She shook her head and grinned.

"It's your birthday, isn't it? I'm here to give you your birthday present." She smiled wickedly, crawling catlike across the bed toward me. When she reached the edge, she wrapped her arms around my neck and kissed me like I'd never been kissed before. It was even better than I'd imagined our first real kiss would be. Sure, we'd kissed before at Joe's, but this was different. This was no heat-of-the-moment kinda stuff that could happen between virtual strangers after a night at the clubs. This was a kiss that told me I was special to her. Our friendship had grown into something beautiful, and Jasmine's kiss told me she felt it, too.

I placed my hands around her hips and pulled her as close to me as humanly possible. I'd been waiting for this day for over two months. I wanted to savor every second.

"Happy birthday," she whispered seductively, her breath warm against my neck.

"Thanks," I murmured between kisses, "but can I ask you a question?"

"Sure." She nibbled on my ear.

"Not that I want you to"—a few more kisses—"leave or anything . . ." She gave me a long, passionate kiss before I finished. "But how'd you get in here?"

"I used the key under your flowerpot." Jasmine was kissing her way down my neck as she spoke. "Smartest thing you ever did was tell me where you hide your key."

"Mmm, I'm starting to believe you." I rolled my neck so that she could kiss the other side. She was making my nature rise. "So what brought all this on, anyway?" I knew why I wanted to be with Jasmine, but I wanted to hear her reasons for wanting to be with me. I hadn't expected this. I figured I'd be the one to seduce her, not vice versa. I had to know what she was thinking.

"Well, I did a lot of soul-searching while you were out of town, and I realized that I don't wanna lose you, Dylan. I just had to stop fighting what my heart had been telling me all along."

"And what's that?"

"That I want you, Dylan. And that I want to be with you." She stopped kissing me and lifted her head so that we were eye to eye. "I have wanted you since the first night we were together."

I stared at her, processing everything she'd just said. This seemed like such a quick change from the woman who could only talk about her love for her man in jail.

"What about Derrick?"

"What about him?" She took my arm from around her waist and placed a condom in my hand. "I'm not gonna lie. I still love Derrick. But I love you even more, and you're the one I wanna be with."

"I'm the one you wanna be with, or I'm the one who's available? Would you feel this way if Derrick wasn't locked up?" I had to ask.

She looked me straight in the eye and answered, "Look, we can discuss this all you want later. Right now, you're gonna have to trust me when I tell you that this has nothing to do with Derrick. Even if he wasn't behind bars, you would still be the man I want to be with. That's why I'm here." She kissed me again and gestured toward the condom I was holding. "Now, are you gonna use that thing, or what?"

"You're serious, aren't you?" I still couldn't believe this was happening.

She nodded, and it finally sunk in. Everything I'd been hoping for was coming to fruition. I wanted to pinch myself to make sure it wasn't all a dream.

"Hey, you. What does a girl have to do to get a kiss around here?"

Jasmine snapped me out of my fog with her question. She gave me a beautiful smile, and I responded with a long, passionate kiss. I felt like I just couldn't get close enough. I'd been waiting for this moment for so long, and it was even more powerful than I'd imagined. I didn't ever want to let this girl go.

She pulled me onto the bed. We rolled around that bed kissing and feeling on each other for the better part of half an hour, and I enjoyed every last sensation like it was my first time. My hands roamed up and down her satin nightgown, and every touch made me want her more and more. Finally, I just couldn't take it anymore. I had to have her.

I slipped the strap of her nightgown over her shoulder, exposing the most perfect breasts I've ever seen. I kissed my way down until my lips could caress her nipple. I sucked gently and she moaned with pleasure, but to my surprise she grabbed my head and pulled me away.

"Stop."

She didn't have to tell me twice. My hands went to my side right away. We'd gone down this road once before, that first night at Joe's. I was not about to go there again. I cared for Jasmine, but the last time this happened, she tried to accuse me of rape, so I wasn't taking any chances.

"Look, Jasmine, maybe this wasn't such a good idea. I mean, maybe we're better off as friends." I tried to get out from under her, but she placed her finger over my lips.

"Please, don't get up. I didn't mean it that way. You're just moving a little too fast. I kinda had the night planned out. Just let me do things my way. I promise you won't be disappointed."

"Are you sure about this?" I was still a little hesitant after her Dr. Jekyll and Mrs. Hyde act. One minute she's with the program, the next she's not; then all of a sudden she's with the program again.

"I swear, Dylan. I've never been so sure about anything in my life. Just bear with me and everything is gonna be fine." She crawled off the bed and walked to my night table. She gave me a nervous smile and picked up a box of matches to light some candles. I guess we were both feeling a little strange now that this was finally happening. I know I was nervous like it was my first time.

"Turn the radio on," she whispered as she turned out the light.

I did as I was told and watched her sway to the smooth rhythm of Usher's "U Remind Me." I don't think I've ever seen a more erotic sight than Jasmine dancing in that candlelight. Ever since that night at Joe's, I knew she had a nice body. But the way things went down, our clothes never fully came off. So I didn't know just how nice it really was till then. She did a slow, seductive striptease that had my heart racing and my brow sweating. When she finished, she was wearing nothing but a thong, and I was rock-hard.

"Come 'ere," she called. "I wanna show you something."

I stood up. She reached for my collar and started unbuttoning my shirt. When the last button was undone, her fingers went to my belt buckle. My pants fell to the floor. I closed my eyes and let out a soft moan when her fingers reached into my boxers and wrapped around my manhood.

"Lay down, Dylan," she whispered, still holding onto the elastic of my boxers. I gladly did as I was told. She removed my boxers and my socks, and I was completely naked, ready for whatever she had to give me. Jasmine crawled on top of me and rubbed her hands over my chest as she placed long, slow kisses around my face. The kisses went lower and lower until she had covered every inch of my torso and found her final destination.

"My, my, my. Aren't you a big one?" She smiled. Of course, I was beaming with pride. If there's one thing we men like to hear, it's a compliment about the size of our dicks.

Jasmine wasn't just down there to compliment me, either. She had other things in mind. Very pleasurable things. And without giving it a second thought, she swallowed half my manhood. I moaned my appreciation. That shit felt so good. It had been a long, long time since someone had done this for me, and I'd forgotten just how good it could be. During the six years we'd been together, Monica wouldn't even discuss the subject. She always complained that it was nasty and unsanitary. Although she never seemed to have a problem when it came to me doing her. She was just selfish that way.

"Oh, God. Oh, God. Ohhh, my God." I was gasping for air as I held onto the sheets with all my might. I was making a conscious effort not to grab hold of Jasmine's head, because someone told me once that women hate that. That was easier said than done. My natural instincts were telling me to hold her head and make sure she didn't stop.

"Damn, baby, if you're trying to get me open you're doing a damn good job. You really got skills."

I think my words must've invigorated her, because she started to work even harder. If she kept it up, it wasn't gonna be long before I erupted. At least until I heard the doorbell and lost my concentration. I tried my best to ignore it, but whoever it was kept on ringing.

"Hold on a second, Jazz." I lifted her head.

"What's the matter? Was I doing something wrong? Don't you like it?" She sounded disappointed.

"Oh, no, baby, I liked it. Shit, I loved it." I told her with excitement.

"Then, why'd you stop me?" She looked confused. "Sounded like you were enjoying it."

"I was. Trust me. The only reason I stopped you is 'cause someone's at the front door. Didn't you hear the bell?"

"The doorbell? You stopped me from going down on you because you heard the doorbell ring?" Now she was definitely insulted. "Just pay attention to what I'm doing. They'll go away."

She lowered her head to finish what she'd started and I lay back to enjoy it. She was right. Whoever was at the door would go away. All I had to do was concentrate on her and the phenomenal job she was doing down there.

Unfortunately, it was almost impossible to concentrate. The unknown visitor didn't seem to be getting the hint. They'd stopped ringing the doorbell and started banging.

"Goddamn it!" I yelled. "Let me go see who the hell that is. It's probably Joe's stupid ass. He's the only one who'd come knocking on my door at this time o' night."

"Whatever," Jasmine whined as she lifted her head. She rolled her eyes at me and I knew I was in trouble. She was obviously losing her enthusiasm quickly.

"I'm sorry. I'll be right back." I bent over to kiss her, but she backed away with an attitude.

"Just hurry up, okay? My jaw's starting to hurt. You seem to forget I don't do this very often, Dylan."

"I know, I know. Please don't be mad. I'll be right back. I promise." I got up in a hurry, grabbed my robe, and headed down the stairs. Joe was about to get cussed out, even though I couldn't wait to tell him who was upstairs waiting for me.

"You know Joe, you got the worst fuckin' timing in the world," I swore as I swung the front door open. When I saw who was there, I gasped, immediately closing the door without a thought. It wasn't Joe at my door. Oh, no. Not by a long shot. It was Monica, and she had the nerve to be holding a suitcase. I was so puzzled by her sudden appearance that I just stood there like a fool until she knocked again.

"Monica, what're you doing here?"

"Freezing my ass off. Can I come in?" She was clutching her suitcase and shivering. Just looking at her made me tighten my robe to protect myself from the cold.

"Why? What d'you want?" I eyed her suspiciously.

"I wanna talk to you, Dylan. It's important." She tried to step around me, but I blocked her. For the first time in five months, I was eye to eye with the woman I thought I knew better than I knew myself. That is, until she abandoned me for Jordan. I studied her. She looked the same except for a slight weight loss and a fucked-up do. The Monica I knew never went anywhere without every hair being in place.

"To be honest, Monica, tonight really isn't a good time."

"Well, make it a good time. What I've got to say is important." Her demanding tone hadn't changed a bit, and it made me cringe a little to remember just how often she'd used it on me.

She gave me this innocent-yet-determined look that under

normal circumstances would've melted me. But tonight was not normal circumstances. Tonight I was gonna make love to Jasmine, and there was no way I was gonna let Monica or anyone else screw it up. Sure, there were plenty of things I still wanted to talk to Monica about, but it would have to be another time. I'd waited five months to find out just why I wasn't enough for her, so I could wait a little longer. I had better things to do tonight than dig up that past. Much better things.

"I can't talk. I've got company."

I don't think she heard a word I said beyond "I can't," because all she did was suck her teeth as she dropped her suitcase on my foot. When I reached down to pick it up, she pushed her way past me and entered the living room.

"Goddamn it! Why the hell you playin' games, Monica? You know I didn't invite you in." I said it loud, just in case Jasmine was listening at the top of the stairs.

She ignored me as she walked around the living room, sighing every time something nostalgic caught her eye. She was taking her own personal trip down memory lane. I almost felt sorry for her. It was actually looking like she regretted the day she walked out on me for Jordan.

"You haven't changed anything since I left, have you?" she asked.

"Nah, not really."

"I figured you would have gotten rid of all this stuff and moved some woman in here. I guess I was wrong. No woman would let you keep this." She picked up the picture of the two of us standing in front of the house. "We really had some good times in this old house, didn't we?"

"We sure did," I smiled. "I thought we were gonna spend the rest of our lives in this house."

"So did I," she said sadly. "I love this house. I love you too, Dylan."

"Monica, why are you here?" Her confession came totally out of the blue, and I definitely wasn't prepared for it. My mind was still on Jasmine, waiting for me upstairs.

"Well, to start with, I wanted to say I'm sorry." She walked up to me and touched my robe. I took a step back, trying to be subtle so I wouldn't hurt her feelings. Sure, she'd ripped my heart out, but I'd loved this girl too much to do it back to her.

"I didn't mean to hurt you, Dylan. I swear I didn't mean to hurt you. I was just mad. I wanted to get married."

"Oh, so you thought Jordan was gonna marry you?" I couldn't help it. I had to laugh.

"Jordan's an idiot." She pouted. "He doesn't care about me. He never cared about me. He was just using me."

"You know, Monica, I hate to say I told you so, but I told you so." There was silence between us for a few seconds. I guess Monica was digesting this huge slice of humble pie. I couldn't believe I was actually hearing her admit she had been wrong.

"You were right. I was a fool to think I could have with him what I had with you." She straightened out the collar on my robe. "I know I did you wrong, Dylan. I'm sorry about that. Can you ever forgive me?"

I sighed loudly.

"Yeah, I'll forgive you, Monica, but I won't forget. You don't know how much you hurt me. How much you embarrassed me. We weren't even broke up twenty-four hours and Jordan was driving by my store in your car, blowing the horn." I was starting to get emotional and tears were welling up in my eyes. I needed to get Monica outta there before I started crying. "I was in love with you, Monica. True, deep love. I never felt that way about anyone else in my life. So yeah, I'll forgive you, but don't ever ask me to forget." I handed her the suitcase. "I think it's time for you to leave."

Jasmine must have been listening, because at that moment she yelled down the stairs like she'd been cued. "Dylan, is everything all right?"

"Everything's fine. I'll be right up!" I turned to Monica, who was staring at me with a jealous, flabbergasted expression. Now she looked more like the Monica I remembered.

"Who the fuck is that?"

"I tried to tell you I had company."

"Dylan, are you sure everything's all right? You been down there an awfully long time." Jasmine walked down the stairs. She was wearing only my shirt, and looking mighty good in it if I do say so myself. I just prayed she wasn't gonna have an attitude when she saw Monica standing in the living room. I figured that was too much to expect, but she surprised me. When she got to the bottom of the stairs she placed her hand on my shoulder, all cool and calm, kissing my cheek and smiling at Monica.

"Hi. How you doin'? I'm Jasmine." She extended her hand. I was so proud of her. What a classy way to handle a bad situation. Unfortunately, Monica didn't show nearly as much composure.

"Didn't I buy you that shirt?" Monica's voice was cold as she glared at Jasmine, then at me.

"Oh, excuse my manners," I said. "Monica, this is Jasmine. Jazz, this is Monica. My *ex.*" It was quite obvious by her expression that Monica did not like the way I introduced her. But that was her problem. My problem was getting rid of her and getting Jasmine back upstairs to finish what we'd started.

"So, Dylan," Monica hissed, "I guess Jasmine's your new girlfriend now, huh?"

I placed my arm around Jasmine to reassure her. We hadn't discussed where our relationship was going or what our status was, but I wasn't about to make her look like a fool in front of Monica.

"She's here, isn't she?" I shot back with a little sarcasm of my own.

"Yeah, I guess she is. Look, Jasmine, is it?" Monica eyed her competition from head to toe with a sneer. "You don't mind if I talk to Dylan alone for a minute, do you? I have something very important to tell him."

"Sure. Go right ahead." Jasmine gave a condescending smile, like Monica was some beggar off the street. "I'll be upstairs if you need me." Jasmine kissed me, then patted my butt, her eyes on Monica the whole time. "Try not to be too long, Dylan. You haven't finished unwrapping your birthday present yet." She winked at me before she turned to the stairs. I grabbed her wrist before she could take a step.

"Hold on, Jazz. You don't have to go upstairs. Whatever Monica has to say she can say in front of you." I wasn't sure this was the best move. God only knew what Monica was about to say to me. I just figured it would be better to have Jasmine witness it, so there would be no misunderstanding later. I turned to Monica and yawned.

"It's getting late. If you have something to tell me, spit it out. I don't keep secrets from Jasmine."

"Oh, isn't that special?" Monica cooed sarcastically. She stood up. "Don't worry, I'm leaving. I just need some money." She stuck her hand out.

"Money! I'm not giving you no money. You better go ask your boyfriend Jordan."

"I would, but I'm not with Jordan anymore. He kicked me out when he found out I was pregnant. So I need some money to get a hotel room if I can't stay here. I'm also gonna need some money for an apartment."

I couldn't believe what I was hearing. I knew Jordan was a lowlife, but this was worse than even I expected of him.

"You're carrying his child and he put you out on the street?"

"No, Dylan. I'm not carrying his child." Monica spoke as if she were explaining something to a first-grader. "He kicked me out because I'm pregnant with your child." I could feel Jasmine's fingers wiggling free from my hand.

"What do you mean, my child?" I took a step back and eyed her from head to toe. She didn't look like she was pregnant, but even if she was, it couldn't be mine. Could it? "How can I be the father? I haven't slept with you in five months," I protested.

"Gee, what a coincidence. I just happen to be five months pregnant." Monica didn't even look at me, but she gave Jasmine a nasty smile.

"Well, maybe it's Jordan's baby," I shot back. "Ain't no way for me to be sure you wasn't sleepin' with both of us back then."

"I doubt it. He had a vasectomy five years ago. That's why he kicked me out. He can't have kids."

"Well, who else were you messing with?" Now I was grasping at straws.

"Don't play yourself, Dylan. It's your baby. And if you don't believe it, you can have a blood test." She folded her arms across her chest, but then her tone softened a bit. "Look, I could've gotten rid of this baby. But I remembered how much you love kids and wanted to be a parent. I didn't wanna deprive you of a chance at fatherhood."

Maybe it was her tone of voice, or the fact that she volunteered to let me have a blood test, but I believed that baby she was carrying was mine. All of a sudden, a flood of emotions came over me. A flood of electrifying, positive emotions.

"Oh, my God. I'm gonna be a dad. I'm gonna be a dad!" I kept repeating.

I jumped up in the air and I felt like I could fly. In my

euphoria, I turned to Jasmine and repeated the words again with even more enthusiasm.

"I'm gonna be a dad!" She took a step back to avoid my attempted embrace. Her icy-cold stare made it obvious she was not ready to share in my excitement. So instinctively I reached out and wrapped my arms around Monica, kissing her right on the lips.

"Oh, no, you didn't! No, you didn't just fucking kiss her." Jasmine's shout snapped me back to reality. But by the time I let go of Monica, she was already halfway up the stairs, yelling more obscenities. I had really fucked up, and Monica's next comment summed it all up perfectly.

"Uh-oh, Dylan. Looks like trouble in paradise."

"Shut the fuck up, Monica," I spat, glaring at her.

It took me a few minutes to gather enough courage to follow Jasmine up the stairs. It wasn't that I didn't wanna talk to her; I just didn't know what the hell I was gonna say. I left Monica standing in the living room. Of course she protested, tellin' me I didn't need "that bitch" making my decisions for me, but fixing things with Jasmine was my first concern. Monica and her mess would have to wait. I'd be dealing with her for the next eighteen years.

When I got to my room, Jasmine was fully dressed, tossing all the trappings of our romantic evening into a small black duffel bag. All that was left to remind me now was the wax that had dripped from the candles onto my nightstand.

"Jazz? Jasmine?" I called, but she didn't answer me. I stepped in front of her, hoping to at least make eye contact. I wanted to explain, to get back some of the closeness we'd felt just minutes before. But she never even glanced my way. Out of frustration, I grabbed her arm.

"Jasmine, you gotta listen to me. This is all—"

"Get off me!" Even if I'd wanted to hold on, I couldn't.

She slapped me so hard across the face, I had to take a few steps back, and I let her go.

"Don't you fucking touch me, you bastard!" she yelled. "How could you do this shit to me? I was ready to give up everything for you!"

Her expression was a mixture of ferocious anger and genuine hurt. I wanted to say something to her, to make her understand I felt just as strongly about her. But for a man who always has something to say, I was speechless. Monica's announcement had totally floored me, and I could barely think straight to make my next move. All I could do was watch Jasmine pick up that duffel bag and head for the stairs.

"Jasmine, where are you going? Please don't leave," I pleaded.

"I'm going to Roanoke to be with a man who really cares about me. It's pretty obvious you don't." Her words cut me.

"That's not true. I do care, Jasmine. This is all just a misunderstanding."

"You know what, Dylan? You can save that 'misunderstanding' crap for your baby's momma. I know what I saw. That shit wasn't no optical illusion. You kissed that bitch!"

"Yeah, okay. You're right. I did kiss her. But it wasn't a kiss of passion." I pleaded with her to understand. "I was just excited by the news, is all. There was nothing sexual about it."

"You expect me to believe that shit? You were going with that woman for six years. Anything you two do has to be sexual in some way." She moved toward the door, but I tried to block her exit.

"If you don't let me out, I swear we're gonna be fightin' up here." She tried to shove her way past.

"So that's it?" I sighed. "You're just gonna forget about us?"

"What do you want me to do, Dylan? Go downstairs and sit down so the three of us can talk about raising the baby? We ain't got nothing to talk about." She started to cry. "She's having your baby, Dylan. I can't compete with that. Shit, I don't wanna compete with that. I know how much you want a child."

"Why do you have to compete, Jasmine? Why can't you be a part of it?"

"You just don't get it, do you?" She let out a faint laugh.

"What?"

"If you had to choose between Monica and the baby or being with me, which would it be?" I hesitated, and she folded her arms across her chest like she'd just made her point.

"Why can't I pick the baby and you? Monica doesn't have to be part of the equation."

"What are you, stupid? Monica comes with the baby. You can't get around it. Trust me, I've tried."

"But I don't love her, Jasmine. I love you." I thought these words might help, but she seemed unfazed.

"Oh, you love her. You may not want to, but you love her. And you'll love her even more once she has that baby. That's just the way you are, Dylan."

"I don't believe that. If we care about each other, we should be together. Can't we just look at this like a minor setback? We were just starting out."

"Maybe that's the point, Dylan."

"What's the point?"

"Have you ever heard of kismet?"

"Yeah, it's like fate or destiny." She had me totally confused now.

"Well, I'm starting to believe that your destiny is to raise a child with Monica and my fate is to be with Derrick. Maybe it was kismet that she showed up here tonight before we could really do anything." She took a step toward the door, and I sadly let her pass.

"I'm not mad at you, Dylan. I just wish I hadn't taken a chance on you."

I was about to protest, but she raised her hand and headed down the stairs. When she reached the front door, she glanced over at Monica, who was on the couch, all spread out like she owned the place.

"You leaving?" Monica gave a satisfied smirk.

"Yeah, I'm leaving. He's all yours."

"He always was."

Jasmine took a step toward Monica but stopped. I know she wanted to run over there and smack the shit outta her like she'd done to me in the bedroom.

"You know, bitch, you just ain't worth the energy." Jasmine shook her finger at Monica as she headed for the door.

I called out to her, hoping there was still a chance to make things right. She didn't even turn around, just raised her hand to wave good-bye as she walked out my door and probably out of my life.

# 24

# Jasmine

*Slam! Slam!*

"Who's the man?" he shouted.

"You are, baby!"

"Who?"

"You are, Derrick! You're the only man for me!"

*Slam! Slam! Slam! Slam!*

I was sure my headboard was about to break, the way it was slamming up against the wall. Derrick was on top of me, pushing himself inside me with all his might, and I was screaming at the top of my lungs. Only I wasn't screaming because it felt good. I was screaming because it felt like he was gonna rip me wide open. He was having such a good time, he didn't even notice that I was in pain. As far as I could tell, he thought my screams of agony were cries of pleasure and he was doing his job. Every time I opened my mouth, he pushed himself deeper and harder inside me. I wanted to tell him what the grimaces on my face really meant, ask him to slow down, and at least be a little less rough, but I was afraid I'd hurt his feelings. And that was the last thing I wanted to do, especially since he'd been waiting for three years to make love to me.

I'd gone to pick Derrick up right after I left Dylan's house. Oh, I struggled with the idea the whole ride up. I even pulled over a couple of times and contemplated turning around and going back to Dylan. But each time I pulled over, I'd think about Monica being pregnant and the way Dylan kissed her, and I'd get back on the road headed west, convinced that being with Derrick was the right thing to do.

I still wasn't sure about my feelings for Dylan. I wasn't sure if I loved him or hated him. The pain was too raw for me to really deal with yet. But when I finally got up to Roanoke, I was glad I hadn't turned around. All my uncertainty vanished when the gates of that prison opened and Derrick walked out a free man. I wanted to cry, I was so happy. There he was, standing in front of the car, looking as fine as ever, showing off those sexy dimples of his.

"What you gonna do, baby? Sit in that car, or come over here and give your man the love he's been missing?" Derrick stood by my car door with his arms wide open. I jumped right from my seat into his arms. This was the first contact we'd had in three years without guards breathing down our necks, watching our every move. I was so elated! I held him as tight as humanly possible. He was mine again, and as God was my witness, I was never gonna let him go. I can't ever remember being that happy before in my life. All the doubt I had about our relationship vanished with just one kiss. I guess that deep down I had never really imagined this day would come. Maybe that was why I had let myself start to fall for someone else. But now that I was back in Derrick's arms and we had our whole future ahead of us, I wasn't about to let go.

Derrick and I stood in the same spot for at least half an hour, and our lips barely parted in all that time. There was so much pent-up passion and desire between us, it was incredible. I wanted to make love right then and there. I begged him to let me find a secluded spot where we could park, but he told me he'd waited three years to make love to me and he wasn't about to cheapen it by doing it in a car. That made me feel so special that any thoughts of another man, including Dylan, went right down the drain.

When we got back to the apartment, Derrick carried me over the threshold like we were newlyweds. As soon as the front door closed, we were headed straight for the bedroom. He laid me on the bed and started to slowly take off his clothes. He'd always had a nice body, and all those years working out in the prison gym had defined his muscles even more. I almost didn't wanna wait. He was so damn sexy and I was so damn hot for him, I just wanted him to hurry up and get naked. I couldn't believe that after all that time behind bars, he was being more patient than I was. In fact, I don't ever remember him being as attentive as he was that night during foreplay. The Derrick I remember wasn't all that creative in bed, and he definitely never gave me oral sex. All those years in prison must've given him lots of time to dream up new ways to please me. He took his time, kissing every part of my body until I literally begged him to make love to me. He obliged and entered me with one long stroke.

I would love to say it was the greatest experience of my life, and I'm sure Derrick thought it was. But I hadn't felt that much pain since I lost my virginity.

I was hurting so bad I tried every trick in the book to help him finish his business; I was screaming, scratching his back, faking orgasms, but he just kept going and going like he was the fucking Energizer bunny. Finally I just gave up and lay there, taking the pain. Would you believe that's when he finally finished?

"Ahhhhhh, shit. Baby, I'm about to come!" he shouted.

His body became rigid and he lunged forward in a spasm. I was sure he had finished his business when he collapsed on top of me and moaned.

"Damn, that shit felt good," he huffed. "Wasn't that shit

good, boo? I've been dreamin' about doin' that to you for three years, baby."

It wasn't exactly the same kinda sex I'd been dreaming about all this time, but I smiled at him, just glad the ordeal was over.

A few minutes later, he was curled up next to me, snoring. I watched him sleep for a while as I stroked his soft, black hair. After the throbbing between my legs subsided, I actually enjoyed the feeling of lying naked next to my man. I had missed this kind of intimacy.

A knock on the front door interrupted my thoughts, and I panicked. Maybe it was Dylan. After all, I had left his house in a huff, and it would be just like him to try to mend fences. Even if I did want to clear the air with him and let him know I was moving on, I knew I couldn't talk to him now. Not with Derrick here. I eased myself outta bed, the whole time praying I wouldn't wake Derrick. I didn't know what I was gonna do, but I did know I had to get rid of Dylan in a hurry. Fortunately, when I looked through the peephole I was able to relax. I didn't have to deal with Dylan quite so soon. I opened the door and smiled at my sister.

"Girrrrllll, you just don't know. I ain't never been so happy to see you in my entire life."

"That's nice. Now, can you get out the way? It's starting to rain out here." Stephanie pushed her way past me. "It's kinda late to be wearing a housecoat, ain't it? I guess you and Dylan had a late night."

I hushed her and gestured toward the bedroom.

"Will you be quiet?" I whispered.

"Oh, my bad. I didn't know he was here." She sat down next to me on the sofa.

"He's not here. Derrick is."

"What? Get the hell outta here!" She went bug-eyed.

"What happened? Big Momma told me you wanted to be with Dylan. Boy, is she gonna be disappointed!" She was trying to whisper, but she was about as quiet as a jet plane. I glared at her and reminded her to keep her damn voice down.

"Well, I did wanna be with Dylan—until last night."

"Last night? What happened last night?" Now she looked even more confused.

"Steph, it was a mess. His ex-girlfriend showed up at his house." I offered the shortest explanation possible, but of course my sister wanted all the details.

"Oh, no, she didn't." Stephanie leaned forward, waiting to hear more.

"Oh, yes, she did. We were just about to do our thing. I had the candles burning, I had just done my little striptease. Hell, he had the condom in his hand. And this chick has the nerve to knock on his door at two in the mornin', talkin' 'bout she's pregnant." I rubbed my temples, wishing I could erase the humiliating image from my memory.

"Well, what he say? Did he believe her?"

"Hell, yeah, he believed her. He was jumpin' around like it was the got-damn Fourth of July."

"Oh, no, Jazz. I know you wanted to kick his ass."

"Wanted to? Shit, he pissed me off so bad I slapped the hell outta him."

"What? You oughta stop. You ain't slap that man."

"The hell I didn't! You should've seen the way he kissed that heifer in front of me."

"He kissed her? Damn, and here I am thinking he's a nice guy."

"That's the problem, Steph. He *is* a nice guy," I said quietly.

"You sound like you still care about him."

"I do, as silly as that sounds." Even though I could hear

snoring from my bedroom, I whispered. Maybe if I spoke them quietly enough, these feelings would just go away.

"You really got hooked on that guy, didn't you?"

"Look, I don't feel like talking about Dylan right now, all right?" I pointed toward the bedroom, but it was just an excuse not to deal with my feelings.

"Okay," she agreed. "I understand."

"So what brings you over here, anyway? I thought it was your weekend to take Big Momma to church."

"Oh, my God. I completely forgot. Big Momma's outside in the van. She wanted me to make sure you were home."

"What? Why'd you bring her over here? You know she can't stand Derrick."

"Hey, don't be blaming this on me. Big Momma said something about you and Dylan was supposed to take her to Morrison's for dinner tonight. Besides, I didn't know Derrick was home."

Of course, you know, three seconds later there was a knock on the door.

"Oh, shit! Now what am I gonna do?"

"You better answer the door before she starts knocking louder and wakes up Derrick. You know how Big Momma is."

I did know how she was, so I got up and answered the door, hoping I could get rid of her before Derrick heard us and came out of the bedroom.

"Girl, why ain't you dressed?" Big Momma bellowed. "I thought we were going to Morrison's."

"I'm sorry, Big Momma. I forgot all about it."

"Well, I didn't. I been thinkin' about their banana pudding all day. Now, go on and get dressed." She ambled past me and sat on the sofa next to Stephanie. "Where's Dylan, anyway?"

"Oh, Big Momma he . . ." I glanced at the stairs, praying for some way out of this.

"He in the bedroom, ain't he? That's why you got your robe on at three o'clock in the afternoon." Big Momma shook her head. "Lord, you young people sure work fast. Last week you were trying to tell me he was just your friend." Stephanie laughed and I cut my eyes at her.

"He *is* just my friend, Big Momma. Look, I gotta tell y—"

She cut me off again. "Then what's he doing in your bed?"

"He's not in my bedroom. . . ."

"Baby, where's the car keys?" All eyes turned in the direction of the voice. Derrick was walking down the stairs fully dressed. "Oh, excuse me. I didn't know you had company."

"Oh, Lord," Big Momma mumbled under her breath to Stephanie. "What's he doing here? I thought they sent him up the river."

Stephanie shrugged in reply.

"And where's Dylan?" Big Momma continued questioning Stephanie. I rushed to Derrick and gave him a hug, trying to keep some distance between him and my mumbling grandmother on the couch. I talked loud to drown out the questions she was asking Stephanie.

"Derrick," I started nervously, "you remember Big Momma and my sister, Stephanie, don't you?"

"Yeah. What's up, Big Momma? How you doin', Stephanie?" Derrick approached them, and Big Momma leaned back and glared at him. He did his best to ignore her dis and addressed my sister. "So, Stephanie, I hear congratulations are in order. A new baby, huh? What's that make, two?"

"Yeah, a boy and a girl." Stephanie smiled proudly.

"I'm happy for you. I can't wait till me and your sister

have some kids." Derrick put a hand on my shoulder and joked, "We gonna have to hurry if we're gonna catch up to her, boo. She's gonna mess around and have a basketball team before we have one kid."

"If you say so." I tried not to grimace. I knew it was only a matter of time before Big Momma opened her mouth.

"How you gonna have kids and you ain't even got no damn job? And selling those drugs just gonna wind you right back in that prison."

"Big Momma, Derrick's gonna go to college. He's already got accepted to Virginia Union in the fall."

"Oh, really? What's you gonna do, Derrick? Start selling drugs to the college students? I guess that's the next step in your plan to destroy black people."

Derrick's face became contorted. He looked like he was about to say something we might all regret. So I gently took his hand and spoke before he could.

"Derrick, didn't you say that you wanted the car keys?"

"Yeah, I wanted to go see Tyler." His eyes were still locked on Big Momma.

"Okay. Here they are." I reached in my bag and handed him the keys.

"Why you gonna give him your car keys?" Big Momma asked. "He needs to buy his own car. When you gonna get your own car, anyway, Mister Big Shot?"

"When you gonna get the hell out my—"

I grabbed his arm. "No, Derrick, please don't start no trouble," I pleaded. "Big Momma don't mean no harm. Go 'head and see Tyler."

"Oh, I meant every word," Big Momma spat. But thankfully, Derrick ignored her last insult and headed for the door, turning to me before opening it.

"Hey, baby, you wanna come with me?"

His invitation sounded sincere, and any other time I would

have taken him up on it, because seeing Tyler meant seeing Wendy. Even though I trusted Derrick, I damn sure didn't trust Wendy. This time, though, I was happy to see him go, especially since I was afraid he and Big Momma were gonna tear each other apart.

"No, you go 'head; we're supposed to be going to Morrison's for dinner."

I breathed a huge sigh of relief once he walked out the door.

# 25

# Stephanie

What a long day it had been! Jasmine and I had been at the mall most of the morning looking at bridesmaids' dresses. After picking out what we thought were the perfect dresses, we went to Applebee's for lunch and stopped by the party goods shop. I'd always thought my sister was a real square, but after spending the day with her, I had to give her credit. She was actually a hell of a lot of fun to be with. And she had good taste, too. She was taking as much pride in my wedding as I was, and the dresses she helped me pick out were the bomb. We had so much fun, I hated to leave her. And when I pulled into my driveway, I wished I hadn't.

"What the fuck is he doing here?" I spotted Malek's car parked in front of our house. He wasn't in it, which probably meant he was inside talking to Travis. That wasn't good news at all. Malek had been calling the house more and more frequently in the past few weeks. He was using the excuse that he wanted to find out how Maleka was doing or that he wanted to update me on Nana's condition, but every conversation ended with him asking for some ass. And me telling him to kiss mine. He must have just gotten sick of the rejection and decided to blow me up to Travis.

I stayed in my car almost twenty minutes, trying to decide if I should go inside. Travis finally made my decision for me. He walked outside with T. J. in his arms. I was so scared to death of what Malek might've told him, it felt like my heart had slid down into my stomach. Travis's facial expression didn't give me one damn clue of what he knew. It was just blank, and that made me even more nervous.

"Baby," Travis said, knocking on my window, "you need to come in the house. There's someone here to see you." He opened my car door and handed T. J. to me. He didn't even attempt to give me a kiss, and that worried me. He never forgot to give me a kiss unless he was mad about something. So I just knew I was in trouble.

"Malek's here, isn't he?"

"No, but his mother is." I raised both eyebrows. I was confused but relieved.

"Miss Janet's here? What's she doing here?"

"I think it might be best if she told you." I handed him the baby and walked into the house. Miss Janet was sitting on the sofa, and Maleka was sitting on her lap. They both had Barbies in their hands.

"Mommy! Look what Grandma Janet brought me!" Maleka jumped off of her grandmother's lap to show me the dolls.

"Wasn't that nice of her?" I smiled at my daughter, never taking my eyes off of her grandmother. I didn't even know she knew where I lived, so her presence had me worried. After everything I'd gone through recently, I didn't need any more drama. It was time for me to leave all that shit behind and concentrate on my upcoming wedding. I just hoped Malek's mother hadn't come over and messed up my plans by saying the wrong thing to Travis.

"Hey, Miss Janet. What you doing here?" I hoped she didn't notice the suspicion in my voice. When she gave me her news, I felt bad for even thinking about myself.

"Momma died last night, Stephanie."

"Nana? Nana's dead?"

I knew Nana didn't have much time, but I at least thought I'd see her before she passed.

"Have you made the arrangements?" My voice was choked up.

"Uh-huh. The funeral's on Friday." Miss Janet wiped away a tear from her cheek. "I was hoping you'd do a reading."

"Oh, I don't know about that, Miss Janet."

"Come on, now. You know how much Momma loved you. Least you could do is read at her funeral."

I glanced at Travis. I felt real bad about Nana dying, but I wasn't sure if I should be reading at her funeral. Don't get me wrong. I wanted to read. I wanted to do anything I could for Nana. I just didn't want Travis getting upset. Things were just starting to get back to normal in our house. After the night he left, I had promised things would change. And once I took care of the problem with the STD, I really had been behaving. I'd been coming home straight from work, acting like the perfect fiancée and mommy. But going to the funeral meant I'd be seeing Malek, and I knew Travis didn't want that to happen. That's why I was surprised when he put his hand on my shoulder and told me it was okay for me to go.

"Okay, Miss Janet. I'll do it. I'll read."

Miss Janet smiled. "Good. You gonna bring Maleka, right?"

Travis answered Miss Janet before I could.

"Yeah, Maleka will be there. And I hope you don't mind if I come, too? I'd like to pay my respects to your mother. I know how much she meant to Stephanie."

Miss Janet hesitated, but she looked like she was about to agree when I cut in.

"No, Travis. You stay here with T. J."

"Why?" He took his arm from around my shoulder and frowned at me.

" 'Cause Nana is Malek's grandmother, and you two

don't get along. They were very close, and this is gonna be hard enough on him as it is. Things will only be worse if you're there. You understand, don't you, boo?"

I knew I was taking a big chance asking him to stay home, but I figured he wouldn't protest, at least while Miss Janet was there. Sure, we might have an argument about this later, but I had to keep Travis away. I knew why he wanted to be there, and I didn't blame him for wanting to keep an eye on Malek. But I also knew that if Malek was upset enough, who knew what would come out of his mouth? Shit was already crazy enough between me and Malek. I did not need a scene at Nana's funeral. I would go and pay my respects, then finally be done with Malek. It was time to get myself back on the straight and narrow.

# 26

# Jasmine

Our apartment was hooked up with streamers and party favors. Sabrina, Becky, and I had spent all day decorating it in Derrick's favorite colors, red and white. This was really gonna be a party to remember. I had spent over five hundred dollars on food and drink, and had gotten Derrick's friend Devin to DJ so nobody could complain about the music. I was proud of the job we had done. It all paid off, too. When Derrick walked through the door with his buddies, he was surprised as hell. I'll never forget the way he kissed me and announced to everyone how much he loved me. I thought for sure that was the start of a beautiful evening, but it turned out to be the beginning of a nightmare.

Originally, I had planned on a small surprise party a week after Derrick's release from prison. Except for sex, things were going so well between us, I just thought he deserved it. I thought a couple of his closest friends and family for dinner would be nice. Kinda like what my family does on Sundays. But after I asked his mother to make a few calls and invite some of the family, things got out of hand. She gave me a list of over forty people. She musta called everyone she knew, from the car dealer to the drug dealer. And before I knew it, I had over fifty people in my apartment, all of them hungry and wanting to get drunk.

Even that would've been cool if they all acted civilized,

but those fools were the most triflin', ghettofied people I'd ever met. To start with, Derrick's Aunt Jean and Uncle Roy tried to rob us blind. I caught them filling up a shopping bag with all the meat from our freezer. I grabbed that damn bag out of Roy's hand and headed straight for Derrick's mother, who invited their low-rent asses in the first place. I wasn't trying to make a scene at Derrick's party or anything, but I wanted those two out of my house. Would you believe that woman sucked her teeth and told me if her brother and sister-in-law had to leave, she was leaving too? You should have seen the attitude she gave me. She turned her back on me and marched right over to Derrick like he was supposed to be mad with me or something. Well, believe it or not, that woman knew her son, 'cause next thing I knew, Derrick was glaring at me like I'd beat his sister. He came over, grabbed my hand, and led me upstairs. I could hear his mother, uncle, and aunt all laughing and slapping each other five as we walked up the stairs.

My stomach was in knots when Derrick got to the top of the stairs and turned to speak. I knew I had to keep myself under control, 'cause right before he went to prison I said something smart about his mother and he locked me in the closet for an hour. Don't get the wrong idea; I deserved it. When you call your man's mother a piece-of-shit project whore, you should expect a beat-down. I got off easy bein' locked in the closet. At least he didn't lay his hands on me.

"Thanks." He gave me a gentle kiss.

"You're not mad?" I was amazed.

"No." He kissed me again. "Mama's just tryin' to start some trouble, and Uncle Roy and Aunt Jean think we rich 'cause we don't stay in the projects. Let them have the meat, baby. I'll go grocery shopping in the morning." He kissed me again and left me with my jaw hanging. He turned to speak again when he was halfway down the stairs. "Oh, baby, you did a great job with the party. Thanks."

So I thought I was through with the drama for the night. That is, until I heard noises coming from my guest bedroom. Now, I know I wasn't throwin' no kind of party where I expected some nasty-ass people to be doin' their business on *my* clean sheets. I wasn't havin' that. And I didn't give a damn about no one's privacy, so I barged into the room. The view was more than I'd bargained for. There was Derrick's sixteen-year-old sister, Vicki, butt-naked with a teenage boy trying his best to split her in two. The two of them looked like they were going to die when they saw me. Vicki was pleading and crying as she scrambled to put her clothes on.

"Please, Aunt Jasmine, don't tell Mommy or Derrick. Please!"

Out of everyone in Derrick's family, I liked Vicki the most. Probably 'cause she gave me respect when the two of us had traveled together upstate on occasion to visit Derrick in prison. Plus, Vicki had always sent a few dollars from her McDonald's job to Derrick's commissary each month, which is more than his own mother ever did. So I was definitely leaning toward not telling her mother. Telling Derrick was a different story. Derrick was my man, and the last thing I wanted to do was lie to him. If I lied to him about this and he found out later, he'd wanna kill me. He was so proud of Vicki, who he thought was still a virgin. She was the first woman in his family not to get pregnant before graduating high school. Derrick was hoping that she might be able to attend college and really make something outta herself.

I watched Vicki as she sat on the bed and put on her shoes. The guy she was with had bolted as soon as his pants were up from his ankles. That just proved that he wasn't about shit. How these young girls get hooked up with these half-ass men, I just don't know.

"Okay," I finally told her. "This is what I'm gonna do. I'm not going to say anything to your mother or Derrick. But if Derrick asks me anything, I'm tellin' the truth."

I thought Vicki would go through the ceiling, she jumped so high. She threw her arms around my neck in a grateful hug.

"Thank you, Aunt Jasmine. Thank you so much!"

"Give me the condom and the wrapper. The last thing we need is your brother finding a used rubber lying around. Then we'd both be in deep shit."

I knelt down to search for the wrapper under the bed, until I realized Vicki had not moved. She just sat there with this dumb-ass, blank stare.

"Don't tell me you didn't use a condom."

Her answer was silence.

"Damn, Vicki! What the fuck is wrong with you?" I spent the next half hour trying to explain the importance of birth control and disease prevention. I'm not sure if it did any good, but at least it made me feel a little useful. Not to mention the fact that it gave me a chance to be away from Derrick's pain-in-the-ass mother.

When I finally got back to the party, things had thinned out a bit. Derrick's mother and his older relatives had left with most of the food from the dining room, which really wasn't a problem for me. I didn't want to clean up all that shit anyway. Besides, I had much bigger problems than Derrick's family. Right in front of my eyes, standing in my living room, drinking my liquor, talking to my man, was Wendy. I ain't gonna lie. I was about to kick that bitch's ass. Derrick must've seen the look in my eye. He hauled ass over to me and dragged me into the kitchen.

"What's that bitch doing in my house, Derrick? I want that bitch out my house!"

"Look, baby. I know you don't like Wendy, but my mom

asked her to come over. Besides, she ain't hurtin' nobody. Why you gotta be so paranoid? Stop trippin'."

"Your mother ain't even here! Get that bitch out my house!"

Derrick raised an eyebrow. I hated when he did that, because it usually meant he was about to give me an ultimatum.

"Okay. Ah'ight, check this out. If Wendy has to leave, I'm leaving, too."

He looked at me like I should care. I did, but I sure as hell didn't intend to show it. He could leave with her if he wanted. I'll tell you what, though, that bitch Wendy was not about to leave my house with my man without an ass-whipping.

"Well, then, get to steppin'," I challenged.

"Ah'ight." He grabbed my hand and dragged me into the living room, where he pulled the plug on the DJ's equipment.

"Excuse me, everybody. The party's over."

"Yo! Dee, man. What up with that? I just got here!" a man said from the crowd.

"Yeah, it ain't even eleven o'clock!" another angry voice called out.

"Look, y'all, I wanna party just as much as you. But my old lady doesn't like the company I keep. She wants me to kick a few of y'all outta here. But y'all my peeps, so I told her if my peeps gotta go, so do I. So since the party was for me and I'm leavin', the party's over."

I had never been so embarrassed in my entire life. The last thing I expected was for Derrick to do something like this. All I wanted was for him to stop disrespectin' me with his baby's bitch-ass momma, and he had blown the whole thing out of proportion. Every eye in that room was on me and there was no escape, 'cause Derrick had his hand on my arm in a vise grip.

"Cut it out, Derrick. Can't you see you're embarrassing me?" I was talking through clenched teeth.

"This is what you want, ain't it, baby?" he whispered.

"Of course not. I just want that bitch out of my house."

"Well she's out, and so am I. For good. Either you trust me or you don't. I'm not gonna play these games with you, Jazz."

His tone was dead serious, and I was scared. The last thing I wanted him to do was walk out of my life right after I'd finally gotten him back. Reluctantly I decided to put my own pride aside and keep my man. Big Momma always told me to keep your friends close and your enemies closer, so I was about to take her advice.

"Don't do this, Derrick. She can stay." I was about to cry.

"You sure?" He wrapped his arms around me when I nodded. "Now, that's my girl."

"Hey, y'all. I was just playin'," he laughed. "The party's still on. My lady loves all my peeps. Don't you, boo?"

I nodded weakly, but it wasn't like any of these triflin' folks even cared what I thought of them. When Derrick said the party was back on, they just plugged the DJ back in and went back to partying. I pushed Derrick away and walked to the bar, pouring a straight glass of something brown. I tilted my head back and let the liquid slide down my throat, burning so much I almost gagged. I didn't give a fuck, though. I just wanted to get drunk as fast as I could. This whole damn night had been enough to damn near drive me crazy. And for the first time this week, I missed Dylan. I missed him a lot.

"Wake up, Derrick wants you outside."

It was almost midnight when Malcolm, one of Derrick's teenaged drug-dealing friends, woke me from my drunken nap on the sofa. It took me a while to come to my senses, but after a few seconds I realized where I was at. There were still plenty of people in the house and the music was blasting, but everyone seemed to be congregating at the front door.

"Derrick wants you outside." Malcolm repeated.

"For what?" I rubbed my eyes as I tried to stand. I was still drunk and my knees gave out, so I plopped back down on the sofa. "What's everybody doing at my front door? Y'all better not have the police at my house." I gathered my strength, got up from the sofa, and pushed my way through the crowd. What I saw at the other end of the door made me scream. Dylan was on the ground, being held down by three of Derrick's friends. He was barely moving, and blood was coming from his nose and mouth. Derrick was standing over him with his foot on Dylan's throat. He looked like he was gonna kill him.

"Jasmine . . . help . . . me. Get him . . . off me." I could barely hear him between gasps for breath.

"Stop it, Derrick!" I shouted.

Derrick turned to me and glared. "You know this nigga?"

My eyes roamed to Dylan, then back to Derrick. I didn't say a word. I was afraid of what Derrick might do if he didn't like my answer. I didn't want to see Dylan hurt even more than he was. I wouldn't be able to forgive myself.

"I asked you a question, Jasmine," Derrick repeated. "Do you know him?"

I tried to avoid his glaring eyes, but eventually we made eye contact. And during that split second, I'm sure he could read my mind. His eyes became small and he pushed down on Dylan's throat. I was frozen with terror. He knew about me and Dylan; that much looked certain. Thank God Sabrina was there to save Dylan—and rescue me.

"Yeah, she knows him." She shoved her way to the front of the crowd. "He's my boyfriend. Now get the fuck off him unless you plan on going back upstate."

Then she did exactly what I wish I could have done. She shoved Derrick out of the way and bent down to help Dylan.

"Get away from him!" she yelled at Derrick's friends. I still hadn't moved. I'm not sure if it was shock or alcohol, but I was stuck in my place.

"Dylan, are you all right? They're not gonna bother you anymore, baby." Sabrina cradled his head, and I felt a twinge of jealousy. That should have been me helping him, holding him. "I hope you're fucking proud of yourself, asshole. You must really like it upstate. I hope they put your fucking ass *under* the jail for this!" she yelled at Derrick.

"That nigga was tryin' to break into my car," Derrick replied defensively, like that made what he did right.

"Oh, yeah? What was he trying to do, break the glass with roses?" Sabrina grabbed a handful of flowers off the ground and threw them at Derrick. Then she turned her eyes on me, but I couldn't make eye contact.

"Yo, Jasmine. You need to keep your man in check or he's gonna end up back in jail." She sucked her teeth at me, then turned back to Dylan. I cringed as I watched her murmuring to him, stroking his hair. I wanted to strangle her when she kissed him, even if it was only for Derrick's benefit. That's when I knew I was in love with Dylan. Damn, was I in a bad situation.

# 27

# Stephanie

"Young lady, that was a beautiful poem you read. I don't think I've ever heard 'Phenomenal Woman' read so well," Reverend Clarke complimented between bites of his fried chicken. We'd just returned from Nana's funeral. I was trying to find Maleka so that I could get home to Travis when the preacher pulled me aside.

"Thank you, Reverend. It was one of Nana's favorites, so I thought it would be appropriate."

"And it was. It really was," the preacher praised, then finished off the last of his chicken wing. "You know, we could use an orator like you in our church. Have you ever thought about going into the ministry? What church do you belong to?"

"Ah, well . . . I guess you could say I'm a member of Mount Olive Baptist—"

He cut me off. "What do you mean, you guess?" He looked at me with concern and I tried to avoid eye contact. The last thing I wanted to do was tell that man I hadn't been to church since last Easter. Luckily, Miss Janet rescued me.

"Excuse me, Reverend," she huffed, pulling on Maleka's hand. "Stephanie, have you seen Malek?"

"No, ma'am. Not since we left the cemetery."

"Well, will you go find him for me?"

"Do I have to, Miss Janet?" I whined. "You know me and Malek don't get along."

"I know that, Stephanie. But I got over forty people in this house. And I'm doin' everything from meeting and greeting to servin' the food. I ain't got time to go lookin' for that boy, and everyone in here's been askin' about him. Please do me this favor. All I want you to do is go find him and tell him I wanna see him. That's not too much to ask, is it?" she sighed.

"No, ma'am." I replied weakly, and said good-bye to the preacher. I was happy to get away from him, but I really didn't wanna go find Malek. I'd been avoiding him as best I could all day. After everything that happened with the VD, he was the last person I wanted to be around. Like Mary J. said, I don't need no more drama in my life, and it seemed like every time I got near Malek, it followed me.

After I searched the first floor, I headed for Malek's room in the basement. As soon as I opened the door, I was practically knocked over by a cloud of smoke. It smelled like someone was smoking a pound of weed down there.

"Malek," I called. He didn't answer, so I walked down the stairs. I found him sitting on his bed, smoking a blunt. He'd loosened his tie, but he was still wearing his suit.

"Your mother wants you. There's a lot of people upstairs who wanna give their condolences." He nodded his head and went right back to smoking his weed. I turned to walk back upstairs before I got high from all the smoke.

"Yo, Shorty. Lemme ask you a question." I stopped and turned my head. "You think Nana's in heaven?"

I smiled, stepping down from the stairs. "Yeah, Malek. I think she's in heaven."

"I sure hope so. If anyone deserves to be in heaven, Nana does." His eyes had tears in them, and that surprised me. I couldn't ever remember seeing Malek cry before.

"I miss her, Shorty. I miss her so much."

"So do I, Malek. So do I." I sat on the bed next to him. I wrapped my arm around his shoulder and we cried together.

The two of us had a good cry for a few minutes before he finally lightened the mood.

"She looked good in that casket, didn't she?"

"She sure did." I smiled and wiped away my tears. "She looked like her old self."

Malek reached over and picked up the blunt from the ashtray. I watched him light it, then suck on it gently. When he finished, he gestured for me to take it. At first I hesitated. When I came downstairs, I had intended on giving Malek Miss Janet's message and getting the hell away from him. Now here I was, all sentimental about Nana, sitting with Malek on his bed, about to smoke a blunt. I knew I was in dangerous waters once again, but Malek really looked like he needed some comforting. I took the blunt from him and inhaled deeply. Besides, I figured nothing could happen with all them folks upstairs, anyway.

"You know, Shorty, you was lookin' mighty good today. I like it when you wear dresses." He reached up and removed his tie completely.

"Thanks." I smiled as I exhaled. My eyes roamed up and down his body. "You looked pretty good in that suit."

I took another hit, then passed the blunt. I sighed as I watched him wrap his lips around the brown cigar paper and suck on it. An image of him sucking my breast popped into my mind, and I could feel myself getting moist. What the hell was it about this man that made me want him so bad? When he finished smoking, he handed me the blunt. I inhaled the weed for the third time, finally starting to feel its effects. Malek reached behind me and began to massage my shoulder. I thought about stopping him, but his hands felt so good around my neck and shoulders. He leaned over and blew in my ear.

"Stop it, Malek. You're gonna get my panties all wet." I turned my head and that made things worse because he started kissing my neck. Finally, I couldn't take it anymore and I whispered, "You got any condoms?"

"Yeah," he nodded excitedly. "I got condoms in here."

He reached over to his night table drawer and pulled out an open three-pack of condoms. I took the box out of his hands and smiled.

"Come on." I stood up and headed for the stairs.

"Where we goin'? To the motel?" He followed me eagerly.

"No. I told you before, your mother wants you. There are people upstairs who wanna see you."

"But I thought we were gonna get busy." He raised his eyebrows. "You said I was making you wet."

"I am wet. And extremely horny," I told him honestly.

"Then where you going? The hell with Momma. She can handle them old farts upstairs. I'm horny, too. Look at this."

He reached down and grabbed himself, grinning. I made sure I was halfway up the stairs before I responded to him.

"Just because I'm horny doesn't mean I'm gonna sleep with you, Malek."

"Then why'd you ask me for the condoms?"

"Me and Travis ran out last night. And after smoking that blunt, I'm so horny I can't wait to go home and fuck his brains out."

"What? I don't believe this shit!" Malek yelled. "Now that's some real foul shit, Shorty! Some real foul shit!"

"No, Malek. You wanna know what's foul? Foul is getting gonorrhea from someone you care about. Foul is getting accused of giving it to someone who knows they gave it to you. Foul is not even getting an apology from the person who gave it to you. Now that's foul, Malek. So if you think it's foul that I won't sleep with you, then good. That's exactly what I was trying to get in that thick-ass skull of yours. After what you did to me, you will never put your dick in me again. And I mean never." He looked away from me and I walked up the stairs to find my daughter and go home to my man.

I wasn't in the house more than five minutes before I was all over Travis. The second I saw him I wrapped my arms around his neck and tongued him down. I can't ever remember being that horny in my entire life. If my daughter hadn't walked in on us, we probably would have ended up doing the nasty right there on the family room floor.

"Mommy, can I have some ice cream?"

"Travis," I purred seductively, "do me a favor and give Maleka some ice cream and put her to bed. I'm gonna go upstairs and get into something a little more comfortable." I kissed him as I whispered. "I want you, baby. I want you real bad."

"I don't know what's gotten into you," he whispered back. "But that sounds like a plan to me. Come on, Maleka." He headed for the kitchen.

"Hey," I called, "don't take too long or I might get started without you."

He laughed. "You can be such a freak. You know that?"

"That's why you're marrying me, isn't it?" I blew him a kiss and headed for the stairs, thinking naughty thoughts.

When I got to my room, I immediately stripped off all my clothes and slipped into a sheer white Victoria's Secret teddy. I was about to lie on the bed and wait for Travis when the phone rang.

"Hello?"

"Dammmmn, I never expected you to answer the phone." Every muscle in my body tensed up when I heard Malek's voice. "I figured you'd be getting your groove on by now."

I inhaled deeply and tried to keep my composure. I knew I had to get Malek off the line as quickly as possible before

Travis walked in the room. If he even thought I was talking to Malek, he'd have a fit. As horny as I was, I did not want to be fighting with Travis tonight.

"What do you want, Malek?" I got up and closed the bedroom door.

"We need to talk."

"Talk about what? I said everything I had to say to you at your house, Malek. "

"Well, I didn't say everything I had to say."

"Okay, I'll humor you. What do you have to say?"

"I want joint custody of Maleka. And I want her every weekend. And since you thought you was so slick this afternoon, I want some ass at least once a week."

"Are you fucking crazy? I ain't giving you shit."

"Okay, then. Put Travis on the phone."

"Travis?" He was making me nervous, but I tried to make light of the situation. "What do you want Travis for? He's not about to tell me to give you some ass."

"Just put him on the phone."

"Well, he's not here."

"Then take a message," he taunted. "Tell him that we need to talk before he goes down the aisle. And make sure you tell him I'll call him back."

"Don't play with me, Malek."

"No, Shorty. Don't play with me. You've got a lot more to lose." I hated to let him get the last word, but Travis walked in the room, so I hung up.

"Who was that on the phone?" Travis walked over and I wrapped my arms around his neck.

"Oh, it was nobody. Just a wrong number. Did you put Maleka to bed?"

"I sure did; now it's time to put my other girl to bed. He lifted me up and I kissed him as he carried me to the bed.

# 28

# Travis

"Oh, Travis! Yes, baby! Yes! Don't stop! I'm almost there! Give it to me, boo! That's it! Please don't stop!"

Stephanie was on top of me, doing her thing. I mean, *damn,* she was doing her thing. She was jumping up and down on me like I was a trampoline and she was a world-class gymnast. And from the sounds of her screaming, she must've been having the time of her life. I just didn't understand why she was so worried about me stopping. Shit, she was the one doing all the work. To be honest, I was half asleep. This was our third round since she'd come home from the funeral, and I was dog-tired. I mean, it was nice that she wanted to make love and all, but damn. Three times on a work night was a bit much.

"Waaaaaaaa!"

I cringed when I heard the baby crying. Now I knew I wasn't gonna get any sleep.

"Waaaaaaa!"

"Steph. Steph! Stephanie!"

"What?" she whined, still gyrating on top of me.

"The baby's crying."

"Damn it." She looked over at the crib. "Let him cry, Travis." She ground her hips into mine. "I'm almost there."

"Waaaaaaa!"

"Steph, get the baby," I told her sternly.

"No, Travis! I'm gettin' ready to come." She started to move faster.

"Waaaaaaaa!"

I looked over at the crib, and there was my son, T. J., staring me in the face. He was crying loud enough to wake up the entire south side of Richmond. Just looking at my little boy's face covered with tears was anything but a turn-on. I lost my hard-on in a matter of seconds.

"Stephanie, get the damn baby!" I grabbed her hips to stop her from moving.

"I'ma kill your ass, T. J.!" She glared at him, but that didn't stop T. J. He was quiet for about five seconds before he started again in full force.

"Waaaaaa! Waaaaaa! Waaaaaaaa!"

I pushed her off of me and got out of bed to get my son.

"What's up, little man?" I put his pacifier in his mouth and took him out of the crib. His screams had subsided to little sobbing breaths, but his body was still trembling. I kissed his forehead.

"Gimme my baby. He's probably wet." Stephanie snatched a Pamper off the top of the dresser and walked over to the crib. I handed T. J. to her and she laid him down on the changing table. I lay down on the bed as I watched her changing my son. His little temper tantrum was over now. She was singing a lullaby to calm him down. He even smiled when she handed him his bottle.

Now I was fully awake. And with the baby comfortably settled in his crib, Stephanie's naked body definitely had my attention. She knew it, too. She stood over T. J.'s crib, singing him to sleep, swaying those lovely hips of hers in my direction the whole time. As soon as the baby fell asleep, she crawled on the bed and gave me a sexy smile and a kiss.

"Think we can finish what we started?"

"Damn, woman, you trying to kill me or something? Haven't you had enough?" I whispered jokingly.

"No, you're just irresistibly sexy. I can't get enough of you."

"Well, if you put it that way, I'd love to give you some. The only problem is, I didn't realize I was coming home to a nymphomaniac. I only bought a three-pack of condoms this afternoon."

"Don't worry. I got some condoms." She ran over to her purse and brought back a box. Within seconds, she'd slipped one on and slid down on me. But before we could get into a groove, we were interrupted by the phone.

"I'll get it." I reached for the phone, but before I could get it, Stephanie jumped off me and snatched the receiver from the night table. I had wanted to answer the phone because we'd had a few wrong numbers the past couple of hours. I thought I'd explained to her that if they heard a male voice they might stop calling. But I guess she didn't understand me.

"Hello?" Stephanie answered. "I'm sorry. I told you before you have the wrong number. Please don't call here again." She hung up.

"Give me the phone," I ordered.

She handed it to me reluctantly and I placed it on my night table.

"Next time it rings, I'll answer it. Okay?"

"All right," she sighed. Her entire demeanor seemed to change. "Why don't we just turn the ringer off or somethin'? It's probably just somebody playin' games."

"Well, let's see if they play games with me," I told her, opening my arms for her to climb aboard. "Come 'ere. You still wanna finish what we started, or what?"

She shook her head. "No. I'm not in the mood anymore."

"Huh?" I was confused by her sudden change of tone, but I wasn't gonna argue. She'd given me enough sex to keep me quiet for a week, so if she wanted to call it a night, she was entitled. Besides, it was getting late and I had PT in the morning. I leaned over and kissed her, looking forward to some good sleep. That's when the phone rang again.

Stephanie jumped up and tried to reach over me, but I grabbed the phone off my night table, keeping it out of her reach.

"Just let it ring, Travis. Turn the ringer off so we can get some sleep." She sounded like she was begging. She was desperate to keep me away from whoever was on the other end of that phone line. So desperate, in fact, that she actually attacked me and tried to wrestle the phone out of my hand.

"What the hell are you doing?" I tried to pull the phone back.

"Gimme the phone, Travis. Just give me the phone," she growled as she pulled on it with both hands.

"Have you lost your mind? What the hell is wrong with you?" I yelled.

But she continued to wrestle with me until we both fell off the bed. Unfortunately for her, she hit the ground first, and my two hundred and fifty pounds fell on top of her. That's when I pulled the phone free from her hands. But of course by that time, the ringing had stopped. I stood up and glared at her.

"What the hell is wrong with you? And why don't you want me to answer the phone? Who the fuck keeps calling my house, Stephanie?"

Now I wanted some answers. But even if she wanted to give them, she didn't get a chance before the phone rang again. This time I turned my back and hit the talk button before she had a chance to pounce on me.

"Hello?"

"Yo, this Travis?" I recognized Malek's voice right away. He had that same smug street cockiness he had in front of the house on Christmas Day. Just the sound of his voice made my blood pressure rise, so you can imagine what was going through my mind. Why the hell was this fool on my phone at this time of night, and how the hell did he get my unlisted phone number in the first place? I glanced at Stephanie, who was still on the floor trying to avoid eye contact, and the answer was obvious. She gave him the number.

"Yeah, this is Travis. What you want, Malek?"

"So she told you it was me callin', huh?" He let out a little laugh.

"She's my woman. She tells me everything," I lied.

"Is that so?" Malek snickered. "Well, did she tell you that she gave me gonorrhea?"

"No, why don't you tell me about it?"

"Nah, I'll let her tell you that. Can I speak to her?" I turned and glared at Stephanie. She was now sitting on the edge of the bed, huffing and puffing from our tussle, with a worried look on her face.

"Yeah, you can speak to her, but don't you ever call my house at this time of night again. You hear me?" My words were tough, but my insides felt like they were turning to Jell-O. Both he and Stephanie had disrespected me for the last time.

"Uh-huh. I hear you, boss," he mumbled. "By the way, how'd you like those lambskin condoms I gave her? They're great, aren't they? Sorry I only sent you two, but I had to use one, if you know what I mean." I was so shocked by his comment, I couldn't even reply. I just shoved the phone in Stephanie's face.

"Malek wants to speak to you."

She pulled her hands back and shook her head. "I don't wanna talk to him."

"Take the damn phone! And tell this man to stop calling my house!" I yelled angrily. She finally took the phone from me. I thought about standing over her and listening to her end of the conversation. But then I realized I might not be able to control myself if I heard anything I didn't like. I didn't want to put my hands on Stephanie, so I knew it was best if I just backed off for a minute. I walked over to my son's crib. Just watching him sleep so peacefully helped me to calm myself. I stroked his hair, then bent over and kissed him.

"I love you, son," I whispered as I looked across the room at Stephanie. She was talking very low, so I really couldn't hear much of what was being said. From her body language, it didn't look like she had any kind words to say to Malek. Still, however angry she looked now, I couldn't forget Malek's comment about the condoms. Just the fact that he knew she had them made me wonder. And what else did he know? Stephanie had a hell of a lot of explaining to do.

I grabbed my pants and shirt off the back of a chair and shut myself in the bathroom. I splashed some water on my face, trying to get my emotions in check. By the time I walked out of the bathroom, Stephanie was off the phone, waiting for me.

"Travis, we need to talk about Malek."

"Talk about what? There ain't nothin' to say that ain't already been said. I told you before, I'm not putting up with this shit with you and Malek. I'm a good man who's been good to you. I don't deserve this shit, Stephanie." I tried to walk past her, but she grabbed my arm.

"Don't do this, Travis. This is exactly what he wants you to do."

"Well, whose fault is that, Steph? If you had stayed home with me instead of going to the funeral, we wouldn't have this fuckin' problem. Would we?" I walked over to the bed and sat down to put on my shoes.

"I had to go to the funeral, Travis. Nana was like a mother to me."

"But you didn't have to go *alone,* Stephanie. You were so worried about Malek's feelings, you never thought about mine."

I picked up the box of condoms and stared at the box.

"Now, explain this to me. How the hell did Malek know what kind of condoms you brought home? And how come there were only two in the box?" Her eyes got huge and she stared at me, unable to choke out an answer.

"Travis, I asked him if he had any condoms because I knew we were out. We had smoked some weed and I wanted to come home and make love to you, boo."

There wasn't a damn thing funny, but I had to laugh to keep from crying.

"Tell me something, Steph. If I told you my ex-girlfriend gave me some condoms so I could come home and fuck you, would you believe me? Would you?"

She didn't speak, so I answered for her. "Hell, no! You'd say I was fucking her. Just like you fucked him, Stephanie. You know it and I know it."

"Travis, I swear I didn't do anything with him. This is all just one big misunderstanding. Baby, you gotta believe me."

"Everything's a misunderstanding to you, Stephanie. Oh, and what's this shit about you giving him gonorrhea?"

"I didn't give it to him! He gave it . . ." She shut up before she got herself into more trouble. "He's lying, Travis. If I had gonorrhea I would have given it to you."

"You know what? I don't care anymore. I'm sick of the lies, and I'm sick of you and your baby's daddy." I stood up. "As far as I'm concerned, the wedding is off. I want my ring back." I paused, but she made no move to give me the ring or beg me to change my mind. She just sat there and stared, her body trembling. "Do you hear me? I want my ring back."

* * *

I really didn't know how Brittany was gonna react when she saw me standing at her door at four o'clock in the morning, suitcase in hand. But a few months ago she had given me an open invitation to sleep on her couch if the need ever arose, and it definitely had. So here I was, at her doorstep in the middle of the night.

"Who is it?"

"It's Travis, Brittany. I'm sorry to come by so late, bu—"

She opened the door before I could finish my sentence. "Don't tell me. You and Stephanie had a fight?"

I nodded. "I couldn't take her shit anymore. I left."

"I understand." She smiled sympathetically. "My brother just went through the same thing. Some women don't understand when they got it good." I nodded my agreement.

"That invitation to sleep on your couch still open?"

"Sure. Long as you paying for groceries, you can stay as long as you like. I just have one rule."

"What's that?"

"Keep your woman and your kids away from my house, 'cause I don't wanna deal with no baby momma drama. And from what I've seen, you've got some of the worst I've ever heard of."

"Yeah, I guess I do have more than my fair share."

# 29

# Dylan

I hobbled into the Shoney's in Petersburg, where I was supposed to meet Joe for breakfast. I was almost forty minutes late, and by the expression on his face it was clear he wasn't very happy with me. We were supposed to meet for breakfast before we headed over to his mom's to do some painting. Joe wanted to get started early, 'cause the Duke basketball game was on later. He was a huge Duke fan. It wasn't even a question that he was gonna have an attitude if we didn't finish all the painting by noon.

"Hey, man. Sorry I'm late. I had a rough night."

"Whatever," he sneered, shoveling a forkful of eggs into his mouth. He didn't even look up from the newspaper he was reading. "Sit down and eat so we can get the hell outta here. I ordered your usual."

I slid into the booth with a grimace. Every muscle in my body ached from the beating I took the night before.

"What's wrong with you?" he asked, finally lifting his head. "Damn, you look like shit. What the hell happened to your face?" Joe put down his fork and inspected my bruised face.

"Man, I should've never listened to your ass and went up to see that girl."

"So you went up to Richmond last night, huh?" I nodded and he continued. "I take it things didn't go so well. What'd she do, slap the shit out of you again?" Joe laughed, but I didn't think a damn thing was funny.

I'd gone up to Jasmine's place last night with the intention of mending things between us. I'd been trying to get in touch with her all week, but she'd changed her home phone number and her cell phone number. And when I tried to contact her at the post office, they refused to forward my calls to her office.

I'd been going crazy trying to get in touch with her. I knew I could make her understand that my kiss with Monica meant nothing. I just had to get her to listen to what I had to say. We'd been so close to making things work between us. I just wanted another chance at that. As far as I was concerned, Monica and the baby were just a little bump in the road. Well, maybe a big bump in the road, but we could still work it out. All Jasmine had to do was listen to me. By Friday I was really starting to get depressed, so Joe suggested that I go up to see her in person. He said if I showed up with a dozen roses in hand, she'd at least have to listen to what I had to say. Unfortunately, when I got there the only words I got to speak to her were from the ground. And they were a plea for help.

"So what the hell happened up there, anyway?" Joe asked, snapping me back to the present.

"Derrick is what happened," I told him.

"Derrick, Derrick," Joe repeated like he was trying to remember something. "Oh, you mean her boyfriend? I thought he wasn't coming home for a couple o' months."

"That's what I thought. As you can see, we were both wrong. He and his boys jumped me last night." I lifted my shirt so he could see the bruises that covered most of my body.

"Damn! You want me to call up a few of the fellas? We can go up there and pay this Derrick a little visit if you want."

I took a deep breath. Joe's suggestion was tempting, but not anything I hadn't thought about for most of the ride home last night. After Sabrina helped me into my car, I only had one thing on my mind: I wanted revenge so bad I could taste it. But the closer I got to Petersburg, the more I realized that it wasn't Derrick's fault at all. It was Jasmine's fault. I would never have gone to her place if I had known Derrick was out of prison. All she had to do was answer one of my calls.

Derrick must've been outside with a few of his boys when I pulled into the complex. There's always somebody hanging out in her parking lot, so I didn't pay any attention to them. I was too busy noticing all the cars that were parked around the place. There was definitely someone throwing one hell of a party. And from the blaring music and people around her apartment, it was clear Jasmine was that someone.

I have to admit, I felt left out when I heard all the laughter coming from her place. A week before, I would've been right there, partying with them. Now it seemed like she was getting over me a hell of a lot faster than I was getting over her.

That's why I decided to write a note instead of knocking on the door. The last thing I wanted was to walk in on her party uninvited. There's no better way to make a fool outta yourself than to crash a party and then be asked to leave. I wasn't about to risk that kind of humiliation.

So I sat in my car and wrote her a note. I asked her to please give me a chance to explain and to give us a chance at happiness. I planned to leave it with a rose on her windshield, so I picked up the flower and headed to her car. That was when the trouble started. When I reached her car, the door was unlocked like it always was. She had a bad habit of leaving her car door open, but I'd been trying to break her of that habit.

Not too long ago, she had bought a new car stereo, and I knew she would've been pissed if it was stolen like the last one. So I opened the car door to lock it for her. Big mistake.

"What the fuck you doing in my car, nigga?" I didn't recognize the voice, but when I turned around I damn sure recognized the face. I'd seen it in dozens of pictures scattered throughout Jasmine's apartment. It was Derrick. Only he wasn't supposed to be out for at least two months.

"I asked you a question, nigga. What the fuck you doing in my car?"

"Yo, man. Take it easy." Luckily, it was dark enough that Derrick didn't see me toss the rose and stuff the note in my pocket. I held my hands up and stepped back from the car. "I was just locking your car doors. That's all." I smiled, trying to look cool, but I know I looked nervous. I could take Derrick in a fight. Of that I was confident. But his three friends, they were a different story. Those three brothers were huge, and the 40s in their hands could be turned into some serious weapons. If I was gonna survive, diplomacy was probably my best option.

"Is that so?' Derrick laughed, and they moved in closer.

"Yeah, I was just locking your door. It looks like you got an expensive stereo in there. Can't be too safe these days. You never know who's gonna try and rip you off." I patted the car.

He laughed again.

"Did you hear this, y'all?" Derrick looked back at his friends. "He was locking my car 'cause he was worried about someone ripping me off." They all laughed as they moved in closer. "Damn, that's nice of you, brotha. And to think I thought *you* was gonna rob me of that stereo."

"Who, me? Nah. I wouldn't do that." I shook my head nervously as I scanned the area for an escape route.

"I bet you wouldn't. Why don't you let me thank you

properly?" He raised his fist, but I was ready for it. Before he could connect, I hit him as hard as I could right in the stomach. I didn't get in a second blow, though, 'cause his friends were on me like white on rice. The next thing I knew, I was being stomped and kicked by all four of them. If it wasn't for Jasmine's friend Sabrina, I'd probably be in intensive care right about now.

"Yo, Dylan, you want me to make that call to the fellas, or what?" Joe asked again.

"Nah," I exhaled. "Leave him alone."

"Now that's a first." Joe looked skeptical. "You're gonna let someone get away with jumpin' you without putting up a fight?"

"Only because he didn't do anything I wouldn't have done."

"What are you talking about? The guy kicked your ass for no reason."

"Oh, he had a reason. . . ." I began to explain the situation to Joe, and when I was done, not only did he understand, he agreed we should leave Derrick alone.

"Damn, I thought Jasmine was smarter than this. All she had to do was call and tell you he was home."

"That's what I'm saying."

"You know, you're a bigger man than I thought you were, Dylan. I woulda bet money that you'd be up all night plotting and scheming like you did with Jordan." Joe sat back in his chair and finished the last of his coffee.

"No, Jordan was different. He knew Monica was my woman. Jasmine, it seems, was never mine. I was just borrowing her until Derrick came home." I took a sip of the coffee that Joe had ordered for me. "Besides, I had other things on my mind last night. Some very pleasurable things, I might add." Joe studied my face, then broke out in a big grin.

"You tryin' to tell me, after all this shit, you got some ass last night?" He laughed.

"Yeah." I couldn't contain my pride.

"How the hell'd you do that with all those bruises?" Joe stared at me in amazement.

"Oh, very gingerly," I grinned. "Very gingerly. She did all the work."

Joe laughed. "You are crazy."

"You'll never believe who it was."

Joe stared at me like he was tryin' to read my mind. Then, all of a sudden his eyes got big.

"Oh, shit. I know who it is. You dirty dog. You got with Jasmine's friend Sabrina, didn't you? Didn't you? Damn, I know she got some good-ass booty. Fine as she is." Joe stuck out his hand, but I left him hanging.

"Nah, man. I ain't mess with Sabrina. I'm mad at Jasmine, but I ain't that damn mad. Those two are like sisters."

"Then who?" Joe leaned forward.

"Let's put it this way: she's having my baby."

"What? Oh, shit. Not Monica. Please don't tell me you're fucking with Monica again." Joe's grin turned sour and he lowered his head. "Damn it, Dylan. What the hell were you thinking about?"

"What was I thinking about? You actin' like I was fucking your sister. This is my ex-girlfriend we're talking about, Joe. I went with her for six years. Don't act like you never thought there was a chance we might get back together. Especially since she's having my baby."

"No, I didn't. I thought you were stronger than that. And how the hell do you know that's your baby, anyway? Did you have a blood test? No!" He was really mad. "Don't be tellin' nobody that's your baby, Dylan. You hear me?"

"Why not?"

Joe hesitated. I knew that look on his face. He wanted to

tell me something, but he was afraid I might not like what he had to say. We'd had our wars over the years when it came to Monica. And I knew he didn't especially like her, but true friends never let a woman come between them. So right now I wasn't worried about him hurting my feelings. I needed to know if he had some information.

"Why, Joe? Why don't you want me to claim the baby?"

He inhaled deeply before he spoke. " 'Cause Monica's a *crackhead,* that's why. There's no telling whose baby that is."

"A crackhead? Monica ain't no crackhead." I almost laughed at him as I leaned back in my seat. Usually, Joe's information was good, but this was so far off base, he must've gotten his stories confused.

"Yeah, she is," Joe insisted. "That's the real reason Jordan kicked her out. Not that bullshit she told you about the baby not being his. It's because she was smoking that shit. Man, that brother got three kids. He ain't had no vasectomy."

"Who told you that bullshit, Joe? Monica ain't no damn crackhead. I've been hanging with her all week and she damn sure don't act like no crackhead. Now, she's an arrogant ass, I'll give you that, and she can definitely be a bitch. But a crackhead? No, I think you have the wrong woman."

Joe exhaled loudly. "How does a crackhead act, Dylan?"

"They steal money and appliances and shit. And they all skinny like that Robin chick they call 'Creature Feature.' Monica ain't stolen nothing from me."

"Look, all I'm tellin' you is that my man George seen her coming out the spot on East Washington Street. If it'll make you feel better, maybe she's not a crackhead. Maybe she's just a casual user. But let's get one thing straight, my friend. If she's coming out the spot, she had to go in there for something. Unless she got a job as a cop or a social worker, she went in there to buy crack."

I wanted to call him a liar. I wanted to tell him he didn't

know what the fuck he was talking about. But in our seven years of friendship, Joe's information had almost always been on the mark. And he did look pretty damn determined to convince me this time. Not only that, but an image of Monica snorting coke in Jordan's living room invaded my memory. I didn't wanna tell Joe, but it *was* possible that she had graduated from snorting coke to smoking crack. I hated to even entertain the idea, but I had to at least talk to her about it. Especially since she was moving her shit into my place as we spoke.

"Why didn't you tell me this before?"

"I just found out yesterday. You weren't with her. You were chasing behind Jasmine, so I didn't think it was urgent. I was gonna tell you this morning until you came in lookin' so fucked up."

"I'm not gonna front with you, Joe. I don't think she's using crack. But I'm gonna go talk to her about it. 'Cause if on the off chance you're right, that shit could be affecting my baby's health. And I do mean *my* baby."

"Ah'ight. I can respect that," Joe told me quietly. "I just hope you know I wouldn't tell you this shit if I didn't love you."

"I know that." I stuck my hand out and he grasped it. "I gotta go take care of this. I can't paint Mom's house today. Tell her I'm sorry, but somethin' personal came up."

"Don't worry about it. I'll take care of Ma. You go handle your business."

"Thanks, Joe. Breakfast is on me." I reached in my pocket and pulled out my wallet. My heart sank when I realized there was no money in it. Well, at least not as much as I thought.

"What's wrong?"

"I had eighty-five dollars in my wallet last night. Now I only have five, but I ain't spent no money." Joe and I stared at each other. I'm sure he was having the same thoughts as I was.

"Man," he said, "now you really got to go home and handle your business."

It seemed like it took forever to get home from Shoney's. Then again, that might have had something to do with the fact that I took the long way home, trying to get my head together for the confrontation I was gonna have with Monica. I kept repeating Joe's accusations in my mind. I really didn't want to believe Monica was doing drugs, but the evidence was staring me right in the face when I opened my wallet. As I drove home, I wracked my brain. Maybe I was so delirious after the fight with Derrick that I spent the money and just didn't remember it. I was hoping Monica would have some type of logical explanation for being seen near a crack house.

When I finally walked in the front door, I was met by the sound of R. Kelly's music blaring upstairs. I don't know what it was about that dude, but Monica loved her some R. Kelly. Even after he was accused of child molestation. She played his songs all the time and supported him by buying the CD he did with Jay-Z.

When I reached the top of the stairs, I took a deep breath before I walked into the bedroom. I knew I was gonna have to be real smooth when I approached Monica about this crack issue. She wasn't stupid at all, and even if she was using crack, the chances of her admitting it to me were slim to none. I figured the best way for me to approach the matter was to pretend I had been tempted to try crack myself. They say no true crackhead wants to smoke alone. When I stepped into the room, I realized that approach wasn't gonna be necessary at all.

"What the fuck are you doing?" I screamed.

I couldn't believe my eyes. Monica was sitting on my bed, sucking on a crack pipe like it was an oxygen mask. I was so mad I couldn't control myself. I slapped that damn pipe right outta her mouth, sending her in one direction and the pipe in the other.

"Get the fuck out my house! Do you hear me? I said get the fuck out!" I was so mad I was trembling. How could she do this to me? How could she do this to *my baby?* "You're killing my baby! You bitch!"

My words must have sunk in, because she curled into the fetal position and started crying.

"Oh, God. My baby. What have I done to my baby?" she kept repeating between sobs. She rubbed her hands in slow circles around her belly.

"Don't act like you give a shit now! You should've been thinking about the baby when you were sucking on that glass dick. Now get the fuck outta my house."

"Please, Dylan. Don't kick me out. I ain't got nowhere else to go."

"Go home to your mother and father."

"I can't!" she yelled desperately. "I stole a hundred dollars from my dad and he told me never to come back."

"Oh, and you steal eighty bucks from me and I should let you stay? You gotta be kidding me. Get the fuck out my house, you crackhead."

She crawled over to me with a face full of tears.

"Please, Dylan, please don't kick me out. I'm having your baby, for Christ's sake," she sobbed. I ignored her last comment and shoved her toward the door. That's when she grabbed hold of my sweats and tried to pull them down.

"What the fuck is wrong with you? Get off my pants!"

"You always said you wanted me to suck your dick. If you let me stay I'll suck it every day. I swear." She tried to pull my pants down again. That's when I knew she wasn't a casual user at all. She was a crackhead. Six months ago I couldn't have paid her a million dollars to perform oral sex on me. Now she was offering to do it every day like I had a lobster dinner in my pants.

"I can't believe you even said that shit. What the fuck is wrong with you? Are you crazy? Get off me." I shoved her hands off me, then turned my back. I couldn't even look at her. "You need some help, Monica. Some serious fucking help." I bent over and picked up her clothes, tossing them to her. "Now get your shit and get the hell out my house before I throw you out."

"Dylan, please don't do this. Please don't give up on me."

"It's too late. I gave up on you when I walked in here and saw that stem in your mouth. You're a sick woman, Monica. You need help."

"Then help me, Dylan," she pleaded. "If not for me, then for the baby's sake. Just help me. I'll do whatever you want. Just don't give up on me. I don't have anyone else."

Our eyes met, and hers actually reflected the sincerity of what she was saying. She really did want help. So I knelt down on the floor and wrapped my arms around her.

"Okay, okay. Don't worry, I'm gonna help you and the baby. But you have to be honest with me. Is that baby mine?"

Monica looked me straight in the eye, but she hesitated before she spoke. "Yes, Dylan, the baby's yours. I swear to God it's yours."

I breathed a sigh of relief and held her trembling body as I thought about who I should call first to find her some professional help. I was determined to make her well and save our baby.

# 30

## Stephanie

I'd just come home from work and was about to drive over to the day care and pick up the kids when the doorbell rang. I ran to the door praying it was Travis. I hadn't heard from him since he left a week ago, and I was beginning to think he wasn't gonna come home. I can't even begin to explain how much I missed that man. I opened the front door, and standing right in front of me, grinning like I was supposed to be happy to see him, was Malek.

"What's up, Shorty? What you doin?"

"What am I doin'?" I snapped in disbelief. "I'm thinking about ways to kill your ass for all the trouble you caused me. What the fuck do you think I'm doin'?"

"Damn, why you so hostile? I made sure your boy Travis's car wasn't here before I pulled up."

"Ain't nobody ask you to come here, Malek." I stuck my head out the door and looked both ways. It'd be just my luck that today would be the day Travis decided to come home. "What do you want anyway, Malek? Haven't you caused enough trouble?"

"I just wanted to see if you were all right. Make sure that nigga Travis didn't rough you up after I told him about them condoms."

He had the nerve to laugh. So I reared back and swung at him, but my blow didn't connect and he laughed even harder.

His laughter pissed me off even more. I threw a barrage of punches and slaps at him until I connected, busting his lip.

"Yo, what the fuck's wrong with you?" He rubbed his hand against his lip and got angry when he saw the blood. "You better chill the fuck out before I knock your ass out. I ain't that nigga Travis. You better *recognize*."

"Recognize what? That he's a man and you're not? That you're a loser who can't keep a job at Home Depot? I mean, tell me what the fuck I'm supposed to recognize, and I will. 'Cause what's standing in front of me ain't shit."

"Oh, so it's like that, huh? I ain't shit."

"You damn right. Now get the fuck off my property before I do something we both might regret."

"Oh, please. What you gonna do?"

I held the phone so Malek couldn't see the numbers I was dialing, and called 411. I started talking before the recording even picked up.

"Hello? I need the police at Twenty-one-sixteen Harrogate Road." I said it in a panic as I smirked at Malek. "What's the emergency? My daughter's father just got out his car with a gun. His name? His name is Malek Robinson and he's driving a white Honda Civic. Please tell them to hurry. I have two children in the house." I clicked off the phone and glared at Malek. "You wanted to know what I was gonna do, Malek? That's what I'm gonna do. Now, you probably have about three minutes to get the hell outta here before the cops are all over your ass. And if you don't, you're going to jail, 'cause I know you got weed on you."

"Well, if I'm going to jail, maybe I should slap the shit outta you before the cops get here. At least then I'll be going to jail for a good reason." He lifted his hand like he was about to slap me, and I wished I had really dialed 911 instead of information. Thank God he came to his senses and turned toward his car. "This ain't over, Shorty. Trust me, this ain't over at all. I'll be back, and maybe it'll be when that nigga of yours is home."

"You know what, Malek? You done fucked with the wrong woman. I'ma get somebody to fuck you up." My words were tough, but I didn't have a clue how to back them up. Or did I?

I knocked on Jasmine's door for the third time. Derrick finally answered a few seconds later with a shout.

"Come in!"

I must've been the last person he expected, 'cause when I let myself in, he jumped up and quickly tightened his robe. I couldn't help but smile, though, because he didn't get his robe closed around his johnson quick enough, and what I glimpsed was a hell of a lot bigger than anything I would have ever expected. I mean, he was in Malek's league, and I didn't think anyone could compare to him. Well, good for Jasmine. Now that I saw what she was working with, I could understand why she stood by Derrick all those years. Shit, the man definitely had something worth waiting for. I was sure she was having a hell of a lot of fun now that he and his big old johnson were back in town.

"Stephanie?" He sounded skittish, though I don't know why. This was *my* sister's place, after all. "Jasmine's not here. She's at work."

"I know. I didn't come to see her. I came to see you."

"Come to see me? About what?" He kept tightening the belt of his robe nervously. Maybe he was afraid his johnson would pop out and I'd see it again. Okay, so maybe I was having trouble keeping my eyes away from his groin. But you can't blame a sistah for wanting a little peep show once in a while, can you?

"I got some things to talk to you about." My eyes finally

made their way back up to his face. "But first I gotta use the bathroom. I'll be right back."

You should have seen him. I thought Derrick was gonna break his damn neck trying to leap across the love seat to stop me.

"There's somebody in there. You gotta use the one upstairs."

"No, that's okay. I can wait. It'd be just my luck Jasmine would come home as I was walking down the stairs. I got enough problems. I don't need my sister thinking I'm trying to get with her man." Besides, I wanted to know who the hell he was hiding in the downstairs bathroom.

"No, really. You can use the one upstairs. Jazz won't be home for hours." He tried to guide me toward the stairs, but I shrugged him off.

"Why you so eager to get me upstairs? You got a girl in there or something?" I took a step toward the bathroom, and he stepped in front of me, which confirmed my suspicions. "You *do* got a girl in there, don't you? Does my sister know about this?"

He didn't have time to even make up a lie before the bathroom door opened and a brown-skinned woman about my height and complexion walked out. She looked familiar, but I just couldn't place her, and she wasn't about to give me time to figure it out.

"Who the hell are you?" She eyed me from head to toe and sucked her teeth like she owned the place. If I didn't know better, I'd think she was tryin' to intimidate me. I was about to put her in her place when Derrick cut in.

"Look, Wendy, this is Jasmine's sister, Stephanie, so will you be quiet?" She actually got the look off her face pretty fast. I guess Derrick was in charge when it came to this wench. He turned to me with a lame attempt at an explanation. "This is not what it looks like, Stephanie."

"Oh, no? Then what is it? 'Cause it looks like you got some bitch over here in my sister's place about to get your groove on." I sucked my teeth, showing a little sister-girl attitude of my own. Derrick was visibly nervous, and he hesitated before he spoke. He knew enough to choose his words wisely.

"Nah, it ain't nothing like that. You see, Wendy's my son's mom. And, well, we were discussing his schooling. Right, Wendy?"

"Yeah, whatever." She twisted her lips and shrugged. "Look, Derrick, I'm outta here. I need a hundred dollars to buy Tyler some tennis shoes."

He reached for his wallet on the coffee table and handed her some money. He looked like he was in a big hurry to get her out, 'cause he didn't even bother to count what he handed her. I guess she'd be getting her nails done with the change.

"Get him a pair of those baby blue Jordans. Like the ones I got last week," Derrick suggested. Wendy nodded and headed for the door. She didn't have anything else to say, but she made sure to smirk at me on her way past. I just shook my head and walked into the bathroom. When I came out, Derrick was sitting in the recliner smoking a cigarette.

"Yo, Stephanie." He put the cigarette down and leaned forward. "I hope we can keep this between us. I mean, your sister and Wendy just don't get along. Know what I mean?"

No shit. And after seeing Wendy and her stank attitude, I could see why my sister might have a problem. I was about to jump in Derrick's shit until I remembered why I was there. I needed his help.

"Look, I came over here to ask you for a favor, not to blow you up. Just don't be hurtin' my sister."

"Man, why would I hurt your sister? I love her. Shit, she did a three-year bit with me, so you know I got love for her.

It's just that she don't get along with Wendy, that's all. So I gotta keep them apart and see Wendy on the low, if you know what I mean."

"Whatever, Derrick."

"For real, Steph," he insisted. "Ain't no funny shit going on. My baby takes good care of me."

"That ain't none of my business as long as my sister don't get hurt. Shit, I got my own problems."

"I heard that." I know he was relieved to be changing the subject. "So what brings you over here? You said you needed a favor. I didn't think anyone in your family would ever ask me for a favor."

"Look, I'm not Big Momma," I told him. "I don't care what you do for a living. That's your business. Only thing I care about is that you take care of my sister." I glanced at the new entertainment system that had appeared in Jasmine's living room not long after Derrick got home.

"You know, Steph, I knew there was a reason why I liked you." He gestured for me to have a seat. I sat on the love seat next to him. "So what's this favor you need?"

"Well, I don't know if Jasmine told you or not, but me and my fiancé broke up recently."

"Yeah, she mentioned it. I'm sorry to hear that." He actually sounded sincere.

"Thanks, but I'm gonna get him back eventually."

"That's good. So what's the problem?"

"Do you remember Malek, my daughter's father? He used to rap with KRN."

"Yeah, I remember that nigga. He's the one who stole that bag of weed from my boy, Butter. Man, Butter beat the shit out that nigga." Derrick laughed at the memory. "And that soft-ass nigga is your baby's father?"

"Yeah, and he's also my problem." I was actually glad to

hear that Derrick didn't like Malek. It would make it easier to get his help. "Malek keeps harassing me. And now he's trying to blackmail me into sleeping with him."

"Damn, that's fucked up." Derrick leaned back in the recliner and smirked. "But from what I hear, you were sleeping with him anyway. Weren't you?"

Hadn't he said Jasmine had just "mentioned" that Travis and I broke up? Sounds like she did more than mention it. Shoot, she might as well have taken an ad out in the local paper, as much of my business as she was giving up. I didn't give a damn if it was only to her boyfriend. But I'd have to deal with my sister and issues of loyalty later. Right now I needed help from Derrick.

"Uh-huh," I sighed. "I was sleeping with him, but I stopped. I love Travis, Derrick, and he left me because of Malek. I can't get him back if Malek won't back off. That's why I need your help."

"What you want me to do about it?"

"I want you to go talk to Malek. Tell him to leave me alone. Send him a message."

"Whoa! Hold on a minute." He stood. "This ain't no damn gangster movie or nothin'. And I ain't the Godfather. I'm on parole. How I look sending that nigga a message? You tryin' to get me sent back upstate?"

"Look, I'm just asking for a favor, Derrick. Same way you asked me to do you a favor and keep my mouth shut about your baby momma's little visit. I mean, what would Jasmine think if I told her you were hanging out with Wendy with your johnson hanging out your robe?"

"Aw, shit. Why you gotta go there? Now you trying to blackmail me." He sat back down, looking a little defeated.

"Hey, I'm not trying to blackmail you. But I am desperate, Derrick. He's scared of you and your crew. Especially

Butter. If you pay him a little visit and tell him to leave me alone, I can fix things between me and Travis."

"And if I do this, you're gonna completely forget about Wendy stopping by here?"

"Derrick, if I never came by here, how can I tell Jasmine about Wendy?" I gave him a knowing smile.

"Ah'ight," he sighed. "Where can I find this nigga?"

I wrote down Malek's address and handed it to him.

"You do realize this might not work. This guy might not scare off so easy."

"It'll work. It's gotta work. 'Cause as long as Malek's around, I'm never gonna get Travis back. So do what you gotta do."

Derrick nodded and I smiled at him, taking one last glance at his lap before I left. It was too bad he was my sister's man, 'cause I could work with that.

# 31

# Jasmine

"Damn it!" I stepped off the bus and picked up my broken heel from the ground. This was not my day, not my day at all. I'd just spent the better part of two hours on public transportation, and I still had to walk two blocks before I got home. As if that wasn't bad enough, when I stepped off the stupid bus, I landed in a hole and broke the heel on my favorite pair of shoes. All that because Derrick never showed up to pick me up from work at five o'clock.

To say I was pissed off was an understatement. I was furious. By the time I reached my apartment, I was ready to explode. Only I was gonna have to postpone my explosion, 'cause my car wasn't in the parking lot, which meant Derrick wasn't even home.

I couldn't wait to get inside and take a nice, long, hot shower. Traveling that damn bus route makes me so tense, and those buses are so grimy. Besides, it was best if I relaxed a little before Derrick came home. If I saw him right away, I might just try to take his head off.

When I put the key in the door, my mood just turned from bad to worse. I could hear the TV blaring. I had told Derrick a million times to turn that shit off before he went out. This was just one more thing to add to the list of shit that was really starting to get to me about him. Yeah, I missed him while he was away, but I guess I'd gotten used to the way

Dylan had done things. He may not have bought me things like the entertainment center or the new rims on my car, but he always remembered the little things, and that made me feel special.

Just as I opened the door, I heard Tyler shout, "Watch out for that one behind you, Dad!"

My car wasn't outside, but Derrick *was* home after all. Sitting on his ass, playing video games with his son. Damn, I hoped he hadn't smashed up my car.

"Don't worry, son. I got 'im!" Derrick shouted back, sounding like a kid himself.

"No, you don't! He's still alive! Oh, no! Look out, Dad!"

"Damn." The game made some sort of "game over" noises.

"Oh, well. My turn. You're dead, dad," Tyler laughed.

"Yeah, Derrick. You're dead." I must've scared them both pretty good, because they each jumped about a foot in the air.

"Goddamn it! Don't do that shit, baby! You scared the shit outta me."

"Me, too," Tyler added smugly. Well, at least he didn't curse at me like his father.

"Hey, what are you doing home, anyway? I thought I was supposed to pick you up from work at . . . Uh-oh." He glanced at his watch, then at the clock on the wall. "Baby, I'm sorry. I lost track of time."

"For two and a half hours?" I fumed. Derrick gave me one of his cute little smiles to try to disarm me, but it wasn't working this time. So he tried harder.

"I know, baby, I know. I fucked up. I'm sorry. Come on, let's talk about this in the bedroom, away from Tyler, okay?"

He approached me with his arms open, but I put out my hand to block him.

"Don't, Derrick. Don't even come over here with that mess, okay?" He kept walking anyway.

"Baby, calm down. Don't act like this. I'm sorry. You know I didn't mean it. I was just trying to spend some quality time with Tyler and we lost track of time. It won't happen again, I promise."

His voice was actually soothing. And even though I'd crossed my arms in front of me, he managed to wrap his around my waist. I got a whiff of his cologne when he leaned in to kiss my neck. After two long hours on the bus, I had to admit it felt pretty good to be held, even if I was still upset with him.

"Look, why don't you go upstairs and take you a nice bubble bath?" he murmured. "Read a little bit of that Mary Morrison novel while I fix dinner. I bought us a couple of steaks and some lobster tails this morning. How about some surf and turf with a nice salad? What do you say?" He gave me a peck on the lips, and my frown disappeared.

"Oh, all right," I sighed. Derrick always knew how to handle me. He could push me to the edge with his childish ways sometimes, but then he knew just how to pull me back with his attention and his touch. How could I say no to a nice bath and a great dinner prepared by my man? And if we could get rid of his son later, maybe he could make it up to me in other ways. Things hadn't been great in the bedroom, but they had improved. Who knows? Maybe if I was lucky, he'd slow down a bit and let me enjoy myself.

"Daddy, when is Mommy coming back?" Tyler's mention of his mother put the tension right back in my body. "I thought she said she was just going to the store. She's been gone a long time."

I swear I felt Derrick's entire body tighten up with each word Tyler spoke. He probably wanted to choke that little boy for blowing him up like that.

"Wendy was here?" I tried to pull myself free, but Derrick pulled me back.

"She wasn't here long, boo. She just stopped by to see if I'd watch Tyler while she went to the supermarket." He started to kiss my neck again, but this time it wasn't working.

"Derrick."

"Yes, babe?" He was still kissing my neck.

"Where's my car?" He didn't reply, and I was afraid I already knew the answer. I pushed him away so I could look in his eyes. "Derrick, I asked you a question. Where's my car?" He still didn't answer, and I exploded. "Where the fuck is my car?"

"Now, take it easy, baby. Your car's all right. I just let a friend borrow it for a while."

"A friend, or your baby's momma?"

"Okay, okay. I let Wendy borrow it to go to the store. She should have been back by now."

"What? You lent my car to that bitch instead of picking me up?" That was it. After everything I'd been through the past few hours, I couldn't take any more stress. Now he was letting that bitch drive my car? I'd had enough disrespect. I started beating his chest with my fists, screaming about how much I hated him and Wendy.

"Leave my daddy alone! Leave him alone!" Tyler was shouting as he kicked my ankles. I turned around and raised my hand. By this point, I was so far gone I was about to slap the shit outta that little boy. Derrick grabbed my arm firmly, and I was about to slap his face with my free hand when there was a knock at the door. I pulled myself free and ran to the door. To no surprise, Wendy was standing there like she didn't have a care in the world. She backed up about five steps when she saw me.

"Gimme my keys, bitch." I stuck out my hand.

"Oops. He was supposed to pick you up from work, wasn't

he?" She had the nerve to smirk at me like she'd done the shit on purpose.

"You know what, bitch? I done had about enough of your shit!"

I ran at her like I was a locomotive, swinging my arms like I'd lost my mind. She didn't have a chance. I slapped her face so hard she went flying about three feet back. And I didn't stop there. I grabbed a handful of her weave and tried my best to rip out every last track. She was lucky Derrick pulled my ass off her.

"Jasmine, calm down, baby."

"You calm down! Don't tell me to calm down! Get the fuck off of me!" I huffed, barely able to breathe from the fight. I watched Derrick walk over and help Wendy up from the ground. Her nose was bleeding and she had tears in her eyes.

"I'm going over to Momma's. When I get back I want your bitch, your kid, and your shit out my house. You hear me?" I stormed off to my car, praying that triflin' bitch had left me enough gas to get to my momma's.

I returned home around ten-thirty, just as pissed off as when I left. Derrick met me at the door holding a dozen roses. I just rolled my eyes at him and ignored the flowers he tried to hand me. He must've thought I was playing when I said I wanted him and his shit outta my house. Well, he was wrong. Dead wrong.

"I thought I told you to get out." I glared at him.

"You did," he said humbly. "But I wanted to talk. I wanna work this out."

"I don't wanna talk anymore, Derrick. I just want you to get the hell out my house. I can't take this shit anymore." I could feel tears begin to well up in my eyes. The last thing I wanted was to start getting emotional. I did not want him to see any weakness.

"Look, Jasmine. I'm sorry, ah'ight? I fucked up. I don't know what I was thinking about. You have every right to be mad."

"You damn right I have the right to be mad. You disrespected me, Derrick. You let that woman drive my car while I was taking the bus. Do you know how humiliating that is?"

"Look baby, I know I should have never let Wendy use the car. But she was just supposed to go to Food Lion and back. I didn't know she was gonna joyride around Richmond. She knew I had to pick you up. Don't you see? She was trying to fuck up things between us."

"I'm sure she was, but you should've seen this coming. It's not the first time she's pulled some shit like this, Derrick. Why do you keep letting her come between us?"

"I gotta see my son, Jasmine. You know how hard she would make that if I told her she couldn't come around? I gotta be nice to her, baby." He was pleading with me to understand, but I'd had enough.

"Look, Derrick. I just can't do this anymore. She's been trying forever to fuck things up, and you just don't seem to want to put a stop to it. You have no one to blame but yourself. Now pack your shit and get out my house before I call the police."

"Baby, please don't do this. Give me one more chance. I know that sometimes I let Wendy get away with things, but that's because I don't wanna lose Tyler. Please, baby, come on. Let me make this up to you."

"No, Derrick. I want you out!"

"Damn! Why you gonna do this? I was gonna ask you to marry me tonight." His voice was a mixture of anger and desperation, and although I was surprised, I almost believed him. Still, he'd fooled me before with his lies.

"Yeah, right. Do you really expect me to believe that crap?" I shook my head, chewing my bottom lip.

"It's the truth. That's why I bought the lobster tails and steak this morning. I was gonna make you a candlelight dinner; then right after dessert I was gonna propose."

"You fucking liar. I don't believe a word you're saying. And I don't appreciate you trying to play with my emotions like this." I walked over to the door and opened it. "Get out, Derrick. Get the fuck out my house and don't come back. I'll have your shit sent to your mother's."

He walked to the door and stopped in front of me.

"You want me to leave? Okay, I'll leave. But if I'm lying, why do I have this in my pocket?" He reached into his pocket and pulled out a small jewelry box. My jaw dropped.

"Look. I can understand if you don't want this. But I been waiting to do this all day." He opened the box, and I almost fainted when I saw the size of the rock. It had to be at least three carats.

"Jasmine, will you marry me?"

There was a part of me that wanted to scream, "Yes! Yes! I'll marry you." But after everything that happened today with Wendy, there was no way I could say that. Sure, the ring and everything was real romantic, but things weren't right between us. I was so tired of this triangle between me and him and his baby's momma, and until he put a stop to Wendy's shit, I couldn't marry him.

"I'm sorry, Derrick, but I can't. I can't do it. I love you. I'm not gonna deny that. But I can't marry you. Not the way things are."

"Then I'll change the way things are. I swear."

"How? How you gonna do that? You gonna keep Wendy away from my house?"

"Yeah," he nodded.

I'd heard his promises so many times, I wasn't sure if I

could really believe him. I glanced at the beautiful ring, then handed the box back to him.

"I'm gonna give you one last chance, Derrick. But I'm not gonna take your ring. At least not until I see some changes in the way I'm treated."

He frowned as he took the box, but then he stroked my cheek and smiled at me. "Don't worry, baby. You gonna be wearing that ring in no time. Things are gonna change. You'll see."

# 32

## Stephanie

I'd been tossing and turning for two hours, thinking about Travis and how lonely I was without him, so I was not happy when the phone started ringing and woke me up just after I finally got to sleep. *Damn* Malek! He'd been calling nonstop the last few days trying to blackmail me into sleeping with him. I must've told him no a thousand times, but he wasn't giving up. He was probably hoping that Travis would answer the phone so that he could blow up my spot again. God, I couldn't wait till Derrick and his friends took care of his ass.

"Hello?"

"Steph?"

I recognized Travis's voice right away and sat up in the bed. He'd been avoiding me for quite a while, stopping by the day care center to see the kids or coming to the house only when he knew I wasn't gonna be at home. I mean, I can't lie and say he wasn't handling his business. He was paying the bills and leaving me money on the kitchen table. But he was definitely avoiding me, and it was getting frustrating.

"Travis, is that you, baby?"

"Yeah, it's me. How are the kids?"

"They're good. T. J. sat up today for the first time, and Maleka keeps asking me when you're coming home. She misses you, Travis. And so do I."

"Well, tell her I miss her, too."

"Travis, where are you?" I was trying to hide the desperation in my voice. "I've been calling all over for you. The people at the base said you took leave. Are you all right?"

"I'm okay. I'm staying with a friend for a while. I had to get away and clear my head. Figure out what the hell I'm gonna do."

"And did you figure it out?" I held my breath. I probably shouldn't have asked that question, but I needed to know.

"Some of it. But I still have a lot of thinking to do."

"Stop thinking so much and come home, Travis." I begged. "I'll do whatever it takes. I just want us to be a family again. I don't want you at some friend's house. I want you to come home."

"I can't do that, Steph," he said flatly.

"What do you mean you can't do that? Are you trying to tell me you're not coming home? I don't like the way that sounds, Travis."

"Neither do I, Stephanie, but keep in mind, I'm not the one at fault. I'm the victim here. Remember?" I frowned when he said that. It was obvious he was still mad and probably would be for a while. I was going to have to play this carefully and be as humble as possible.

"What are you trying to say, Travis?"

"I think we need some time apart. Maybe we should date other people or something."

"No, Travis. We've spent enough time apart. And I don't wanna see other people. I want you to come home. Please, baby. Just come on home. I promise I'll make it up to you."

"How you gonna make it up to me, Stephanie? In the bedroom, under the sheets? What're you gonna do, meet me at the door in a teddy?" Damn, he knew me better than I thought.

"Yeah, maybe for starters," I told him. "What's wrong with that?"

"It's only temporary. That's what's wrong with it. Once we leave the bedroom, everything goes back to the way it was. *Fucked up.*" I'm not gonna lie—that hurt. That hurt a lot.

"Travis, you don't mean that, baby. I know you're upset and hurt about the condoms and about Malek calling the house. But you don't mean that."

"Yeah, I do, Stephanie. I mean, you don't appreciate me. I've given you everything a woman could ask for and you still kept disrespecting me."

"Travis, I never meant to disrespect you. Or hurt you."

"Well, you did," he snapped angrily. "Look, I gotta go. I'll give you a call later."

"Wait. Don't go."

"What do you want, Stephanie?"

"Do you think you can stop by for dinner some time? The kids would love to see you, and I think we need to talk some more."

"I don't think that's such a good idea. Not yet, anyway."

"Why not? It's just dinner. It's not like we're going to sleep with each other. You can leave right after dessert."

He hesitated for a minute, but to my surprise, he agreed.

"All right. I'll do it for the kids. How about tomorrow night?"

"That's fine with me," I replied. "The kids are gonna be so happy."

"Okay. I'll see you tomorrow around seven."

"Tomorrow around seven," I echoed. I hung up with a huge smile on my face. I was finally going to get back with Travis. Oh, he didn't know it yet, but when I promised that he could leave right after dessert, I forgot to mention that I was dessert.

* * *

"Mommy? Mommy?" Maleka was standing next to my bed, shaking me awake, which was no easy thing to do. I'd gotten out of bed after my call with Travis. I must've been up half the night, cooking and cleaning, getting things ready for my dinner with Travis. I wanted everything to be perfect when I seduced him. I wanted to make sure he had no doubts about coming home.

"What, Maleka? What is it, baby?" I sat up and rubbed the sleep from my eyes.

"Somebody keeps knocking at the front door." I sat there for a second and listened. She was right. Somebody was at the door. I got out of bed and looked out the window. There was a police car in my driveway. I was scared. Police never showed up in the middle of the night unless they had bad news.

"Maleka, go back to bed, baby. It's only five o'clock in the morning." I escorted her back to her room, then headed down the stairs nervously to answer the door.

"Who is it?"

"Chesterfield Police, ma'am. Are you Stephanie Johnson?"

"Yes, I'm Stephanie Johnson. Is everything all right, officer?" I opened the door and gasped at the sight in front of my eyes. "Oh, my God!"

"What's up, Shorty?" Malek managed to croak, though his mouth was so messed up I don't know how he could speak.

He was leaning against the two officers, 'cause he didn't look like he had the strength to stand on his own. His face and clothes were a bloody mess. It looked like he was in a lot of pain. Shoot, he was so messed up, if he hadn't called me Shorty I might not have recognized him. The officers helped Malek inside, and somehow we got him into the kitchen. He sat at the table and put his head down on it. I stood and spoke with the police.

"What happened to him?" I whispered the question but I knew the answer. Derrick and his friends sent their message, like I asked. Only problem was, I told him to scare Malek. From the looks of it, they tried to kill him.

"He says he got jumped. We found him about two blocks from here in his car. Says he was trying to make it over to your house but he ran out of gas."

My heart started racing like an Indy 500 car. If Malek named Derrick and his crew, I was in some deep shit.

"He got jumped? Who did this to him?" I asked with mock concern.

"He said it was too dark to see his assailants, ma'am." I breathed a sigh of relief.

"Is he okay? He looks like he should be at the hospital."

"The paramedics cleaned up his wounds, but he's still in pretty bad shape. They recommended he go to the emergency room and have some X rays. They think he might have a couple of broken ribs."

"So why'd you bring him here? Why didn't you take him to the hospital?"

"He refused to go to the hospital, ma'am. He said he wanted to come here."

"What do you mean, he refused?" I glared at the officer. "Can't you make him go?"

"No, ma'am, we can't. Not if he doesn't want to. But you're right. He should go to the hospital. There could be some internal damage."

Just the sound of that made me shudder. What if they had fucked him up so bad he was bleeding internally? I did not want to be responsible for his death just because he was too stupid to go to the hospital. I looked over at Malek's motionless body resting on my table and shook my head. If it wasn't one damn thing, it was another.

"Well, why'd you bring him here?" I folded my arms

across my chest and turned back to the cop. "Why didn't you just take him home to his momma's house?"

"He didn't mention his mother. He just asked us to take him to his girlfriend's house."

"Girlfriend! I ain't his girlfriend. I'm just his baby's mother," I protested, but it was useless. These cops didn't give a shit who I was to Malek, as long as they knew they could leave him here.

"Ma'am, we were only responding to what he told us. We can take him home if you'd prefer." It was clear from his expression that the cop did not want to have to do that.

Of course, I would've preferred to have Malek out of my house right then. Shit, I'd spent an hour scrubbing that kitchen floor so it would be sparkling for Travis's visit, and here was Malek leaving bloody footprints all over it. But I also knew I had some responsibility in this whole thing. Malek wouldn't be in this condition right now if it weren't for me. Yeah, I wanted his ass to leave me alone, but I didn't mean for it to be like this. He was my daughter's father, after all.

"Ma'am?" The officer was getting impatient. Probably close to the end of his shift, or something.

"Yeah," I sighed. "You can leave him here."

"Okay, then, Miss Johnson. I'm going to leave you the number to the station house. You be sure to call us if he remembers anything about the people who attacked him."

He handed me a card, went and spoke a few words to Malek, and then they were gone. I looked down at the number he had given me and prayed we wouldn't be needing it. The police said Malek didn't know who had jumped him. That was good news. I might be in deep shit if they found out it was Derrick and his boys. Not only would Derrick probably give me up as the one who ordered the attack, but my sister would never forgive me if her man violated his parole on my account. I had to be as nice as possible to Malek to make sure this whole incident stayed between us.

I wet some paper towels and started to clean his face. "Malek, you need to go to the hospital and have some X rays."

"Yeah, I know."

"Well, then why didn't you let the paramedics take you?"

"I wasn't going to no hospital unless you were the one to take me, Shorty."

I sighed. "Damn, Malek. Why you gotta be so difficult? You almost died tonight, and you're still worried about getting with me?"

"Naw," he managed to explain through his swollen jaw, "this ain't about getting with you. I just wanted to make sure you knew what your boy Derrick did to me. Let you know I got your little message."

I gasped and pulled my hand back from his face. So he did know who jumped him, after all.

"Malek, I . . ." Damn, I felt bad all of a sudden.

"You what, Shorty? You didn't mean it? Please, you told me you was gonna have someone kick my ass. That nigga Derrick made sure I saw his face. And he made sure I knew why he was there." He stopped for a few seconds. It was obviously painful for him even to be talking, but he was determined to make his point. "So I want you to know I got your message."

I looked at him with wide, frightened eyes. My shoulders slumped. This just couldn't get any worse.

"What do you want me to say, Malek? I didn't mean for you to be hurt this bad. You just wouldn't leave me alone. I didn't know what else to do."

"Save your bullshit for someone who cares. I got your message; now here's mine. I *will* see Maleka anytime I want, and you *will* be givin' up the booty, no questions asked."

"Please, Malek. You don't really think I'm gonna do that shit, do you?"

"Oh, yeah, you're gonna do it. Or, if you'd like, I could just regain my memory and call up my new friends at the police department. I'm sure they'd be happy to pay Derrick a little visit, ask a few questions."

I was like a trapped animal. My mind was racing, but I couldn't think of any way out of this. The best I could hope for right now was to buy myself a little more time. I doubted it, but maybe after Malek cooled off a little bit, he'd change his mind. At least I might be able to ensure his silence if I had some time to think of a plan. And it had to be one that would allow him to walk away with some dignity. See, I knew that right now Malek's demands were all about pride, anyway. He was already pissed that he couldn't have me. Before I walked out on him after Nana's funeral, he probably figured he could have me anytime he wanted. Guys can be that way sometimes. They figure once they've hit it, you'll never refuse them again.

But Malek's ego was damaged even more now. Not only was I not givin' up the ass, I'd sent someone to beat him. Talk about humiliating! No wonder he seemed determined to make my life a living hell. Well, he obviously had the upper hand. All I could do for now was be as nice as possible to him. I'd have to talk to Derrick later on and see what he wanted me to do.

"Ah'ight, Malek. I can see you and me have a lot to talk about." I spoke calmly. "But right now we both need to get some sleep."

"No doubt. I do feel like shit." He rubbed his hand gently over his bruised face.

"I'll get some sheets to put on the couch for you. In the morning I'll take you over to the hospital so you can get checked out."

"What? I ain't sleepin' on the couch."

I knew he was gonna do that, so I was ready for it.

"Malek, they said you got broken ribs. What if I roll over in the middle of the night? I don't want to hurt you. We shouldn't risk doing any more damage till a doctor takes a look at you," I explained.

"Yeah. I guess you're right. Go get me them sheets. I'm about to fall out right here on your kitchen floor."

I was so relieved to get away from him, even if it was only for a few hours until the sun came up. I got him settled on the couch and then went to bed, to toss and turn until morning.

# 33

# Dylan

"Okay, Mrs. Turner, thanks. Sorry to wake you at such a late hour."

I watched Officer Ronald Burns hang up the phone with Ellen Turner, a counselor from the Phoenix House Rehabilitation Center. Officer Burns turned to me with a smile. I sighed impatiently as I waited for him to speak. Ron and I weren't exactly friends. We were acquaintances through my buddy Joe. But right then I was hoping he considered me a friend, because I felt like my life was in his hands.

"Well, Dylan, it looks like your story checks out. You can go home right after I get the okay from my sergeant," he told me. "Man, I'm not gonna lie. For a minute there you had me pretty scared."

"Shit, you were scared? I was the one with the cuffs on. I thought I was going to jail." I tried to keep my tone respectful.

"Hey man, I'm sorry about that. I was just doing my job."

"Don't worry about it, Ron. I know you were." I offered him my hand, and he took it with a smile. "I just can't believe I got caught up in some shit like this."

"Who you tellin'? I damn near fainted when I saw my partner walk you outta that crackhouse. I'll be honest with you. I thought you'd turned crackhead on me." We both laughed, but not because anything was funny.

I'd been arrested about an hour before, or at least detained, as Ron put it, until my crazy story checked out. And when I say crazy, I mean craaaaazy. Thank God Ron was willing to hear me out and the people at Phoenix House Rehabilitation Center answered their phones, or I'd be spending the night in jail with the other people who got caught up in the midnight raid.

The whole night started when I got a call around midnight from Ellen Turner, Monica's counselor at the Phoenix House Rehabilitation Center. Ellen had called to notify me that Monica had gone AWOL for the fourth time this month. If she didn't return by eight in the morning, she'd be kicked out of the program.

It had taken just about every contact I had to get her into Phoenix House, and she was slowly but surely screwing it up. I had paid almost ten thousand dollars for her to get into the program, and Ellen made it clear this was her last chance. That was bad news. With the baby coming, I was desperate to keep Monica clean. It turned out she was more hooked on that stuff than I thought. She wasn't willing to quit on her own, like she said, so I had to force her to get help for the baby's sake. That was my child's life she was messing up with every hit of crack she smoked. Unfortunately, she was so hooked she didn't seem capable of considering the baby's health. There was only one thing she cared about, and that's what she went in search of when she left Phoenix House again.

When I got the call about her disappearance, I had a pretty good idea of where to find her. Either she was in the crackhouse on Washington Street, smoking crack, or she was on Halifax, selling her ass to get some money for crack. I decided to check out the crackhouse first, and I was right. But when I went in there to get her out, we both ended up in handcuffs. Now, thank God, I was getting ready to be released, but I wasn't sure what was gonna happen to Monica.

"What about her?" I pointed toward a cell where Monica was sitting with about ten other women who'd been caught up in the raid. "Can I take her back to Phoenix? She's pregnant."

"No. We found paraphernalia on her, along with a couple o' vials of crack. She ain't going nowhere until she sees the judge in the morning." Ron wasn't so apologetic this time.

"Well, can I at least talk to her?"

"Yeah, go 'head. But let me give you a little advice first." He turned his back to the prisoners and spoke quietly to me. "You're a nice guy, Dylan. I know you wanna help her, but trust me. You can't help someone who doesn't want help. If I was you I'd get as far away from her as possible. It's only gonna get worse. Look what happened today, and believe me, this is just the beginning."

"I appreciate the advice, Ron. But I have to help her. Maybe she doesn't want it, but that's my baby she's carrying, and I'm gonna do whatever I can to save my child."

"Well, then, good luck to you, my brother." He gave me a pat on my shoulder.

"Thanks. I'm gonna need it." We shook hands; then I walked over to the cell and spoke to Monica. She was hunched over on one of the crowded benches. She didn't look up, but she knew I was there.

"What do you want, Dylan?" she sneered.

"I just wanted to tell you that I'll see you in the morning. I'm going home."

She lifted her head and glared at me in disbelief. "You leaving me here? You're not gonna bail me out?"

"They found drugs on you. You've gotta see the judge before they'll release you."

"Why? How come you get to go home?" She started yelling. "Didn't you tell them that I'm with you? What the fuck is wrong with you, Dylan?"

"Of course I told them that. They don't care. You had crack on you." I tried to speak in a soft tone, hoping she'd lower her voice, but it didn't help.

"Well, then, make them care!" she cried. "Don't you care about the baby?"

She'd hit a nerve, and it took everything I had to control my own anger. Who the hell was she to ask me that question?

"I'm not the crackhead. So I should be asking you that. And stop yelling at me. You're making a scene." There was no use reasoning with her now. Shit, she was probably still too high to hold a conversation even if there weren't a dozen other crackheads around to hear every word. "Look, I'm outta here. I'll see you in court in the morning. Just pray they're gonna let you back in the program."

"Fuck you!" she shouted. "I'm not going back to no fucking program."

"Yes, you are. Even if I have to drag your ass there. You're not gonna fuck up my baby's life." With that, she jumped up and leaned against the cell bars to get as close as she could while she screamed the most hurtful words.

"It's not your fucking baby, so leave me the fuck alone."

"What did you say?" I could feel a rage building up inside me. I felt like everyone in the station house was staring at me.

"I said the baby's not yours, motherfucker! Can't you hear? Only reason I told you that it was is 'cause I needed a place to stay. And I knew you'd be stupid enough to let me stay in your house." She was spitting as she spoke, shaking her head the whole time.

"Yeah, right. If it's not my kid, then whose kid is it?"

"Jordan's. Who do you think? When this baby's born, he's gonna be light, bright, and almost white. Just like his daddy." She gave me an ugly smirk.

I swear it was a good thing those bars were between us; otherwise, I would have killed her ass.

"Joe was right about you the whole time. You are one hell of a bitch! How could you do this to me? How could you lie to me like that? After everything I've done for you!" Bars or no bars, I tried my best to grab her, and every woman in that cell scrambled. "You think you can play with my emotions? I'm gonna kill you, bitch! I'ma kill your fucking ass."

"Dylan! Come on, man. She ain't worth it." Ron pulled me from the cell and into another room. I sat at the table and wiped my face with my sleeve.

He waited until I calmed down a bit before he spoke. "You ah'ight, man? Think you can go back out there without making a fool outta yourself?"

"Am I all right?" I stared at him like he was insane. "That wench just told me that I'm not the father of her child. And you wanna know if I'm all right? No, Ron, I'm not all right. I just lost a child that hasn't even been born yet."

# 34

# Travis

Brittany passed by my bed on the couch as she walked from her bedroom into the kitchen. I'd been staying at her place for quite a while, so most nights I wouldn't even pay attention to her when she went by to get a midnight snack. But then again, most nights she wasn't wearing a cut-off T-shirt and a thong that exposed every inch of her perfectly round rear end.

"Travis, you awake in there?"

I lifted my head and pretended to be half asleep, but with the TV on she had to know I'd been watching her the whole time. Things had been strictly platonic between us the whole time I'd been staying at her place, but shit, I'm still a man. There was no way I was turning the other cheek when a half-naked woman walked into the room. Especially one as fine as Brittany.

"Yeah, I'm awake."

"Good. We need to talk." She walked out of the kitchen and sat in the chair next to the sofa.

"Ah'ight, what I do now?" I sat up. "Don't tell me you fell in the toilet again. 'Cause I made sure I put the seat down this time." I was trying to keep things light because Brittany sounded pretty serious.

"No, I ain't fall in the toilet again." She pretended to be angry. "Why you always gotta bring that up, anyway?"

" 'Cause the shit was funny, that's why," I laughed.

I will never forget the way she looked that night. Her legs and arms were flailing all over the place, but her ass was stuck in that toilet bowl. She was screaming at me to pull her out, but before I did, I couldn't resist. I had to run into the living room and get my camera. I never developed the film, but man, was that shit hilarious!

"Look, I didn't come out here to get laughed at. I came out here to talk to you about our living arrangements."

"Uh-oh," I sighed. "I knew this was coming sooner or later. You want me to give you some more money toward the rent?"

I didn't really think she wanted to talk about money, but I threw it out there just in case. I had to show her that I appreciated what she was doing. I didn't want her to think I was some deadbeat trying to take advantage of her kindness. But this little conversation we were about to have was about way more than money. This was about Brittany's personal space and privacy, something she'd lost when I moved in to her living room. With me there, she'd been real careful about covering herself up when she came out of the shower, taking her phone calls in her bedroom, shit like that. But I know that had to be bothering her. She should have been able to walk around her place butt-naked if she wanted to.

So I knew what she was going to say. It was time for me to leave. And as a true friend, I could appreciate that. Shoot, I don't think I could ever repay her for her kindness. She hadn't complained once the entire time I was there. As much as I didn't want to go back home yet, I owed it to Brittany to give her back her place.

"This is not about money, Travis," she replied. "You've already given me enough money to damn near pay my entire rent. I just can't have you sleeping on my couch anymore. It's just not right—"

She sounded upset, so I cut her off. "Look Brittany, I can see where this is going, and I appreciate everything you've done for me. I'm gonna go find a place on the base in the morning. I'll be out your hair by tomorrow afternoon, ah'ight?"

"No, it's not all right." Her tone surprised me. She really sounded frustrated. "Damn, don't you men understand anything about women?"

I shrugged my shoulders. "Evidently not, because I don't know what the hell is wrong with you."

She got up and sat on the edge of the couch.

"You don't know what I'm talking about? What I'm talking about is that I want you to move off my couch so that you can move into my bed, Travis." She kissed me passionately and her hands roamed my body until my manhood sprang to attention.

"Whoa. Where'd that come from?" I muttered as our lips parted.

"It came from here." She pointed at her heart, but her eyes never left mine. "Travis, I've tried to be respectful of what you have, or think you have, with Stephanie, but it's been a while now and you haven't even attempted to go home. I hope I'm not overstepping my boundaries, but you're a good man and I'm sick of waiting for you to notice that I'm a good woman."

I'm not gonna pretend like I never thought about Brittany and me getting together. Hell, everyone on base already thought we were together. But the truth is, I didn't know what to do about her. I still thought about Stephanie a lot. I had to get over one hurdle before I could attempt another.

"Are you serious, Brittany? You really wanna be with me?"

"Uh-huh." She bent down to kiss my neck. "I've never been more serious about anything in my entire life." She blew in my ear and I instinctively wrapped my arms around her back, holding on tight. I was ready to give in right then and there. She felt so damn good, and I really missed a woman's touch. But my conscience wouldn't let me do that. At least not until Stephanie and I officially broke up. I mean, hell, she was still living in my house.

"Look, Brittany. I like you. I like you a lot. But I still have feelings for Stephanie. It wouldn't be fair to you, because I wouldn't be giving a hundred percent to the relationship. Not yet, anyway." I removed my arms from around her waist.

"I know you have feelings for her, Travis. I was just hoping that you might let me help you forget about them." She gave me a quick peck on the lips then stood. "I'm going to bed, but my door is always open. Let me know when you're ready to be with someone who appreciates you." I watched Brittany's hips sway in that thong and shook my head. Damn, was I really turning down an offer to get my hands on that? Well, at least Brittany had done one good thing for me tonight. It was time for me to stop feeling sorry for myself and make a decision about Stephanie and me.

I stopped staring at the ceiling and got my ass up off the couch about an hour after Brittany went back in her bedroom. As you can probably imagine, I found it rather hard to fall asleep. Every time I closed my eyes, I'd see an image of Brittany's ass swaying back and forth in that thong, and my johnson would get rock-hard. Unlike me, my johnson didn't have a conscience. It kept trying to convince me to go in there and take Brittany up on her offer. Finally, after a lofty mental debate with my johnson, I caved in. I knocked on Brittany's bedroom door to get some of what my body was craving.

"Brittany?" There was a single candle burning, and she was lying on her bed naked. She wasn't asleep, either.

"Yes, Travis?"

"You really think you can make me forget Stephanie?"

"I sure as hell wanna try. Come on in here."

It was six in the morning when I moved Brittany's arm from around my waist and slipped out of bed. I had to give her credit. She wasn't Stephanie, but she was one hell of a sex kitten in the bedroom. We had two hours of the wildest and most uninhibited sex I'd ever had. And it was just what I needed. Or at least what I thought I needed.

I really liked Brittany. We had a lot in common, with both of us being sergeants in the army and all. And even more important, I trusted her. Long before we had a physical relationship in Germany, we had developed a great friendship. That was something Stephanie and I never had. Maybe that had been our problem. Sometimes we're more faithful to our friends than to our lovers.

All that being said, I was still reaching into Brittany's hall closet for my duffel bags. Even though I had a great time with Brittany, I still couldn't fall asleep. The sex was great, but once it was over, my conscience went into overdrive, and my mind kept drifting back home to my son, to Maleka. And yes, to Stephanie. Yeah, she'd done me wrong, and I'd probably be better off without her, but I owed it to the kids to at least try to figure this mess out. Besides, I'd forgotten something when I went into that bedroom last night. I'd forgotten that I still loved Stephanie. So the best thing for me to do was get the hell outta Brittany's house as quickly as possible. Staying with her just meant I'd end up sleeping with her again, and that would only complicate things more than they already were.

"Travis, what are you doing?" I turned and Brittany was standing in the doorway.

"I'm packing." I zipped up my duffel bag and tried to keep my eyes from wandering over her body.

"I can see that. I just don't understand why."

"Because I don't wanna hurt you, Brittany. Last night was beautiful, but it's not gonna change the fact that I'm still in love with Stephanie. I can't get her out of my head. I really thought being with you last night would help me forget, but it's gonna take more time. If I stick around here, you're just gonna get hurt, and I don't want that to happen."

I walked over and kissed her forehead. "I wish things were different." And I really did. Here was this beautiful, understanding woman offering to love me, and I was turning her down for someone who'd betrayed me over and over again.

"You're going back to her, aren't you?"

"Yeah, I think so." I nodded. "I gotta give it one more try. If only for the kids."

"Lucky kids," she said sadly. "You know, I should hate you for this, Travis. But I gotta take some of the blame. I knew what I was getting into when I asked you to sleep in my bed."

"I would understand if you did hate me, Brittany. Truth is, I hate myself for doing it. But I'd rather do this now than six months from now." I reached into my pocket. "Here's your key."

"No. Just lock the door on your way out. You never know—you may change your mind again."

I smiled at her. "You never know—I just might."

"If you do come back, Travis, just understand one thing. I want you to come back as my man. I'm not some chick you can just lay up with when you're mad at Stephanie."

"I know. And I wouldn't have it any other way."

"Take care of yourself, Travis. I'm gonna miss you."

Brittany's eyes looked misty, and she turned quickly and

headed back into her bedroom. I sighed deeply, then picked up my bags and left.

When I got to the house, I'd barely gotten out of the truck when Stephanie, fully dressed, ran out to meet me. Just the sight of her hurt. I didn't realize quite how much I'd missed her, or how guilty I'd feel about cheating on her.

"Travis? What are you doing here?"

"What do you mean, what am I doing here? I came to see the kids." I glanced at my watch. "Didn't I tell you I'd be here at seven o'clock?"

"Yeah. But I thought you meant seven o'clock this evening, not seven in the morning. We were supposed to have dinner." She looked a little nervous. Same way I felt. There was so much we had to talk about.

"Well, you don't mind if I'm a little early, do you?" I smiled, hoping to relax some of the tension. I held up a box of Krispy Kreme donuts. "I brought breakfast. Your favorite. Apple crumb."

"That's real nice, Travis."

I stepped away from the truck and headed toward the house. I expected her to follow, but she stood in her spot and called after me. "It's nice, but . . ."

"But what?"

"But I gotta pick up Big Momma and take her to the doctors. Why don't you come back this afternoon?"

"Why don't I just go with you?" I had no place else to go, anyway. And after setting eyes on Stephanie and the house that was supposed to hold our happy little family, I wanted it all back. I wanted to work things out. I took hold of her hand and stared straight in her eyes. "I'm ready to come home, Stephanie. What better way to start that than letting Big Momma know we're back together?"

"And I'm ready for you to come home, Travis." She was talking real fast, her voice was all business. She didn't seem to be moved by my little speech at all. "But I don't think Big Momma would feel comfortable having you go with us to her gynecologist."

"Oh, yeah. You're probably right." I didn't exactly wanna be there for that, either. "So why don't I just stay here with the kids until you come back?"

"No. That's not gonna work. Big Momma asked me to bring the kids, 'cause she promised to get Maleka some shoes. You know how she is. She's gonna wanna get T. J. some, too."

"Yeah, I guess you're right. Lemme just go say hi to the kids before you all leave." I stepped away from her, and Stephanie grabbed my hand in a panic.

"You can't go in there. I got a surprise in there." She had quite a grip on my arm. "And, um, it won't be ready till tonight."

"What kind of surprise?" I asked suspiciously.

Something was wrong. She was acting way too funny. I was nervous, too, but this was something else. She had begged me to come home and now she hadn't even given me a kiss. And she was doing her damnedest to keep me out of the house. Desperate, just like she'd been that night Malek was on the phone. My heart sank. Here I was hoping for reconciliation, and Stephanie was still playing games. I was afraid I already knew the rest of the story.

"Look, Stephanie. I'm gonna go kiss my kids; then I'm gonna go make me some breakfast. Whatever surprise you have for me is no big deal, because I'm home." I pulled my arm away from her and headed for the house.

"Travis, don't!" She ran behind me.

"What do you mean, don't? What's going on, Stephanie?"

"I mean, don't go in the house."

"Why?" I halted in my tracks and turned to face her. My arms were crossed tightly over my chest, because I was afraid of how I might use them if she said what I thought she would.

"Because Malek is in the house," she said quietly. I felt like I was gonna explode. My muscles tensed, and it took everything I had not to slap her.

With tears in her eyes, she tried to explain. "It's not what you think, Travis. Not at all. He just—"

My hands flew up in the air and she flinched. I took a few steps back to put some distance between us.

"He's in my house with my kids. With my son! You fucking bitch! You have fucked me over for the very last time." I took a step toward the house, then stopped myself. If I kept going, I'm sure I would have killed Malek and possibly Stephanie. "I want you out my house. You got exactly one month to get all your shit out my house."

Her eyes were wide and her voice trembled. "No, Travis! Please don't do this. Please let me explain. We can work this out. You just have to listen to me."

"Ain't nothing you could say that would make me change my mind." I headed for the truck. "I mean it, Stephanie. You got one fucking month. After that, I'm throwing your shit out."

"What about T. J.? I thought you didn't want him to grow up in the projects."

"I didn't want his mother to be a whore, either, but she is. I'll have my lawyer contact you about custody." I started the engine and watched her crumple to the ground in hysterical sobs as I drove away.

I made it back to Brittany's in record time. When I got to the door, I let myself back in with the key she'd let me keep. She was standing in the kitchen making breakfast.

"You're back? Did you forget something?" She turned away from the stove to face me. Her tone told me she wasn't expecting me—and wasn't too happy to see me. I couldn't blame her, after the way we'd left things this morning. I knew she must be pissed.

"I didn't forget anything." I sat down at the kitchen table. "Except maybe that Stephanie was no good. I should've known not to bother giving her another chance."

"What are you talking about, Travis?" She turned off the stove and came to sit at the table with me.

"She had Malek there. I can't fucking believe it. He was in my house, Brittany, with my kids."

"You didn't hurt anybody, did you?" she asked nervously.

"No. But I'm through trying to make it work with her. I told Stephanie she had a month to get her shit out my house."

"Where's she gonna go?"

"Probably back to her grandmother's house. I really don't give a shit. We're through."

"What about the kids?"

"I ain't worried about that. Stephanie might be a ho, but she loves them kids. She knows I love them, and she knows they love me. If she's got one decent bone in her body, she'll do the right thing."

Brittany sat silently for a minute. I waited to see what she would say. It could go either way right now. I might've been bringing more drama than she could handle. I wouldn't blame her if she put my ass out, told me to find another place to stay.

"So why'd you come back here? This ain't about you looking for revenge, is it? I don't want you comin' back here just to make Stephanie mad for a while, then I end up kicked to the curb so you can make up with her again."

"I meant what I said, Brittany. You know I've never lied to

you. I won't ever be going back to her. I mean, shit, there's only so much a man can take."

Again, she didn't answer right away. Got a faraway look in her eyes as, I guess, she imagined the possibilities.

"Look. I'm ready to move on. If you want, I'll move back onto base. Just don't shut me out. We can take it as slow as you want, but I want you to give me a chance. Let me show you that I mean what I say."

Brittany reached across the table and took my hand in hers. Finally, she gave me a real smile. She pulled me up from my chair and started leading me through the living room, toward her bedroom.

"Well, then. Let's rewind back to last night. Pretend this morning never happened. You wanna start over? Come on in here and show me what you mean."

# 35

# Jasmine

"Jasmine! Jasmine!"

It was Thursday evening, and my whole family was over to celebrate my mother's fiftieth birthday. My aunt Mary made pigs' feet and collard greens, and Big Momma made my favorite homemade sweet potato pie with the coconut on top. We were havin' a real good time. Well, at least I was until Big Momma started yelling my name.

"What you want, Big Momma? I'm right here." She was sitting at the kitchen table with my momma and a few other relatives. I was standing right behind her, slicing the pie at the kitchen counter.

"Whatever happened to that good-looking Dylan Taylor? Lord knows he's the man you should be getting married to next week. Not that no-good, drug-dealin' *Derrick.* I bet it was his idea to have this heathen wedding in Sin City you planning to have."

That's when I knew Big Momma wasn't happy at all with the fact that Derrick and I had planned to elope to Las Vegas next week. She was never one to hide her feelings. And believe me, she let it be known that she did not approve of me getting married away from my family and friends to a man she thought was beneath me. And the fact that I wasn't getting married in church made things even worse.

I knew Big Momma would be mad when she found out I

was marrying Derrick, so I tried to keep the wedding a secret until we came back from Vegas. I was doing pretty good, too, until big-mouth Sabrina started yapping about how she couldn't believe I was getting married next week. And she didn't do it in private. My whole family was there when she opened her damn trap. Next thing I knew, everyone in the house was asking me fifty million questions.

I must admit, though, my momma made me feel good. Whatever she thought of Derrick, she kept her opinions to herself. She kissed me and offered to let me use her wedding dress. But Big Momma wasn't about to let me off so easy. She let it be known, loud and clear, that she thought I was making the biggest mistake of my life. Why couldn't I find a good man, like Stephanie had found Travis? I had to bite my tongue when she said that. Everyone in the room knew how Stephanie had handled her good man. But I wasn't about to bring that up, even if it might've taken the heat off me. So I just shut my mouth tight, hoping that it would all just pass, but Big Momma brought up the one person I was trying to forget. She hadn't stopped reminding me since.

"Child, did you hear me?" she asked again. "Whatever happened to Dylan?"

"We don't speak anymore, Big Momma." I tried to sound matter-of-fact, even though it hurt just saying those words out loud. I really missed Dylan.

"I thought you said he was one of your best friends."

"He was, Big Momma. But things have changed a lot in the past few months, and well . . ." I hesitated. "Dylan and I are better off this way."

"She's lying, Mrs. Washington." Sabrina had come into the kitchen and interrupted. "Derrick and his friends beat Dylan up so bad that he hasn't been around since."

My mother, who was sitting at the kitchen table with one of my aunts, stared at me. In fact, it felt like all eyes in the room were on me. Well, except for Sabrina's. She was avoiding eye contact with me. But what else should I expect from a sister who had just sold me out?

"Is that true, Jasmine?" Big Momma turned to face me. I wiped my hands on my apron.

"He didn't mean it, Big Momma," I explained. "He thought Dylan was trying to break into my car. That's all. Tell her, Sabrina."

Sabrina didn't say a word.

"Don't be making no excuses for him, child. I told you before, that boy ain't no good. Where the hell is he, anyway?"

I couldn't answer her. Derrick and I had had a big fight earlier, because he didn't want to be around my family. He knew how Big Momma felt about him, and he said he didn't need to be treated like shit by my grandmother. I begged him to stick around for my sake, hoping that they could make peace. Derrick just needed to show Big Momma what a great man he really was. But he wasn't having it. He said he didn't need to prove nothin' to no one, and then he stormed out. I had no idea where he was.

"How you gonna call yourself marrying somebody that can't even come to your mother's birthday party?"

"Momma," my mother interrupted the discussion that was about to turn into an argument. I was tired of Big Momma constantly disrespecting Derrick. "Why don't we have our dessert and watch the video of T. J.'s christening?"

"Okay, Betty Jean." Big Momma took her voice down a few notches. "But Jasmine, me and you gonna have a nice, long talk tomorrow. You hear? So just be prepared."

As everybody else took their slices of pie and headed for the living room, I could feel my head starting to ache. I went upstairs to the bathroom and pulled out the Tylenol. This was slowly but surely turning into one of those days.

"There's a lot of pills in that bottle. You're not gonna do anything stupid just because Big Momma pissed you off, are you?" Stephanie had followed me upstairs. I sighed as I opened the bottle and answered her.

"No, I'm not gonna do anything stupid. I just got a headache." I took out two pills and shoved them in my mouth. "Can you believe Sabrina told Big Momma about Dylan getting beat up? I thought that wench was my friend."

"Well, you never know who your friends are these days."

"That's for sure." I placed the bottle back in the medicine cabinet and turned to face Stephanie. She looked so concerned.

"What I wanna know, Jasmine, is why the hell you're marrying Derrick so soon. He's just got outta jail two months ago. Are you just tryin' to rub it in my face 'cause I never made it to the altar?"

"What? Please, this ain't got nothing to do with you. I'm marrying him because I love him, Stephanie. I been waiting for him to get outta prison for three years."

I knew Stephanie was going to be jealous about my engagement. Especially since she and Travis weren't together anymore. But I never thought she'd be judging me for choosing Derrick. Shit, it wasn't like he was any worse than Malek.

"Big Momma's right, Jasmine. He's not a good guy at all." Stephanie was pissing me off with her holier-than-thou attitude. I had Big Momma downstairs to give all the lectures I needed. I did not need one from her. Besides, who was she to give anyone advice after the way she messed things up with Travis?

"How the hell would you know if he's a good man, Stephanie? You haven't spent more than five minutes with Derrick since he's been home."

Stephanie folded her arms across her chest and stared at me, hard and long.

"Are you sure about that? You do a lot of overtime, don't you? How do you know how much time I spend with Derrick? How do you know how much time anyone spends with him and that big old johnson of his?" Stephanie sucked her teeth and smirked at me like she had a secret. What the hell was she up to? And how the hell did she know how big Derrick was? Suddenly, my headache was worse.

"Look, Steph, if you got something to say, then say it. Otherwise, don't play with me about my man. Keep it up and you and I will be fighting, party or no party." I put my finger in her face for effect.

"Look, you don't have to act all shitty with me. Like you used to tell me, I'm your sister. I just don't wanna see you get hurt. All I'm saying is, watch your back. Derrick's not the man you think he is."

"You better not be fucking my man, Stephanie." What the hell was she trying to tell me? Could my own sister really have sunk so low as to sleep with my man?

"You got a lot bigger problems than me fucking him. At least I'd give him back." She turned around and walked down the stairs. "You may not know it, Jasmine, but I love you. Remember that."

She loved me. I sure didn't hear that too often from her. But right now I was more concerned with what else she had told me. I wasn't quite sure what she was warning me about, but I was sure as hell going to find out when Derrick got home. Maybe Stephanie was just making this up so I could join her club of losers who couldn't get married. Or maybe, just maybe, my sister knew a hell of a lot more about Derrick than she was telling me. I was going to have to keep a close eye on both of them.

I went down the stairs a few minutes after Steph and was amazed at how quiet the house was. There were at least fifteen adults in the house and five kids, but I didn't hear a sound except for a few of the kids out back. It was highly unusual to have a party with my family where Big Momma's mouth couldn't be heard from every corner of the house. I was getting nervous and then confused, when I walked into the living room and saw everyone just sitting there. Momma had her hand over her mouth, and her eyes were wet. A million things ran through my mind as I looked around and realized everyone in the room was staring at me.

"What is it?" I asked, afraid of the answer.

"Jasmine, baby, come here." Big Momma put out her cigarette and reached her hand out to me. I went to her chair and sat on the arm. She slipped her arm around my waist.

"Gerald, move out the way."

My uncle Gerald was a big, fat, jolly man who was always smiling. Except for now. His face was as scary-serious as everyone else's in the room.

"Momma, I don't know if this is such a good idea," he said.

"I told you to move, boy!" Big Momma raised her cane as if she were about to knock Gerald out. He moved out the way reluctantly, and I got a view of the TV. That's when my entire life came crashing down on me. There on the television was a video of Derrick in our bedroom. Some woman's head was bobbing up and down in his crotch area, and the two of them were just moanin' away. I tried to make out who the woman was, but the camera was showing more of her ass than her face. One thing was for sure: it wasn't Stephanie. She had a big old birthmark on her ass I remembered ever since we were kids. It was probably that bitch Wendy, but I couldn't be sure.

My eyes were glued to the TV screen, and I started to cry.

That's when I felt Big Momma squeeze me, and I remembered I wasn't alone watching this horror. It had to be the most embarrassing moment of my life. I started screaming.

"Get the fuck out my house! All of you, get the fuck out my house!" I pointed toward the door.

"Now, baby, don't get mad at us." Big Momma was the only one bold enough to speak. "We your family. We gonna be here no matter what."

"I don't give a damn about that, Big Momma. All I want is for you to get the hell outta my house. Can't you understand that? Just get!"

They started to scatter at that point. Even Big Momma gave up and headed for the door. A few people put a hand on my shoulder and tried to comfort me as they walked by, but I wasn't going for it. I just pointed them toward the door.

"You gonna be ah'ight, Jasmine?" Stephanie was the last one to leave.

"What the fuck you think?" I was nearly hysterical by this point, but Stephanie wasn't giving up. She kept talking.

"After all the mistakes I made with Travis, Jasmine, I don't know what to think anymore. I just hope you leave him."

"You knew, didn't you? You knew he was fucking around on me?"

She looked down at the ground. "I wasn't sure what he was doing, but I didn't like what I saw when I came by your house. It wasn't right having that bitch around while you're at work."

"Why didn't you tell me, Stephanie?"

"Would you have believed me?"

I hesitated because she was right—I probably wouldn't have.

"You still should have told me, Steph."

"I couldn't tell you. Not without any evidence. He would

have lied, and you would have believed him. And the only one who would have gotten hurt would be me. I would have lost a sister I'm just now getting to know."

I looked at her sadly as she continued.

"You need to get away from him as fast as possible, Jasmine."

"You think I don't know that? I can't help it if I still love the fool."

I must have sounded as helpless as I felt, 'cause Stephanie didn't stick around with any more words of wisdom. I guess I couldn't blame her. I had just finished kicking everyone out, and they were all probably waiting outside to hear what I said to her. She could only stay but so long before Big Momma got pissed.

"Look, I gotta go. Momma and them are waiting in the van. I love you." She wrapped her arms around me and hugged me tight.

"I love you, too, Stephanie." She went outside and headed for her car. All the others had gone, but there was Big Momma in the front seat of the van, watching us closely. I could only imagine what she was thinking right about now.

"Stephanie!" I yelled, and she turned around. "Who is she?"

"Who?"

"The girl in the video."

"Shit, I thought you knew."

I shook my head. "I didn't see her face."

"Well, maybe that's a good thing. 'Cause trust me, you don't wanna know."

I had to take her word for that, because she wasn't offering any more details. If I could stand it, I'd have to watch the tape again from the beginning. I couldn't hurt any worse than I already did, and at least then I'd know who Derrick thought it was worth losing me for.

Stephanie called out one more time as she started the car. "Jasmine! Call Dylan. I saw him in the mall and he was asking about you. He's the kinda guy you wanna get with. He kinda reminds me of Travis." I could hear Big Momma agreeing from the passenger seat.

I thought about what she said as I watched her drive away. She was right. Maybe I would call Dylan.

# 36

# Dylan

I'd just pulled in front of my store, and like so many other times in the past few months, I found myself daydreaming about Jasmine. It seemed like forever since I'd seen her, and even though I'd gotten my ass kicked by Derrick and his boys because of her, I missed the hell outta that woman. I closed my eyes, and an image of her beautiful face took over my thoughts. Well, at least it did until Joe started banging on the passenger-side window of my car like a madman. That fool scared me so bad I almost peed on myself.

"Hey, man! Open the door. I need to talk to you," his voice boomed, even through the glass.

When I finally regained my composure, I gave him the finger. He stood with his arms crossed and laughed at me. He always did enjoy fuckin' with me.

"Goddamn it, Joe! What the hell'd you do that for? You tryin' to give me a heart attack or something?"

"Sorry, man. I couldn't resist." He reached for the latch. "Open up. I got something important I gotta tell you." I hit the unlock button. He opened the door and slid in. It took a few seconds for him to adjust the seat to accommodate his large six-foot-five frame, but when he was settled, he turned to me with a dead-serious expression.

"Drive."

"Drive? I ain't going nowhere." I took my keys out of the ignition. "I gotta open the store."

"Look, you can open the store when we get back. This is important. Now, come on." He gestured at the ignition.

"What's going on, Joe? Where we going?" I placed the keys back in the ignition and started the car.

"Southside Regional," he said flatly.

"Southside Regional . . . *Medical Center?"* He nodded as I pulled into the street. "Why we going there? You sick?"

"You asked me to find Monica, didn't you?"

"Yeah."

"Well, I found her. She's at Southside Regional."

"Is she all right?" I asked in a worried whisper.

"Yeah, she's fine. But rumor has it you mighta became a daddy last night." My eyes lit up.

"Monica had the baby?" I tried to sound nonchalant, but a wave of excitement passed through me. I know she told me the baby wasn't mine, but I still wanted a blood test. No matter what she screamed at me from that jail cell, my heart leaped at the thought of possibly being a father. I'd invested too much of my emotions in this whole situation and lost Jasmine in the process. I had to see this through. I had to find out if the baby was mine.

"Dylan! Dylan, you ah'ight, man?" Joe roused me from my shocked state.

"I'll be ah'ight, man. I just didn't think this day would come so soon. She wasn't supposed to have the baby for a few weeks," I told him. I really didn't feel like getting into the million other things I was thinking at the moment, such as, was I really the baby's father? And, more important, was the baby born healthy?

We rode in silence the rest of the way as I sorted through the array of feelings that were coming at me in waves. I was so nervous by the time we got to the hospital, I thought my knees were gonna give out. It's a good thing I had Joe with me, because it probably would have taken me an hour to find the maternity ward.

"Excuse me, beautiful. We're looking for Monica Cooper's room." Joe smiled flirtatiously at the woman behind the desk as we stepped off the elevator onto the sixth floor.

"I'm sorry, sir. Visiting hours don't start till noon."

Joe pointed at me. "What about him? He's the baby's daddy."

"Oh, that's a little different. Let me see what I can do. What's her name again?"

"Monica Cooper," Joe replied.

The woman looked down at a chart, and I got even more nervous. What if there was a note alerting her that Monica didn't wanna see me or have me see the baby?

"Cooper, Cooper. Monica Cooper. Here it is." She looked up at me. "Looks like she had a C-section last night. What's your name, sir?"

"Dylan Taylor," I told her nervously.

She picked up the phone, dialing some numbers. "Hi, Monica. This is Carol, from the nurses' station. There's a gentleman out here by the name of Dylan Taylor." She listened for a few seconds. "All right, I'll send him down."

"You're gonna have to wait here with me." She smiled at Joe. "But *you* can go see Monica. She's right down the hall on your left. Room six twenty-three. Congratulations."

"Thank you," I told her halfheartedly as I turned to Joe. "I'll be right back."

"Don't worry about me. I'll be here when you get back." He glanced at the woman's name tag. "Won't I, Carol?" Joe grinned and the woman blushed. I just shook my head as I walked down the hallway. That Joe sure had a way with women.

So while he stayed at the desk and flirted, I headed down the hall, more scared than I'd been in a long time. Joe had no idea how much I really wanted him to go with me. I didn't know what I was about to walk into. Would Monica scream on me again as soon as she saw me, or would she welcome me and let me hold the baby? And of course, there was still the question of how I would feel about this child, who may or may not be mine.

When I first walked into the room, I was relieved. It was a big room with four beds in it. Only one other bed was occupied on this morning. The curtain was drawn around it, so I didn't see the couple, but I could hear the murmurs of proud new parents cooing at their infant. This was good news for me. I figured that with strangers in the room, Monica would at least have to try and act civil. When I saw her in the bed in the back, I was pleasantly surprised to see that she was more than civil. She was smiling at me.

Monica was propped up in her bed, holding the baby. And believe it or not, she looked pretty good. I was expecting her to look all skinny and cracked out, but she didn't. She almost looked like her old self. I mean, she was obviously tired from giving birth, but that was it. If you didn't know her, you wouldn't guess she was a drug user.

"Hi, Dylan," she said quietly as I crossed the room to her bed.

I was so mesmerized by the sight of the baby in her arms that I didn't even answer her. I'm sure this must have offended her, 'cause as I got closer to look at the baby, she kinda hunched over like she didn't want me to see the bundle in her arms.

"I just had a fucking C-section and you can't even say hi?" Her voice was a little harsher, but she was trying to keep it down so as not to disturb the other couple in the room. So maybe she was still mad about our last encounter, but at least she wasn't screeching at me the way she was in the jail.

"I'm sorry. Hi, Monica, how you feeling?" I replied quickly, making sure to keep any trace of attitude out of my tone. I didn't wanna fight with her. I had more important things to do. And she obviously knew what I was there for, 'cause once I acknowledged her, she gave me what I wanted: a view of the baby.

"I'm all right, I suppose." She sat up and loosened the blanket from around the baby. I swear, my heart felt lighter in my chest when she exposed the small, brown face. I know it's not scientific, but that baby's dark pigment meant the world to me. Oh, I knew there was still the possibility that the baby could be Jordan's, but now the odds were considerably in my favor. I smiled softly at the beautiful child.

"Is it a boy or a girl?" I mumbled.

"A boy. His name is Davon."

"A boy . . . a boy. I always wanted a son." I was choked up. "Can I hold him?"

"Okay. Just be careful."

I pulled a chair next to the bed and sat down, arms outstretched. Monica placed Davon gently in my arms and I cradled his tiny body close to mine. My heart was pounding till it felt like it would burst. He had to be the most gorgeous baby I'd ever seen. It was love at first sight. I didn't wanna ever let him go. Sadly, as I gazed at this beautiful child, reality set in.

"Is he healthy? I mean, he doesn't have that shit in him, does he?"

"I don't think so," Monica answered honestly. "I mean, I haven't been getting high lately, if that's what you're asking."

"You haven't been getting high?" I made sure she heard my disbelief. "You broke outta rehab four times to get high.

And now you expect me to believe you just stopped using? Please, Monica. Do I look stupid?"

She actually looked insulted! But I didn't care. Somebody had to be straight with her. There was no reason to avoid the issue now. In fact, with Davon here, it seemed even more important to face it.

"I just did thirty days in the Petersburg jail for having drugs during that raid. How the hell did you expect me to get high?" she tried to explain. But I wasn't about to let her off so easy.

"You can get drugs in jail. You think I don't know that?"

"Yeah, you can get high if you got money. I didn't even have money for cigarettes, so I damn sure wasn't getting high."

I let the issue drop for now. That was her story, and it looked like she was stickin' to it. I made a mental note to ask the doctor later if the baby was checked for drugs in his system.

"Well, let's hope the other eight months you were getting high doesn't affect him. . . ." I kissed the baby, suddenly sorry for the life he would have to lead with Monica as his mother. "So, you're probably gonna get high the second you get outta here, aren't you? I bet you wish you could get a hit right now." She looked away, answering my question without saying a word. "You're pathetic, Monica. You know that?"

"Look, I didn't ask you to come here and lecture me, Dylan. So just gimme my baby and get the hell outta here." She pointed at the door.

"You want me to leave?"

"You don't understand English? Yes, I want you to leave." She raised her voice and looked at me like I was stupid.

"Keep it down, Monica," I warned her. I felt bad for the

other couple, who had suddenly become silent. Our drama was definitely intruding on their happy little family moment.

"Okay, I'll leave," I whispered. "All you gotta do is tell me the truth. Is Davon my son? 'Cause if he is, you ain't getting rid of me. I'm not gonna abandon my child. You know me better than that."

Monica's expression relaxed, but she still didn't answer me. She wouldn't even make eye contact. I repeated the question.

"Is the baby mine, Monica?"

"I don't know," she said sadly. "I hope so. 'Cause Jordan's ass ain't worth a shit."

"Damn. This is bullshit, Monica. What the fuck happened to you? You weren't like this when me met." I was trying to keep my voice down, but it was getting harder to keep my emotions in check. Luckily for everyone in the room, we were interrupted by a knock on the door.

"I heard you wanted to see me, Ms. Cooper. How you feeling?" A short, balding white man wearing a lab coat walked into the room.

"I'm doing all right, Dr. Benson. Just a little tired," Monica answered.

"How are your stitches?"

"A little sore."

"Well, that's to be expected. I'll see if I can get you something for that." The doctor turned and smiled at me kindly. "And who is this young man holding the baby? Is he the father?"

All of a sudden, Monica was speechless. The Monica I once knew would have been totally embarrassed to be in the situation she was in now. I guess she still had a little pride left, 'cause she was not about to admit she couldn't name the father of her child. I didn't give a shit about her pride. I answered the doctor.

"That's up in the air, doc. We're still trying to sort that out."

I expected a disapproving look from the doctor, but I guess he'd seen it all before.

"Well, if it's a matter of paternity," he suggested, "we can give you a simple swab test here and take care of that. It'll take a couple of days to get the results, but by the time Monica's released, you should know."

I didn't bother to ask for Monica's opinion. My only concern was finding out for sure about this beautiful child in my arms. I needed to know if I was his father, so I could start making plans.

"Sounds good to me, doc. When can we do it?"

"Just let me finish my rounds and then I'll be back with some consent forms. We can do it this morning if you're both in agreement." His eyes moved from me to Monica. She nodded her approval, though she refused to make eye contact with me or the doctor.

"Okay, then. I'll be back in a little while." The doctor turned and left us alone. I'm sure the happy couple was relieved that Monica and I didn't speak at all until the doctor came back to give us the test that would determine the course of the rest of my life.

I stepped off the elevator and into the maternity ward of the hospital, carrying a car seat in one hand and my paternity papers in the other. Joe's new friend Carol was sitting at the nurses' station. I gave her a smile and a warm hello. She didn't respond, though. Matter of fact, she actually frowned when we made eye contact. I ignored her and walked past the station toward Monica's room. I guess her date with Joe last night must not have gone too well. I wasn't gonna let that bother me, though. Especially since, after three painful days of waiting, I'd finally received the paternity results proving Davon was my son.

"Excuse me, Dylan?" I turned around and saw Carol. She had come from the station and was standing in the corridor.

"Were you calling me?"

"Yes, I was." She hesitated. "I just wanted to tell you she's not there."

"What are you talking about? Who's not there?"

"Ms. Cooper. She's not in her room. She checked out a few hours ago."

"Monica checked out?" I froze. Carol nodded.

"Where'd she go?"

"I don't know. She left with an older man, but I don't think they knew each other very well."

"Why's that?"

"When he came to ask for her, he didn't know her last name."

"And you let her leave with him? They're probably going somewhere to smoke crack. What's wrong with you people?"

"We can't tell patients who they can and cannot leave with. The only thing we require is a release from the doctor and a car seat for the baby."

"Car seat for the baby! Oh, my God! Please, tell me my son's still here. Please." I held my breath and said a prayer as I waited for her answer. When she didn't respond quickly enough, I ran straight to the nursery. I looked in every single bassinet they had, but couldn't find my son. I finally stopped dead in my tracks when I looked up at the big board they had on the wall. My son's name had a black mark through it and *discharge* written in red.

That's when I realized I couldn't breathe. My heart began to race, and my chest tightened up. A knot developed in my stomach that dropped me to one knee. I swear to God, I thought I was having a heart attack, the pain was so bad. It took me a good sixty seconds to recover from what I soon realized was not a heart attack but an anxiety attack.

"Dylan? You all right?" It was Carol.

"My son's not here, is he?"

"No, she took him with her," Carol replied tentatively.

"This can't be happening. This can't be happening to me," I repeated.

# 37

# Jasmine

I must have watched that video twenty times before Derrick came home. He was calm, cool, and collected. Judging from the way he strolled in, he had no idea what had gone down earlier in the day. He had no idea that right now all his clothes and personal shit were on the lawn below our bedroom window. Just knowing that shit was out there made me feel a little better. At least enough that I could look at him now without crying.

"Hey, baby, everything go ah'ight with your mom's party?"

"Yeah, I wish you could have been here." I smirked at him. "You were the main topic of conversation. In fact, my family saw a part of you they'll never forget."

"Is that so?" He looked puzzled.

"Yeah, let me show you." I clicked the remote for the VCR and watched Derrick's skin turn pale.

"Oh, shit." He collapsed onto the couch, his mouth hanging open.

"How could you, Derrick?" I finally broke down in tears. "And with Sabrina! That's my best fucking friend!"

I couldn't believe it, but he wasn't trying to come up with some creative lie. All he did was stand there and stare at me. I wanted to get up and smack the shit out of him. My world was crumbling around me, and he was as calm as a meditating monk.

"Where'd you find it?" he finally asked.

"Big Momma found it in the camcorder. They thought it was the tape from T. J.'s christening."

He turned his head and bit his lip. I wondered what was making him feel worse, the fact that he was stupid enough to leave the evidence in the camera, or the thought that my whole family had watched his damn freak show with Sabrina. I looked at him from where I was sitting, and I just wanted to explode. But it wasn't all about Derrick. Oh, he and I were through. There was no question about that. But I was just as angry with Sabrina. She'd broken every rule in the friendship book.

"Why Sabrina, Derrick? Do you hate me so much that you had to fuck my best friend?"

He started to sniffle like he was holding back tears. As if it was going to get him sympathy or something.

"What the fuck are you sniffling about?" I shouted. "I'm the one who should be crying! I'm the one who got fucked over! I could have fucked a hundred men while you were upstate, motherfucker! But I didn't do shit! So tell me, what the fuck are you crying about?"

He turned around to walk up the stairs, probably to get his shit. He couldn't possibly think I was gonna let him stay. But I had to make it perfectly clear he was out of my life.

"You ain't staying here, motherfucker! And your shit ain't upstairs, 'cause I tried to do a Terry McMillan on your ass and burn it up!"

"My comic books," he mumbled.

"You damn right! That was the first shit to go." Believe it or not, that was the first thing that got him to show any real emotion since he walked through the door. It was sickening how important those damn comic books were to him.

"Bitch, you burnt up my comic books!" he yelled, stomping toward me. "Do you know how much them things are worth? I'm gonna kill yo' ass."

I believed him, too. He grabbed me by the shoulder and raised his fist high above me. I struggled to get loose.

"Come on, motherfucker! I wish you would hit me! But if you hit me, you damn sure better kill me, 'cause I'll have your parole violated before you get out the door."

I'd hit a nerve. He sure wasn't ready to give up his newly earned freedom so quickly. The grip on my shoulder loosened. I wiggled free and ran to the other side of the room.

"I love you, Jasmine. I've never loved anyone more than I love you."

"You don't know what love is, Derrick." We were both panting from the exertion. "Now, get the fuck out my house. And I better not catch your ass trying to stay with that bitch Sabrina."

"You're making a big mistake, Jasmine. Let me stay and we'll work this out, boo," he pleaded.

"Get the fuck out. Now!" I turned my back and waited until I heard the sound of the front door slamming.

My eyes were stinging from holding back the tears, but I was not about to cry now. That man had hurt me so many times, and I was furious. I thought it was bad, way back at the start of our relationship, when I found out he was really a drug dealer. But even that lie wasn't as bad as what he had just done to me. I'd been faithful to Derrick for three long, lonely years while he was away. Shoot, I'd even made nice with his pain-in-the-ass baby's momma, bringing her money and watching her kid. And this was how Derrick repaid me. I guess all my sacrifice meant nothing to him if he could throw it all away for a damn blow job.

I looked around the apartment at all the photos of Derrick and me. Him with that pretty-boy smile, always with his arm around me. And me looking up at him like he was the best thing that ever happened in my life. I felt like such a fool. Just the sight of those memories made me hurt. I had to get out of the apartment. I grabbed my keys and headed for my car, not sure where I was going.

I got onto U.S.1 heading south, thinking that a drive might clear my head. And it did help a little. I drove for at least an hour, surfing through radio stations to avoid hearing any romantic song that might remind me of Derrick. My mind wandered back over so many incidents in our relationship that at the time seemed minor. In the bigger picture, though, it was becoming clear that Derrick really never was the great man I thought he was. There were so many times he'd manipulated me. I was forever giving in to his demands, doing things a real man would never have asked of his woman in the first place. And yet with Derrick, not only did he ask me to do them, but he worked every possible angle until he got me to agree. But I guess I was at fault, too. I should have been stronger, said no a lot sooner. The more I thought about it, the more I realized we were both just really bad for each other. After all we'd been through, I doubted I could ever hate Derrick, but I was pretty sure that soon I'd be happy to be without him.

So as I drove, my mood started to improve a little bit. I was actually singing along with a song on the radio when I got the call that put me right back in a foul mood.

"Hello?"

"Jasmine."

"Who is this? I can barely hear you."

"It's me. Sabrina." I almost swerved into another lane.

"What the fuck do you want, bitch? You already fucked my man." I hung up the phone, but she called right back.

"Stop calling me!" I shouted.

"Jasmine, you gotta listen to me." She spoke fast. "I'm sorry. It was an accident. I didn't mean for this to happen."

"An accident! What? Did you accidentally wrap your lips around his dick so that my whole family could see you suck it? Please, bitch, don't insult me. You already got an ass-kicking coming to you. Don't make it worse than it already is." She had me so pissed off, I ran a red light.

*Whoop! Whoop! Whoop! Whoop!*

I looked in my rearview mirror and saw the flashing lights of a police car.

"Damn it! See what you did, bitch?" I clicked off the phone. "Shit! What the hell else is gonna happen today?"

I pulled over to the side of the road and waited for the officer to get out of his car. A tall, broad-shouldered cop approached my car. He shined his flashlight in my face.

"License and registration, please."

I thumbed through my purse and handed the information to him.

"You know you just ran a red light, don't you?"

"I'm sorry, officer. I didn't realize it until I was halfway through."

"Well, this is a heavy pedestrian area. You might wanna stay off that cell phone and pay attention to the road."

"I know, officer. I'm just having a bad day. I just found out my boyfriend is cheating on me with my best friend."

"Is that so?" He actually looked sympathetic as he handed back my license and registration. "Look, I'm gonna let you off with a warning, but—" Something in the car caught his eye and made him pause. "Ma'am what's that?" He pointed at my ashtray. I gasped when I saw the half blunt lying there. Once again, Derrick had screwed me over.

"It looks like a blunt," I admitted. "But I swear it's not mine. My boyfrie—"

He didn't let me finish. "Have you been smoking marijuana, ma'am?"

"No. I don't mess with that stuff," I told him honestly. "I

work at the post office. We have random drug tests." I guess he'd used up all his sympathy with my first story, 'cause now he wasn't hearing it.

"Ma'am, can you step outta the car, please?"

"Step out the car? For what? I told you it's not mine."

"I understand that, but I'm gonna have to search the car. So I'm gonna need you to stand over here." He pointed to the spot on the curb where he wanted me to go, and then he opened my car door. I was not happy, and I let him know it.

"Go 'head. There's nothing in my car but that blunt."

"Well, if that's the case, you're lucky, because we only give citations for that amount of marijuana. Now, can you sit on the curb, please?"

I sulked over to the curb and sat down to watch the officer begin his search. After a few minutes, another squad car pulled up, and an officer got out to assist. The two of them looked through the car pretty quickly, and they didn't find anything, just like I knew they wouldn't. I smirked at them as they headed for the trunk. I couldn't wait to get back in my car and go home. One of the officers stepped away from the trunk and gestured for me to get up.

"Ma'am, can you please stand up and place your hands behind your back?"

"Hands behind my back? For what?" I asked as he came near.

"Ma'am, you're under arrest for possession and intent to distribute a controlled substance." His partner held up a sandwich bag full of white powder.

"What? That's not mine. That's Derrick's." I was so shocked, I couldn't even cry. "It has to be his, 'cause it ain't mine. It's not mine."

"Well, it's in your car and you're driving," he stated with no emotion. "So I have to inform you of your rights. You have the right to remain silent. . . ."

# 38

# Stephanie

"Commonwealth of Virginia versus Jasmine Johnson. Possession of a controlled substance with the intent to distribute," the clerk shouted as he handed the judge a folder.

A door to the right of the judge swung open. The occupants of the courtroom watched as three sheriff's deputies escorted my sister to the front of the courtroom. She looked like shit in those orange overalls. Her hair was a mess, and you could see from her smudged mascara that she'd been crying. I've never felt so sorry for anyone in my entire life.

I'd gotten the news that Jasmine had been arrested late last night, when the operator woke me with a collect call. Jasmine never called collect, so I was nervous as I accepted the charges.

"Stephanie?" Jasmine's voice was low.

"Are you all right? Did Derrick do something to you? You're not at the hospital, are you?"

"No, I'm not at the hospital."

"Thank God," I sighed with relief. "So why the hell are you calling me collect?"

"Stephanie, I'm in jail. I got arrested." Her voice cracked like she was about to cry.

"Arrested? For what? Don't tell me. Your license was suspended?"

"I wish it was that simple." Now she was scaring me.

"You did something to Derrick, didn't you? Oh, my God, you didn't kill him, did you?" I knew my sister was upset about the video, but I didn't think she was that upset. To be honest, I didn't think she was capable of hurting anyone enough to get herself locked up.

"No, I didn't do anything to Derrick; he did something to me. He left drugs in my car."

"Oh, shit. No, he didn't."

"Yes, he did," she sobbed. "Look, Steph I need you to call Big Momma and see if you can get me a lawyer. Tell her I need a good one, 'cause they're talking about giving me fifteen years."

So now here I was the next morning, watching my sister trembling in front of the judge, waiting for her lawyer. It was obvious she hadn't slept a wink. She sighed when a tall, wiry, baldheaded white man stepped forward.

"Robert Smith for the defense, Your Honor. Waive reading." The judge wrote something down on the file, then turned to the Commonwealth attorney. "Mr. Green, what have you got?"

"Your Honor, Ms. Johnson was pulled over for a routine traffic violation. Her car was searched after the arresting officer found marijuana within her immediate reach. During the search of her car, the arresting officer and his partner found approximately twenty grams of cocaine."

"This looks pretty serious; Mr. Smith, how does your client plead?" the judge addressed Jasmine's lawyer.

"Innocent, Your Honor. There are some mitigating circumstances involved in this case that the Commonwealth is unaware of."

"I see. Well, you'll have to discuss that with them." The judge looked at the prosecuting attorney. "Bail, Mr. Green?"

"In light of the amount of cocaine, the Commonwealth suggests a fifty-thousand-dollar bond, Your Honor."

"Mr. Smith, I'm sure you have something to say about that?"

"We feel that's excessive, Your Honor. Ms. Johnson is a citizen with no criminal record and heavy ties to the community. She's a supervisor at the United States Post Office and is not a flight risk. We ask that she be released on her own recognizance."

"Considering the amount of cocaine in her possession, we're not going to release her that easily, but we will reduce the bail. Bail is set at fifteen thousand dollars, cash or bond."

The judge banged his gavel, and Jasmine's body sagged. Her lawyer had to grab her arm to keep her from collapsing on the floor. I wanted to cry. My sister and I might've had some rough spots in our relationship, but she didn't deserve this. That's why I was glad that I'd called the right person to help her out of this.

"Where the hell is she?" I was pacing across the tile floor in the lobby of the Richmond city jail.

"Stephanie, relax. The deputy already told you it's gonna take a while. They have a lot of paperwork to take care of before they can release her." I nodded my head at Dylan but continued to pace.

I had called Dylan right after I hung up the phone with Jasmine last night. Once I explained what had happened to her, he didn't hesitate to offer his help. The first thing he said was that he'd have his lawyer represent her. And I didn't even have to mention bail before he started talking about going to the bank first thing in the morning. The way he was acting, there was no doubt in my mind about how much he cared about Jasmine. I mean, when it came down to it, the brother put up his house as collateral after the judge announced Jasmine's ridiculously high bail. If it wasn't for him, Jasmine's ass would be sitting up in that jail cell a hell of a lot longer than this.

"Hey, Stephanie. I'm gonna go get us a couple of sodas. You wanna come?"

"No. I'm gonna wait here in case they let my sister out a little earlier."

"Suit yourself. I'll be back in a sec." I watched Dylan walk out and had to smile. He was all right. Jasmine should've held on to him when she had the chance, even if he did have a little baby momma drama. Hell, these days it seemed like everybody had some type of drama. Especially me. But shit, who was I to criticize anyone after all the mistakes I made with Travis? I'd lost a damn near perfect man, and there was no one to blame but myself. In the two weeks since Travis had ordered me out of the house, we only spoke two times, and that was because he wanted to know when I was moving out. Malek had called with his crap a few times since then, but I let him know there wasn't shit happening. As far as his demand for on-call booty, he hadn't been pushing the issue. Rumor was that LaKeisha Nixon was nursing him back to health since the night he got jumped. I guess she was making him feel good enough that he didn't need me anymore. And if he wanted to go to the police? Well, that was his prerogative. But he knew better, 'cause even if he did get me or Derrick locked up, Derrick had plenty of boys out there who'd be more than happy to finish the job for him.

So I stayed home with my kids most nights, wondering why I'd let my life become such a mess. How could I have been willing to risk everything just to mess around with Malek? I knew his ass was no good. I knew he hadn't changed. Maybe I just got too comfortable with Travis. I got too used to being treated like the world was mine.

Now, don't get me wrong. I'm not saying that a girl deserves to be treated like shit to keep her in line. I'm saying that Travis was almost too good to me. He just gave and gave and gave. He was the most generous man I'd ever known, with his money and his heart, and he hardly ever asked for anything in return. I got so comfortable with receiving things from him, I forgot to think about giving back. Not that I had a lot of money to be buying him things, but I should've given him my total devotion. Instead, I just coasted along, taking his gifts and figuring he was satisfied as long as I kept him well fed and well sexed. I had a lot to learn about truly being in love, and I was sorry for all I had to lose before I could start learning.

And my poor kids. Maleka had lost the only daddy she'd ever known, and T. J. would grow up never knowing what it was like to have a father living under the same roof. Sure, they'd be able to spend plenty of time with him after we finalized a custody agreement. I wasn't about to fight over that. But it wouldn't be the same. If I had used better judgment, they would have had both of us, together, all the time.

Thank God for my family. Big Momma offered to let us stay with her once I told her Travis wanted us out of the house. Of course, I had to listen to her rant and rave about how stupid I'd been, what a good man I'd lost. But what could I say? She was right, and we both knew it. So after she ranted for a while, Big Momma opened her heart and her home to us. I was packing a little bit each night after work, and we would be out of the house before the month was up.

Jasmine had also been really supportive through the whole ordeal. I never once heard her say "I told you so," which is exactly what I would've expected from her. Well, maybe that's what I would've expected in the past. But ever since she'd busted me at the motel with Malek, our relationship had been changing. She'd actually spent hours on the phone with me since Travis ended things, listening to me cry or scream or whatever I felt I needed to do. Maybe both of us were starting to realize that our lives were more similar than either of us had ever thought. After years of competing with each other for Big Momma's approval, we finally realized it was pointless. We'd both made mistakes through the years, and Big Momma still loved us both, no matter what. We were her family, and we'd finally learned to start acting like family. It felt so good to have a sister now. That's why I was so anxious for Jasmine to be released from the jail so we could get her home.

I walked over to the deputy behind the desk and asked the same question for the tenth time. "How long did you say it was gonna take before they release my sister?"

"Actually, ma'am, your sister's being released right now." He pointed toward a metal door. I looked up and saw Jasmine coming through the door with her lawyer.

"Jasmine!" I ran up and embraced her. We twisted and turned and cried for a full minute.

"Thank you, Steph. Thank you so much for getting me outta here." She held me tight.

"Come on, Jazz. That's what sisters are for. Isn't that what you've been trying to get through my thick skull?" I stepped out of our embrace and looked in her eyes. "But it wasn't just me."

"Yeah, I kinda figured that." She inhaled and braced herself for what she thought was coming. "Where's Momma and Big Momma? I know I'm gonna hear it from them."

"They're at home. I didn't tell them you got arrested."

"Really?" She looked surprised but relieved.

"Please, you got enough stress right now. You don't need Big Momma making it worse. I love that old girl to death, but trust me—she don't know how to let shit die."

"I know that's right," Jasmine smirked. "But if Big Momma didn't bail me out, where'd you get the money? And who paid for my lawyer?"

"Dylan."

"Dylan," she repeated. "Dylan Taylor? Are you serious? He paid for my lawyer?"

"And your bail, too. He put up his house." I smiled.

She shook her head in amazement.

"That man never ceases to amaze me. What made you call him, anyway?"

"I figured, why not? I couldn't let you sit in jail. And he was the only one I could think of other than family who might be able to come up with the money. Besides I told you I saw him and he asked about you."

"Yeah, you did, didn't you. But just because he asked didn't mean he would go out on a limb like this. I still can't believe he did."

"Look, Jasmine, whether you believe it or not, Dylan still cares about you. He wouldn't have come here today and sat in that courtroom if he didn't."

Jasmine's eyes darted around the lobby. "He's here? Where is he?"

"I'm right here, Jasmine. You okay?" Dylan had come up behind us while we were talking. I don't know how much he'd heard, but I don't think it mattered. His eyes were glued on Jasmine like she was the only thing that did matter to him.

"Dylan, I don't know what to say. I can't believe you did this after everything that happened." She was so choked up.

"I'm your friend, Jasmine. When your sister called and said you were in trouble, I knew I had to help. I couldn't bear the thought of you sitting up in here for something you didn't do, while Derrick's roaming the streets."

"But what about Monica? I'm surprised she let you out her sight." Poor Jasmine. I know she didn't really wanna hear about his baby's momma right now. But then again, as fucked up as things had become for everyone involved, they might as well be up-front about the whole situation.

"I'm not with Monica," Dylan said.

"You're not?"

"I never was. That's what I wanted to tell you."

"But, what about the baby?"

"Just because she was having my baby doesn't mean I wanna be with her. Besides, she disappeared with the baby. I don't know where they are."

"Oh, Dylan. I'm so sorry."

"Don't be. She's a crackhead. Sooner or later she's gonna need money to get high, and when she does, I'll find her. I just hope she takes good care of my baby until then."

We were all silent for a few moments as we digested that scary thought. That poor baby could be anywhere with that crackhead right now. I think the thought was too much for Dylan, 'cause he changed the subject in a hurry.

"Listen, the important thing right now is that we get you out of this mess."

"Don't I know it!" Jasmine shuddered. "Thank God for that lawyer you got me. He thinks he might have a way to get the charges against me dropped."

"That's great news." Dylan smiled. "I knew Robert would do a good job for you. So what about now? What are you gonna do?"

"I don't know yet. I can't go back home. I don't wanna be alone there, just in case Derrick tries to come by. I can't deal with that now. I might kill him."

"No, you're already in enough trouble; you don't need to kill nobody," he joked, trying to lighten the mood. "But on the serious side, if you need a place to stay, you can always stay with me."

Jasmine shook her head.

"Thanks, Dylan, but I can't. I gotta do this by myself.

I've been relying on men all my life. I gotta do me right now. I'm probably just gonna go stay with Becky or my grandmother."

"Sure is gonna be crowded over there," I interjected. "You know, me and the kids are moving over to Big Momma's next week."

Jasmine shot me a look. She knew exactly what I was trying to do. Dylan had offered her a place to stay. I just thought I'd help move things along between them. But my sister's eyes told me she wasn't having it. She didn't look mad. More like she was begging me to just leave it alone for right now. I knew we'd talk about it later, but for now I just hoped that it didn't mean she was letting this brother slip away again.

"Well, we'll all just be one big, happy family then, won't we?" I said as I wrapped my arm around Jasmine's shoulder.

We all gave an uncomfortable laugh. There was definitely a lot that Jasmine and Dylan still needed to talk about. Maybe my sister could have the good life that I'd messed around and lost.

"You know, Dylan, Big Momma always did like you," I reminded him. "When Jasmine is there, we can count on you to come around and visit, right?"

"It's the only way I would have it," Dylan answered. "That okay with you, Jazz?"

"I'd like that," she answered before her lawyer approached.

"Hey, Dylan, how are you?" He stuck out his hand to shake Dylan's.

"Good, Robert, but I'll be better if you get my friend off."

"Well, that's what I'm trying to do," he sighed, turning to my sister. "We've got to speak to the Commonwealth attorney now."

"Okay." Jasmine turned to face us. "I can't thank you enough for being here with me today."

Jasmine's eyes got misty, and she gave me a hug. Then she turned to Dylan.

"Thanks, Dylan. I can't tell you how much it means to me that you're here." She leaned in and kissed his cheek. He wrapped his arms around her and held her tight. The tension in her shoulders seemed to relax for just a second when she leaned into his embrace. She took a step back, gazed into his eyes, and said good-bye.

Things were still not perfect. Jasmine was still gonna have to fight to get herself out of this mess. She was still gonna have to deal with getting Derrick and his shit out of her life for good. But I saw the way she and Dylan were looking at each other as she left with her lawyer. I had a good feeling about them.

# 39

# Jasmine

Seeing Dylan and Stephanie after I was released made me feel a hell of a lot better. That feeling didn't last long, though, once my attorney took me to meet with the assistant Commonwealth attorney, Anthony Green, the man in charge of my case. On the way into the room, Robert explained to me what I could expect. He said they'd already met with Mr. Green to discuss the possibility of dropping the charges, but he didn't tell me how he'd gotten them to agree to that. So at least things looked a little more hopeful, but not enough to keep my knees from shaking as I sat down in front of Anthony Green. I hadn't even gotten comfortable before he started drilling me with questions.

"Miss Johnson, do you know Derrick Winter?"

That question caught me off guard. And I wasn't sure if I should answer it, so I glanced at my attorney. That upset Mr. Green.

"Mr. Smith, did you explain to your client that if she cooperates with us we are willing to drop the charges against her?"

Robert patted my shoulder. "It's all right, Jasmine. You can answer Mr. Green's questions."

"Well, Miss Johnson," Mr. Green continued, "do you know Derrick Winter?"

"Yes, I know him. He's my boyfriend—well, ex-boyfriend. We broke up last night."

"And did you know he was a drug dealer?"

I glanced at my attorney again and he nodded.

"Yes, I knew he was a drug dealer," I told him, lowering my head. "But I'm not. Derrick knew better than to bring that shit around me."

This answer put a smile on Mr. Green's face. He leaned back in his chair and folded his hands on the table. "So, does he know you were arrested?"

"No."

"Are you sure?"

"Yes, I'm sure. The only ones who know I was arrested are my sister and my friend Dylan."

"So as far as you know, he thinks the drugs are still in the car?"

"Yeah. There's no chance anyone in my family would have talked to that motherf—uh, I mean, to Derrick."

"Well, Miss Johnson"—the Commonwealth attorney was looking happier by the minute—"it appears you are in a position to help us."

"Help you how?"

"We've been aware of your boyfriend's activities ever since he was released on parole. He's only been out a few months, and he and his boys have taken over the West End from the Dominicans. It won't be long before they go after the Browns in Southside and Big Boy Johnny Ray in Petersburg. We wanna stop him before he does, and this time we wanna put him away for good. Have you ever heard of the 'three strikes' law?"

"I think so."

"Well, under that law, Derrick already has two felony convictions. If we can somehow arrest him for a third, your ex will be going away for good."

*Damn.* Now I knew where this conversation was headed. I felt like I was in an episode of *Law & Order.* This man was about to ask me to set Derrick up.

I looked at Robert, but I couldn't read any expression on his face.

"So you're asking me to help you get Derrick, is that it?"

"No, Miss Johnson. I'm asking you to help yourself."

"How is this helping me? You don't know him. If he finds out I had something to do with his arrest, he'll have someone kill me. Even if I wanted to testify against him, I wouldn't make it to the stand without a bullet in my head."

"We need some assurances, Mr. Green," Robert finally chimed in. "My client cannot agree to anything unless we have absolute certainty that Mr. Winter will not know of her involvement."

"We understand," said Mr. Green. "What if I can guarantee that no arrest will take place in the presence of your client? Her part will be done before we take him into custody."

I looked at Robert for some kind of reassurance. Maybe he was comforted by what the lawyer had just said, but I wasn't. This guy would say anything to get me to agree. For all I knew, he'd make these promises and then I'd be standing right next to Derrick's ass when the cops came to get him. That would be the end for me. I guess Robert trusted this guy, because he nodded and told me the deal was okay.

"What do you want me to do?" I asked, hating Derrick even more for getting me into this position in the first place.

Mr. Green handed me my cell phone, which they had taken when I was arrested. Now I knew why they hadn't given it back to me with my other things when I was released. I figured some crooked guard had stolen it.

"Since your arrest, your phone's been ringing quite a bit. We figure he's been looking for you. Do you know any of these numbers?" He handed me a piece of paper.

"The top one's his cell phone and the second one's his mom's number. I don't know who the third number belongs to, although it does look familiar."

"Do you know a Wendy Wood?"

That sleazy motherfucker. I should've known when I kicked his ass out that he'd end up back over there with that ho. And now he had the nerve to be calling me from her place.

"Yeah, that's his baby's momma." I answered. "When we broke up, I kicked him out my place. He probably went to stay with her."

"Well, we'd like you to call him back and set up a meeting."

That made me nervous. Not only did I not want to be involved in this sting, I didn't want to see Derrick face-to-face. I was still so pissed at him for that video, there was no telling what I would say when I saw him. But from the glance my lawyer gave me and the determined look on Mr. Green's face, I knew I had no choice. Not if I didn't wanna be the one behind bars. I had to get over my fears and do what they were asking.

"What should I say to him?"

"Call him on his cell. Tell him you want to see him, to talk about your fight. Tell him you'll meet him in a Starbucks in the West End."

"Alone?" I didn't like the way this was sounding.

"Well, he'll think you're alone, but we'll have undercover people stationed throughout the shop."

"And what am I supposed to say to him once we're there?"

"Ask him for your keys back. Tell him you hate him. It doesn't really matter. The important thing is that he knows where you parked your car, and that you don't leave with him."

"Why does he have to know about the car?"

"We assume he'll go looking for the drugs after your meeting, so park it in an obvious place. Once he's been spotted with the drugs, we'll arrange an arrest away from the coffee shop."

This whole thing made me nervous. I was feeling sick to my stomach. What if Derrick got there and I chickened out? He had a way of talking me out of some of our biggest fights, and no doubt he'd be trying to do it this time. It was not gonna be easy, getting him to leave without me after I told him to fuck off. He would put up a good fight, for sure. I prayed I'd develop some real courage to deal with him, before I had to face him. I turned on my cell phone reluctantly and dialed Wendy's number with trembling fingers.

I was sitting in the back of Starbucks, drinking my third cappuccino. It was decaf. My nerves were already a wreck, so I didn't need any of that high-potency Starbucks coffee to make things worse.

There was a couple next to me holding hands, poring over the real estate section of the newspaper. They looked so totally in love, searching for a home. Actually, they were there for my benefit. They were undercover officers, ready to pounce on Derrick if things got out of hand. I was just praying that wouldn't be necessary. I wanted to avoid it at all costs, actually, 'cause I was still terrified that Derrick's boys would kill me if they knew I was doing this to him. A car with two more undercover officers sat outside in case they were called in as backup. My lawyer was in the car with them, and he'd promised me he'd be in there with me as soon as Derrick was gone.

Derrick was supposed to be there at 3:00, and it was now twenty-five after. I wondered if he was making me wait as a punishment for kicking his ass out the other night. When I talked to him on the phone, I played it as cool as I could. I didn't beg him to come meet me, but I also didn't give him shit. I just told him we had a lot of things to talk about, and we should get together in a neutral place to decide how we were gonna handle our "little issues." He was so damn cocky.

When Derrick finally walked in at 3:30, I put my drink down.

"What's up?" he asked. "You been here long?"

My mouth was dry, and my mind was a complete blank all of a sudden.

"I hate you," were the only words I could get out.

I wanted to slap him right about then, but I pulled myself back together and did my little act for the benefit of all the officers who were eavesdropping. Actually, there was no acting necessary here. Tears formed in my eyes as I remembered the images I saw on that video.

"I know, Jasmine. I never meant for you to see that tape."

"You never meant for me to see it? How 'bout you never meant to do what you did with my best friend? That shit should've never happened."

"C'mon, baby." He tried to win me over with one of his puppy-dog looks. "You know I never wanted to hurt you. I made a little mistake, that's all. Can't we just forgive and forget?" He reached out for my hand. I pulled it away.

"Hell, no. I ain't forgiving and I damn sure ain't forgetting. I just wanted to know why. Why would you do this to me after everything I've done for you? Why would you fuck Sabrina?"

"Look, Jazz, I'm sorry about what happened with your friend, but it's partly your fault."

"My fault?" I shouted. The cops at the next table shifted in their seats to remind me where I was and what I was supposed to be doing.

"Yeah, your fault." His dimples retreated into a hard frown. "Everything woulda been cool if you would've been a little more open in the bedroom. And you shouldn't talk so much to your damn friend."

"What's that supposed to mean?"

"It means you should have never told Sabrina how big my johnson is. That woman was coming over every day, talking about she just wanted to see if you were lying. Finally, I just showed it to her." My stomach lurched when I heard that. Shit, I knew Sabrina was a ho, but I thought our friendship was sacred ground.

"Oh, so when she saw it you just fucked her right then and there, huh?"

"No. I fucked her after she told me you said I was too rough. She said *she* liked it rough. After that, it was a wrap." He got up from his chair. "Like I said before: you talk too much, Jazz. Don't you know you never tell your friends what you're working with in bed?"

I shuddered. There was some truth to what he was saying, but it hurt to realize it.

"Now, are you gonna let me come back home, or what? 'Cause I got shit to do. I ain't got time to be baby-sitting you and your little tantrum."

I thought I was so in love with this man, but it was so clear now that he'd never really cared about me. Sure, he bought me lots of things. And at one time I guess I confused that with loving me. But Derrick was never concerned about my heart. He kept me on a leash, and I was willing to do anything for him. He let his baby's momma disrespect me more times than I wanted to count. And I was a fool. I stayed by his side, gave up my own life to wait for his ass for three years. Now here I was, scared as shit, trying to keep my own self out of jail. Well, those days were over. I was ready to live my life on my own terms. I was ready to say good-bye to

Derrick. And I was doing it for me, not for any cop, not for the lawyers. Just for me.

"No. I'm not gonna let you come back home."

It felt so good to tell him that. And I couldn't believe his response. He didn't fight at all. He reached into his pocket, pulled out my keys, and slid them across the table to me.

"Your loss," was all he said as he left.

I sat alone at that table for five of the longest minutes of my life. I couldn't wait to get the hell out of there, but I had to get the word from the cops. Even the undercover couple next to me were still playing their part, pretending they didn't know I existed. Finally, my lawyer came through the front door, and he was smiling. I felt like I could breathe at last.

"He's gone, Jasmine. You can relax now," Robert told me.

"Did he go to the car?" I asked.

"No." My heart sank when he said that. But then he explained, "While he was in here with you, he had one of his friends get the drugs out of your trunk."

"What? Does that mean he's not gonna be arrested?" I was so nervous.

"No one's been arrested yet. The friend was waiting outside when Derrick left. Derrick got into his car, and the undercover car is following them now. They're hoping that at some point Derrick will take the drugs into his possession so they can get him."

"So what do we do now?" I asked. "I thought I was gonna be done as soon as I talked to him."

"Your part is done for now. Now we just have to wait. As soon as I know something, I'll call you."

"Does this mean the charges are dropped?"

"Technically, no. We have to go in front of a judge to have that done. And the Commonwealth won't do that until they have Derrick in custody."

"Damn." My shoulders sagged. "How long do I have to wait?"

"Hopefully, not long. Try to relax."

Easier said than done. There was no way I was gonna relax if I thought Derrick was still out there. What if his friend kept the drugs after all this? Then they couldn't pick him up. Might even stop trailing him. For all I knew, he'd come looking for me if he decided he didn't like the outcome of our little conversation today. I walked to my car feeling like I had a lead weight tied around my neck.

Stephanie sat on her couch with me for almost two hours when I got back to her place. The kids were off at the day care center, so I had her undivided attention. It didn't matter, though. It's not like I could even talk. I was so upset by this point, I just sat and cried until the phone finally rang.

"Jasmine? This is Robert. He took the drugs back to Wendy's house and they got him."

My knees gave out and I grabbed the couch before I ended up on the floor.

"Thank God."

"With what they found in that house, they arrested him *and* Miss Wood." That put a little smile on my tearstained face.

"So does that mean I'm free?"

"Yes, Miss Johnson. It means they're dropping the charges. First thing tomorrow, I'll appear before a judge to finalize everything."

I started crying—this time, tears of relief. Derrick was going away, and it was time to start my life over.

# 40

# Dylan

"Child, where have you been? We almost finished eating." Big Momma scolded Stephanie as she walked into my dining room and took a seat.

"I told you this morning I had to drop the kids off at Travis's," Stephanie replied as she looked around the table at all the food. "Lord, this stuff smells good. Who cooked it?"

"Dylan," Big Momma answered. "Can you believe he cooked all this food? And Stephanie, you got to try them ribs. The meat just falls off the bone."

"I don't see no ribs." Stephanie frowned.

"There's some in the kitchen. I'll go get you some. Anyone else want ribs?"

Big Momma headed to the kitchen as she offered everyone a second helping. Not one person other than Stephanie took her up on the offer. We were already beyond stuffed after tons of hamburgers, hot dogs, spare ribs, and other grilled goodies. I'd invited Jasmine and her family over for a barbecue as a way of thanking them for their kind treatment the past few months. Thank goodness I'd finished most of the cooking right before it started raining, but we had to eat in the house.

Since Jasmine had gotten out of jail, her family had done their best to thank me for getting her such a good lawyer. Both Stephanie and Big Momma had gone overboard to make me feel like one of the family. And Big Momma didn't hide the fact that she hoped I'd be a member of the family through marriage someday. She couldn't go five minutes without complimenting me on something or telling me what a good grandson-in-law I'd be. And from what Jasmine told me, she was getting the same pro-Dylan speech just as often.

But Jasmine and I were still taking things slow. She'd gotten rid of Derrick, and I hadn't seen or heard from Monica since she disappeared from the hospital. I didn't give a damn about Monica, but I spent lots of time worrying about the baby. I had Joe on the case, so I wasn't worried. If Monica was in Petersburg, sooner or later he'd find her. In the meantime, Jasmine had become a great listener whenever I needed her. And I continued to do the same for her as she worked through her feelings about the whole situation with Derrick. There was no doubt that I had strong feelings for Jasmine, and she felt the same for me. If her family had anything to say about it, we'd be on our way down the aisle already.

But we'd both been seriously hurt by our past lovers, and neither one of us saw a reason to rush into anything until our heads and our hearts were straight. We were content to spend as much time together as possible but still let our relationship grow at its own pace. Sure, I knew that if things continued the way they were going, I would be giving her a ring in the not-so-distant future. But I didn't share that information with Stephanie, or she and Big Momma would start picking out names for our firstborn child.

As for Stephanie, she was happy to be meddling in our relationship, since she didn't have one of her own. Actually, it wasn't as bad as it sounds. She and her sister had developed a much closer bond than they'd ever had before. Stephanie honestly seemed to be interested in keeping her sister from making the same mistakes she had made. And in that respect, she was trying to make the best of the damage that had been done to her family after she stepped out on Travis.

Not long after she moved out of Travis's place, her daughter's father, Malek, left town again. He went back to D.C., this time with a girl Stephanie couldn't stand, named LaKeisha Nixon. Stephanie seemed so relieved to have him gone, and her family had actually hoped that would be the deciding factor to getting her and Travis back together. But by that time, Travis had moved on, started a new relationship, and seemed pretty adamant about being through with Stephanie.

From the way Jasmine described her, the old Stephanie would have tried to manipulate her way back into Travis's life. But she didn't. She worked with him peacefully, to figure out a way that the kids could get plenty of time with both of them. He got to see the kids twice a week, and they stayed with him every other weekend. Stephanie actually seemed satisfied with the arrangement, and hadn't tried to make any problems for Travis and his new woman. Her family was very proud of her, and they made sure to tell her as often as she could stand to hear it. Yeah, all around, things were headed in the right direction for the Johnson girls.

"Come 'ere and give me a kiss." Jasmine wrapped her arms around me and pulled me into the hall as I walked out of the dining room. I was more than happy to do as she asked. I gave her a quick kiss and she peeked around the corner, pretending to be nervous.

"I better be careful," she joked. "Your girlfriend Big Momma might get jealous if she knew I was doing this." She pressed her lips against mine and we kissed passionately until we heard footsteps.

Big Momma walked into the hall and we started to laugh.

"Mmm-hmm, what y'all up to?" she smirked. "Don't y'all be doing all that kissing and hugging around me unless y'all getting married some time soon." Like I said, Big Momma took every opportunity she got to put in her vote for a quick marriage.

"Big Momma, why don't you leave those two alone?" Stephanie chimed in from the dining room. "Can't you see they're trying to get their groove on?"

"That's just what I'm sayin'. If they wanna act like that, they should hurry up and get married."

I had to laugh at her persistence, but the phone rang.

"I'll get it," Stephanie offered. "Y'all keep on doin' your thing out there in the hall." She got up and headed for the kitchen. Jasmine and I went back into the dining room, but before I could sit down, Stephanie called me to the phone. I gave Jasmine another quick kiss and headed to the kitchen to take the call.

"Hello?"

"Dylan, this is Ron Burns." It was the police officer who'd helped me out the night I was picked up in the crack house.

"Hey, Ron, what's up? Everything all right?"

"Well, I'm not sure. Joe was telling me a while ago that you've been trying to find your son."

"Yeah. Do you know something?" My heart jumped. Maybe there was finally some news about the baby.

"We just picked up your ex for possession."

"Monica? She's there now?" I hadn't heard any news about her in so long, I was starting to think she'd left town.

"Yes. Monica's here."

"What about the baby? Was the baby with her?" I held my breath as I waited for his answer.

"The baby's right here," Ron answered. He sounded uncomfortable. "We were hoping you'd come pick him up. Otherwise, we have to turn him over to child welfare."

There was no way I was gonna let that happen. Ever since

that first day that I held him, I'd been waiting to have my son in my arms again. Now that I finally knew where he was, I didn't want to waste any time getting to him.

"I'll be right there, Ron."

"Good. But listen, you need to do one thing before we can let you take him home."

"Just name it; I'll do it."

"We just need to see some type of proof that he's your son."

"What about the lab results from my paternity test? We had it done right after he was born."

"That's perfect. Just bring those so we can make copies to keep on file here. You understand. We just have to keep everything documented."

"No problem. I'm on my way." I hung up the phone and went into the dining room, where everyone was listening to Big Momma tell a story about her own wedding.

"I'm sorry folks, but I have to go out for a minute," I announced. "Just make yourselves comfortable till I get back."

"Is everything all right, Dylan?" Jasmine asked as all eyes turned to me.

"Yeah, I guess. They found my son. I'm about to pick him up."

"Who found him?" Big Momma was the only one talking. Everyone else had their mouths hanging open.

"The police. They arrested Monica, and they have the baby at the station now."

The room fell silent. No doubt everyone was as shocked as I was at this point. My mind was racing. I couldn't even think straight enough to give them any more details.

"Well, go on, then, son," Big Momma broke the silence. "We'll be right here when you get back."

# 41

# Jasmine

I threw my napkin on the table and got out of my seat.

"I don't believe this shit!" I shouted to no one in particular as I headed for the back door.

"Where you going?" Big Momma demanded to know as she followed behind me. Stephanie was right on her heels.

"Jasmine, what is wrong with you?" Stephanie shouted at me.

I stopped and turned around to look at them.

"What do you think is wrong? I can't believe he's gonna bring that baby back here. Just when things were starting to get good between us."

Big Momma raised her eyebrows and shook her head.

"Child, what else did you expect him to do? He can't just leave that baby there, now, can he?"

My shoulders slumped. "No. You're right. It's just that I went through so much baby momma drama with Derrick and Wendy, I promised myself I'd never do it again. No more men with children."

"Please, Jasmine." Stephanie sucked her teeth. "You knew Dylan had a baby. Shoot, you been the one listening to him talk about how bad he wanted to find his child. Did you think this couldn't happen?"

I couldn't answer her. Of course I knew that this could happen. It's just that things with Dylan had been going so well, I'd lulled myself into a false sense of security. Even though I never said it to Dylan, part of me thought Monica was long gone and she'd never become an issue.

"Child, don't you see?" Big Momma said. "The fact that Dylan has a child don't have to scare you away. You oughta be proud of him."

"Proud?"

"Yes. Proud. How many baby daddies you know are even willing to acknowledge their children, let alone take them in and raise them without the momma?"

"I know," I sighed. "But how do we know it's gonna be without Monica? Eventually, she'll get out of jail and she'll be knocking on Dylan's door. Then what?"

"You deal with that when it happens," Stephanie said.

"Dylan is a good man, Jasmine," Big Momma told me. "If you ask me, this just proves it even more. He ain't the kind of man who's gonna let Monica ruin things between you, even if she is his baby's momma."

Stephanie agreed. "She's right, Jazz. If you'd stuck around long enough last time, he might've been able to prove how he could handle Monica. You never gave him a chance."

I had so many regrets. So much of what had happened to me since Derrick got out of prison could have been avoided if I had just given Dylan the chance he'd asked for. He'd tried to tell me he wouldn't let Monica ruin what we were just starting. But I was too scared to trust that. It was easier to stick with the baby momma drama I was already living than to take a risk with someone new who might bring me the same kind of shit. I wasn't ready to take that risk, so I ran right back into Derrick's arms. This time, I still wasn't sure. But at least I could make my decision without another man complicating my thoughts.

"I don't know if I can do it," I said. "I'm really scared."

Big Momma put her arm over my shoulder. "It's all right

to be scared, child. But don't let that stop you from living. We're here to help you if things get rough. And Dylan is a good man. I have faith that he'll do right by you. Just give him a chance to prove it."

Big Momma led me back to the living room. Someone turned on the TV, but I couldn't tell you who did it or what we were watching. I was lost in my own thoughts until Dylan came back with the baby.

"He's here!" Stephanie yelled when we heard the car door closing outside. They jumped up and ran to the door to greet him, but I couldn't. I wasn't excited about seeing the baby, and I knew I wouldn't be able to hide my feelings. It would ruin Dylan's moment for me to walk over there with my face all screwed up.

Dylan had a nervous smile on his face when he came through the door. Even if I had wanted to glimpse the baby from my seat on the couch, I couldn't, 'cause Big Momma and Stephanie and Momma were all over him in a flash. From all the *ooh*s and *ahh*s they were yelling, I guess the baby was pretty cute, all bundled up in his daddy's arms. It didn't take long before Big Momma told Dylan to hand the baby to her so she could hold him. Now the minicrowd gathered around her.

Dylan spotted me on the couch and left his son with the group of cooing women. I tried to smile, but I know I must've looked sad, because his face changed to reflect my mood as he approached. He sat down next to me.

"You okay over here?" he asked.

I shrugged my shoulders. I hated to be ruining this for him, but I couldn't lie. "I don't know. This is really scary to me."

"Me, too." He took my hand gently. "I've wanted this moment for months, but I can't describe how nervous I was, walking out of that police station with my baby. I kept expecting someone to come tell me it was a mistake. Tell me to give him back."

"What about Monica? Did you see her there?"

"Yeah. They let me talk to her for a few. She looked real bad."

"Where'd they pick her up?"

Dylan explained to me the little bit that he knew. Monica had gone to Richmond with the baby right after she left the hospital. The guy who'd picked her up at the hospital was some old guy she'd been with a few times before. He took her back to his place in Richmond. They had an arrangement. She could stay there with her baby, and he'd supply her with enough crack to keep her flying high, as long as she was willing to give him some ass every day. That lasted for a few months, until Monica was so cracked out she lost her figure and her beauty. The guy drove her back to Petersburg in a hurry and dropped her in some rundown neighborhood where he knew Monica would find her way to the nearest crack house.

That's where the police found her and the baby. She'd only been there a day or two when they picked her up.

"What about your son, Dylan? Is he all right?"

"Yeah, thank God," he sighed. "They had him checked out. Said other than a little dehydration, he seems to be okay. She managed to take care of him the best she could. I'm gonna take him over to the hospital tomorrow just to be sure everything's all right."

We looked over at the women, who were still cooing at the tiny baby. They all burst out in excited laughter when he gave them a tiny smile.

"Ooh, Dylan. This one's gonna be a heartbreaker," Stephanie said from across the room.

Dylan smiled as they headed outside to the porch with the baby. He looked back at me.

"It was so sad seeing Monica like that. I can't believe it's the same woman I used to love."

I gave him a halfhearted smile. Sure, I felt bad for her. No one uses crack because they want to end up like that. She couldn't help herself. But I hated her for doing this to her baby, and for getting in the way of Dylan's and my happiness.

"So what's gonna happen to her?" I asked.

"They said she'll be going before the judge tomorrow. Chances are, she'll be locked up for a while this time, since it's not her first arrest for drugs."

There was a strange relief, knowing she wouldn't be around for a while. But I knew there were no guarantees.

"And the baby can stay with you? What about after she gets out? Aren't you scared of getting too attached to him? She'll probably come out and wanna take him right back."

"I don't know. I suppose it's possible that she could want him back. But for now, she knows she fucked up. She knows that baby is better off without her."

"She does?" I was surprised. I know it must've been hard for a woman to admit her child didn't need her.

"She never wanted to hurt him, Jasmine. That crack just had a hold of her senses. She actually told me she's glad they arrested her. At least now our son has a chance."

"So she's okay with you keeping him?"

"Yeah. She told me to get a lawyer to draw up papers giving me full custody."

My mood was starting to brighten just a little. Maybe things could work out. It wasn't gonna be easy, but at least I could now see that it might be possible. Someday down the road, we might have to deal with Monica. But Dylan had shown me over and over that he was a good man. A strong man, who wouldn't let his baby's mother put me through the shit that Wendy did.

"Jasmine?" He put his hand under my chin and turned my face toward his. "I love you."

My eyes filled with tears. He'd never said those words to me before.

"And I love you, Dylan."

"I love my son, but I love you, too. I want both of you in my life. I know it's not gonna be easy, but I'm willing to do whatever it takes to make this situation all right for you. Can you bear with me, give this a try?"

It was time. Time to let go of my fears and trust what my heart was telling me. I took Dylan's hand and led him out to the porch. When we got outside, I made my way through the circle of women surrounding the baby.

"Momma, gimme my turn to hold that beautiful little baby," I said. Everyone turned to look at me. Big Momma had a huge, satisfied smile on her face. They handed me the baby, and I held his tiny body close against my chest. My heart was pounding, but it felt good. I was so full of love and so full of hope. The baby looked up at my face and smiled at me.

"Well, little Davon. It looks like it's gonna be you and me and your daddy from now on."

The following is a sample chapter from
Carl Weber's eagerly anticipated upcoming novel
SO YOU CALL YOURSELF A MAN.

This book will be available in January 2006
wherever hardcover books are sold.

ENJOY!

# 1

# James

Call me kinky, but there is nothing in the world that turns me on more than hearing a woman scream pleasurable obscenities as I make love to her. And that's exactly what my lovely wife, Kathy, was doing as I held onto her hips and made love to her from behind for the second time tonight. Our two boys, James Jr. and Michael, were with my mother-in-law for the weekend while Kathy and I were taking advantage of their absence by spending some quality time together. We'd gone out to dinner, taken in a movie, then come home and finished off a bottle of wine before making love on the living room carpet. We were now on our second round in our bedroom, going at it like two lusty college students in heat.

"I love you, James," my wife moaned affectionately, clutching the sheets just as an orgasm overtook her body.

"I love you too," I growled back as my body stiffened and my own pleasure erupted.

Totally spent, Kathy lay flat on her stomach while I gently collapsed onto her back, gasping for air. After a brief recovery, I slid my sweat-soaked body off of hers. She snuggled up next to me and I wrapped my arms around her, pulling her in close, her back to my front. I was so exhausted, I wanted to just close my eyes and let the sedative of sex take me to dreamland, but I couldn't do that because it was against the rules we'd created almost a year and a half ago to keep our marriage together. Somehow, I was going to have to force myself to stay awake at least ten more minutes and talk to her before allowing myself the enjoyment of sleep. I kissed her neck, whispering in her ear, "You okay? Do you want me to go down on you or anything?"

"No, baby. I'm fine just like this. All I want you to do is hold me." I did as I was told and she snuggled her backside against me. A few seconds later I could hear her snoring lightly.

I loved Kathy more than anything in the world. Sure, we had our problems like most couples. Hell, I even thought we were gonna break up a few years ago, but we worked it out and now things had never been better as far as I was concerned. I'd loved her since the day we met in our junior year at Virginia State University. She was my soul mate, and I'd do anything and everything to keep her and my boys safe and protected. I kissed her neck again then dozed off to sleep.

I couldn't have been asleep more than five minutes when the phone rang. Instinctively, I reached over and picked it up from my night table, glancing at the caller ID before hitting the talk button. The screen read PRIVATE NUMBER, and my eyes wandered to the clock radio on my night table. *One twenty-one A.M. Who the hell is calling me at this time of night?* Then it hit me. There was only one person who would call me at this time from a private number—my fraternity brother, Sonny. He lived in L.A. and was flying in sometime tomorrow. I was supposed to pick him up at the airport, so he was probably calling to let me know what time his flight would arrive. Sonny always had a beer or two after dinner, so knowing him he'd probably just forgotten about the time difference.

"Hello?"

"James?" It wasn't Sonny as expected. It was a woman, a

familiar voice, but in my tired state I just couldn't make out the voice. "James?" the woman asked again.

"Yeah, who is this?"

"It's . . . it's Michelle."

The hairs on the back of my neck stood up and every muscle in my body tightened. I could feel Kathy start to stir next to me and fear ran through my body. I immediately cupped the phone and rolled over on my right side, away from my wife.

I'd met Michelle about two years ago during the time Kathy and I were having problems and contemplating divorce. She was living with her mother and their house was a daily stop on my UPS route. Her mother was addicted to the Home Shopping Network and was constantly ordering nonsense she didn't need. Looking back at things, I wished I had never met Michelle, but in all honesty, she was exactly what I needed to realize that what I had at home was worth fighting for.

In the beginning, I never even thought about having sex with Michelle. She was just the girl in a beat-up housecoat who answered the door when I dropped off her mother's packages. But as time went on, her appearance started to change. At first it was subtle; the scarf she usually wore to cover up her rollers disappeared and her hair was now combed every day. Then one morning she started wearing makeup. I knew something was definitely up when she stopped wearing the beat-up housecoat and started to answer the door wearing silk pajamas or a negligée. Being a harmless yet flirtatious guy, I gave her a few compliments on her improved appearance. Yeah, I know I was a married man, and even though things with my wife were rocky, I really didn't think anything would start with Michelle. I was just seeking some attention. That changed, though, when she was more than a little receptive to my flirtation. We started flirting back and forth over the next couple of weeks. I don't have to tell you what happened after that. Let's just say it happened every day for six months, even when I didn't have any packages to deliver to her house.

"I thought I told you not to call me on this phone." I was whispering but my voice was cold and serious.

"I know, but I've been calling your cell since five o'clock and it just keeps sending me to your voice mail."

"That's because I'm busy." I glanced at Kathy to see if I was talking too loud. She seemed to still be asleep.

"You don't have to get nasty, James. What is wrong with you? Is your wife right next to you?"

"Yes. Now look, it's late. Don't call me anymore, okay?"

"No!" she shouted. "We need to talk now. I really don't care if you wife is there or not. I need to talk to you."

I didn't like her attitude and was thinking about hanging up. The only thing that stopped me was the fact that she could call back. One call at 1:30 in the morning Kathy might ignore or sleep through, but a second call would have her radar up like she was NASA waiting for the space shuttle to land. "Look, I don't have time for this."

"Well, make time. Unless you want me to show up at your doorstep with your son."

I swear I could feel my heart stop. "Hold on a sec." I cupped my hand over the phone, then swung my feet off the bed to sit up. Kathy turned toward me.

"Baby, who's that on the phone?" She was still half asleep.

I turned toward her and forced a smile. "Oh, it's just Sonny. I've gotta write down his flight information. I'll be right back."

"Aw'ight. Tell 'im I said hi." She rolled back over, pulling the covers around her neck. I left the room, heading downstairs as quickly as possible. When I reached the family room, I turned on the television for background noise and brought the phone to my ear.

"What the hell is this about, Michelle? You told me the baby wasn't mine." Now that I was not within earshot of Kathy, I had a real attitude.

"I know that, James, but I was wrong." There was a strange tone to her voice, not the attitude I expected. It was more like exhaustion. If I didn't know better, I might have thought she didn't want to be having this conversation with me. But I did know better, and I was sure Michelle was up to something.

"What do you mean you was wrong? Why you trying to play me, Michelle? You know that baby ain't mine. He looks just like your boyfriend. He don't look nothin' like me."

"Ain't nobody trying to play you, James." The attitude had crept back into her voice. "I just want you to take care of your responsibility. I can't do this by myself."

"What responsibility? That baby ain't mine. I saw you and his daddy pushing a stroller down the street just the other day. You looked like one big happy family. Why you trying to put this on me now? I ain't rich. I ain't got no money. Damn."

"You think I want this? I wouldn't even be talking to you if Trent hadn't failed a paternity test. The baby's not his, James. DNA tests don't lie."

There was silence on my end. I wasn't sure what to say. I wanted to ask, "Well, whose baby is it?" but common sense told me that wasn't a good idea, especially since she had my cell number, my home number, and my address. If she wanted to, she could make my life a living hell.

As if she was reading my mind she said, "You're the only other one I was sleeping with, James, so don't come out your face with any stupidness."

*God, I wish I had never met her.*

"What do you want from me, Michelle?"

"I think we should sit down tomorrow and talk. All I want you to do is take care of your son, James. I don't want anything else."

"I can't do it tomorrow, Michelle. It'll have to be Sunday."

"Sunday it is. Call me after church with the time. But don't make me call you, James, 'cause I ain't calling your cell phone anymore. I'm calling your house."

"Aw'ight. I'll call you." I clicked off the phone, then walked up the stairs as if I was in a trance. How the hell was I gonna tell Kathy that I had another son?